LIVING
IN THE SHADOWS

Living in the Shadows (The Foundling's Path - Part 1)

Copyright ©2017 Jemima Brigges

EBooks by Design
queries@ebooksbydesign.co
www.ebooksbydesign.co

ISBN: 978-1-910100-85-1

British Library Cataloguing in Publication Data
A catalogue record for this book is available from the British Library

Typeset in 11pt Aldine font

Cover design by Aimee Coveney
www.authordesignstudio.com

Living in the Shadows

(1808 - 1816)

The Foundling's Path
(Part 1)

Jemima Brigges

Other books by Jemima Brigges

Brothers at Arms
Counting the Cost

A Marriage of Convenience:
1: Held to Ransom

The Foundling's Path:
1: Living in the Shadows

Dedication

To my paternal and maternal grandfathers who were born during the reign of two different English monarchs of the 19th Century; one grandparent, the son of a gentleman farmer; the other a countryman, who became a local celebrity – a raconteur, and singer of country songs – from whom I learned many aspects of rural life. A historical fact that is stranger than fiction.

Author's Note

What chance has a girl, born into poverty and viewed with suspicion, of achieving a position of trust, unless a person in authority deems her worthy? Things might be different for women living in modern times, but in the Pre-Regency Georgian era, the answer would have been virtually none, had it not been for the beneficence of a gentleman – with a reason to help.

In 1808, the majority of the working classes only knew about servitude and obedience. That is where we find Nell Walcote at the beginning of The Foundling's Path Trilogy...

Jemima Brigges

In Dire Straits

(1808 - 1811)

Chapter 1

August 1808 – on a wooded Shropshire hillside

"Please help me, Meg; I have nowhere else to go."

Through a haze of exhaustion, Nell Walcote saw the tall figure moving towards her. She felt herself falling, but strong hands caught her and she had the sensation of being carried.

"Meg…" she whispered.

"I have you safe, little one," said a familiar voice, in which Nell had absolute trust. Sleep beckoned and she slid unresisting into its welcoming arms. She awoke some time later surrounded by a herbal scent to which she could not give a name, and lay wondering where she was, until the sight of the frayed grey blanket strung on a rope between two walls told her that she was in the woodsman's hut in the clearing.

Without thinking, Nell swung her legs off the straw mattress covering the pallet in the corner, and stood up. Her legs still ached but the soreness of her back did not bother her as it had done before.

Gradually, memories returned to her and she began to recall the problems she had encountered on the previous day, which had followed her to Hillend Rectory, where she worked. No, that was in the past, for she had been dismissed. A wave of sadness welled up inside before she could suppress it.

Nell's problem involved men, one bad, the other… She sighed and touched her lips with the tip of her tongue, tasting salt and the memory of a

1

kiss. At least, that is what she supposed it was for no one had ever kissed her before. She had no memories of her mother, only Peggy Walcote who fed her when she was a baby and grumbled every day thereafter saying that she was a bastard found in the church porch.

Nell could not imagine why anyone would want to kiss a foundling, and yet in recalling the moment it happened, a warm feeling came over her, and her head felt as if it was floating. Sensing that she might fall, she slipped back under the covers of the bed and slept.

★★★

"I have you safe, little one," Meg Chapel said, wondering what Nell was doing here in a state of collapse, when last night she had taken the girl back to Hillend Rectory, shaken and bruised after being molested by a farm labourer. What had happened since to reduce her to a state of abject exhaustion?

Knowing that questions must wait, she carried the girl to the hut in the woodland clearing, pausing only to stoop under the door surround to gain entry. That was the problem with being tall like a man; but in other ways her height was an asset, and one she used to her advantage.

The girl flinched as Meg laid her gently on a pallet mattress, and half-turned her over to unhook the fasteners of the work frock she wore.

"I'll have to leave you like this, Nell," she said, setting aside the fine woollen cape, and deftly peeling back the sodden pads on the girl's back to reveal a dozen bloodied lash-marks from a birch.

At the sight Meg, who had long since dispensed with emotions, felt a brief surge of anger at the perpetrator who inflicted the damage. Then it was gone for she knew that such feelings were futile.

"Stay there," she said. "I'll find some clean dressings."

Outside the door, she took a deep breath and strode back to the vardo. Minutes later, she returned with a kettle of boiled water in one hand, and a bowl containing a bundle of clean cloths, torn into strips, various jars of salves and padding in the other. Any change of clothes could wait until later.

Nell was dozing when Meg re-entered the hut, and remained so until she had completed the dressings. The girl's eyes opened in surprise as Meg pulled off the dusty boots and applied salves to the blisters on her sore feet. A wash in warmed water would help, but that too must wait.

"I'm sorry, Meg," the girl whispered. "I don't want to be a nuisance, but I couldn't think of anywhere else to go."

"Don't worry, little one," she said, gruffly. "Go to sleep. You can explain later."

"Thank…you…" The girl's eyes were already closing.

Meg nodded, recalling the tattered clothes and state of distress in which Nell had arrived the previous day. On that occasion, she had smeared salves on a few scratches to Nell's face and arms and repaired, as best she could, the torn bodice of her frock. Her friend had said little about the fine woollen cape that covered her state of undress, or the young gentleman who had rescued her. She did not need to, for Meg knew quality when she saw it.

She stood for a moment, watching the girl sleep, before going outside to resume her preparations for a visit down the valley to see one of her pregnant women whose delivery was due. She had little doubt that Annie Longden would shell this one out as she did the previous eight, but Meg needed to know that the head and not the breech or shoulder was presenting. The last three babies had come into the world in a rush, and with nine pregnancies in twelve years the woman needed help to prevent another.

If only that brute of a husband would give Annie time to recover from the birth before mating with her again. Knowing the man would not, Meg added a small pouch of herbs for the woman to mix with hot water, which should give her a few months' peace from another pregnancy.

Nobody questioned the use when she said, with some authority, that it was a herbal remedy to regulate the woman's monthly flow. Men shied away from any mention of such things. So Meg, who did not suffer the problem herself, was happy to mystify them. In her lone situation, it was just as well she did not.

With the girl's immediate needs in mind, Meg decided that her visit to the valley must wait until the morrow. In the meantime, she doubled her stocks of herbs and food and collected extra water from the nearby spring in a couple of leather bladders. Several times she looked into the shed at her sleeping visitor, and as the hours passed, she folded more bundles of dressing strips and mixed herbal paste for salves, all the time pondering the

3

cause of the girl's distress. Whatever it was, she sensed it had something to do with the gentleman's cape lying across the girl's bed.

As darkness fell, she settled in an old wooden chair in the hut, her eyes apparently closed, but she instinctively knew when the figure on the pallet moved and roused ready to give a sip of spring water.

"Meg." The voice was hardly a whisper. "I must tell you…"

"Yes, little one, what is it?"

"I missed evening prayers…" Nell sniffed. "Miss Snitterfield caught me on the back staircase, and beat me."

"What happened then?" she said, knowing that Nell would not rest otherwise.

"I don't know, except that I heard Miss Dinchope telling them that visitors had come, so they left me and went downstairs."

From that, Meg guessed that Parson Snitterfield had been in the room with his sister. It did not surprise her, for she had heard bad things of him from other village folk.

"Who put the dressings on your back?"

"The housekeeper did," said Nell. "She was kind at first, but then told Mr Jemkins, the gardener, to see me off the premises. Instead, he let me rest in the potting shed and gave me food this morning. I came here because I didn't know where else to go."

"You can rest now, Nell. We'll talk more of this later."

While the girl slept, Meg shaded her eyes in a half-sleeping state that she practised. A woman living alone could not afford to drop her guard.

At first sight, Meg Chapel looked like a man in her black coat and breeches. She was lean and lanky, with big feet and no feminine features. Her one redeeming factor was that she had the hands of an angel. But in that, nature had prepared her well for the harsh life she led.

Meg was a lone soul inured to the discomforts of life, but occasionally she admitted to a desire for company, left over from her youth. Mother Chapel had, for many years, filled the space left by another. Now she lay beneath the turf where the bluebells grew in the spring. After her passing, Meg continued her mother's work, helping others but taking only the necessities to keep herself alive.

When she was young, she had trusted all would be well, but when doors closed in her face she had grown accustomed to living in exile. Unlike her mother, she would never feel the hand of a lover or bear his child. Nor would she cause a jealous woman grief – of that she was certain.

This young woman was her final chance to right a wrong from days gone by.

***

Awake at first light, Meg replaced the soiled dressings and applied extra padding to the girl's wounds. Breakfast for both was herbal tea, dipped with crusts of bread, and then she helped Nell to move a few steps to the couch in the vardo, which she brought close to the hut.

"I'll leave the door ajar until we reach the road, and then close it so that nobody sees you," she said, and heard Nell murmur a sleepy agreement.

There was a chill from the heavy morning mist, hanging low over the river, as Meg led the horse along the woodland path and manoeuvred the caravan down the slope to the drovers' road. She knew when the sun rose above the trees, the mist would burn off as it had on the afternoon, a couple of days ago, when Nell had visited her before.

"Are you all right?" Meg called as she pulled the door shut and took her place on the driver's bench. The sleepy silence in the van told her all was well.

***

Nell drifted on a cloud, feeling the sway of the gypsy caravan as it moved. Her eyelids felt heavy, her mind a mass of conflicting thoughts as she viewed shifting scenes, seeing the surrounding light change to increasing darkness as unpleasant dreams intervened. She relived the stark shock as icy water closed over her head when she fell in the stream, and felt again the terror of being swept away by the current, sure she was going to be drowned – and then immense relief when a trailing tree root caught in her clothes.

She did not know for how long she had clung to the lifeline before finding the strength to inch her way to the riverbank. Had she known what awaited her at Hillend Rectory, she might have let go of the tree root. Instead, she lay for a while on the riverbank, soaking up the warmth of the afternoon sun.

5

In another change of scene, a rough hand snatched at her clothes and she tumbled backwards through the scratchy undergrowth and struck the forest floor with a thud. Confused, Nell lay still, aware of the bruise on her hip, tender now, but it was nothing to the sick feeling that followed as the mists shifted again, and a harridan screeched like a crow, *Harlot – you've been with a man…*

Nell flinched as the stinging swish of a birch caught her on the raw. The sickly scent of violets and roses made her feel sick thinking about it. As did the realization that the nightmare she had known as Reverend and Miss Snitterfield had finally caught her. Tears of relief filled her eyes when she heard the housekeeper speaking, kindly at first, but then the woman's voice hardened when she told Mr Jemkins to send Nell away. The banishment hurt more than Nell's smarting back.

Once again, she had been sent away. It had happened when she was but a baby, and again to avoid trouble with Ted Walcote at Oak Apple Cottage. And now she had been expelled from Hillend Rectory. Would she never lose the stigma of being a foundling? Nobody ever believed anything good of them.

★★★

Almost two hours and three winding miles later, Meg brought the caravan to a halt outside the Longden dwelling, just as two gentlemen emerged from within. The property was one of three tied cottages for workers on the Neathwood Park Estate, its occupation being dependent on the job, as was the custom. Everything was of the most basic in such places: four stone walls at ground level with a loft bedroom above, and a lean-to wooden outhouse at the back.

She recognised the older gentleman, clad in the formal black attire of a physician, as Dr Althorpe from Middlebrook village six miles away. She judged from his companion's style of dress and autocratic demeanour that the younger man with fair hair was of the gentry.

Expecting to be ignored in full view of other houses, she waited for them to leave, but instead the physician approached her.

"Good morning, Mistress Chapel," he said, in a brisk tone. "It is fortunate that you are visiting Mrs Longden in her time of need."

Meg nodded, and waited for him to continue.

"I have to tell you that she is in a sorry state of distress. Her husband has just died from injuries sustained in an accident with a horse from the Linmore Hall stables, a few days ago."

Ah, so it was Squire Norbery's horse that put an end to the villain, was it? Meg felt a savage sense of satisfaction that the blighter had his just deserts for attacking Nell.

"I should also mention that Lady Chetton of Neathwood will be visiting the bereaved woman this afternoon," said the physician. "I would be obliged if you could prepare the deceased for burial. It would not be seemly to neglect such a matter in her presence. You will, of course, be recompensed."

Meg unconsciously stiffened at the name, and her response was sharper than it would otherwise have been in speaking to the gentry.

"I make no charge at a time like this," she said, intending to do the work to help Annie Longden. The suggestion that she might wish to impress the lady from Neathwood found no favour in her eyes.

"Your generosity of spirit does you credit, Mistress Chapel," the physician said firmly, handing her a shilling, "Nevertheless, you will require an assistant who will expect payment."

Accepting the coin he offered, Meg watched him climb into his gig and drive away. Then she turned her attention to the younger man who was wearing a mid-grey tailored riding cape and standing beside his horse, a big chestnut gelding. Even from where she stood the garment looked remarkably like the one covering the bed in the caravan, which suggested that Nell's rescuer was Squire Norbery's son. He had the look of his father.

Meg waited for him to leave, but instead the gentleman looked enquiringly at a young girl watching them from the doorstep, and then turned his gaze to Meg and back to the child.

Letty, the oldest of the Longden brood, was quick to understand. "That's Meg Chapel," she said, "Her comes to see our mum."

Turning to Meg, he said, "Do you often travel the roads around here?" His voice was deep, but clear and cultured.

"From time to time, sir," she said, watching closely as he paused to moisten his lips. She sensed what he wanted to say, but could not help him find the words.

"Have you by any chance seen a young person with…um…red hair travelling this road in the last few days?"

Meg could easily have denied seeing a girl of that description, for the vibrant shade of Nell's tawny hair was nothing as common as red. Alternatively, she might have admitted that the subject of his enquiry was in the caravan. Instead, she pretended to ponder, and the girl listening to their conversation, saved her the need to answer.

"That sounds like Nell Walcote from the rectory at Hillend."

Meg noticed that his expression brightened, as if he recognised the name, for he promptly rewarded Letty for her trouble. The girl gazed in wonder at the sixpence in her hand, and rushed indoors to proclaim her newfound wealth.

Unable to resist the temptation, Meg said, "Would there be any message for the girl, sir; just in case I see her on the road?"

Her voice brought him back to the present.

"No, thank you," he said, "I…um…wondered if she had recovered from her mishap."

Watching him through half-closed eyes, even Meg, who was immune to the attractions of men, could see his face was distinctive. On their own his aquiline nose and grey eyes might be unremarkable, but there was something about his mouth that brought the face together. What it was she could not decide, but knew the young girl in the caravan would have no defences against him, and it was obvious that Nell had made an impression on him as well.

After he rode away, Meg peeped through the caravan door at the sleeping girl, and then went into the house to examine her patient. A quick assessment told her that the only suitable place to palpate the pregnant woman's belly was on the bed beside her dead husband, lying with a sheet drawn over his face.

Having ushered eight curious children of various ages from the room, and requested the woman brought in to clean the house to boil water, Meg said, "Lie down there for a minute, Annie. You're quite safe. He can't touch you now."

Her comment elicited a weary sigh of relief as the pregnant woman struggled to ease her bulky frame into place. Once settled, Meg ran her hands lightly over the taut skin, feeling an occasional tightening and when it relaxed, noted that the head was in the birth position. Labour would start soon, but was not imminent.

"It's not long now, Annie, a few days at most," she said, as she helped the woman to sit up again. "There's plenty of time to see the lady from the big house."

"I'm not one for talking to the gentry, Mother Chapel," said the woman. "Artie always told me to keep me mouth shut. They weren't interested in what I had to say."

Meg put the use of her late mother's name down to the stress of the moment. She did not mind what people called her as long as they trusted her to do the work. Sometimes it helped to be anonymous.

"I daresay he did," she said, knowing the woman's husband had been a brute and a braggart. "What happened to him?"

"A horse from Linmore kicked him in the head, close by the river. I don't know what he was doing there. He should have been harvesting with the other workers."

"Maybe he answered a call of nature," said Meg, knowing that in reality, the woman's husband had stalked Nell along the drovers' road, and attacked her by the river. It was only the young gentleman's arrival that saved her life. Afterwards, the girl had come to Meg and told her story.

"He'd been warned before about not doing his fair share of the work," said Annie. "I can't help thinking that Squire Norbery's son might have done us a favour."

"I daresay," said Meg, noting the widow's simplistic assessment of the situation. Artie Longden's dismissal would have been swift and poverty inevitable for his growing family. Eviction at such times meant the poorhouse for all of them. It might still do, but Lady Chetton would have to make the decision, in full knowledge of the Linmore involvement.

"Mr Joshua paid for the physician when the accident happened, and he came here the following day with his aunt, Miss Littlemore. They brought food and bedclothes for us, and this purse of money from Squire Norbery to pay for the funeral. I don't know what I'm going to do with it all. I've never

9

seen so many coins in me life."

"It's good that the Linmore folk accepted responsibility," Meg said, nodding at the leather pouch that the woman was clutching. "Keep the purse out of sight and don't tell anyone about it – for it might be a temptation for some folk."

"I've got that worked out," said Annie. "It'll be safe under the mattress."

Meg nodded, wondering how many other folks knew of its likely hiding place, and how long it would remain undetected. More than a few, she imagined, but if it was lost she, as a gypsy, would be the first to be suspected. It was ever thus.

Afterwards she enlisted the help of the next door neighbour to prepare the deceased for burial. Having been paid for the task, the woman readily agreed to be on hand for the delivery. She would have stayed to talk longer, but Meg sent her on her way saying that she needed to instruct Annie in the use of a herbal remedy in the weeks after the delivery. There might not be a husband in the house but it would not do any harm to be sure. Other men might chance their luck with a widow.

Not wishing to be present when the gentry visited, Meg climbed back into the vardo and set off along the road. Half a mile further on she pulled over to allow a groom driving a black high-perch phaeton to pass. The lady passenger, clad in a dark blue habit, inclined her head in acknowledgement and Meg did likewise.

So that was the new Lady Chetton from Neathwood Park. She looked a kinder woman to the harridan that Meg remembered as her predecessor, in a different lifetime.

★★★

In the caravan, Nell struggled to shake off the unaccustomed languor, but Meg's relaxing potion was too powerful to resist. A recurrent dream drifted through her subconscious state. It was the memory of a kiss, light as the touch of a butterfly's wing, then a savage beating and an inexplicable dismissal. Somehow, they were interlinked, but she was too weary to understand.

In a daze, she heard Meg speaking to her, and swallowed a mouthful or two of water before drifting off to sleep. Later, she heard the dull sound of hoofbeats, and thought she heard a man's voice, but decided she must be mistaken. She touched her lips and murmured contentedly, knowing that whoever her rescuer was, she would know him again. Then, feeling the sway of the caravan starting to move again, she drifted off to sleep.

The following morning she awoke feeling little refreshed. When she sat up and put her feet to the caravan floor, her slender frame ached with inactivity; but taking a few hesitant steps to the door, she pushed through the discomfort.

All was quiet in the woodland clearing. Meg was sitting on a box beside the campfire, plaiting rushes to make into baskets. As if sensing Nell's presence, she looked up and smiled a welcome.

"Have I overslept?" Nell said.

"No, it's early yet," said Meg. "How does your back feel?"

"It's a bit stiff," she said, "but not so sore."

Meg nodded and said, "You'll hardly notice in a few days. I'll find you some different clothes to wear when we go out. We'll wash the ones you're wearing later and leave them to dry in the hut."

"I'm sorry," said Nell. "I should help you, but couldn't stay awake."

"That was the idea," said Meg. "Animals rest when they're injured. It is nature's way to ensure they heal faster."

Nell nodded and sat on another box by the fire. It was not cold, but the kettle which hung on a hook was singing to show it had boiled.

"Are you hungry, little one?"

"Yes," she said, realising she was famished.

Within minutes Nell held a bowl half-filled with broth in her hands, and in the absence of a spoon, sipped the contents until it was empty. She did not recognise the taste but the nourishment it gave was exactly what she needed.

"Thank you, Meg. Where do I wash the bowl?"

The question was instinctive, drummed in by her work at Hillend Rectory.

Meg smiled, pointing to the kettle, and in minutes the bowl was clean. It was not at all like washing dishes at the rectory. Nor was Nell accustomed to having idle hands. "What can I do to help?" she said.

11

"Can you plait rushes?" Meg said, holding up a long strand she had already made.

"Yes," said Nell, thinking back to the time at Oak Apple Cottage when she made rush mats for the earthen floor. It seemed so long ago, and yet it was only four years since she was a skinny little girl of ten, starting work at the rectory. A lot had happened since then. When Ted and Peggy Walcote died, their children were sent to the poorhouse. Being a foundling, Nell was not really part of their family.

"What's the matter, little one? You look sad."

Nell sighed, but her fingers did not stop plaiting.

"I wish that I knew where I belonged, and to whom," she said.

Meg looked up from her work. "Never mind what went before. How would you feel if I said that your life began here with me on the hill?"

"I would like that, Meg," she said, "but I must do something…"

"You can spend the winter with me, if you like," Meg said, without hesitation, "and we'll see what next year brings."

"Stay here?" said the girl. "But what will I do?"

"Come with me on my travels. I'll take you beyond the hill and show you places that you never dreamed existed."

"Won't I be a nuisance?" said Nell.

No, little one, you won't be a nuisance, Meg thought. Aloud she said, "There are times when I could do with company. We might find somewhere for you to work."

Even as she said the words, Meg knew there would be difficulties to overcome. Hardships for Nell to endure living outdoors which Meg had similarly encountered as a child.

"Wouldn't people know that I was turned off from my other job?"

"Not if we don't tell them," she said, shrugging her shoulders. "We could always say that your employer died, or that you weren't needed any more. They wouldn't know any difference."

Despite her assertion, Meg knew that some folk might question the presence of a fair-skinned girl travelling with a gypsy, but would deal with the problem if it occurred.

She could tell from Nell's intense expression that she was mulling the idea over. Then the girl nodded and said, "Yes, I'd like that. What can I do to help?"

"We'll start the hedgerow harvest tomorrow. Usually I gather fruits and berries alone, but with you here we'll pick more. Then we'll prepare them for drying and storage. I'll show you what to do. First, of all, you need different clothes to the ones you're wearing."

Chapter 2

Nell lay in her narrow bed, listening to the silence that preceded the onset of bird song. She knew she should move, but the ache in her back reminded her that only two days had passed since she arrived in the wood asking for help, and Meg had made her welcome. Guessing that the hour was not yet four, she drew the bedcover and the warm grey cape her rescuer had given her over her shoulder, closed her eyes and allowed herself the indulgence of a few more minutes rest.

Sleep was impossible after the first blackbird's call, so she looked around the vardo in the half-light, seeking her clothes. Then she recalled that last night, before Meg left her to sleep, she had sorted through a box of second-hand garments and left them on the old wooden chair by the door.

Discarding the stained uniform frock, full of memories, Nell laced a high-necked bodice over her shift and added a fichu. Then she pulled on a gathered skirt that she hitched up before wrapping a thin leather belt twice around her waist to ensure a closer fit. She draped a woollen shawl about her shoulders, and reached for a faded blue scarf, but no matter how she tied the cloth around her head, her tawny hair refused to be contained. One little red-gold curl after another peeped out.

"What can I do, Meg?" she said. "People will know who I am if I leave it uncovered."

It was another tainted memory from her childhood. As long as Nell could remember, her hair had shone like a beacon, marking her as a foundling. There was not another red-haired woman in the district, and she did not want Meg to be blamed for befriending her.

14

Meg rummaged in the box for a boy's cap that fell down over Nell's ears and half-covered her eyes. "Does that make you feel better, little one?" she said.

Nell looked up at her from under the brim, and laughed. "Yes, thank you."

"Your pretty hair is worth looking at, girl," Meg said, "and don't ever forget it. Folks would go a long way to see curls like that."

"I know," said Nell. "I should be grateful, but I don't like people looking at me."

"They stare at me as well," said Meg, with a wry smile, "for different reasons. We just have to live with the fact."

"I suppose you're right," she said. "I'd never thought of it before."

★★★

No, but Meg had, many times over the years. With no other option, she had accepted the life that was dealt her, but knew it would have been different if she had been born a boy. That was why she sometimes put it to the test.

A woman found to be dressed as a man was treated harshly, but Meg had a disregard for the law ever since Mother Chapel's older sons were transported to the southern ocean on a trumped-up kidnapping charge. Two fine boys, on the brink of manhood, who had done no harm to anyone.

It was the old matriarch of the gypsy camp who had allowed the black-haired girl of the gentry to stay when she wandered in claiming to be lost. When her kinfolk came looking for her, the girl had told lies and been damned for her trouble.

Meg remembered the day it happened, and the old woman's harsh words when her favourite grandsons were dragged away in shackles, expecting to be hung for a crime they had not committed. They might well have been, had not Squire Norbery of Linmore interceded. Not in their defence, but he must have known the girl's free and easy ways. His intervention saved them from the gallows, but nobody knew what happened after the prison hulk set sail, or if they ever made shore again.

When the gypsy mother turned her venom on the girl, she wished her no luck in her lifetime. Not a curse in the true sense, but once spoken the bitter words could not be recalled.

Almost a decade had passed since then. The "Ancient One", as Meg called her, died within months, poisoned by grief. Mother Chapel followed two years later, leaving Meg alone. Now she realised that she had someone to look out for. Nell was more than a babe in arms, but no worldlier than the first time Meg had seen her. One day soon she would have to tell the girl the truth of her birth.

★★★

Being dressed in strange loose clothes reminded Nell of her early days at Hillend Rectory, which she tried to stifle, only to have other memories come to the fore. What had Maisie Jemkins thought when Nell disappeared? Had she pestered Miss Dinchope with questions, and how had the housekeeper replied? She hoped the woman had not scolded the gardener's daughter for her curiosity, which was considerable. Nell sighed and pushed the thoughts to the back of her mind.

After breakfast, they set off to walk along the lower ride that bordered the hill, an uneven path more wearing than any she had used before. Meg moved with easy strides, while Nell, afraid of tripping over her skirt, stopped every so often to tighten the belt, just as she had done with the strange new undergarments in her first days at the rectory. Clothes which she had left behind, but secretly missed wearing.

It seemed strange to be walking in the fresh air at the time of morning when she would normally have been on her knees scrubbing floors or brushing carpets. Other days, she had helped Mrs Jemkins with the laundry, or made butter in the dairy.

A memory of roasted ham wafted back to torment her, which she resolutely pushed aside knowing that such food had never graced her plate. Only Reverend Snitterfield and his sister, in the rectory household, were allowed such luxuries.

Turning her mind to the task of gathering whimberries, Nell was surprised to see that a dozen or so women and children had appeared on the hillside with the same intention. At first, she was fearful of being recognised, but soon realised that with Meg beside her, no one gave her a second glance.

Despite not knowing which fruits to gather, she was intrigued to find that Meg knew which part of the hillside yielded the juiciest whimberries. Having filled their baskets, Nell took a rest while Meg carried the fruits back along the path to the wood. On her return, they ventured down to common land running beside the hill, where Meg located a big bramble bush loaded with blackberries; an elder tree, whose berry-covered twigs Nell could pick when Meg reached up and pulled the branches down, and bushes of rosehips bigger than anyone else could find.

When the baskets were again filled to overflowing, Nell stood, wriggling her aching shoulders. "Have we finished now?" she said.

"Yes, for today," said Meg. "We'll find something else tomorrow."

"What shall I carry?" Nell said as her friend effortlessly picked up all three baskets, two large and a smaller one filled with rosehips and haw berries.

"You can take the little one when we get to the top of the slope," said Meg, but when they reached that stage, she strode ahead, and Nell followed wearily behind.

She soon found, however, that their day was not over. After a warm drink and a bite to eat, they began to prepare their finds for use later in the season.

Despite her aching shoulders, Nell's nimble fingers quickly mastered the art of bunching up heavily laden sprigs of elderflower and berries to hang from hooks in the shed roof, and then she helped spread out the rosehips and haw berries.

"How do you remember the names?" she said, yawning.

"Mother Chapel taught me and made sure I would never forget," said Meg with a grimace.

"Was that your mother?" she said, not liking to ask any more.

Meg nodded, and turned away to reach for a sheet of parchment, which she placed on the table and took a bone-handled blade to sharpen a pencil; such quality items were surely unusual in a gypsy caravan, Nell thought.

"If you write them down," Meg said, "it's easier to remember."

When Nell had itemised each name of the day's collection, she found to her surprise that Meg could also read the words aloud. She did not question her friend's ability, but thought about it later in the evening when they walked out to the spring at the edge of the hill and stood looking across the valley. Something in the peaceful glow of sunset told her the time was right to ask.

"Have you always lived on the hill, Meg?"

When Meg seemed lost in her thoughts, Nell half-wished she had not spoken.

"No, I lived down there in the valley," Meg said, pointing into the middle distance, "but came here with Mother Chapel when I was seven years old."

It seemed strange to call her mother by that name.

"She went down as a midwife for the gentry, and stayed too long. Her family didn't remember me, so we came to live in the wood and I have been here ever since. Before she passed on, she chose her place to lie under the trees amongst the bluebells, so I buried her there. Maybe someone will do the same for me when my time comes."

Nell shivered at the thought, and wondered if she would be the one to fulfil Meg's wish. She wanted to ask what Meg meant by saying her mother's people refused to take her back. Did she mean the gypsies – and if so, why?

"Don't you have any more family, Meg?"

Her friend looked at her and gave a wry smile.

"I once thought I had a brother, but he's too grand to know me now."

Nell wondered if he was as tall and black-haired as Meg and whether he had strange green eyes and wore riding boots of fine black leather. If he did, she would be sure to know him. Somewhere in her mind was a memory of such a man, but she could not recall where and when she had seen him.

They spent much of the next day gathering acorns and beechmast in the wood. Nell was glad it was on relatively level ground, and easy to drag her hessian sack along the tree-lined path to the woodman's shed, where the space was rapidly reducing, while Meg slung a larger one over each shoulder.

"You're carrying all the weight," Nell said, "I should have put more in my bag."

"I'm used to carrying sacks," said Meg, "but I wouldn't be any good at making butter."

Nell, knowing that she had the skill, felt comforted by the thought.

18

Two days later, they walked further into the wood seeking wild garlic, pungent in its freshness, and various kinds of fungi that grew in abundance. Meg pulled up roots; some to cut in slivers to dry, others in chunks to be prepared later. Finally, they collected twigs of willow bark, which Nell learned was to treat fevers. When they returned to the hut, Meg told her the names of each item, which Nell tried to memorise before she went to sleep.

Each night, she went to bed weary with aching shoulders, but glad that she was being of use. She tried not to regret the loss of her feather bed in the rectory attic bedroom, or bemoan the strange sounds in the woodland that sometimes made it difficult to sleep, but she did not blame anyone for her change of circumstances.

Nell had always known her place and done as the housekeeper told her, apart from one occasion when she was contrary. Honesty made her admit the fault, for she had known before she set out to see Meg that her old work frock was too small, which was why she left off her shift to make it fit, thinking it would not matter. That was only the beginning.

Usually, when she walked along the drovers' road to the crossroads, she turned up the hill path to the wood. Perversely, feeling hot, she ran down a track to paddle in a stream that she had found in the coppice of silver birch trees.

If she had not crossed the stepping stones, she would not have fallen in the stream and soaked her clothes. Nor been tired and gone to sleep on a slab of rock, and when she awoke, the farm labourer, who looked like Ted Walcote, would not have been watching her from the bushes.

She shuddered, recalling how easily her frock tore when he grabbed her, and she fell back through the bushes out of reach. Then she opened her eyes, and saw him prostrated on the riverbank, with a second, younger man lying stunned on the floor and the horse he must have been riding grazing beside him.

The same gentleman had covered her state of undress with his cape. When he asked her name, she said, "Nell," without knowing who he was or from where he had come, but she would never forget his kindness.

She sighed, remembering how clean he smelled, when everyone else she knew was sweaty. To her, he was like a god. Not with a halo and wings as she had seen on the stained glass church windows, but with light-coloured hair that fell in a wave across his face.

If he had been an angel, she would not have dared touch his cheek, or felt a tingle rippling through her at the slightest rasp of bristle. Nor, when he awoke, would he have touched her lips so softly with his own.

Oh, yes, she had been severely whipped and dismissed from service, but she did not regret everything that happened.

★★★

When Nell awoke the next morning, she saw a row of stone herbal jars on the ground beside the vardo, and Meg placing them carefully in a cupboard underneath.

"What are you doing?" she said.

"I'm getting the stores ready for when we go to Caitlin tomorrow."

Nell felt a bubble of something well up inside, which could have been excitement, or maybe trepidation. Whatever it was, the thought ensured she was awake on the morrow at the break of dawn. She knew from the sounds of movement outside that Meg was already in the clearing, with the fire lit and the kettle boiling. It made her wonder how much Meg actually slept, but she did not like to ask.

Where was Caitlin, and by which path would they travel? She assumed that Meg would drive the caravan further along the road past where they had found the blackberries. She waited, expecting to walk beside the vardo, as Meg led the horse down the slope.

Instead, Meg climbed up onto the driver's bench and sat looking at her. "Aren't you coming with me?" she said with a lopsided grin.

"Which way are we going?" Nell said, wondering where else there could be.

"Climb up beside me and I will show you," said Meg, pausing before taking the horse deeper into the wood.

It was soon apparent that Hillend village had been too close to Linmore Hill to give Nell any idea of the size of the woodland that enshrouded the western side. Although she had always lived in the countryside, there was much she was seeing for the first time. Becoming aware of the faint rustling of leaves and changing colours, she looked up at the canopy of branches above her head, wondering what type of tree it was.

"That oak is probably two hundred years old," Meg remarked, casually supplying the information as they trundled past.

Nell noted the details, and then recalled something she had meant to ask. "What were those people doing in the wood the other day?"

"Collecting acorns and beechmast for their pigs," said Meg. "The hill is common land but the wood and the hut is owned by Squire Norbery of Linmore Hall. He gave Mother Chapel leave to use it when we performed a service for him at the time his son was born."

The gentleman's name struck a chord of memory.

"I've heard of him," said Nell. "Mrs Grimble, from Hillend, told me that he took an interest in my welfare when I was a baby. That's why I had to work hard at school and learn my letters. I don't think he'd be pleased with me now."

She had also remembered him in her prayers.

"He certainly wouldn't be happy with the folk who did that to your back."

"It was Miss Snitterfield, but her brother was in the room as well," Nell said, shivering at the thought of the parson revelling in her humiliation. Then she remembered, "What about my dirty work clothes? I should have washed them."

"There's no need," said Meg, "They're drying in the shed, but I'll leave the mending to you. The frock might be useful in the colder weather."

Nell realised that Meg must have gone down to the stream while she was asleep. Nothing more was said on the subject, but she was intrigued when Meg drove the vardo further into the wood. Gradually the path became steeper and she realised that they were going uphill.

The horse plodded steadily onwards, unconcerned by the sloping ground that dropped away a few feet beyond the vardo wheels, but Nell noticed and held her breath until the road levelled out again.

Her fears were calmed by the gentle clop of his hooves and muffled sound of turning wheels, while any birdsong merged into the silence. The woodland had a homely feel, as if it belonged to a world in which Hillend

Rectory might never have existed, even though she knew that it did. *Had done*, she corrected the thought.

Meg's voice broke through her reverie.

"The oak tree up ahead is older than the other one we saw, for they become more gnarled and wider with age. The other trees are ash, beech and horse chestnut, but birch, with the silver bark, grows faster than the others."

Nell remembered seeing oak trees in the open parkland hidden away behind wrought-iron gates along the road from Hillend, when she had visited Mrs Ferndale, the dressmaker. The same gateway where she first met Meg and the place where Maisie Jemkins had slipped through a hole in the hedge and Nell had followed to bring her back.

A few yards beyond the gates, a birch coppice had screened a mound of stones from a long demolished house, overgrown with grass. There was a sad looking dovecote with the branches of a birch tree growing out the top and ducks on the lake in the distance, which Maisie was determined to see.

Nell shivered at the recollection of her struggle to persuade a simple-minded girl, with no perception of danger, to return to safety; and of how the notion of dirty boots and Miss Dinchope's good opinion had been the deciding factor.

She felt sad, thinking about the clothes that she had made from remnants of material given to her by Mrs Grimble. She had so looked forward to wearing them, but knew she would never see them or the people she had known again. Worse still was that Maisie would never see the skirt that Nell had made with loving care, knowing the different colours of blue, green and russet brown would delight her.

"Are you all right?" said Meg. "You're quiet."

"Yes," said Nell, in a husky voice, brushing away the tears that contradicted her words. "There's so much to see, it is confusing."

"This is only the beginning," said Meg.

As if to prove the point, the path started to level out at the top of the rise, and more sky became visible. As they emerged from the trees, Meg stopped to look around and Nell gasped in astonishment as the vista of the heather-topped hill unfolded before her eyes.

"Oh, Meg, it's huge," she said, her voice muffled with emotion. "I never realised it would be like this." Her voice broke, and tears blurred her vision.

The prospect of so much open space and not another person in sight was overwhelming. Despite that, Nell found Meg's silence comforting.

"I'm sorry for being silly," she said.

"No, little one." Meg's voice was gruff. "I feel like that every time I see it, just as you will when we return home."

The word *home* had a strange ring to it that gave her a sense of belonging.

"How far does it go?" she asked.

"Seven or eight miles to the far end of the hill, but there are rides that come up at different levels from the drovers' road," said Meg, pointing towards the land edging the valley.

"What's that?" said Nell, who had heard the name before, but not understood the significance.

"It's where herds of Welsh cattle are driven in the spring and autumn. There can be two or three hundred head at a time. And sheep or geese as well."

"Why?" said Nell.

"They are taken to market, but have to be fattened up along the way. The drovers try to avoid the toll gates, because they are charged so much per animal, which adds to the cost of the journey."

"What about their feet?" Nell said. "Wouldn't they be sore?"

"The cattle are fitted with metal shoes, called 'cues', by a blacksmith. Geese sometimes have leather boots, or they might have their feet tarred for protection."

Nell was intrigued by the thought of that but she could see the sense.

"Will we see them on our travels?" she said.

"I try to avoid them," said Meg. "All those animals frighten the horse. Coming this way, we cover the ground better than down in the valley following every rise and fall of the roads."

It made sense, but somehow Nell guessed that it was not the only reason.

"Where do all these tracks go?" she said, pointing in various directions through the heather. "There are so many of them."

Meg gave a low chuckle and began to speak. "The one we are following

23

leads to the end of the hill, and turns down to Caitlin Vale. Another one halfway along the hill goes to Brackenridge Common, where we go in the spring. Then there's one that heads out towards the town of Norcott, with Bredenbridge a distance beyond that, and Westbridge is in another direction across Linmore Dale."

The places were just names, but Nell determined to recall them. The mention of being with Meg in the spring gave her a sense of belonging. It was a reassuringly long time away and something about which she did not need to worry.

Even so, a little voice in her mind told her that she would have to play her part in finding work to pay for their food, even if she had no idea what she had eaten for breakfast.

"How far is Caitlin?" she asked.

"Six miles as the crow flies," said Meg, "or eight if you follow the road."

A distance further than Nell had travelled before in one direction.

"What do you do in these places?" she said.

"Visit the hamlets and farms. Catch up on the news and supply herbs to the village carers that treat remedies in the winter. Sometimes I help a baby to come into the world, or deliver things for people between the villages."

"Do you think I could be a carer?" said Nell.

"I don't see why not, when I have taught you a few things about my work. You're bright, so you can learn as we go along."

"It might take a while," Nell said.

"We've got plenty of time," said Meg. "In the meantime, can you sew a straight seam or do darning?"

"Yes," said Nell. "Mrs Ferndale, the seamstress at Hillend, taught me basic sewing and dressmaking. I can also wash clothes and scrub floors as well."

"Sewing will do for now. The coaching inns often need someone to repair torn sheets. It might even lead to a job if the place is right."

"Wouldn't they want to know where I'd worked before?" said Nell, worried at having to admit that she had been dismissed.

"Not necessarily, people move all the time. We might find work for you on our travels, but folks don't always trust gypsies too well."

Nor had they trusted the folk from Oak Apple Cottage.

★★★

The silence under the great expanse of sky was both calming and frightening at the same time. Striving for a degree of normality, Nell wondered what time it was, and who was doing her work at the rectory and if anyone would miss her. Then she chided herself for being silly, for apart from Maisie, she doubted if anyone cared.

The sun was shining when she bowed her head to hide her feelings. When she looked up, minutes later, the view was hidden under wisps of chilly cloud. The change came suddenly, but Meg seemed unperturbed, as she reached for a shawl that lay on the bench between them. "Put that around your shoulders," she said.

As she complied, Nell realised that she had learned her first lesson about living on the hill. That the weather, which had seemed benevolently warm, could change in a few minutes. The horse, however, plodded onwards.

"How does Loadstone know where to go?" said Nell.

"Animals rely on instinct and the blinkers stop him from being distracted."

Within half a mile, the clouds had gone. When the sun reappeared, Meg stopped the vardo to water the horse, and before they resumed their journey, they took a drink of water and chewed on a crust.

Nell got down from the bench and stretched her legs, but did not stray too far in case the weather changed again. She yawned, and resumed her seat.

"Do you want to rest?" said Meg. "Sitting here takes some getting used to."

"Would you mind?" she said.

"I'm used to it, little one, and you'll grow accustomed. Maybe not by next week, but it will be second nature by the time we reach the end of Caitlin Vale. There's no shame in taking a rest after what you've been through."

Nell could not deny that her back ached from the unaccustomed posture on the driver's bench. She was more than ready to be lulled to sleep by the gentle sway of the vardo, her eyes half-closing the minute her head touched the pillow.

"Don't forget the cape to keep you warm…" Meg's voice followed her through the door.

She smiled contentedly as she snuggled down into its comforting warmth and thought of the owner.

★★★

"Oh, Mother Chapel," muttered Meg, to herself, "if I'd been born a boy, none of this would have happened."

As a girl, Meg was a misfit, living between two worlds and rejected by both. Supposedly a babe-in-arms when her mother wet-nursed a nobleman's only living son, she stayed to bear him company, and when he called her sister, she in her innocence believed him. Until, at seven years old, he went to school and left her to weep tears of humiliation when she learned the ugly truth of her existence.

"Enough of that noise, girl," Mother Chapel had told her.

"Where are we going, Ma?" she had asked in a state of confusion.

"Up on the hill where my kind belongs."

"Why must we leave?" said Meg, wanting to stay.

"You heard her ladyship, child. We've served our purpose and these people have no use for us. The young master will live a different life to you."

"He said I was to be his sister," insisted Meg.

"That's what he wanted to believe, but we know different."

Do we know for sure that's what his father intended? thought Meg.

When Mother Chapel had taken Meg home to her kinfolk, the gypsy matriarch made the decree. *Renounce the baseborn child if you want to see your real family again.*

Instead, her mother had walked away and taken Meg with her.

That was the real reason that Meg came to live on the hill. After the first rejection she had wept silent tears in the night and, when they were dry, decided that emotions were for fools, and that gentlemen could not be trusted to keep their word.

The second time she felt nothing. Since that day, she had only once shown her feelings for another person, until she saw the bloodied stripes of a birch across Nell Walcote's back, and a deep smouldering resentment against the gentry had threatened to erupt. Necessity, born of habit, made her suppress the emotion as she carried on dressing the wounds; but with the knowledge of having befriended Nell and invited her to the woodland, Meg knew she should have ensure the girl's safety. As she had not, she must make amends.

Chapter 3

Nell had her first view of Caitlin Vale in the late afternoon. She slept for several hours and awoke to find they had reached the end of the hill. From the top of the slope looking down, the valley appeared narrow and steep-sided with a stream running parallel to the single-tracked road that hugged the edge of the hillside. In the distance, she noticed forested hillocks and undulating ridges that might hide other roads from sight.

By the time darkness fell they had made their painstakingly slow way down the winding road to the foot of the hill, and parked the caravan alongside a stream where they replenished their water supply. For Nell, it was a day fed by excitement and trepidation, so sleep came easily, but Meg seemed to carry on regardless.

In the early morning when Nell climbed down from the vardo, the hill was shrouded by mist, which gave the valley an almost ghostly appearance. She shivered, feeling a sensation of being cut off from the world she had known.

Things looked better when the sun made its presence felt, so they took breakfast and continued their journey, turning first towards what Meg told her was the head of the valley.

As they progressed, Nell saw several piles of broken rocks along the roadside verges.

"What are those stones for, Meg?"

"For road repairs when there's someone to do the work," said her friend. "Each parish is responsible for the pathways within its boundary, and itinerant workers do repairs in exchange for a meal and bed for the night."

From the unkempt state of the road, Nell guessed that not many people travelled through Caitlin Vale. The land had a wild, overgrown look with fewer enclosures than she had seen in Linmore Dale. She had no reason to consider such things at Hillend, but she saw it now.

At the approach to a hamlet, Meg forded the stream and drove the caravan towards a cluster of cottages and stopped. All was quiet, but within minutes, people came out of their dwellings to see the herbalist.

Watching from inside the van, Nell could see what was going on, but she waited for Meg to complete her business, and then emerged as the caravan trundled down a narrow cart track towards a farm.

No sooner had the wheels rattled on the cobbles of the fold, than barking dogs rushed out of the barn, and a cockerel vied with honking geese to warn of the visitors' arrival. Meg parked the caravan in the farmyard, and went off to speak with the farmer's wife. Sitting alone on the driver's bench, Nell noticed a group of workers gathered around a pigsty. After a while, curiosity overcame her and she climbed cautiously down to peer over the low stone wall, where a farrowing sow lay on her side suckling her piglets.

For several minutes, it seemed the process was complete, but then Nell realised another piglet was about to be born. No sooner had its feet touched the ground, but the shoulders shrugged, and four tiny trotters propelled it forward with accompanying squeals and grunts towards the source of nourishment.

Nell watched enthralled, as several more followed, with larger ones pushing the smallest aside in their rush to get food. She wanted to help, but one of the workers warned her not to touch the runt because the sow might tread on it. Recognising the danger, she returned to the caravan and found Meg waiting to resume their travels.

On reaching the outskirts of the next village, she noticed a boy sitting alone by the signpost. At the sight of them he dashed off into the distance.

"Did we scare him away, Meg?" she said.

"I expect he's been told to wait until he sees any strangers, and then pass the message on." Meg obviously knew the local practices, and before the caravan reached the houses by the church, a group of people was already waiting.

At the sight of them, Nell retreated inside the vardo but left the door ajar to listen. The first customer was a seamstress who needed a remedy for headaches. The schoolmaster came next, seeking advice for various ailments within the schoolroom, and finally, a farmer asked for a supply of bloat mixture, ready for when cattle strayed into spring grasses. After that, a few more people drifted by, unsure whether their problems warranted the time or effort of asking for help.

She heard everything Meg said, and watched to see whether people understood the instructions. Seeing some puzzled looks she wondered if they could read or write, and was pleased when Meg suggested they brought an older child that understood his numbers to count out the doses. Nell thought if she wrote it down they could ask the schoolmaster to help, but then realised it would draw unwanted attention to her presence.

★★★

Within minutes of solving the last villager's problem, Meg was on the move again.

"Where are we going now?" Nell's anxious voice came from the vardo doorway.

"To see a woman I know," said Meg, noting that as they approached the carer's cottage at the edge of the village, Nell retreated out of sight.

Hardly had the horse drawn to a halt, than Molly Hardwick, a homely-looking woman, came out of her house.

"Where's your little friend?" the woman asked. "Billy Bosbury came running in ten minutes ago to say you were on your way and that you had a passenger. I told him to mind his own business, but I daresay that he'll have told everybody from here to the Hall before nightfall."

"In the vardo," said Meg, nodding towards the closed door. "She's doing some sewing for the farmer's wife down the road. I said we'd take it back later."

"And old Mother Huffer agreed?" Molly Hardwick said, incredulous. "That's the first time I've heard of her trusting anyone...um...well...not that she has reason to think you're dishonest."

30

Meg gave a wry smile, knowing that gypsies were the first to be suspected if anything was missing – and even if it was not.

"Who is the girl, and what kind of background does she have?"

Knowing that Molly liked to be the first to hear the news, Meg chose her words carefully. "An orphan who lost her mother at birth and the family that adopted her died in the Linmore epidemic, a couple of years ago. She was in service at the time, that's how she survived."

"What about her employers?" Molly said.

"The lady of the house died at about the same time," said Meg, recalling what Nell had told her about Reverend Snitterfield's wife, "and the housekeeper turned off the younger maids."

"I expect she was one of those that had her eye on the master of the house," said the carer, with a snort of derision. "How do you come to be involved?"

"I knew the girl's mother before she was born," said Meg, knowing she was telling parts of the story that were likely to draw sympathy.

"If you'd been here a few weeks ago, she might have found a job at the rectory, but my girl, Elsie, started work there at the beginning of the month."

"Does she like it?"

"Yes, Elsie says that the parson and his wife are lovely folk to work for. She had the chance to be dairymaid up at the Hall, but said she preferred to be nearer home. The truth is, Meg, I thought she'd be safer at the rectory than in Squire Whitcott's household. He's the parson's older brother, but only by a few minutes. They're twins, you know, and both wanted to marry the same lady."

Meg nodded, having heard the story before of how the daughter of a baronet had chosen the younger son, a man of the cloth, in preference to his bombastic brother who was heir to the family estate. A severe blow to his ego, by all accounts, and he promptly married an heiress whose father had made his money in trade.

"The Squire's wife is a rich woman, but not quality born like Mrs Whitcott at the rectory. Nor are the sons from the Hall proper gentlemen either, unlike Mr Adam, the parson's son. Captain Adam, I should say, for he's an officer in the army."

31

"Has he been home lately?" said Meg.

"No, and the parson worries about him. Wishes he'd taken to the ministry, but when Miss Lavinia from the Hall, who he was supposed to wed, ran off with a groom, he'd have enlisted as a common soldier if the squire hadn't insisted on paying for his commission or whatever they do. Mortified, he was, by her behaviour."

"What about the sons?"

"Don't take your little girl anywhere near Caitlin Hall. She wouldn't be safe. Oh, that reminds me, Meg, I'll need some more of the herbal tea you gave me last year; as much as you can spare if we're to avoid those two from the Hall littering the district with their by-blows. The pair of them need gelding, and if they don't mend their ways, one of these dark nights, some of the girls' fathers will do it to them – and then we'd all be in a pickle.

"That's why I didn't want our Elsie working there. The squire wanted to send Mr Cedric to the war with his cousin, when he came home from school, but his wife wouldn't hear of it. She didn't like him spending her money on Mr Adam, but couldn't deny he had good reason to go with Miss Lavinia being their daughter."

"The gentry always have one in the litter like her," said Meg, recalling another such feral female on the other side of Linmore Hill. "Did she marry her groom?"

"No, she soon tired of him," scoffed Molly. "The last I heard from the housekeeper, who told me in confidence, was that Miss Lavinia had found herself a wealthy protector in Bredenbridge, and was living the life of a lady at his expense. Not a young man by any means, or a proper gentleman, but she wasn't choosy."

"Anyone we know?" said Meg, feigning indifference.

"Some factory owner…or was it a foundry from out Bredenbridge way? I can't remember. It seems he's married, and if what the housekeeper said was right, the father of one of her fancy school friends. But they don't like that being talked about."

"I bet they don't," said Meg, gathering her things together. "I'd better be on my way, Molly. Otherwise the farmer's wife will think we've stolen her sewing."

"Be careful where you're going, Meg. The squire's sons are out hunting today, and I wouldn't like Mr Cedric to see your young friend and cause trouble. He's feral, and it's just as well that she's not a boy, for the servants at the Hall say that Mr Barnaby, who'll be the next squire when his father's dead, is differently inclined."

"Mmm," said Meg, in a dry tone. "I don't have any potions for his complaint."

She prepared to go on her way, somewhat disappointed that Elsie Hardwick was wasting her time as a lady's maid. A pity about that, for Meg thought she had the makings of a carer like her mother. *Ah, well...these things happen.* Then she remembered something she meant to ask.

"Do you know anybody that might have any old clothes to spare?" she said. "The little one will need something warmer to wear around her legs for the winter."

She did not mention breeches, but Molly seemed to understand.

"Elsie was telling me that the parson's wife has kept all Mr Adam's clothes from when he was a boy. I can ask Mrs Rumble, casual-like, to see if there's anything similar at the Hall. I daresay there's plenty for the squire's lady don't give much to the poor," Molly Hardwick said with obvious disapproval.

"Thank you," said Meg, casually. "Boy's clothes would do just as well. I'll come back in a couple of days to see what you've managed to find."

★★★

Nell, sitting in the caravan, heard every word that was spoken. She had already finished her linen repairs for the farmer's wife and was engrossed in a book of sermons that she had found, which bore a faded inscription: *To Margaret on your seventh birthday, 1780.* There was also a signature, but it was indistinct.

She wondered if Meg had ever been called Margaret. Or had she happened upon it by chance? The latter seemed more likely, for Nell was sure Meg was older than that. What puzzled her most was Meg's reference to knowing her mother.

At the village limits she resumed her seat on the driver's bench, but scarcely half a mile beyond along the narrow road, they encountered two gentlemen on horseback approaching at a canter, their hunting togs splattered with mud.

"Get out of our way, filthy peasants," snarled the thinner of the two riders.

Ignoring the insult, Meg drew to the side to allow them to pass.

"What are we going to do?" said Nell, nervously.

"Stay where you are, little one," murmured Meg, "they'll go by."

Nell hoped they would, but as the one riding a roan started to pass, the other on the showy chestnut stopped directly in front of the vardo.

"I say, Barnaby," he said, "it's damned back luck we lost the fox, but this gypsy wench can compensate for the lack of a kill."

"Leave her alone, Cedric," said the other one, evidently his brother, "the sport is over for the day and in any case, we're too close to the village."

Ignoring him, the other one said, "Get down from there, wench, and lift your skirts or I will make the old crone suffer."

Nell froze as he raised his riding crop threateningly. Meg did not appear to move, but Nell heard a sound, more a hiss than a whistle, and suddenly, all was confusion as one horse bolted, while the animal nearest the vardo reared in a panic, stepping back over the edge of the village duck pond and shedding its rider in the process.

There was a roar of obscenities, and then a dull splash as the huntsman landed in a puddle of stagnant water. His mount followed the first horse, with its frantically clinging rider, past the vardo and on through the village.

"That should cool him down," said Meg, grimly, as she flicked the reins, and encouraged Lodestone to break into a trot for half a mile before turning down a cart track towards the farmhouse they had visited earlier in the day, to return the sewing.

"What did you do?" said Nell, astonished at Meg's unconcern.

"Something I'll have to teach you, little one," Meg said softly. "But for tonight, we'll stay here out of sight."

The experience had an unsettling effect on Nell, but Meg, possibly more accustomed to abuse, seemed unconcerned.

As dusk fell they parked the caravan near a coppice within sight of the farm, and sat around the campfire talking. "Does that happen often, Meg?"

"Not all the gentry are like those two. From the name, I reckon they were Squire Whitcott's sons that Molly Hardwick told me about."

"Do they...?" Nell stopped, not knowing how to phrase the question.

"With me?" said Meg with a humourless laugh. "They'd have to be blind to try that, and they'd have no joy of it."

Not knowing how to respond, Nell said, "I hope you don't mind, Meg, but I found your book in the vardo."

"You can read it," said Meg. "That's what it's intended for. I've had it a long time."

With that Nell had to be satisfied, but a few minutes later, she wondered, "Did you bring it up from the valley?"

"Yes," said Meg. "One day, I'll show you the place where it came from."

Nell wished she could ask who gave Meg the book of sermons with the fine brown leather cover. An item of quality, such as a gentleman would have. Was he the one whose son Mother Chapel had fed, and had he been sad when they left?

Instead, she said, "Did Mother Chapel have any other children besides you?"

"Three boys and a couple of girls by her husband. The two oldest sons used to slip out of the camp under cover of darkness to visit their mother in the wood. They were the ones to be transported."

"Were you lonely, not having anyone to talk with?" Nell asked, but then remembered that nobody bothered to speak to her either.

Meg shrugged her shoulders. "It's no good worrying about things you can't change. I learned to work early and have been doing it ever since."

Much as Nell had done.

★★★

When Nell woke the next morning, Meg was nowhere in sight. Nor was the horse, so she assumed that Meg had ridden Lodestone back to Caitlin village. It was the first time she had been aware of her friend's riding ability.

When she returned, it was obvious that Meg had an excellent seat, far better than the huntsman from Caitlin Hall who ended his ride in the pond.

Nell smiled at the thought, but sensed that Meg had made an enemy who might seek retribution – and it was her fault for being there. When asking Meg for help, she had not realised the position in which she placed her.

"Did you wonder where I was?" said Meg, as she tossed down a bundle to Nell, before dismounting.

"I guessed that you went back to see Mrs Hardwick," she said, catching it lightly.

"That's right, and she sent some warm clothes for you to wear in the winter. We'll sort them out later."

"Did anyone know what happened yesterday?"

"About the squire's sons, you mean? Yes, Molly told me that the news arrived back in the village before they reached home – or a version of it did. Not that they're likely to admit the truth in a case like that."

"What did she say?"

"That the blacksmith owed me a tankard of ale, for starters. His late brother's daughter was the last of the local girls that Cedric Whitcott spoiled, and he'd go to strong lengths to avenge her if he could avoid being caught. A few other men hereabouts feel similarly inclined."

To Nell, having someone that cared seemed a remarkable thing. She, of course, had no one. "Where do we go now?" she asked, feeling her eyes water.

"After that nonsense yesterday, we'll take a few back roads," said Meg, "but in a week or two I need to meet up with some of Mother Chapel's people."

Nell waited to hear more but Meg changed the subject. "The farmer's wife said to give you this," she said, jingling some coins in her hand and counting out six pennies. "Said that she's pleased with the repairs, and when we come this way again she'd find some more for you to do."

"Thank you," Nell said. The praise brought tears to her eyes, and the recollection of how she had learned to sew. Mrs Ferndale, her mentor, had been similarly pleased with her progress. It was a world to which she had once belonged, now gone forever.

Chapter 4

After the unpleasantness of the previous day, the next one seemed to acquire a sense of purpose. It was a dull morning that looked as if it would turn later to rain. Whilst Meg made no reference to what had occurred, Nell assumed it was to avoid the sons of the gentry that they drove briskly along winding country roads, through wooded coppices and up slopes and over the brow of hillocks and down the other side. All the time Meg seemed to be on the lookout for someone.

If Nell was impressed by her friend's ability to ride the cob like a man, she was doubly so by the light-handed skill in manoeuvring the vardo over rough terrain. In other circumstances she might have been tempted to ask who taught Meg to drive, but on this occasion remained silent.

After an hour, they came to a halt in a hamlet where a man and a youth stood waiting in the middle of the road.

"She needs you," said the man, running alongside, pointing the direction for Meg to turn the vardo along a forest trail.

Nell did not know whom they were going to see, but she recognised the sound of Meg clicking her teeth, and the flick of her wrists as she urged the horse to hasten.

Within minutes they arrived at a lone cottage set back amongst the trees. Someone took the reins and Meg jumped down and strode through the open front door, leaving Nell to follow her inside. Cries greeted them from an upper room, telling of a person's distress. Ones that Nell had heard in the past, and recognised for what they were.

A woman was in labour, and by the sounds of things, Meg had arrived at the optimum time. Nell ran up the flight of stairs and watched as Meg laid her gentle hands on the woman's swollen belly, palpating with sure fingers that slowed when the skin tightened, and moved again when it relaxed.

She met Meg's eyes and spoke without thinking. "What can I do to help?"

"Ask the men to bring the chair contraption from the store under the vardo."

Nell nodded and went down the staircase to the front door. "The midwife needs the birthing chair," she said. "Can you carry it inside, please?"

"What's that?" said the older man.

"I'll show you," Nell said, and with that, dashed to open the drop-down flap of wood that served as a door. A contraption it certainly was, but until it was assembled, she did not know what it would look like. Once the menfolk had, with much muttering and cursing, bundled it up the narrow stairs, Nell saw the assembled tool for what it was – a wooden chair with an open hole in the seat; the back of which could recline or have pillows for support, and footrests that slotted into place.

"Is it fitted together properly, Meg?" she said, hoping she had performed her task correctly.

A brief nod gave Nell the answer she needed, which pleased her. Within minutes the young woman, who had been wallowing on her back, was supported on the chair looking at Meg, where previously she had gazed at the ceiling unable to see what was going on.

"That's better," said Meg. "Now we can give nature a helping hand."

"Is there anything else that I can do?" said Nell.

"You don't have to stay and watch," said Meg, aside.

"If I'm going to be a carer then I have to learn, if you will teach me. I've seen births before. Peggy Walcote had several, but they didn't all survive," she said in a whisper, realising what might be the outcome of the process.

"It happens sometimes," Meg said equally quietly, and then turned aside to the woman of middle age waiting anxiously with the birthing woman, who Nell realised was younger than she first thought. "We'll need fresh water from the spring to drink, and a cloth for my friend to use – and keep the kettle on the boil."

Discarding her shawl, Nell was soon engrossed in giving sips of water and wiping the sweat from the woman's brow, then rinsing the cloth to do it again. She tried, with a hand that shook, to smooth back tresses that had once been flaxen fair; and calm the fear of the unknown, which filled the pale blue eyes.

It was a relief to attend to the needs of others, rather than recall the times as a child when she had seen a neighbour from Oak Apple Lane doing the same for Peggy Walcote. On those occasions Nell's task had been to fetch and carry.

Having triggered memories from the past, Nell saw in the face of the middle-aged woman who watched her someone she recognised. The clothes she wore were a faded grey but the weary look of sad resignation was the same as the day when Nell had seen her waiting outside Hillend School wearing a black frock. She hoped her suspicions were wrong, but did not think so.

Hearing the birthing woman's breathing change, she sensed the moment was close and watched Meg on her knees before the chair, with one deft hand supporting the lower belly, the other ready to carefully check the cord and guide the baby's head into the world. She held her breath in wonder, heard a newborn cry, and felt tears on her cheeks.

"It's a boy," said Meg, as she placed the baby on its mother's belly. "That's the first part over. Now we'll have to wait a few minutes for the afterbirth to come."

The girl looked at her, bewildered. "What's that?" she said in a dull voice.

"It's what's been feeding the babe all these months, and you've done it well. He's a good size."

"I didn't want him," she said, with tears running down her cheeks.

"Maybe you didn't," Meg said, "but he needs you, and that's what matters now. Come on, girl; let me put him to the breast. It'll help deliver the afterbirth."

Firm in her manner, but gentle, Meg wrapped the baby in a dry towel and fixed his questing mouth to the nipple. At his touch, Nell saw the look of distaste on the new mother's face turn to wonder. Within minutes, there was a trickle of reddish fluid, and then a slithering sound as the afterbirth slid into Meg's hand.

Supporting the weight, she laid the organ on the sodden sheet that covered the floor, and checked it. Seeing the scrutiny, Nell determined to ask the purpose, but Meg, as if sensing it, answered, "To see that nothing's left inside to cause bleeding. Now we can clean her up and get her back into bed."

"How did you know about this woman?" Nell whispered. She said *woman*, although it was obvious the new mother was no older than she was.

"Molly said that Lily's time was due, and told me where to find her."

"Lily…?" Nell said, recalling a friend of that name from Hillend School.

"Larkspur, that was, although her mother married again when the girl's father died in the war."

Nell looked at the girl and their eyes met. Then she looked away, not knowing whether it would embarrass the girl by speaking. Wordlessly, she pressed the other's hand in sympathy, knowing that she too could have been in that situation, had not a real gentleman happened along to save her. Where was he now, and was he aware of how grateful she was?

"Will she be all right, Meg?"

"She should be, but we'll see her a couple of times tomorrow to make sure."

That night, they curled up together on the vardo couch for warmth, but although Nell was tired, she did not sleep. Her mind was on the process she witnessed in the labourer's cottage. She had seen Peggy Walcote give birth several times at Oak Apple Cottage, but this came too close to her age for comfort. Poor Lily Larkspur's life had been ruined.

For the first time in her life, Nell felt anger against a living person, and was glad that the man who forced himself on the other girl had his just deserts with a ducking in the pond. Not that his kind would feel regret for his actions, for to his mind, the common folk were there for his use.

When morning came, Nell found to her relief that Lily was alive, together with her son. She did not know what would happen to them now, but could not help her actions as they turned to leave the dwelling. Dipping in her pocket, she took the six pennies that she had earned with sewing, and

40

pressed the coins into the girl's hand.

"It's for you, Lily," she said, "and your baby."

"Bless you," said the girl, her eyes filling with tears. "I think I knew you at school, when I stayed with my grandparents in Hillend village before my father died. Was your name Nell?"

"Yes," she said, unable to deny it.

"How do you come to be with a gypsy?" The words were almost accusatory.

"Meg is a herbalist and midwife," Nell said with dignity. "She knew my mother."

"I'm sorry," said the girl. "I should be grateful to her, and I am, but I don't know what will become of me or the baby. I can't work, and we'll probably end up in the poorhouse. It might have been better if I had died."

Lily's words stayed with Nell as they left the house. "I wish I could have done more," she said.

"What you did meant a lot to her," said Meg, "and there is something else we might do for them. Let me give the matter some thought."

★★★

That evening when Nell was asleep, Meg took a sheet of parchment from her secret store and sharpened a quill, which she dipped in newly moistened ink. She thought for a moment, set the pen to paper and began to write in a firm hand.

> *To Squire Whitcott, Caitlin Hall, Salop.*
>
> *If you wish to acknowledge your grandson, he can be found in Merry Dingle with his mother who did no wrong, but is in need of sustenance.*

Before folding the paper, she reached for the leather-bound book of sermons, and looked long and hard at the inscription before resuming her writing.

From someone who wishes the girl well. It was as much as Meg could do. Only time would determine the outcome. The newborn child might be the only grandson the squire had to give his name, and a few shillings would keep him alive.

She also knew that, before the next moon cycle began, there was another matter that she must explain. In the event, it was Nell who asked the question before another day passed.

They were sitting by the campfire, watching the sun setting over Linmore Hill to the west. Meg revisited Lily Larkspur in the morning and evening to ensure no problems had occurred, and left a sufficient supply of herbs for her mother to administer, which would ensure the girl's monthly flow came on time for the next year. Beyond that she could not say.

Similarly, she gave them the letter she had written, with instructions for it to be placed in Molly Hardwick's hand, knowing the carer would ensure its safe delivery. The church at Caitlin was the obvious place for it to be found by the squire's brother, someone who could not be ignored.

"What did you mean by saying to the carer in Caitlin that you knew my mother?" Nell asked hesitantly.

Meg would have welcomed a little more time before facing the question, but she knew it must be answered as truthfully as possible.

"I was with her when you were born," she said. "If I'd had the means to feed you, Mother Chapel wouldn't have left you in the church porch at Hillend. As I didn't, we risked losing both of you. Down in the village, you stood a chance of being adopted."

Nell was quiet for a moment. "Where was I born?"

"In the woodsman's hut on the hill. We met your mother a few months before the birth, and she stayed with us until her time came."

There was no point in saying that, if Nell's mother had taken the final step to the water's edge before Meg reached her, the baby would not have survived long enough to be born.

"I see," said Nell, quietly.

"She had childbed fever," said Meg, hoping the explanation would suffice. Too much time had passed for the absolute truth to be told, and no good would come of it now.

"I hope Lily doesn't die of childbed fever."

"I hope not," said Meg. "I've left several herbs for her mother to give

42

her, and Molly Hardwick knows what should be done at such times. She'll watch over her."

She was relieved when Nell's thoughts turned in another direction.

"What was my mother like? Did she have hair the colour of mine?"

Meg thought back to the time, fourteen years ago and smiled. "Her hair was a beautiful auburn shade, but it was straight where you have curls."

"Did my father have curly hair, Meg?"

"I think she said that he did, but of a rich gold colour."

"Mine is neither. It's too light to be auburn, and too dark to be golden."

"You have the prettiest red-gold hair I've ever seen, and don't you forget it."

"She wasn't married to my father, was she?"

"No, she wasn't," said Meg, "but who told you that?"

"Peggy Walcote said I was a bastard, and everyone at school knew I was a foundling. They used to laugh at me."

What a cruel word to use for a gentle soul like Nell.

"There's a better name that applies to the pair of us, little one," said Meg. "You and I are *barley children*." It was not quite the truth, but it would suffice.

"Yes, I like that…"

Meg saw a questioning look that she was beginning to recognise, and guessed the portent. One day Nell would ask why, if Meg had been a babe in arms when Mother Chapel went to attend the lady of the gentry, no one claimed her as their daughter. It was too complex to explain, and on one side, not her secret to divulge.

★★★

When they moved on, several days of rain ensured that the weather turned colder. After years of living with nature, Meg was inured to the cold and dampness of the autumn nights, but could see that Nell was already beginning to suffer. She had warmer clothes for the girl to wear, but a female problem threatened to interfere, one that Meg had long forgotten, but recognised in others. When it began she could deal with the matter – but not before, which was why she waited.

On one occasion, after a thunderstorm, she approached a fording place on the road that was a torrent of water. Knowing the futility of attempting to cross, she turned the vardo around and set off along the twisting road that followed the length of Caitlin Vale, keeping the river on their left.

It took several days, and the only vehicles they met were farm carts trundling slowly through the mud about their business, but no other vehicles came to meet them on the main road. Towards the far end of the valley, they turned a corner to approach a river crossing, and the reason for the lack of traffic became clear.

The road ahead stopped on each side of the river. There was no sign of the rustic bridge that had once crossed it, apart from the shattered wooden supports and debris that clung to the sides. Evidence that the flood had swept away the centre section and no one had time to repair it. Most likely no one knew it had happened.

"What do we do now?" Nell said.

"Hold those steady," Meg said, handing Nell the reins, before stepping down from her seat to coax the horse to back up as she turned the vardo to face the way they had come – a skill acquired from long practice on other occasions when it had been done before.

Built at the time of her mother's passing, Meg's vardo was small, but sufficient for her needs and lightweight enough for a woman to manoeuvre on the narrow roads she travelled.

★★★

It was a relief to leave Caitlin and its bad memories behind. With the broken bridge making the road impassable, their only option was to follow a winding track, scarcely wide enough for a cart, which took them over a steeply wooded hillside. The terrain was bleak but the trees, although shedding their leaves, offered some shelter from the bitter wind that razed the ground, cutting through everything it touched.

To keep warm at night meant huddling close to share body heat and the comfort of another person's breathing. In the daytime, Nell was chilled to the bone, despite the three shawls and the grey cape that she wore under a waxed sheet that Meg had given her. She was sure that she would never be warm again.

"You shouldn't be up here, little one," said Meg, sounding concerned. "We'll find somewhere better for you by next year."

Nell looked at her, bemused, wanting to ask if she meant the time after Christmas when the year changed, or sometime later. Whenever it was, Nell hoped, if it was not too much trouble for Meg to keep her that it would not be too soon. "I don't mind," she insisted, "as long as I can be with you."

"We'll get the little stove lit when we stop," said Meg. "Then you can sit in the chair and keep warm."

The one to which she referred was in the corner of the vardo near the door, with a little chimney stack through the roof. "Do you use it?" said Nell.

Left on her own in Caitlin, she had looked inside and found dry kindling, but no sign of the stove having been used.

"Not often," said Meg, "but that's what it's there for and I can't have you being ill out here on the road."

Nell guessed that Meg probably realised she was about to decline the need, and was grateful. "Thank you," she said. "I don't want to be a nuisance."

"I'll tell you when you are," said Meg, in a dry tone, which Nell recognised as humour.

They put the plan into action when they sheltered overnight near a derelict hovel. Nell noticed the difference in warmth immediately, and even Meg acknowledged the fact. Clothes that were damp could be draped over a rack to dry. In the morning, when the rain stopped, they put fresh kindling inside from Meg's secret store under the vardo.

"You'll need different clothes where we're going," said Meg, after breakfast.

"Where's that?"

"I have some folks to see out Norcott way, so we'll have to take the road through the mining valley, and around the end of Linmore Hill."

Nell was only just getting used to her gypsy girl clothes, but on this

45

occasion, Meg tied two dark-coloured scarves turban-like around her head, under a boy's hat with a wide brim that slipped down to cover her ears. She accepted it for the protection it gave, recalling from her days at school that fair-skinned girls with tawny hair stood out like a beacon. Now she was glad of the extra warmth.

Wearing breeches came as something of a shock after skirts, but they were practical, if she did not mind the rough material chafing her thighs. Then she realised that if she stuffed her shift down inside, it was warmer still. Similarly, the longer socks and boots came up to her knees.

"Meg," she said, bethinking a problem in the weeks ahead. "What will I do when *that time of the month* comes?" It was an expression used by Dora Peckledy, a maid at the rectory. Miss Dinchope, however, had called them *courses*.

"We'll sort it out, little one, so that it doesn't last long. You can wear a skirt when it happens."

That was a relief, because the housekeeper at Hillend Rectory had been most particular about everyone keeping clean at such times. Nell presumed that Meg would organise that, but could not see how she could have a bath.

When nature decreed that the following day was the time for her women's problems, Meg gave her a cup of warmed herbal tea and it was soon over. A strip wash in the caravan by the stove followed and after that she was free to wear breeches, just as Meg did.

Once free of the worry, Nell resumed her seat on the driver's bench beside Meg. She felt conspicuous at first, but realised that a man travelling with a boy passed unnoticed, whereas two women would not, and yet it was apparent that Meg slipped easily between the two.

Ever reliable, Lodestone took them through the unfamiliar terrain at a steady plod and Nell noticed that despite his age, the horse never failed to reach the top of a steep slope or refused to allow Meg to guide it down again.

★★★

It came as something of a shock when Nell realised that three weeks had already gone by since they left home and they were halfway through another. Similarly, she had not noticed when they had left the farmland behind, until she saw areas of hillside denuded of growth. As they rounded one of the many corners, she looked up at the hill that ran alongside, and gasped in sheer wonder at the rock face that seemed to have been sliced in half.

"What happened to it, Meg?"

"Folks hereabouts say that in olden times, all this was under a river of ice. When it started to melt the weight shifted and left deposits of quartzite strewn along the top of that hill. Mining has been going on in these parts since the time of the Romans."

Before Nell could ask the source of Meg's knowledge, her friend reached through the vardo door and took a little flask of what looked like wood ash.

"You're too clean to live round here, little one. If you're going to dress like a boy, you'll need a dirty face," she said, lightly dusting a coating on Nell's cheeks.

"And do I?" Nell said.

"I daresay that you'll pass for one in the half-light, if nobody looks too close," said Meg, and resumed driving along the road.

★★★

Nell's first sight of the mining village was a bird's-eye view of a collection of wooden buildings, seen between the trees as they started down a long slope, with her holding the horse's reins and Meg on foot gripping the bridle to keep the caravan steady. It was a ponderously slow descent but Nell knew, by now, that it was the only way to proceed. Any faster and they might go over the edge of the road.

Seeing it from above, she was immediately aware of the difference in size. Whereas most villages were a scattering of dwellings along the sides of the road, this collection covered a much larger area.

"What is this?" she said, wondering where all of the buildings had come from.

"Part of the mining community," said Meg, "where the miners that work above and below ground live and sleep when they get the chance."

A little chapel and school lay half a mile beyond, perched precariously on the edge of the hillside. People came out to look as the vardo approached and

Meg stopped to speak with the womenfolk, young and old alike with dusty hair and weary faces. Children peeped out of doorways, looking uncertain.

Sad-faced toddlers with hollow cheeks and dark weary eyes watched them as they drove on through the village. Their skinny little bodies and hacking coughs reminded Nell of Joseph, her three-year-old half-brother, who died before she went to work at the rectory. Until that moment, life at Oak Apple Cottage had been a distant memory, but the recollection brought it back.

★★★

They came upon the next village quite suddenly on a level patch of ground. To one side of the road, Nell saw an outcrop of jagged rock in the hillside that formed a sheltering overhang. Meg had told her, along the way, that sometimes quarrying was done on the hillside in the wish to scrape every ton of mineral from the slab. More often it was carried on underground, and the workers hardly came to the surface.

It was true what Meg said about this being a "dark place", and it was not only the layers of mining dust that coated everything. There were high fences around the buildings, on which a faded sign declared that the Myndstone mine was "Private" – a word that Nell recognised from the old estate out beyond Hillend village.

Beyond the signs for the mine was another steep hill that Meg started to negotiate with extreme care in the fading light. Halfway around the sharp corner at the bottom, the sound of jeering and shouting erupted. Nell looked at Meg, uncertain what was going on, just as a man appeared by the horse, blocking their way.

"Are you coming to watch the fight?" he called to Meg.

"I'll need to find somewhere to park the van," said Meg, without hesitation.

Nell noticed that her tone of voice had instantly roughened.

The man moved away down the slope towards the mine, saying over his shoulder, "There's plenty to drink. Bring the boy with you; it'll put hairs on his chest."

"Good," growled Meg, "I've got a thirst on me."

"There'll be a bout for the youngsters as well, so we'll see how he measures up against our lads." The man's voice faded into the shadows.

"Are we really going down there, amongst all those men?" said Nell, peering out from under her hat with startled eyes.

"Hush…" said Meg, and kept driving briskly around the next corner. Once clear of prying eyes, she turned the vardo sharply through an ivy-clad stone arch, which led down a weed-covered driveway that muffled the sound of the wheels.

They continued into the trees and sat listening as the remaining daylight merged with the deepening dusk. The sounds from the revelry at the mine could be heard in the distance, but only faintly now.

"We'll stop here for the night," Meg said, "and be away at first light."

"Are we trespassing?" Nell said in a whisper, wondering where they were.

"You might say that, but no more than anyone else who comes here."

After the previous upset with the gentry at Caitlin, Nell imagined that Meg would wish to avoid men, but the ones they saw on the road were evidently mine workers from the village through which they had passed.

"It's likely to get a bit rowdy down there before midnight," said Meg.

"What were they doing?"

"Bare-knuckle boxing; and they assumed, as a traveller, that I'd join them."

"But you're a…" said Nell.

"I'm whatever they expect me to be," said Meg. "That's how I survive."

Nell had to admit that, in the shadows, Meg looked a convincing man in her buckskin breeches and black boots, with her long hair tied back. It was only when she donned a skirt and a shawl that she looked remotely like a woman.

Sleep came slowly and was uneasy. In the early morning, Nell awoke to find that an eerie silence hung over the place where they had parked the vardo around the back of a ruined building.

The house must once have been tall and imposing. Now, it was derelict, its timbers blackened by smoke, with the roof open to the elements. She shivered, sensing something she could not explain. Last night she was too tired to feel fear, but was aware now of an unfriendly presence.

"Shall I fill the kettle from the well?" Nell said, pointing to a water pump.

"Not from this one or any in the area," said Meg in a sombre tone. "We'll use the water bladders, and find a spring of clean water down in the valley."

Nell frowned. "What's the matter with it?" she said, knowing that Meg never spoke lightly of such things.

"They say that too much lead in the water drove the gentry, who lived here years ago, mad. Wild garlic and red clover might help cleanse the system, but those who stay around here don't usually make old bones. Mind you, working in the mines doesn't help them either."

Nell could feel the bleakness in the chill air. "Where are we?" she said.

"This is all that remains of Myndstone Manor," said Meg. "It was owned by the family that ran the mine until one of them won Norcott Abbey in a card game. Someone else must have bought the mining rights."

"What happened to the house?"

"Fire destroyed it forty-odd years ago. The Strettons were a wild bunch given to holding orgies. Rumour has it that they were the spawn of the devil from amongst the quartz stones up on yonder hill. That might well be true for they all carried the curse of the "great pox" that drove them to madness in later years.

"On that particular night, Matthew Stretton, the eldest son, was accused of cheating at cards, so he shot and robbed several guests and set the house ablaze. They caught him at the coast, heading for Ireland, and sent him to the gallows. Those of his family who survived moved to the Abbey and caused trouble elsewhere."

Nell shivered, not wanting to admit that she had heard cries in the night, and thought it was only the howling of the wind in the trees. Now she was not sure.

Whatever it was, she was glad to be moving on.

Chapter 5

Mid-September 1808

They were on the move before the first streaks of daylight brightened the sky, glad to be heading away from the overhanging hills. Before they had travelled half a mile they met a long line of horses and empty carts trundling back the way they had come. As they approached the first cart, Nell said, "Where are they going?"

"Up to the mines to collect the ore that's been quarried," said Meg.

That supplied an answer to a question Nell had wanted to ask the night before. Now she knew, but had no idea what happened to it next.

A short distance beyond, they came upon the tail end of a line of loaded carts that had crawled downhill, and filled the road. There was shouting and cursing ahead as drivers of other vehicles struggled to pass in the opposite direction.

Meg waited for the loaded carts to trundle a distance ahead before following at a slower pace. On reaching a clump of trees, she turned the vardo deftly along a bridle path out of sight.

One minute there was noise, dust and confusion, the next tranquillity as they left it behind – but not before Nell had seen a milestone that pointed fifteen miles to Bredenbridge in one direction, and twelve to Norcott in the other.

"I usually go this way to avoid other folks," said Meg.

Dressed as a man, Nell could understand her reasons.

"Is this the way to Norcott?" she said, recalling the name on the milestone.

"Yes," said Meg, "but we'll stop overnight along the way and see the folks I told you about in the morning."

Nell tried to recall what had been said, but could not. It did not matter, for she would see who they were when they got there.

A sad little hedge-pig, which had expired, provided a tasty supper. Meg showed Nell how to wrap the carcase in clay ready to bake in the base of the fire, leaving the skin and tender meat ready to fall off the bones.

"How do you think it died?" she said.

"Who knows?" said Meg, "Nature provides for those that know where to look."

By now, Nell knew that Meg would go hungry rather than kill an animal or bird. She also noticed that the occasional rabbit or bird appeared out of a pouch that Meg wore at her waist. From this she deduced that people who lived at peace with nature were provided for. But it did not do to advertise the fact for fear of being accused of stealing. As Meg had told her, gypsies were first to be blamed.

That night along the bridle path, they stayed within sight of a circle of stones that appeared out of the moorland. Some stood tall while others had fallen over.

"What are they doing here, Meg?" she said, meaning the stones.

"Nobody knows," said Meg, "or how long they've been here. Some folks say it might have something to do with the Devil's Hill back yonder."

It was a bleak place, with a keen wind that cut through Nell's clothes and whistled around the vardo, but it scared her less than the derelict manor house had done. When they set off again, in the quiet hours of the dawn, it had a peace that Nell would remember.

★★★

Everything changed when they crossed over the wooden bridge that led to the market town of Norcott. There were people and horses coming and going everywhere. Nell had never seen so many people or animals in one place and looked to Meg for a reason.

"What are all these people doing here?" she said.

"They come for the horse sales. There's one here and on Brackenridge Common at the far end of the hill, every year," said Meg, and with that, she joined the line of brightly coloured gypsy caravans parked along the field. Nell stared at the gathering in amazement, and listened to the hum of voices, speaking a strange language she did not understand.

The first person Meg spoke with shook his head, so she turned aside to question another, who pointed to the far side of the camp. Then she beckoned Nell to follow and they set off to walk towards a large old caravan, and when they arrived, Nell waited outside whilst Meg entered the van.

From her position by the open door, she heard a murmur of voices speaking in a foreign tongue. All around her, she heard different voices in the same alien sound, going back and forth from one person to another all unintelligible to her ears.

She wandered a few yards away, to watch a woman stirring the contents of a stockpot over a fire, adding water and herbs to taste. Eventually, the woman looked up and offered her a spoonful of the steaming liquid, but she shook her head and hurried back to where Meg beckoned from the caravan doorway.

When she entered the dark interior, Nell had to blink to adjust her eyes to the lack of light. Gradually she made out the seated figure of an old man, whose skin was browner and more lined than any person she had ever seen in her life.

In assuming that Meg had explained the purpose of their visit, Nell was at a loss to understand her next words. "Your kinswoman, Mother Chapel, gave me responsibility to bring this girl to you, even though she is not of your blood."

How could that be when Mother Chapel had been dead for several years?

Standing motionless before the old man, Nell felt her fears melting away as his soft brown hands reached out and gently traced the contours of her head and face. Even in the half-light of the caravan, she could see that his eyes looked strangely cloudy, and yet she sensed that his touch made him aware of what his sightless eyes could not see. Even the fact she was a girl, wearing boy's clothes.

53

She listened in amazement to the old man's pronouncement to Meg.

"My kinswoman was right. I can see that this child has the inclination to learn the old ways. You must teach her well, Meg Chapel."

Soon they were on the move, travelling towards the head of Linmore Dale, in advance of the storm clouds. Only then did Nell venture to ask, "Who was the old man in the caravan, Meg?"

"That was Wisdom Hawk, the *Chell* or chief of the gypsy clan. I wanted him to see you," Meg responded.

Nell thought about it for a moment, before saying, "I think he was very old, because his hands felt like soft leather. But I wasn't frightened of him."

"You have no reason to fear Wisdom Hawk," said Meg, "but he did once stand by whilst one judged unworthy to remain was banished."

Something about the way that Meg said the words made Nell feel uneasy, but she could not tell why. She looked at her friend, but nothing more was forthcoming.

After they had travelled for another day, Meg parked the caravan on a rise overlooking the head of Linmore Dale. When she looked down the valley, Nell noticed trees that had been green, gold and yellow as they set off were losing their leaves.

As the full length disappeared into the distance, she tried to judge the width looking from one ridge of high land to the other, but suspected the wooded hillsides in the centre might hide secret valleys, much as she had seen in Caitlin Vale.

The next day the caravan crossed over to the other side of the valley, and Nell learned how many villages, hamlets and farms existed in Linmore Dale. She had never imagined there were so many people living within a few miles of Hillend.

Everywhere they travelled, people came to Meg for advice on all kinds of conditions, from lung fever, to relief of bellyache, boils and piles, needing prescriptive potions and a supply of herbs, balms and pastes in readiness for winter ailments.

Nell noticed that in most cases, the people who sought help were women, and Meg told her that many menfolk were afraid to admit to having problems in case it put them out of work. The thing that surprised her most was how people paid Meg for her services.

With little use for money, Meg received payment in produce, which could be anything from a flitch of salted bacon or loaves of bread, to pieces of cheese and a few eggs, often with a flagon of cider or assortment of vegetables.

Sometimes a farmer's wife bundled up a collection of old clothes for them to use or to distribute along the way in exchange for food. Wherever they went, people were pleased to meet Nell, and many gifts of milk, butter and beef dripping appeared in the caravan for her.

At one smallholding, a tenant farmer's son donated a warm fleece to place on the foot of Nell's bed, to keep the little maid warm until next year, when he hoped to see her again. It was just as well that he did not know about the breeches she wore under her skirt.

★★★

"Where do we go next?" said Nell, astounded by all she had seen and learned.

"Down the back road to Middlebrook, and up across the hill," said Meg.

To Nell it meant they were going home after a long journey and what a wonderful feeling that engendered. She was a different girl to the one that set out seven weeks ago; someone who could never go back to the life she led before.

Having seen the post road from the hillock, with its overloaded coaches and vehicles driving at a furious pace, each trying to get ahead before another came in the other direction, Nell was glad that Meg chose to drive along the quieter road.

"There's one more visit to make before we get there," said Meg, as she turned off the road along a rutted cart track, towards a farm.

"Where are we?" said Nell.

"About a couple of miles from Middlebrook," said Meg. "That's the River Linmore down across the flood plain."

There was little time to look at her surroundings before Meg had taken the vardo to the farm gate, and into the yard at the back. The scullery door was open and a scolding voice could be heard. "Oh, do give over, Mother-in-law. I can't be stopping to answer your questions all the time. I have work to do."

When Meg appeared at the door, the farmer's wife issued a flurry of orders to her housemaid and scullion, and sat down at the kitchen table with relief.

"I'm glad you've come, Mother Chapel," she said. "I could do with some of your tonic."

"How's the old lady?" said Meg, who obviously knew the family.

"She's getting her winter cough early this year, and wearing me out with her demands for attention."

"You'll be wanting some lungwort for her, I expect?" said Meg.

"Well, it works better than Dr Tilbury's bloodletting ever did. I never saw such a mess as he created, but you can't say anything, when the only other thing is a purge."

"Would you like me to read to the lady?" Nell said, forgetting that gypsies didn't usually have that ability.

"That's a good idea, it might send her to sleep," the woman said, and handed Nell a well-thumbed book of sermons. Then she looked at Meg with suspicion. "Where did you find this little wench, Mother Chapel? She's a bit out of the ordinary."

Anxious to avoid being asked questions, Nell opened the book and began to read and within minutes the old lady's eyes glazed over. Clearly, all she wanted was the comfort of hearing the sound of someone's voice.

"Over Caitlin way," said Meg, in the background. "She's hoping to find a situation somewhere down the Dale. I told her mother I'd look out for her."

"She's a bit thin and will need warmer clothes for the winter. I haven't anything for a girl, so you'll have to use the boy's clothes that I have until you find something suitable. How old would you say she was – about twelve, if I had to make a guess?"

"Something like that," said Meg, "by what her mother told me."

Nell wanted to say she was fourteen, but stopped as she recalled something Meg had said. *Don't argue with folks. Let them think they're right.*

The woman gave a nod of approval, as if having family gave Nell a touch of respectability. "Work shouldn't be too hard to come by, particularly as she seems to be book-learned. With a good wash she'd look quite presentable. I'll find you some soap, if you like," said the woman, going off to her store cupboard.

"I'm obliged to you, lady," said Meg, as the woman returned. "It'll do the job, wonderful well. She'll scrub up a treat."

Nell wondered what the farmer's wife would have thought of her previous attire. A little forethought on their approach to the farm decided that a hasty change of clothes to a skirt and washing Nell's face would make her respectable enough to be admitted to the house. Meg, similarly, wrapped a long skirt around her breeches, and affected a shuffling gait so nobody would recognise her as the tall old man with the clay pipe.

Despite knowing that the bar of soap would be of the coarse kind, used for washing clothes, Nell was grateful.

Take what's freely offered, little one, even if you only get it outside the door. You never know when it will come in useful. Meg's words from a previous occasion came back to her.

In this case, Nell knew exactly how she would use it, for it meant that she could have a proper strip wash and feel clean again. She might even manage to wash her hair before winter – just like she used to do before she went to school. It was exactly the same kind of soap that Mrs Grimble used when she sat Nell in the stone sink at Oak Apple Farm to be bathed. No scent, no lather, and lots of grime on the sink, but she was clean and it was always the thought that counted.

She continued reading, with one ear on the conversation going on behind her. It was obvious that despite having several indoor servants, the farmer's wife wanted company. Every time Meg made a move to be on their way, the woman started another topic. In many ways, she reminded Nell of Mrs Grimble.

"Have you heard about Mr Blacking, the headmaster from Hillend School, who dropped down dead in the classroom in front of his pupils a week ago?" said the garrulous soul, bursting with news. "You'd have thought he'd have gone somewhere quieter, but I suppose he couldn't really in the circumstances."

Meg made some murmur of acknowledgement as the woman continued, "What do you think Miss Peartree, his assistant, did when the gardener and the lad from the rectory, brought a handcart to carry the teacher outside?"

Anxious to hear more, Nell held her breath, but the querulous old woman in the daybed demanded that she should keep reading.

"Picked up that short strap she keeps on her desk as a threat, and walked to the front of the class ready to carry on as if nothing had happened."

The image of the worn strip of leather, shiny with use, came to Nell's mind, and a recollection of the pain she endured when she took punishment for others.

"No sooner had they gone than she threw the head teacher's birch on the fire, and him not even in his coffin. That's a bit disrespectful, to my mind."

"Well," said Meg, dryly, "he had no further use for it where he was going."

"I suppose you're right, Mother Chapel," said the woman, nodding agreement. "I did hear that the folks at Linmore Hall are paying Miss Peartree to do the job until they find another man to take charge. That's always the way, but who'd want to go to a miserable place like Hillend, particularly with the goings on at the rectory? Did you know…?" The woman stopped abruptly, as if remembering to whom she was speaking. "Oh, is that the time? I'd better find those clothes for you."

Nell sighed, disappointed that she was not going to hear what had happened at the rectory since her departure.

"Keep reading, girl…"

"Yes, ma'am," said Nell, as the farmer's wife returned to the room carrying a bundle tied up with string.

"I daresay Miss Peartree might be glad of some help with the little 'uns. I'll mention it to Mrs Grimble of Oak Apple Farm, the next time I see her. The girl reads well, and if she had a tidy set of clothes to wear, nobody would guess her origins."

Miss Peartree would know me, thought Nell, and I would have to explain my absence to Mrs Grimble and I doubt if she would believe my version of events.

"I'll bear it in mind when we go down that way in the spring," said Meg, "but I'm thinking that my little friend will amount to more than a teacher."

★★★

When autumn slipped into winter, Nell had to get used to living close to nature. Whilst the rest of the countryside lay dormant, she listened to the changing sounds of the forest and wondered how many little creatures had hibernated.

Often in the depths of winter before Nell was awake, Meg went out to search for victuals to sustain them. The first thing that she knew of them was when Meg returned and took the contents from the pouch she wore at her waist and showed Nell how to prepare nature's latest bounty for the stockpot.

Sometimes, she plucked a bird's feathers, and other times skinned rabbit fur from the carcass, and if she thought it had a strong smell, Meg taught her to add wild garlic or herbs and dried berries to counter it. Irrespective of the food ladled into her bowl, Nell never complained because she was grateful that nature had provided for their needs.

As winter progressed, snowdrifts kept the women isolated from the outside world, but despite this they managed to break ice from the waterspout and fill their water container, and most days found kindling for the fire.

Nell only realised that it was Christmas when she heard the eerie sound of carol singers rising from the churches in the valley, and then a few days later, church bells rang to herald in a new year. She shed a silent tear, wishing she could hear the sound of Maisie Jemkins's joyful singing.

By now, time had ceased to have meaning. There was no need to get up before five o'clock to clean a scullery floor or hide from folk who handed out punishments on a whim. Only rarely did Nell miss the company of her friends at the gardener's cottage or the welcoming smells of cooking from the rectory kitchen. She grew accustomed to her new diet and lived one day at a time with no thought for the future, or worries about things she could not change.

It seemed strange to be near and yet so far away from other habitation, but living with Meg she had everything she needed. There was warmth, sufficient food for their needs, and the knowledge that she was safe from harm.

A few weeks into the new year when the snow melted, Nell looked down to the valley and saw how the landscape changed as overflowing streams flooded fields and spilled onto the roads. In some places, the rain caused landslips, and high winds brought trees and boughs crashing down, making country roads impassable.

She soon discovered that travelling in the vardo was a luxury, and when Meg had to attend anyone living on the side of the hill, there was only one way to reach the patient. Whether she liked it or not there were times when they walked over rough or marshy ground, or rode the old horse to reach the out-of-the-way places. Some weeks Nell's waxed cape was permanently wet from being caught out of doors in a heavy downpour. Meg's response was to administer a timely potion of lungwort that served to ward off chest complaints.

After a while, Nell did not question the need to be out in all weather conditions, because she knew that without help, lives could be lost. Often they arrived just in time to help a woman in labour. An infusion of oak bark or acorns could stop bleeding; marshmallow in a potion helped to release a retained afterbirth, or as a cream to relieve soreness of the breasts.

When the first snowdrops peeped above the ground, Nell knew it was spring. A few weeks later she saw the site of Mother Chapel's grave under a blanket of bluebells and shed a tear for Meg's loss.

In the lambing season, the air rang with the sound of ewes calling to their newborn lambs, and Nell learned about the practice of matching up ewes that had lost their young, with orphans. The recollection that Peggy Walcote had looked after her in a similar situation touched a chord.

She set the memory aside, and wished she could help feed them, but realised in her gypsy clothes there were some things she could not do.

Chapter 6

Spring 1809

They set off again in the last week of April when the blackthorn was in blossom, but this time Meg drove the caravan over the hill towards Brackenridge Common at the lower end of Caitlin Vale, which Nell had missed seeing on the previous trip due to the broken bridge. The journey was shorter by several miles, and they went immediately to the circle of gypsy caravans.

Having shared Meg's home and food for more than half a year, Nell was beginning to know some of the practices in her work. Anonymity suited her well. Usually, she stayed in the background watching, yet ready to help if needed.

During the autumn, she had stayed close by Meg's side, fearful in case anyone recognised her, but now she began to look around. She was enthralled seeing the horses, but had no idea what lay ahead until Meg approached one of the younger men on the periphery of a fenced enclosure and they began to talk.

Being tall, Meg could easily see over the fence into the ring, but Nell peeped between the lower horizontal bars, until she felt brave enough to climb higher and hang her arms over the top. Fascinated, she watched the gypsies drilling the animals to run around the course. All shades of light and dark brown, black, or dappled white and a mixture of colours that Meg called piebald.

She noticed that most of the prospective purchasers were gentlemen with their grooms, and working folk, whereas the few women she saw gravitated towards the gypsy caravans. Knowing they were mixing with men, they were dressed in black coats, boots and breeches. Whereas Meg's tailored garments gave her the appearance of authority, Nell's oddments fitted where they touched.

Suddenly, the man with Meg climbed the fence and sat beside Nell, before he leapt down to the other side.

"Are you looking for a horse for the boy, Meg Chapel, or something bigger that you can ride as well?" the man that Meg called Abel Hawk asked with a laugh.

"What have you to show me?" said Meg, ignoring his blunt manner.

"There's an old cob that's been brought in as being a bit contrary. He's strong enough to ride and pull the vardo – or a dappled mare for the boy that's too short in the leg for you."

"Try him on the mare first," said Meg, "and then we'll see the cob."

"Come here, young fella," said the man.

Before Nell knew what was happening, she was lifted bodily from the wooden rail where she sat, and tossed onto the back of the mare. Terrified, she clutched at the horse's mane, gripped with her knees and felt it move forward.

Belatedly remembering that she was supposed to be a boy, she took a deep breath, straightened her back and, with an assurance she was far from feeling, stared between the horse's ears as the gypsy led the horse around the paddock on a rein, back to where Meg stood watching. Her breeches felt strange, but despite the coarse material rubbing her thighs, Nell knew they were the right clothes to wear.

"Not ridden a horse before, by the looks of him," said the man with a knowing grin. "A bit delicate, so you'll have to keep a close eye on the lad, Meg Chapel."

"As you say, Abel Hawk," said Meg in a gruff voice.

There was hard edge of warning in Meg's tone that the gypsy seemed to recognise, for he stepped back a pace. "Now for the cob," he said.

"Don't put that young boy on him," said the farmer who had brought the horse to the sales. "He bites."

Meg stepped forward murmuring softly as she produced an apple from the pocket of her long black coat. "No, you won't, will you, you old fool?"

The horse, cantankerous with men, almost gave away her secret.

"Well," said the farmer, "I never saw anything like that before in me life. If he's that tame, maybe I should take him back home."

"No, I'll try him for size," said Meg in a firm voice, as she hoisted herself onto the cob's back, and leaned down to take Nell's hand. "Use my boot as a step, boy," she said. "I'll take you up before me."

Nell complied and after one turn of the ring, Meg said, "I'll take him."

"Yes, your lordship," said the farmer. "You've got a good horse there, and worth every penny."

Nell glanced at Meg in amazement, but her friend simply rubbed her nose.

"As long as he doesn't bite me," she said, in a deep voice quite unlike her own. "I think you said that was his main failing, which should reflect in the price."

"Only with the missus, sir, and women ain't got much idea about such things."

"As you say," said Meg, tossing the gypsy a coin before dismounting and lifting Nell down. "Where's the Chell?"

It was a name that Nell had been told referred to the gypsy chief.

"In his vardo," said the gypsy.

Meg nodded and turned away. "Come, boy," she said.

"Thank you," Nell said hesitantly to the gypsy, and received a nod of acknowledgement.

"I'll collect the cob when I've spoken with the old gentleman," said Meg, striding away across the field.

Nell ran after her, unsure what the exchange meant. "Meg, what did the man mean by calling you 'his lordship'?"

"A case of mistaken identity," said Meg, with a wry smile. "It happens sometimes."

It was not only the farmer who made the mistake that stepped back, but others who stood in her way that allowed her to pass. If anyone hesitated

Meg gave them a hard stare and they retreated. Nell sensed that she enjoyed the moment of their discomfiture, and strode onwards. Almost as if she was playing another part.

The old gypsy leader waiting in the caravan was, as Nell suspected, the ancient one that they had seen in the autumn, looking older still. The woman sitting with him left at Meg's approach, and Nell, not understanding the tongue in which they spoke, similarly left them alone to talk.

Within ten minutes, Meg came back to see her. "Are you ready, little one?" she said. "We need to see a few herbalists and then be on our way."

As they walked through the collection of caravans parked amongst the trees at the edge of the field, Nell noticed that Meg adopted a similarly direct way of speaking to the women that she used with Abel Hawk, who must, she deduced, be related in some way to the old man, Wisdom Hawk. Apart from the names they exchanged, she did not understand a thing they said.

An hour later, Nell clambered up beside Meg on the driver's bench, and they set off with the new horse tethered to the back of the van. She had to wait until the following day before Meg tossed her onto the horse's back but this time, knowing what to expect, she was ready. It was just as well she did for the animal's back was broader than the mare's.

"What shall we call him?" said Meg.

Nell, quick as a flash, replied, "William…brown, because of his chestnut colour."

"William it is."

As they left Brackenridge Common; Nell tried to work out in which direction they would travel next, but trusting Meg's judgement, forbore to ask. She had already asked more questions than she had asked in her life.

Meg pointed out several landmarks. But when Nell's eye caught a glimpse of a large timber-framed property through the trees, she had to ask.

"What is that house called?"

After a brief hesitation, Meg said, "The manor house of the raven was a place that your mother knew."

From that, Nell deduced it was called Ravensbury Manor.

"Did she live there?" she said.

"For a time, I think."

Hearing the reserve in Meg's voice, she said, "Is that where he lived? My father, I mean?"

When Meg nodded, Nell knew she would hear no more of her origins today. Instead, she started to recognise familiar landmarks that she suspected would lead to Hillend village. The thought of being seen caught the breath in her throat. How would she explain her absence of, she calculated, more than six months.

After a mile or two they stopped, as Nell feared they might, halfway along the narrow lane between the drovers' road and the one through Hillend.

"Stay here," said Meg, "and if anyone wants to drive past, you can walk the horse around the corner to the other road."

Before Nell could ask how it was to be done with a second horse in tow, Meg had walked through the wicket gate into the shrubbery out of sight of the rectory. Nell did not know how she would explain their presence if anyone came.

Feeling anxious, she reached for Meg's leather-covered book of sermons. Lines of difficult words that seemed to exchange other letters for those she had learned in school. After the second page, she set the book aside and was tempted, by her wish to see Maisie Jemkins, to climb down and follow Meg through the trees towards the gardener's cottage.

The recollection of the last time she had been there made her hesitate. Would they want to see her? Did anyone care? She stopped, intending to turn back the way that she had come when she heard voices.

★★★

"I won't be long," said Meg, as she slipped through the side gate to Hillend Rectory. The air felt still in the unusual warmth of the afternoon sun. It was early days for much sunshine, but welcome nonetheless.

A strange atmosphere, almost of sadness, hung over the shrubbery as she approached the open door at the back of the gardener's cottage. Quietly, she watched the man's wife sitting at a table with face in hands, and sensed the portent. There was no sound of the daughter's presence, as there usually was.

She waited for Mrs Jemkins to become aware of her presence.

"How's Nell?" the woman said without preamble. "I assume she came to you?"

"Yes," said Meg. "She's well enough, considering the winter we've had, and her not being used to it."

"Poor little soul, sent away and all because of them two sinners that didn't stay more than a quarter longer."

"The parson, you mean?" said Meg.

"And his evil witch of a sister, Miss Petunia. Miss Dinchope put paid to their nonsense, and Mrs Grimble arranged with Dr Althorpe to send them to the Westbridge Asylum. They're still there, for their kinfolk at Norcott don't want it known that there's madness in the family – as if it was news to anyone here."

"How did that come about?" said Meg.

"It started the night that Nell left here. The parson fell out of bed and cracked his head after drinking too much of the strong brew from the Bluebell Inn, and a bit of extra help from one of Miss Dinchope's special potions. The Middlebrook physician suggested that he went to stay with his relations at Norcott and take his sister with him. That was after Miss Petunia refused to pay his fee.

"When they came back, just before Christmas, Miss Petunia called the housekeeper a thief for taking money from the parson's cashbox. It was no such thing. Jemkins had told Mrs Grimble where it was kept and she decided how much should be handed out. Anyway, the housekeeper spoke her mind and threw a vase of water over the woman for having a tantrum, which tipped Miss Petunia over the edge into madness. I'd seen it coming on for years."

So that was what the farmer's wife, up the dale, had meant about the goings-on at Hillend Rectory. "Is that all that's bothering you?" said Meg.

"No," said Mrs Jemkins. "The housekeeper left us in the New Year. Maisie went off looking for her and didn't come back. She did the same with Nell, but Miss Dinchope had always been here before…"

"Where was the girl?" said Meg.

"She had a habit of watching the ducks in the millstream, but this particular day, she went to the lake on the old Littlemore estate. She's in the churchyard now, and has been these last few months. Jemkins keeps telling me that at least we know where she is, rather than worrying how she'd cope without us."

When her voice broke, Meg placed her hands on the grieving mother's shoulders and closed her eyes, knowing that it could have been Nell. A second before she began to hum, she heard the sound of a soft footfall outside and knew who else had heard the words.

It took but a minute for the gardener's wife to compose herself, but as Meg looked towards the door, the woman said, "Is Nell with you, Mistress Chapel?"

"She was waiting in the vardo," said Meg, "but I expect that I'll find her in the churchyard with Maisie."

★★★

How could Miss Dinchope go away and leave Maisie to fend for herself, when she knew how much the girl doted on her – especially after turning off Nell, who would have looked after her.

Nell stopped at the lych-gate to catch her breath and remember other times when she had walked along the road in tears, on her way home from school.

Wiping her eyes on her sleeve, she set off across the churchyard not knowing where Maisie had been laid to rest. She glanced at the stone shelf in the church porch; wondering if that was where Mother Chapel had left her as a baby. Onwards, past the three gravestones named Grimble...she saw fresh blooms on the Littlemore memorial, no doubt added by Mrs Grimble...until she saw a simple mound of soil with a plain wooden cross, bearing the name *Maisie Jemkins*.

Wanting to leave a tribute, Nell picked a few prickly blooms from the pale pink dog-rose bush in the hedgerow that bordered the lane to the Church Farm and, with tears in her eyes, laid them on the grave. "God bless you, Maisie," she whispered. "I hope your father told you that I wanted to come back to see you."

Another mound to the one side bore the name *Mabel Hopkiln, wife of Jimmy, aged eighteen years, and her infant son.* That was the girl who, within a couple of months of taking over the butter-making at the rectory from Nell, had married the cowman from the Church Farm. She remembered Mrs Jemkins's words at the time, saying that Nell could do better than to marry a cowman. Marriage for her was no more likely now than it had ever been.

Mabel had probably died from childbed fever, the same condition that Meg said had afflicted Nell's mother. The sombre sound of the church clock striking three roused her from her reverie, and she sighed, knowing that it did not matter where in the church porch she had been left as a babe-in-arms. The time was long past and she did not belong here any more.

Warned of Meg's approach by the gentle sound of hoofbeats, Nell hurried back the way she had come, anxious not to be seen. She clambered up into the vardo, while Meg turned the vehicle around and headed back down the lane by the rectory towards the drovers' road.

"What have you done to your hands?" said Meg.

Nell looked at her bloodstained fingers in surprise. "It must have been the dog-roses that I put on Maisie's grave," she said. "I didn't notice."

"Never mind, bind this cloth around your hand until we find some water to wash it," said Meg, handing her a narrow strip of torn cotton sheeting.

As she complied, Meg said, "The gardener's wife gave me some clothes for you that the housekeeper left behind. You can take a look at them later."

Nell sensed that Meg was talking to take her mind off Maisie.

"Where did Miss Dinchope go?" Nell said, knowing she was admitting to having heard their conversation.

"To be housekeeper to one of the gentry, after the parson and his sister dismissed her." Meg equally made no pretence.

"Why did they turn Miss Dinchope off?"

"It seems she spoke her mind about the bad way the parson and his sister treated you, and they didn't like it. If you read the paper she wrote, you'll know her opinion of you."

Had Nell really heard Mrs Jemkins mention the asylum?

"Where is the asylum?"

"In Westbridge, next door to the poorhouse," said Meg. "With any luck, we should reach Crofton Green crossroads tonight. Tomorrow we'll head towards Westbridge along the bridleways, and then go back up Linmore

Dale. I'll see a few folk along the way."

At the junction, they turned left along the drovers' road by a way that Nell had not known existed. Half a mile beyond, they came to a hamlet with tied estate cottages, the occupancy of which depended on the job. A woman with a baby called a greeting from a doorway as they drove past and Meg waved back.

"This is where I came, the first day after you came to the wood," said Meg. "That's Annie Longden, and the baby must be the one she was expecting at the time. He's the ninth of her brood. I haven't heard if she's married again."

"Married again?" said Nell, wondering if she had heard it right.

"Her man succumbed to his injuries after a horse kicked him," said Meg.

"When was that?" said Nell, knowing how badly injured the man had been. She wondered who had taken the labourer home from the riverbank. The young gentleman had told her that the man was alive at the time, but maybe he was wrong.

"He passed on the morning we came here," said Meg. "You were asleep, and there was no point in waking you up to tell you something like that."

Nell felt pleased that the gentleman had not lied about the injured man's condition, as he might have done.

Meg's words about that time brought back memories of other things. The former owner of the cape she wore was the most memorable recollection.

★★★

When they stopped to water the horse, Meg handed Nell a neatly tied roll of cloth.

"Mrs Jemkins said that the housekeeper left this for you."

Opening the bundle, Nell found the second-hand clothes, which the Hillend dressmaker had helped her to alter. They smelled slightly stale, but it was nothing that hanging in the fresh air would not improve. The sight of the dark blue, green and russet velvet garments brought back bittersweet memories of Nell's anticipation of wearing something special – cut short when she was sent away. She hugged the garments to her, wondering if she would ever have the chance to wear them now.

Then a rolled up piece of paper caught her eye. "What is this, Meg?" she said.

"It's something the housekeeper left for you, so you'd better read what it says."

Nell carefully straightened out the creases in the paper…no, parchment, she thought. The words scripted in a familiar hand, enumerating her abilities, swam before eyes that suddenly filled with tears.

Overcome, she bowed her head and wept, recalling the night when Miss Dinchope had tenderly dressed her wounds, and kept her safe from discovery; but within an hour, she banished Nell from the house. *Honest, respectful, diligent…* The sight of the words was almost too much to bear. How could they refer to her?

She felt Meg's comforting arm slip around her shoulder, and heard the gentle hum, which preceded the warmth that always seemed to make her relax. This time was no different. After a few minutes Nell felt strong enough to say, "Thank you. I feel better now."

"Good," said Meg.

"Why did she write such nice things after turning me off?" said Nell, handing over the testimonial to Meg, knowing that she could read.

"I think that these words tell us what she thought of you," Meg said, quietly, "but circumstances forced her to send you away for your own safety."

"I thought bad things about her, and wish I had not," said Nell.

"There's no need to worry about seeing her again, is there?"

"I suppose not," said Nell. "But it's unlikely."

"Stranger things have happened."

"I meant that, if she works for the gentry, I'm not likely to go wherever she is."

"Who knows what the future holds for any of us?"

★★★

After a night's sleep, they set off early along a bridle path that ran parallel to the busy coaching road between Crofton Green and Westbridge. Meg harnessed William, the Irish cob, to the vardo, and Nell noticed the difference in his strength, compared to Lodestone's. The knowledge that they would travel faster pleased her, for she dreaded seeing someone who might know her.

For the time of year, the weather was fair, but chilly. Nell tried to gauge the distance they travelled as she listened to the bustling sounds of the coaching road in the distance, and was glad they were not obliged to drive the same way. It almost seemed as if the bridleways by which they travelled were Meg's own private roads so unconcerned was she by any labourers they saw along the way. A nod of acknowledgement was all the notice they received.

As they emerged onto a country lane, halfway through the second day, Nell saw a weathered signpost indicating that Featherstone Grange Farm lay in one direction, and Winterton Hall, the other. "Who lives there?" she said.

"Your mother lived at the farm when her mother remarried," said Meg.

"Do you know who lives at the Hall?" she said.

"The Morville family. I have a feeling there might have been some connection with them as well, but she didn't tell me what it was."

Looking across the expanse of parkland, Nell saw high imposing chimneys amongst the trees that surrounded the mansion, which stirred an unaccountable memory. The image of a pretty girl, with rich tawny hair, came to mind, but quickly merged with the shadows. Was it someone her mother had known? Or had *she* looked like that? Nell wished she knew.

They stopped for the night on a wooded hillock within a mile of Westbridge, which gave Nell her first sighting of the flood plain that lay at the confluence between the River Linmore, and another watercourse, whose name she forgot.

In the morning, when she climbed down from the vardo, she saw a ruined castle on an outcrop of rock, and a majestic church steeple that towered over the surrounding rooftops. From the distance it seemed quiet, but as they drew closer to the town she realised there was a maypole on the level land, with music playing and people dancing. She looked at Meg in enquiry.

"It's the time of year for the May Fair. There might be a hiring fair as well."

"Will we stop there?"

In response, Meg parked the vardo off the road. Nell half-wished she could join the merrymakers, but turned aside to view the farm workers who sought employment for the coming year.

She noticed there were farmers standing on one side and on the other, groups of workers exhibiting an emblem of their calling. A wagoner signified his trade by wearing a piece of whipcord tied to his hat, a cowman a lock of cow-hair in his, and the dairymaid carried her dairy stool.

Once the hiring process was finished, she watched fascinated, as dozens of farm servants, all dressed in their best clothes, with a year's wages in their pockets, set off to the stalls to buy new clothes, ribbons and trinkets.

Nell wondered the purpose for which Meg had brought her to this place.

"Is that how people find work?" she said.

"Some do," said Meg, "but not the kind for which you'd be looking. You're not ready to leave yet. There's a lot more to learn."

Meg's words sent a glow of warmth through her. The notion of work did not bother her, but she was not sure that she had the courage to show anyone Miss Dinchope's neatly written testimonial. Maybe she would feel better next year.

Nell thought this as they crossed an old bridge over the River Linmore, and up a steep winding hill on which the town was built. She guessed it was not the main route through the town, and learned the reason why when they passed a dreary five-storey structure, built of limestone.

The outside looked horribly dark and gloomy with high windows in the walls, and tiny panes of glass to let in a sliver of light on the occupants. She knew by the sign that this was the Westbridge Asylum, next door to the poorhouse.

"The Infirmary is further along the road," said Meg, "with the mortuary."

There seemed a cold inevitability about the proximity of one building to the other.

"Is that where they were taken?" said Nell. "To the Asylum, I mean?"

"Looks like it," Meg said, and flicked the reins to urge the horse forward.

Nell took one last look at the poorhouse and shuddered. "That's where

72

I would have gone if my mother had lived?"

"Not if I'd had any say in the matter," said Meg.

"Peggy Walcote told me that was where I should have gone, but I think Mrs Grimble paid her to feed me, and as the Grimbles owned the cottage in Oak Apple Lane where we lived, she didn't argue."

They drove on in silence. Nell was glad to leave the town of Westbridge, with its dismal buildings, behind. She hoped she never had cause to visit the place again.

★★★

Beyond the outskirts of the town, Meg took the vardo along a rutted road that led to hamlets that Nell never dreamed existed, with hills in the distance that she imagined must rival Linmore Hill in size. By the time night fell, she was exhausted by all she had seen. Fatigue made her feel chilled to the core, and she was thankful for the warmth of the grey woollen cape lying across her bed.

"One of these days, I might take you along the back road from Westbridge to Norcott," said Meg. "This time, we'll stay on the home side of Cleestone Burf. I don't want to take the horses up those steep hills without a good reason."

Nell could understand why, after seeing the terrain around the mining villages in the autumn, and the difficult situation that forced them to take that route. The recollection of that tortuous journey reminded her of the first birth she witnessed with Meg in Caitlin Vale, and wondered how Lily Larkspur had fared in the winter. The little boy would be half a year old now, unlike Jimmy Hopkiln's son, who died with his mother in childbirth.

She felt a twinge of pity, but was glad that she had not, unlike Mabel at the rectory, been tempted into marriage. Nell did not like men any better now than she had when she left school – or at least, most of them. Only one had ever been kind to her and he belonged to another social world entirely.

Nell had no idea where they parked the vardo the next night, but in the morning when she awoke, Meg had already gathered food for the day.

"Where are we?" she said, looking around.

"On the Neathwood estate," said Meg, "I'll show you the big house when we go through the village. I come this way most years."

Her mood was strangely winsome, and Nell sensed that this was a place that Meg knew well. Instead of asking questions, she noted the newly painted black metal entrance gates, and at the end of the drive a fortified manor house whose crenellated tower could be seen through the trees.

Half a mile beyond they reached a village that was more of a hamlet, which contained a church in good order, a tavern along the road and half a dozen dwellings spread out on either side. Nell was reminded of Hillend, but realised that for all its sparsity of houses, Neathwood had a lord of the manor.

Further on, she saw a couple of farm tracks leading away from the road, but Meg looked neither to the left nor right. She drove briskly onwards through another hamlet, before slowing to cross the main post road between Norcott and Westbridge.

Seeing the names on the milestone, one in each direction, Nell realised that they had travelled in a complete circle, and from there continued up a slope that led to one of the shallow rides on to Linmore Hill and the woodland that she now called home. The thought gave her a warm feeling.

Chapter 7

Early Summer 1809

Wherever they travelled in the summer months, there were new signs to read, and Nell had to learn what these might portend. She accepted Meg's words that nature provided for its own, but it came as a shock to hear that the death of one species nurtured another.

One day as the caravan approached a farm, Meg pointed to a flurry of feathers scattered across a field, and said, "What do you think caused that?"

Nell stopped to think before venturing a horrified suggestion. "Did a fox do that to the chickens?"

Meg nodded. "I expect the vixen has some young somewhere."

Whilst Nell pondered the realities of life, Meg drew her attention to a lone figure digging a hole in the corner of a field. Sitting higher than the hedge, they could observe him, and saw the broken wire cage of the chicken-run a few yards beyond.

Seemingly unconcerned by the smell of rotting birds, the young lad slung the stinking carcasses into the hole at the side of the ditch, and covered them with soil, before trampling the ground down firmly. When his task was finished, the farm worker bent down to extract a single chicken from the grass and walked on his way.

Nell did not know what she was supposed to learn from this situation. The farm boy was short and skinny, like many others she had seen on their travels. When he became aware of the occupants in the caravan, Nell saw him look in Meg's direction and raise a finger to his lips, and she noticed that Meg tapped her nose in response.

"Why did he do that, Meg?" she asked.

"He was telling us not to say a word of what we have seen. I expect the missus told him to go out and find the best of the kill so she can use it for the stockpot, and he had a better idea of what was a fitting bird to eat." Meg seemed to have seen this sort of thing before.

"Do you mean that he killed the bird in the grass and took it back to the farmer's wife?" Nell was learning fast.

"Yes, he probably found a plump bird in the hen coop, wrung its neck, and left it in the damp grass to make it look like it belonged with the others. When he had buried the chickens killed by the fox, he could take it back and offer to feather it so that no one would be any the wiser," Meg said with a chuckle.

Nell was amazed at his audacity. It seemed to her that the fox was not the only wily one to have been amongst the chickens in the farmyard.

Often it was a mealtime when they reached the outlying farms, but irrespective of how poor the household or meagre the offering, Meg and Nell were offered a share. In many households, the workers had a serving of broth thirteen times a week, together with a thick crust of bread for each place setting.

Sitting around a crowded table with the working men, Nell quickly learned to bread her own bowl, before the farmer's wife ladled in the steaming broth. On the coldest of days, it was a welcome relief, and would sustain them for hours.

"You'd better come in out of the rain and have some broth," Lizzie Diglis called. Then turning to the farm labourers sitting at the table, she shouted, "Move up a couple of places, young Ted, and let the women sit down."

The poor hapless youth of that name blushed fiery red and gawked, whilst amongst the shuffling and scraping of chair legs, one of the older men solemnly warned him, "Be careful not to touch the young maid, because the owd woman might turn you into a turnip. And then, where would you be?"

Fearfully, the young man relinquished his seat, and waited by the door until the women had eaten. Nell felt sad to think they made fun of him on her behalf.

In the early autumn, they took the vardo down the hill and along the drovers' road, to a site approaching the village of Middlebrook, and there Meg found a spot to park the van under the trees, to ply her trade, well away from other folk.

"Go and have a look round the stalls," Meg said. "I'll join you later, if I don't have many visitors."

"If you're sure that I can't help you?" said Nell.

Within minutes, a number of women started to gather outside, so Nell set off down the slope, reciting the items she wanted to buy: a bar of soap, if she could find one, a reel of white cotton thread for repairs, with a couple of sewing needles – and a thimble as well. Her finger still hurt from the last time she pierced it with a needle.

Basking in the warmth of the afternoon sunshine, it never occurred to her to question her attire, thinking only that her gypsy clothes provided protection for her to wander unrecognised amongst the ordinary folk who might have seen her at Hillend.

Halfway along the line of stalls, she caught sight of a painted sign bearing the name *Adam Whitcott, Country Artist, Caitlin Vale.* Recalling others with the same name, Nell moved quickly on, not wanting to draw his attention. She stopped a few feet beyond to study the haberdashery goods on a stall, and selected the articles she needed. She said nothing when the woman charged her more than the advertised price. Moving on, she saw a tablet of soap on the next table and without thinking, lifted it to her nose to appreciate the lavender scent.

Memories came flooding back of summer evenings she had spent in the herb garden at Hillend Rectory surrounded by the scent.

"Put that down," a harsh voice broke through her reverie. "And don't touch anything else."

"I want to buy it," Nell said. "I have money to pay."

But her protests fell on deaf ears and the cry went up, as one onlooker after another started to sound like baying hounds. What could she do to convince them of her innocence?

"A likely story," said one person. "Empty your pockets and let us see."

"Where would the likes of you find money for such things?" said a rough voice from nearby.

"What's that stuff in her other hand?" someone else piped up. "I bet 'er pinched that off Mother Doverdale's stall."

"No, I paid for it," she said, backing away from them, but it was obvious that no one, not even the woman who had accepted her money, was prepared to believe her.

Nothing has changed and nobody trusts the likes of you... Memories of Oak Apple Cottage came flooding back as people advanced on her, calling for her arrest.

Suddenly, a hand caught her arm, and a commanding voice said, "You, girl, come with me."

"No, sir," she said, "I'm not a thief."

"Don't argue with me, you foolish child."

Unable to resist, Nell followed where she was led.

"But sir," one of Nell's accusers said, "that gypsy wench pinched them things from Mother Doverdale. I saw her..."

"Then you are either short-sighted or dishonest, for I saw her pay good money for her purchases. Considerably more than the advertised price – did she not, Mother Doverdale, if that is your real name?"

When a voice of authority spoke, others fell back not wanting to be involved.

"I don't rightly remember, sir," said the woman, with a sly wink.

"Then maybe you should seek help for your ocular affliction. It would help you to see better," he said contemptuously, tossing a coin on the table and turning away as the woman shamefacedly accepted it. Others, standing nearby, waited to see what he would do next.

"I haven't done anything wrong, sir," Nell repeated, struggling for release, as she recalled Meg's story of family members being transported for crimes they had not committed.

"I know you have not," said the tall, dark-haired man of medium build. A gentleman in his manner, but the paint-spotted smock he wore confirmed the occupation of country artist listed on the wooden sign.

Nell stood bemused, waiting for him to continue.

"I need a model to sit whilst I sketch," he said. "I will pay for your time. Don't worry, they will soon go away."

She gave a start, realising that they had been followed.

"Begone from here," the gentleman shouted at the encroaching crowd. "I will have none of your nastiness."

Some hastily dispersed, while others woodenly gawked.

"I fear that we must accept the inevitable. The mushrooms have taken root."

Nell sat down where he told her, eyes moist with relief at his understanding. As he worked quietly with quick strokes, she pondered the events that preceded this. In her naivety, she had not realised that dressed in gypsy garb people would not trust her.

Suddenly, there was a stir as the line of onlookers parted to let a commanding figure in black pass between them. Not in a slouch, as was Meg's custom to avoid attention, but upstanding and imperious.

As Nell sensed her friend's approach, the artist said, "No, do not move your head. Keep your expression just so…"

Nell maintained her pose knowing that Meg awaited her, while the crowd that would have threatened her moved back to a respectful distance.

The artist smiled as he worked. "I have seen your tall friend before, and wished that I could sketch her. She is magnificent, for she presents two opposing images – one a guise of almost servility, the other autocratic command. Someday, I hope that she will allow me to transpose her image from a vardo to holding the reins of a gentleman's carriage. That, I feel, is her true milieu."

His reference to her "friend" told Nell that he knew Meg's secret, and yet he said nothing. Gradually, she relaxed.

She cast a curious look in his direction, wondering if this was the parson's son, who had joined the army when his betrothed had run off with another man. If it was, she sensed that the experience had not harmed him. Maybe, if he had taken the groom with him, the young man might have survived.

Nell was glad when he signalled that she could move, but as she turned towards Meg, he said, "Do you not wish to see the picture?"

She looked at him, puzzled, unable to understand how the outcome concerned her. He beckoned, and she moved forward to look. Her eyes widened in amazement as she took in her image. A few black lines represented the shape of her head, covered by the faded scarf, a shawl around her narrow shoulders, with a hint of white bodice, and the long flowing skirt covering her feet.

Was that really her? She looked at him, and he nodded, and drew a coin from his pocket. "This is for you, young woman," he said, "with my thanks."

Nell looked at the shilling in her hand and smiled. "Thank you, sir," she said, remembering to bob her knees before turning towards where Meg stood.

"What else did you intend to purchase before the women turned you away?"

At his words, she stopped and looked back at him. "I had bought two reels of cotton thread for the sewing that I do, with a packet of needles and a thimble, but they took it away from me. They refused to sell me the lavender soap I wanted."

"Wait there," he said, and turned aside, to return minutes later with the items she had specified, and a tablet of lavender soap which he pressed into her hand. "This is with my compliments. I will always think of you when I smell the scent of lavender."

"But I must pay you for it, sir," Nell insisted. "I have the money."

He shook his head with a smile, and said, "My father would say that you have shown true generosity of spirit in giving me the opportunity to sketch your likeness, and for that I thank you."

Nell looked at him bemused, not knowing how to respond.

"Who are you?" he said. "I can see that you are not a gypsy by birth."

Unable to answer his question, Nell shook her head and turned to follow Meg through the crowd, back to the safety of the caravan.

★★★

After that, it was a relief to find occupation with the golden harvest. A year ago, Nell knew nothing of such things. Now she recognised the signs of a good crop of hedgerow fruits, and knew how things should be prepared and stored before they set off across the hill for Caitlin.

She felt a moment of doubt as she viewed again the wide vista of Linmore Hill in all its heather-clad glory, recalling the incident of last year with Squire Whitcott's sons. How different they had been to the gentleman artist, of that name, which she had seen at the Middlebrook Fair. What would happen if they met the riders again? Would they be on the lookout for a gypsy caravan? And would Nell, being with Meg, lead her friend into trouble? She hoped not.

"Don't worry, little one," Meg said, with understanding. "We won't see them this time."

Nell did not know how it was, but she had learned that Meg seemed to have a keen sense of what lay ahead of them.

Her mind turned back to the previous year when she sat on the driver's bench for the first time. Meg had been right in saying she would grow accustomed to so many things. Riding the older horse bareback came as second nature. She knew how to groom the animal and pare its hooves with a knife. It made her feel useful.

She was learning many things about Meg's work. Some joyful, and others sad: even when healthy babies were born the mother could be lost, which brought home the reality of Nell's existence.

★★★

Caitlin Vale was reached without event. Meg visited her usual farms and hamlets and saw the usual people, who repeated the same things they said last year.

When there were no more questions to be answered, Meg moved on again. As they approached the church gate in the middle of Caitlin village, Nell felt nervous when she saw a tall gentleman in clerical grey that she hoped would ignore them. Instead, he gave a cheery wave and Meg drew the horse to a halt.

By then it was too late for Nell to hide, even if he had heard of a missing girl from Hillend village. As she looked in his direction, she found his questioning gaze on her face, which turned immediately to Meg.

Fearful of what he might be thinking, Nell held her breath and studied the church, a small, squat building in local stone, with oval windows to show its Norman origin, but unlike the one of a similar type at Hillend, there were no missing slates on the roof to let in the rain, or draughty gaps under the heavy oak door.

★★★

"Good day to you, Mistress Chapel," the rector said. "Is it really that time of the year for you to visit us again?"

Meg sensed Nell's embarrassment and waited for the questions that could not be avoided. Whilst other clergy ignored her existence, Reverend Joseph Whitcott greeted her with a smile. Sometimes, the former was easier to deal with.

"It is, sir," she said, anticipating his next comment, "but this time I have brought my young companion."

He looked again at Nell. "Is it your intention to assist the young woman to find useful occupation, Mistress Chapel, for she is not, I think, of your family?"

Knowing that the law could be funny about such things, Meg said, "No, she is not, sir, but I knew her mother, and she would wish me to be Nell's friend."

"Her mother is dead?"

"She had childbed fever, sir," said Meg, telling the truth, but not the events that followed.

"Oh, dear," he said, looking concerned. "Does that mean that you have looked after the young woman since childhood? I have not seen her with you before."

"No, sir," said Meg, "Squire Norbery took an interest in her welfare and she was given a home in Linmore Dale. I met up with Nell a few months ago and found that she has a natural ability for the kind of work I do with birthing women."

He looked impressed at the mention of the Squire's name.

"So you do not plan to keep her with you indefinitely?"

"No, sir; she wasn't born to this outdoor life," she said. "The physician

82

from Middlebrook has also spoken with me about her."

Meg knew that it was early days to make such claims, but it brought a look of approval to Reverend Whitcott's face.

"Dr James Althorpe is a good man and a worthy physician. If he could find her a position she would be set up for life."

"Thank you, sir," said Meg. "I must be on my way to see Mistress Hardwick."

Her practice of adopting a respectful demeanour with the gentry served her well, but she wondered what he would say if he knew she was the person who had written the letter to his brother at Caitlin Hall.

"I will not delay you further," he said, stepping back to allow them to proceed.

"Where are we going?" Nell whispered anxiously from the vardo doorway.

"To see Molly Hardwick," said Meg, but on the approach to the carer's cottage at the edge of the village, she was not surprised when Nell retreated out of sight. No doubt to think about Meg's comment about the physician's interest in her.

Explanations must wait until later, for she needed to hear what had been going on in the village since her last visit, and it was not only ailments she wanted to discuss. There were winter supplies of lungwort, wild garlic, valerian, calendula and willow bark to dispense, and other items to acquire without delay.

***

"What happened after we left last year?" said Meg, when they arrived at the carer's house. Nell remained in the vardo as usual.

"There was a lot of running about shouting and cursing, with Cedric Whitcott claiming he'd been attacked by a gypsy, but those of us that knew the story made sure the right people knew the truth. The parson, for one, and his word carried a lot of weight. He ensured that the squire received the letter about the baby, and took care of the girl's family."

"Where's Lily now?"

"Married to the farrier's son, like she was meant to be, and living in a village out Norcott way. The Squire insisted on that. He didn't want any talk of bastards in the village, or anyone taking revenge on his sons, especially when they had finally found a woman desperate enough for a husband to marry the eldest son. I doubt if anyone could stomach his brother. Adam, their cousin, is a different proposition altogether. Most women would be lining up for a chance to marry him."

"Is he still at home?" said Meg. "We saw him over at Middlebrook last month."

"No, worst luck," chimed in Elsie, the carer's daughter, who was leaning against the vardo. "He went back to the war a couple of weeks ago. The parson and his wife are missing him, as we all are. He's a real gent."

★★★

From there, they continued on their travels around Caitlin Vale and found the bridge, swept away by the previous year's floods, had been repaired. The journey to Norcott was easier too, and they called first by the horse sales to see the gypsies.

Meg was met by Abel Hawk, with the news that the Chell had passed on, and a cairn of stones erected in his memory, close to where the gypsies had once lived on Linmore Hill.

"He's up there, where he always wanted to be. He left a message for you, Meg Chapel, to say that he wouldn't have turned you away when your mother brought you to us."

"A lot of water's passed under that particular bridge," said Meg. "It doesn't bother me now. I know where I belong."

"No grudges?"

"I never held one," she said, "even if others did."

"You'll come again?"

"If I'm passing," she said with a careless shrug of her shoulders.

"Look after the boy, Meg Chapel. He still looks a bit delicate."

"I'll do that, all right, Abel Hawk."

★★★

Standing aside by the vardo, Nell heard their conversation and understood all that was not put into words. The Chell who died had been Mother Chapel's father, but it was her stepmother who banished them. Hence the reason that Meg had spoken of his kinswoman.

From there, they moved on to the blacksmiths' shop in a village on the edge of Norcott. Lily Larkspur, as she had been called, greeted them with her babe on her hip, and a gentle swell of her belly to show another was on the way.

"Thank you, Meg," she said. "You were right about the baby being wanted. I'll be having another in a few months, for company."

"The next delivery should be easier," said Meg.

Nell, taking the child that was offered, cuddled him, and felt a slight pang of regret knowing she would never have one of her own. Then she returned him to his mother.

"It suits you, Nell," said her old friend from school. "You need to find yourself a husband and have a baby. Clem, my husband, has a brother looking for a wife. Maybe you two…"

Nell shook her head but said nothing.

"When she's ready," said Meg, gathering up the reins ready to depart.

"I'll see you again next year, Nell," called Lily as they drove away.

"Maybe," said Meg, "maybe not."

★★★

At the farm, approaching Middlebrook down the drovers' road, they learned that the old woman to whom Nell had read passed away in the final days of winter.

"Granny liked you, girl," said the farmer's wife, as she wiped away a tear. "I'll give you one of her handkerchiefs in her memory."

"Thank you, ma'am," said Nell, dutifully bobbing her knees.

"With manners like that, I know you're not what you pretend to be," the woman said, peering at her. "I don't know what it is about this young woman, Mother Chapel, but she reminds me of someone I've seen before, and I can't think who it is. I said as much to Dr Althorpe, only the other day."

"I daresay it'll come back to you," said Meg. "I have thoughts like that as well."

Yes, but Meg had known Nell's mother, whereas the farmer's wife could not possibly have known her – could she?

Once Nell had heard of the Middlebrook physician, it was inevitable that they would meet him on their travels. To her surprise, he acknowledged Meg by name, whereas other people, with less reason to be high-minded, ignored her.

Meg, similarly, treated such people with disdain. It was a particular way she had of looking down her hawkish nose that disconcerted the would-be haughty folk, which had come to Nell's aid when they went to the Middlebrook Fair.

★★★

Autumn slipped into winter, a time of coughs and chills, when calls for assistance were frequent. Several times, Nell was asked to sit with an old lady on the other side of Linmore Dale who suffered with dropsy, and she often did sewing repairs for the lady of the house to while away the hours while her charge dozed.

Once, the physician from Middlebrook visited his patient, and Nell stood up on his arrival, but he seemed not to see her. She, however, observed him from the corner of the room and listened to his conversation with the lady's daughter.

"Might I suggest that you contact Mistress Chapel, and ask for one of her remedies? I have nothing better to offer, and some of her herbs might help."

"Oh, but this young person works with Mother Chapel," said the woman.

Noticing her for the first time, he said, "I see, and where is Mistress Chapel, young woman."

Before Nell could speak, the woman answered for her. "She's attending Mrs Brockmere at the next farm along the lane, sir. She went into labour in the middle of the night. It's lucky the midwife was already here, for she went as soon as she heard the news."

"In that case, I will leave you, ma'am, and visit your neighbour," he said as he turned to leave the room. "I doubt if your mother will suffer a relapse before Mistress Chapel's return. The young woman seems to have a calming influence about her."

"She has a lovely reading voice that settles the old lady in no time."

"Reading?" he said. "How interesting and unusual."

"They say that Mother Chapel can read and write as well," said the woman.

"You intrigue me, ma'am."

Nell wondered if he believed what he was being told, and how the farmer's wife could possibly know such things about Meg, when she called her by the wrong name, as many people did.

Meg brought news within hours of a successful delivery, and a remedy of crushed foxglove leaves for the old woman. Nell packed up her sewing materials, not intending to leave them behind. "Where have you left the vardo?" she said.

"At Brockmere Farm," said Meg. "I brought the horse to get here sooner."

"The physician came from Middlebrook."

"Yes," said Meg with a yawn, "he told me what was needed here, and I said that I'd take you back to look after the nursing mother for a few days."

"Won't he mind?" said Nell, surprised.

"No, for some reason he thought it was a good idea."

Chapter 8

Spring 1810

Meg did not set out to be a teacher, but imparted knowledge by drawing Nell's attention to their surroundings and pointing out the wild flowers and shrubs growing in the hedgerows and ditches. *See it, touch it and smell it,* was her maxim, and soon Nell began to gather an assortment of herbs, berries and flowers with odd pieces of bark, together with roots of garlic and fungi.

Gradually, she learned to look around and recognise what she had seen, listen to the sounds of nature and understand the significance; to smell rain on the wind and feel the textures of flora and fauna. From that, she could identify what was edible and what was not.

At first, she had no answers to Meg's questions, but gradually she ventured a suggestion and as her confidence grew, began to recognise the telltale marks left by animals and know the kind of homes they had.

She learned that badgers lived in a burrow known as a sett, and red squirrels inhabited a drey high up in the trees, and the tiny dormouse, being nocturnal, only came out of its nest when most of the other animals were settling for the night.

This was Nell's favourite, and once or twice she glimpsed the elusive rodent scurrying along the hazel branches in the twilight, and later found neatly chiselled nutshells on the floor, a sure sign of the dormouse's presence.

She felt sad on hearing that this little creature hibernated through the winter months, but then learned that they might not survive the cold without it.

Nell was puzzled when Meg pointed out birds on the wing and asked her to identify the species by its song, but soon ventured to make suggestions and was pleased when Meg nodded approval to her answers. In time, she managed to recognise the snipe, a game bird whose song was supposed to foretell the coming of rain, and recited sayings from country folklore that said how a red sky at night could forecast a good day on the morrow, whereas a morning splash of colour was supposed to forewarn of bad weather.

★★★

Once or twice they visited farms at threshing time, and Nell sat in the caravan, watching the dusty process through the great barn doors as the farm workers beat corn with flails to separate it from the husks and chaff.

She was intrigued when she saw a deep piece of wood placed along the floor between the open doors; and realised it was put there to hold the newly threshed corn inside, whilst the wind blowing through the doors on the opposite side of the barn took the waste to the yard beyond.

Listening to the farm workers talking, she learned that nothing was wasted, and every night, the waggoners prepared chaff to supplement feed for the horses and in the stack yards, any straw left over from the previous year was used for thatching new hayricks.

Seeing that some of the farmers in Linmore Dale had started to plough the fields, she asked, "Why do they use those big horses instead of oxen like we saw in Caitlin Vale?"

"I expect the horses can move faster and cover the ground better. The bigger farms hereabouts sow seeds with machines instead of sprinkling on the surface by hand, as they used to do," was Meg's reply.

"A machine to sow seeds! What does it look like?"

"I've only seen one, which could sow several rows of seeds at a time. I dare say the land is covered faster, but whether it is any better, I couldn't say."

Travelling through the villages, Nell was fascinated when she saw stonemasons building walls at the roadside, and carpenters repairing wooden buildings, while thatchers stripped off and replaced the worn out straw roofs; but in other areas through which they passed, she saw dwellings deteriorating and thought they looked sad and dilapidated.

"Meg, why do they leave buildings to fall apart?"

"It depends on the landowner," said Meg. "A bad one takes money out of the estate, and a good one ploughs it back in. Look at the farms and you will appreciate the difference."

Nell felt sad thinking about the hovel in which she had grown up. Whoever owned that did not care about it – but maybe there was a reason of which she was unaware. It was not her place to sit in judgement on her betters.

High Summer 1810

The leather thong that hung around Meg's neck was a mystery. Nell had hardly noticed it until the day when Meg, dressed as a man, untied her belcher kerchief, and left the neck of the collarless shirt open.

The long summer day had become increasingly humid, foretelling rain after a long dry spell that was perfect for the harvest in the valley. Now the stooks of corn, stacked on wagons, were being transported back to the farms before the storm broke. Meg, knowing the urgency for them to do so, had drawn the vardo aside on the grass verge, and waited for them to pass.

At supper, it was too hot for a campfire, so they made do with spring water, bread and cheese. Nell was glad to be wearing her girl's clothes, yet for once; she wished she could remove them and take a dip in the stream. It was something she only did when there was a real necessity to wash all over. Usually, she made do with a strip wash in the woodsman's hut, or the vardo if they were on the road.

When Meg removed the kerchief and wiped her neck, Nell untied the fichu and let it hang loose around her shoulders. The momentary relief of fresh air to the skin was a joy, but it did not last. The trundling sound of an approaching cart forced her to cover her exposed chest. It would not do to have any men see her like that.

In restoring the kerchief, Meg withdrew the leather strip from her shirt front. Nell stared in amazement at the bauble looped on the end. Keen green eyes met blue, and Meg smiled. "Did you want to see it?"

When Nell nodded, Meg placed the leather strip in her outstretched hand. "It was something Mother Chapel brought back from the valley," she said. "Now it is mine – for what it is worth. Anyone found in possession risks ending their days on the gallows."

Nell could see, on closer inspection that it was not an ordinary strip of cow hide, but a beautifully finished narrow belt of intricate design. Its purpose was to keep safe a ring, heavily engraved around the band and the setting for a fine green gemstone, the like of which Nell had never seen.

She shivered, without knowing why. "It's heavy," she said.

"So is the responsibility of wearing it. When I'm gone, it will have to be taken back where it came from."

"The Neathwood estate?" she said.

Meg nodded. "If anything happens to me; bury me with the bluebells by Mother Chapel. Then, wrap the leather strip with the ring in a cloth and place it in the high-sided pew, under the pulpit in Neathwood church, and leave the book of sermons with it."

"Will the people there know to whom it belongs?" said Nell.

"Yes," said Meg, "they will."

Then the rain came, beating a tattoo in slow patters on the vardo roof. Nell had not noticed the storm clouds gathering overhead, but somehow it seemed symbolic. Was that Mother Chapel's payment in kind, for wet-nursing the gentleman's son, and bringing him through a healthy childhood? It seemed an extraordinary gift for a gypsy woman – but who was Nell to question it?

★★★

"Can I stay with you in the vardo today…out of sight?" Nell did not mean to say the extra words but they slipped out in her anxiety. The time of the Middlebrook Fair was approaching, and all she could think about was the unpleasantness she had encountered on her last visit. Something she did not wish to repeat.

Meg, gathering her herbs together for the occasion, gave her a long look before responding. "You can, if you like, but why don't you wear one of the frocks from the rectory – otherwise, they'll be outgrown before they see the light of day."

Nell complied, knowing the truth of the statement. She was taller than before, and her fuller chest necessitated a slight easement of the darts in the bodice of the russet-coloured frock, which was more sombre than the dark green or blue velvet. Then she added a white frilled cap she had made with Mrs Ferndale and a light shawl around her shoulders which made her look suitably anonymous.

An hour later, Meg stopped a distance along the drovers' road and left Nell to walk to the field where the fair was being held. At first, she felt nervous amongst so many people, but gained in confidence when she passed her accusers of the previous year with no sign of recognition.

She felt a touch of what she supposed was vanity in her appearance, which made her feel better. Armed with a confidence that she had never felt before, Nell walked along the line of stalls, hoping to see some of the pictures drawn by the country artist from Caitlin.

Seeing no sign of him, she recalled being told that the gentleman had gone back to the war in Spain the previous autumn. Avoiding contact with the harridan who had lied about her honesty, Nell purchased some lavender soap and haberdashery items from the next stall. The vender, a stranger, treated her with courtesy, and Nell assumed they thought she was someone in service. Armed with the knowledge, she moved on.

A chance glimpse of Mrs Grimble from Oak Apple Farm in Hillend in the distance made her start forward. Then she noticed the peeved expression of the lady's daughter, Betsy, at her side, looking decidedly overdressed in frills and flounces. She chided herself for uncharitable thoughts, knowing that she was wearing Betsy's hand-me-downs. Although wishing she could speak to the mother, the daughter's presence made it impossible. Likewise the need to explain her absence from the village made her retrace her steps to the vardo.

"How did it go?" Meg said when she arrived. "Did you see anyone who recognised you?"

"No one who would have spoken to me," she said. "The gentleman who sketched my likeness wasn't there."

"Apart from not seeing him, did you find the things that you wanted?"

"Yes," said Nell, feeling pleased. "Everything I needed."

Including the indulgence of two tablets of lavender soap, rather than the one she had intended, and a length of muslin to make a fichu. The knowledge that she was smartly dressed had given her the confidence to do so. Of course, it would be some time before she found a reason to dress like that again, but she had enjoyed it.

★★★

Sometimes things happened to make Nell remember the life she had left behind. It was strange to be outside in the fresh air watching the gathering in of the harvest, yet not playing any part as she had as a child. In a year of abundance, the farm barns were full to capacity, and they were approaching the time of the harvest festival when churches were decorated with fruits of the fields and orchards in readiness for the celebration.

Three years on since the last time, she remembered the bustle of preparation, helping to clean and decorate Hillend church. The pleasure she had derived in listening to Miss Dinchope's tuneful rendition of the harvest hymns, and the joyful, if inaccurate, version by Maisie Jemkins.

The thought brought tears to her eyes, so to counter the emotion Nell added her own contribution. *All is safely gathered in, ere the winter storms begin,* she sang softly, with no one but Meg to hear her. Then she wiped her eyes and wondered what news Molly Hardwick would have to tell them.

Rather than a celebration of the season, there was an inexplicable air of sadness as they drove past Caitlin church where Nell had met the gently spoken rector the previous year. Of him there was no sign.

As usual, Meg drove to the carer's house, and Nell stayed on the driver's bench to mind the horses, while listening to the sound of the women's voices.

"Lung fever it was that carried him off in the spring. He caught a chill riding home from the Hall in a storm, because his brother's wife refused to give him shelter," said Molly Hardwick with an angry sniff. "We lost the school teacher as well, so the parson's wife is helping to teach the little 'uns. It stands to reason with her being book-learned. The poor lady needed something to take her mind off being turned out of the home she'd lived in for over thirty years."

"Where is she now?" said Meg.

"In the old lodge at the end of the park, but it's nothing like as comfortable as the rectory. That's her sister-in-law's spite for you. The Squire should have put his foot down, but he never did have the manners his brother had. Things might be better when Captain Adam comes home for good. I'm glad he managed to get leave to see his father before...it happened."

The name stirred a recollection of the country artist that sketched Nell's likeness the previous year at Middlebrook Fair – a gentleman who had treated an unknown gypsy girl with kindness.

"Where is he now?" said Meg.

"Elsie," Mollie Hardwick called through the open door. "Where did Mrs Whitcott, from the lodge, say her son was?"

"In Spain or Portugal, or one of them countries where they're fighting the Frenchies, I think," Elsie said, breaking off from speaking with Nell to answer. "It's dreadful hot, wherever it is, according to his mother."

"How are things at the Hall?" said Meg, meaning the Squire's sons.

"They're as bad as ever, so I'll need as much of your herbal mixture as you can spare."

"I thought you said the Squire had found a wife for the older son."

"Nothing came of it after the young lady met the younger brother. Once she saw the influence Cedric Whitcott had over Mr Barnaby she took her fortune elsewhere. Served them right for what their sister did to Captain Adam; not but what I think he had a lucky escape."

"When will he be coming home?" said Meg.

"Hard to say, but it won't be soon enough for his mother," said the carer.

As they prepared to drive on, Molly Hardwick said, "If you're looking for more clothes for the girl, Elsie can ask the new parson for permission to look in the clothes box they keep in the attics. She used to work for Reverend Whitcott, but when he died, his widow left her with the new people. She still goes in to help the lady, when she can, but it's not the same."

At the edge of the village, they came to a stone gatekeeper's lodge at the end of a drive leading to a house with tall chimneys half-hidden by trees. The cottage looked a tranquil place, surrounded by the red-gold leaves of autumn, but Nell had a feeling that it would be bleak in winter.

"Ah," said Elsie, knowingly. "There's no smoke in the chimney, so that means Mrs Sarah Whitcott is down at the school. I'll look in on her next time I'm passing to see if she needs anything."

Walking alongside the vardo, Elsie kept up a steady stream of conversation.

"I'll see what I can find, although I can't promise anything," the girl said. "Mrs Sarah, from the lodge, kept a store box of clothes for folks in need. Good quality stuff, if a bit old-fashioned now. Had we known the lady would be moving in a hurry, when the new parson brought his family from Bredenbridge, Mother and me could have carried it down to the cottage. Shameful of the squire, that was, to treat his dead brother's widow like that. Nobody speaks well of him now."

Elsie ran off along the drive and came back within minutes gesturing for Meg to turn the vardo along the lane to the rear of the three-storey house; with little windows on the top floor that reminded Nell of those in the attics at Hillend Rectory.

Instead, Meg stopped the vehicle under the trees, and handed the reins to Nell. "You stay here," she said, climbing down from her seat to stand by the horse.

"The poor lady, to lose her husband and her home," Nell said, finding it hard to believe that even the gentry were treated with disrespect when their circumstances changed.

"Yes," said Meg. "It seems there's no honour amongst the folks that come from Bredenbridge."

Nell decided that Meg must be right because Reverend Snitterfield and his sister had come from there, and they treated people badly.

Elsie came back within minutes, looking angry. "The miserable old devil," she spat. "He didn't even know it was in the attic, and now he's refusing to let me take a look. I expect his wife will try to sell the things in Bredenbridge, the parsimonious..." Words failed her.

Then she looked more cheerful, as she revealed a cloth-wrapped package concealed under her coat. "The cook sent this fresh-baked loaf of bread and a piece of cheese from the dairy, Meg. She's Lily Larkspur's aunt, and never stops telling me how grateful they were that you brought the wench safely through her first delivery. She had another little boy last year, and I suspect she might be carrying the third."

That made three children in as many years, thought Nell, knowing that it would never happen to her.

"I'm sorry, Meg," said Elsie. "I'd help if I could, but any question about ownership of the clothes box will have to come from Mrs Sarah Whitcott."

Meg nodded, and quickly turned the vardo around, intent on driving back to the road, while Nell secreted the victuals out of sight. It would not do for them to be seen in case someone accused them of thievery. And she knew just the villain who would do it. One day there would be an accounting for the dip in the duck pond, but she did not intend Nell to be used as a pawn in the encounter.

★★★

Nell thought about her conversation with Elsie, who made no secret of the fact that she envied Nell her position. "I'd love to work with Meg, like Mother does, but she won't hear of it. Says I must be in service with the gentry, and yet look at the way the Squire treated his brother's widow, even if his wife made him do it."

Elsie's next question caught her unawares.

"How do you come to be with Meg when you're not related?"

"She knew my mother," Nell said, glad to have a valid reason to offer.

"When was that?"

Before Nell could reply, Elsie asked another question. "How long do you think you'll stay with her? Maybe Mother would let Meg teach me her ways."

Although Nell made no response, it was something about which she secretly wondered. Meg did not seem overly bothered about change, but Nell sensed it was creeping up on them like a shadow.

She was already turned sixteen, the age when most women she met had at least one child, and often more. She wondered if her years in the wilderness would, like Meg, affect her ability to bear children – but maybe, as a foundling, it was better if it did.

★★★

Sometimes, when passing country inns, Nell sewed torn sheets or washed clothes to make a little money to buy bread. Often Meg went off alone to see patients, and Nell wondered if her friend was preparing for the time when they would not be together. It made her consider how best to find suitable work, but it would be difficult to take a lesser job when she knew her midwifery skills were in demand.

It was something in which Nell had gained considerable practice. Sometimes, while Meg stayed to finish one delivery, Nell went ahead on horseback to assess another woman in the early stages of labour – a routine that worked exceedingly well.

In the early months when Meg delivered babies, all Nell could do was watch and listen to the words of wisdom. As time went on, Meg placed Nell's hands on the swollen belly to feel the baby moving, and soon touch brought understanding.

It taught her how to identify the position of the baby in the womb, and feel the difference between the rounded cranium and the softer breech, or curve of the back, and irregular feel of the limbs. As the process became more familiar, she listened to the pounding heartbeats and recognised when contractions were growing stronger.

Most babies delivered with the back of the head coming first and she watched in awe as a tuft of hair appeared, then the head emerged. The next pain released the shoulders, and then Meg delivered the baby's body up over the woman's belly into her waiting arms. A lull usually followed whilst the mother suckled her young, and then nature began to expel the afterbirth.

Nell had learned that this part of the birth process needed extra vigilance, because until the intact organ was delivered, bleeding or infection could rob a child of its mother and a man of his wife. When the process was complete, Meg told her that a properly cooked afterbirth could give nourishment to the woman.

With every delivery, Nell's hands shadowed those of the midwife, until the time when Meg stood back and watched her deliver the baby. When Nell's hands were sure and confident, she practised manoeuvres for the safe delivery of a breech and supported the after-coming head.

Only rarely was it necessary to summon a doctor, but when the physician arrived, Meg remained in the background ready to help the woman after the surgical intervention was complete. Normally, she was the one to extract the afterbirth, control the bleeding and dispense herbs to safeguard the woman from infection, but all this was with an unseen hand that challenged none of the conventions to which physicians prescribed.

Nell could not understand why only a handful of doctors knew of Meg by repute, or even fewer respected her contribution. Then Meg told her that medical science scorned the traditional ways, and outlawed anything construed as being akin to witchcraft.

When a miscarriage occurred, Nell realised that although the loss of a pregnancy was a sad occasion, few women had the luxury of sympathy from their menfolk at such a time. Instead it was get up, and back to work, because there were other mouths to feed.

Sometimes, Meg was able to help these women, by giving them herbal remedies to suppress lactation and alleviate depression. The majority of women scarcely had time to recover before they were pregnant again, and the cycle of birth rolled onwards.

Chapter 9

Late Autumn 1810

From Caitlin village, they drove down the valley and along the road that took them through hamlets on the Norcott end of Linmore Hill. It took two days to achieve, but such places were becoming familiar to Nell, as were people she recalled meeting the year before. It gave her a sense of belonging.

Usually, when they crossed the old river bridge in Norcott, Meg followed the direction of the drovers' road that skirted the side of the hill. On this occasion, however, she omitted to visit the gypsy encampment and set off in an unfamiliar direction. All Nell knew, was that the mound of high land, which directly faced Linmore Hill across the valley, was on their left.

"Is this the road to Westbridge around the back of Cleestone Burf?" she said, recalling that Meg had mentioned it the first time they travelled up the dale together. Now she was seeing a different aspect of the valley.

"We won't travel that far," said Meg, "but I want you to see parts of the dale that you've missed."

Nell was eager to know more.

"There's mining on parts of this hill," said Meg, "but not in the same way as over by the Myndstone mines."

Most of the land, along the side of the wooded hillside, was given over to sheep farming. Before settling for the night in a clearing amongst the trees, they shared a supper of herb broth, thickened with remnants of the loaf that Elsie Hardwick had given them. Tomorrow, they must find more victuals.

Covered by her cape, Nell went to sleep surrounded by silence and the starlit sky. She awoke in the early hours feeling a distinct chill in the air, and, looking outside the vardo, saw tendrils of mist that reminded her of the time two years ago, when she sought help from Meg. It seemed a lifetime ago.

Breakfast, to Nell's surprise, was a change from broth, in the form of a dead hedge-pig that Meg found on their journey and baked in clay overnight. Tasty though the morsel was, it would probably be many days before they ate meat again.

When they emerged on the other side of the woodland, Nell saw, through the remnants of mist, the upper part of Linmore Dale spread out at their feet. And across the valley, Linmore Hill stood proud above the other land in all its glory.

That is my home, she thought, and was glad.

From there, the land descended through the mist towards the valley floor. Meg had harnessed William the cob to the vardo, while Nell rode Lodestone beside them along the bridle path. At first, she had no idea where they were going, but after a couple of hours, the sky cleared and familiar signs came to mind. Soon, she thought, they would pass the entrance to Neathwood Park – Meg's one indulgence.

The sighting was brief, but she noticed that, since the previous year, several cottage roofs in the hamlet were newly thatched: a sign that someone cared about their tenants' welfare. Nell knew that it was not her place to have an opinion about the gentry's actions – but in this case she did, and Meg similarly nodded approval.

From there, the tracks they used enabled them to avoid people by skirting the edge of hamlets. Before she knew, a tiny river bridge was crossed and the post road was in sight. Once they were safely across, Nell knew they were almost home. The land immediately started to rise on the approaches to the lower rides, but instead of taking the familiar path across the hill, Meg turned right along a narrow country lane that Nell had not noticed before.

"Where are we going?" she said.

"There's a pregnant woman I need to see. It's near her time, and I want to know she's all right."

"How did you find out?" said Nell.

"I saw her in Middlebrook. She lives out along Callow Edge."

"How far is that?"

"There's a crossroads up ahead, and it's a couple of miles beyond."

Before that, they came to an old tavern, with a rickety sign that proclaimed it to be The Baker's Dozen. Meg stopped at the water butt to let the horses take a drink. When the landlady came out to enquire their business, Meg asked, "Have you any sewing that needs doing, lady?"

It seemed the woman had, and so Nell stayed to repair torn sheets while Meg went on with the vardo to see her patient. Things went well for the first few hours, until the son of the house, a gangly youth in his teens, espied her. Nell ignored him as best she could, but realised as the day went on that Meg had been delayed. Most likely the woman she went to see had gone into labour, which could mean a few hours or a couple of days before she returned.

Anticipating a delay, Nell offered to help the scullion wash the bed linen in exchange for her company. By nightfall, six pairs of sheets had been repaired, scrubbed clean and hung out to dry. Thankfully, there was a brisk breeze, and as long as the dry weather continued, she would help to iron them on the morrow.

It was late by the time she had hung the sheets over the rack and cleaned the washroom floor. Not a drop of sustenance had passed her lips, but the scullery maid had slipped out with an offering of weak ale, which Nell gratefully drank, and found to her surprise, a half-soaked crust of bread surreptitiously placed there.

"Thank you," she said.

"Don't tell the missus about it, or you'll be charged out of your pay," said the woman, snatching the cup back and disappearing before Nell could say more.

Know your place and do as you're told. An old rhyme came back to Nell from her childhood in Oak Apple Cottage at Hillend. Living with Meg, she had acquired new skills and had a different set of values, but to the likes of the landlady, a gypsy girl was no one of importance.

★★★

It was six o'clock, as the dawn started to break over the silent inn, when Nell made her way across the back courtyard. Had she been closer to the scullery, she might have claimed to be visiting the privy, but before she could reach the door it opened to reveal the landlady, taking her ease, clad in her night attire and curling rags. Nell, fully dressed from the previous day's work, hesitated and was seen, so she waited for the inevitable tirade.

"And where did you spend the night, young woman?"

A truculent question received an honest answer.

"In the stables, ma'am," Nell said, about to explain that she hated to be confined within doors, but the woman interrupted.

"Sharing your favours with the grooms and ostlers, I daresay, like the trollop you are."

Appalled at the venom, Nell retorted, "No, ma'am, the horses made better company than their riders."

The woman stared at her with malicious disbelief. "What's wrong with a perfectly good bed in the attic – or are you too choosy to sleep with another woman?"

"Because it was already occupied by two people, with no room for a third," Nell said, wishing she had the courage to add that one was the woman's husband, and even if he had left before dawn, the thought of sleeping on sheets where he had lain made her skin crawl.

Oh, please, Meg, come back today. I don't want to stay here any more.

The woman stomped away, with a look of dawning realisation in her eyes. "Make sure you get the ironing done today, or there'll be no food for you, my wench," she said spitefully over her shoulder.

Nell had only been allowed a morsel the previous day, but it was easier not to argue the point. "Yes, ma'am," she said, omitting to bob her knees, for she was fast learning that whilst some people deserved respect, others did not.

★★★

The events that had driven her out of doors reminded her of the night when Reverend Snitterfield had appeared at the door of her attic bedroom. The same presentiment of trouble warned her when, creeping up the backstairs after everyone else had gone to bed, she heard a bedroom door open along the landing, followed by the stealthy footsteps of a lustful overgrown boy.

She had guessed his intent from the way he gawked at her standing in the scullery when everyone else, even the barmaid, sat around the kitchen table. It was obvious that he felt a gypsy girl was fair game by the disrespectful way he talked about her breasts in her presence.

Later she felt his lascivious gaze following her when she helped the scullion to carry heavy washing baskets from the laundry room to the washing lines, and cringed at his look of eager anticipation when they met in a doorway. Knowing his intention, she crept downstairs and melted into the cloaks alcove in the hallway. Minutes later, she heard his descent, one creaking step at a time.

Nell crouched down out of sight, and through a gap in the cloaks at floor level, saw his hairy shins beneath his nightshirt, in a shaft of moonlight through the window above the door. She knew, from the rank stench of his unwashed body, that he was close enough to touch her, which gave her the impetus to hold her breath.

When clouds finally obscured the light, she heard the first sign of his return up the staircase. She sensed that he hesitated and looked around before making his way back to the upper floor. Even then, she heard his heavy breathing on the landing, and then the shuffling footsteps back to his room. Only when the door had finally closed did she dare to venture out to the stable. A whisper in Meg's gypsy-talk brought a soft snickering response that assured her of the equine's compliance that no human would pass unnoticed.

A few hours later, Nell awoke and set out across the courtyard, intent on cleaning the heavy irons she had found in the storeroom, ready for pressing the newly washed sheets – but before that could be achieved she was harassed by the publican's wife, and so the day continued.

By the evening, Nell was exhausted. A thin dry crust of bread was all she was allowed to break her fast, but the landlady, not knowing it was a feast, watched her swallow every single crumb. There was no time for more food in the day, only a sip of water from the pump when she dampened the sheets for ironing.

Her memories of helping Mrs Jemkins with the washing at Hillend Rectory gave her strength; and the thought of Meg's imminent return. If not tonight, it would be tomorrow at the latest. Nell knew that if she had not agreed to do the work at the inn, she would have gone with Meg to attend the woman in labour. But once an agreement was made, she would never break it.

Abandoned by her scullion helpmate, Nell wielded the irons with an expertise she had forgotten she possessed – helped through the day by the memory of Maisie's joyful voice singing her tuneless songs. Back and forth she walked to the fire knowing that, with a heavy iron in each hand, she was safe. Now, having finally finished the work and placed every sheet on the rack to air, she had gone to the kitchen to eat a bowl of broth, only to find a congealed globule awaiting her, stone cold.

Undeterred, Nell raised a spoon to her lips, but before the first unpalatable taste registered, she looked up to find the landlord glowering at her. She had heard the furious tirade to which his spouse had subjected him for his absence in the night, but thought that would have been infinitely better than his unprepossessing presence.

"Put that down," he said, "and get yourself into the taproom. I'm not paying you to eat when there's customers waiting to be served."

The fact that the regular barmaid, employed for such work, sat taking her ease, seemed to escape him. But Nell, used to such abuse, set down the spoon on the table, her belly protesting at the misuse. Then she told herself it was only a few hours more before Meg returned and they would be moving on.

"Yes, sir," she said, and prepared to follow him into a room where she had never ventured before.

The barmaid, having had her ears boxed by the landlady, took a delight in Nell's predicament.

"If you're not going to eat that soup, give it to me. I'm going to need my strength later," the girl said with a smirk.

Pushing the bowl across the table, Nell followed the landlord out of the room, guessing that she would spend another night in the stables.

The taproom air was thick with smoke, and the dirty oil lamps smelly. The brightest glow was a tree trunk spitting in the inglenook, but for Nell there was little light to see where she placed her feet as she edged between the tables gathering tankards and wishing she could take them out to the kitchen to wash.

When she moved in the direction of the bar, she was called back by one or other of the customers whose voices she could hear, while their faces remained in shadow. She knew they were there by the rank odour of unwashed bodies.

How different to… A memory came to her mind, which she quickly banished. Not permitting her the luxury of thought for fear she might let her attention lapse and find herself bundled into a corner by customers who could not keep their sweaty hands to themselves. Nell was one woman amongst a dozen men, with no hope of a gentleman coming to her rescue – or even a landlord with an ounce of decency.

This time she knew she was alone as she approached a table by the fire, carrying a large jug of ale. Something the other girl would have relished doing and welcomed hands touching her bottom, whereas, Nell was revolted by the thought of such familiarity.

"I bet you I'll have her first," said a loathsome voice of the young man sitting at the table to the one side of the inglenook.

"How much?" said the slurred voice of his companion on the wooden settle.

"Half a crown, says I'll be the winner," boasted the landlord's son. "Come over here, wench."

"Are you speaking to me?" she said.

"Ooh, listen to her fancy talk," said a drunken voice in the dark corner to which Nell could not put a face. "Her ladyship won't want a common chap like you."

"I'll give you a florin if you'll oblige me," said the tavern lad, boastfully.

A stunned silence followed the declaration.

"What do you mean, sir?" said Nell, feigning ignorance.

"Two shillings, my wench; more than you've ever seen before, I'll warrant."

"Oh no, sir," she said, meeting his bleary eye. "I know the value of the coin, but what I have is not for sale."

There was a burst of mocking laughter from his companions.

"You've got a high opinion of yourself, for a gypsy wench. Take yer hat off, and let's be having a look at you," he said, scrambling to his feet in his haste.

"No," she said, backing away. Even in a murky taproom, she knew better than to reveal her hair. Therein lay disaster.

"Leave…the…wench…alone, peasant. She is under my protection."

Nell froze as a masculine voice, chill and intimidating, suddenly emitted from the gloomiest corner of the room. When the bully similarly wavered, she backed away, while the rabble by the fire shouted encouragement, urging their friend to challenge the newcomer. The young man, too stupid to see danger, complied.

"And who might you be to give orders in here, my fine buck?"

"My name does not concern scum like you, boy." The harsh voice oozed contempt, as the chair legs scraped the flagstone floor, "but I think this bauble will."

A flash of green gemstone set in a heavy gold ring, arrested the man's attention, when the clenched fist that it adorned stopped inches from his nose. The threat was implicit, but the newcomer's haughty manner imbued it with infinitely more menace.

Nell was astounded by the change in the bully's demeanour. He stumbled back in alarm, knocking over the heavy wooden chair next to the settle, which bumped against the table and fell with a crash on the hearth amongst the firedogs. Several tankards slopped over as others distanced themselves from their friend.

Hearing the commotion, the landlord rushed forward to fawn over his unexpected guest. "Begging your lordship's pardon," he said, "I didn't know you was in here tonight. There's no call for you to be sitting with these common folk when the parlour's empty." Then to his son, "Damn your hide, Sam Whittingslow, get out of his lordship's way."

But in the ensuing uproar, the dark-clad stranger melted into the night, and Nell, with no reason to stay, followed him. Introductions could wait for later.

★★★

106

Earlier in the evening, a shadowy figure had slipped from the surrounding trees to approach the inn. A dog barked for several minutes in an outhouse but, apart from a curse to quell it, nobody paid it any heed. The ostler and groom in the stables were more intent on washing down a crust of bread and cheese with a tankard of heavy wet, and talking about the landlord's son and his designs on the gypsy wench.

Meg sensed, from the raucous noise in the taproom, that she had arrived not a minute too soon. The previous day had been tedious in the extreme, when the delivery of a multigravid woman presented her with a potentially life-threatening problem. It was a time when she would have welcomed Nell's help in releasing a loose cord from around the baby's neck and foot.

The labour culminated in the birth of a much-wanted son, for a mother with seven previous daughters. After an initially slow response, the baby cried and took to the breast, but delivery of the afterbirth was protracted.

All the time, Meg's mind was straying to where she had left Nell, in the assumption that she would be safe darning and washing sheets. But some deep instinct warned her that all was not well.

She had not intended to delay, but the hours of the previous night had slipped by and half the afternoon before the weary mother was safe to be left.

Caution warned her not to arrive back dressed as a gypsy woman, so she parked up the vardo and took a chance on being seen in her gentleman's suit of black clothes. A risk worth taking even though it was within three miles of Neathwood Park. The thought of it spurred her on.

Hearing an argument between women in the scullery, she crossed the courtyard in three strides, and slipped through the taproom door to a shadowy corner table. A task made easier by the landlord's absence, and his son, a boastful lout, who was more interested in swilling tankards of cheap ale and exchanging lewd stories with his friends, than attending to any prospective customers.

Meg spent the next half hour in the obscurity of the shadows, for no one came through the outer door to disturb her. Usually, a barmaid waited at table, but tonight the idle slut stayed out of sight, probably copulating with the landlord in the cellar.

She had overheard people at the farm talking of this during the delivery, foretelling the landlady's anger if she caught the couple together, with bets being taken on the girl being turned out of doors. That was their problem to deal with, whereas Nell's safety was her responsibility.

The atmosphere was tense with anticipation as Nell entered the room carrying a tray of drinks. When she hesitated to look around, the swarthy individual following cursed her slowness in attending customers. Meg might also have demanded attention, but bided her time to achieve surprise.

Watching from the shadows, Meg knew that she could not, in a roomful of men, win a fight based on brute strength. As she loosened the silver knob-headed swordstick brought for defence, she heard someone offering money for services to be rendered and Nell's polite refusal that ridiculed the braggart.

As the lout lunged forward, Meg, unable to remain silent, infused her voice with all the haughty menace she could muster. A lesson learned at her father's knee.

The room fell silent, apart from the crackle of the burning tree trunk on the hearth; but the lout, determined not to lose his prize, came to a halt before the table.

Confronting him, Meg was sorely tempted to use the tip of the blade at his throat to dissuade him. Instead, she implied the ultimate punishment – of eviction, which his father recognised. All hell was let loose as the man savagely turned on his son, but not before trying – and failing – to placate his illustrious visitor.

"Get out of my way, scum, if you know what is good for you."

Meg smiled grimly as she strolled away from the inn, her arm protectively around Nell's shoulders. "Keep walking to the trees, the horse is waiting for us there," she said softly, half-expecting someone to follow, but there was only an uneasy silence hanging over the inn.

Once more she had deliberately tested her luck to achieve her objective, but how many more times could she play Lord Chetton's part in front of his tenants. One day they would surely meet in the flesh, but would he recognise her for whom she was – or accept her story of their parting? There were many faces like his in Linmore Dale but only one of them, to her knowledge, claimed to be a female.

★★★

The following morning when Nell returned to the inn, there was no sign of the innkeeper or his son; and the publican's wife had other ideas about paying her due.

"Two days washing and sewing is no good to me," she said. "If you'd stayed the full week, I'd have paid you thruppence, and your board. I might even have found work for you next week as well."

It was a derisory offer, considering that Nell had already spent one night in the stable, and had anticipated the need for another.

"No, thank you, ma'am," she said, politely. "I have other work to do."

She did not know whether washing and mending dirty linen for a pittance was worse, or listening to lewd remarks made by customers with wandering hands, who thought she was there for their use. Either way, it was time to move on.

"I'll bet you do – but not as respectable as working here, I'll be bound. It's the best rate in the district that the likes of you can expect."

The likes of you... The woman's words followed Nell through the door, bringing back memories of life with the Walcote family at Oak Apple Cottage. Nevertheless, she was glad she had the choice to walk free; an option that she did not have before.

She found Meg waiting with the vardo a short distance along the road, a troubled look on her face. The taproom scene had proved that she was a burden to her friend, and although she declined work at the inn, she could no longer wait for another Miss Dinchope to employ her, with or without the testimonial.

Meg, similarly, was feeling sad about the future. She knew that she had, in leaving Nell alone at the inn, misjudged the situation and put the girl in danger.

Whilst her work as a herbalist and midwife would continue unchallenged, Nell was too pretty to pass unnoticed. Last night had tested her protection to the limit. If the innkeeper or his customers had suspected Meg's true identity, her life, and that of Nell would not have been worth a groat. For her safety alone, it was time to be planning a parting of the ways.

Similarly, by making an enemy of the gentry from Caitlin, she had stirred up a hornet's nest that would not save Nell if she was caught. Now other men in Linmore Dale were lusting for her, awaiting their chance, but if Lord Chetton saw her first...

Chapter 10

Winter, going on Spring 1811

In late February, the heavy rain that followed recent weeks of snowstorms led to flooding of many roads around Linmore Hill.

Meg, called out to a delivery in an isolated village, was forced to abandon the vardo at a farm where she was known, and in it she left the birthing chair that often eased the process for many women. From there, she and Nell continued the two miles over Squilver Ridge, in the Bredenbridge direction, on horseback.

The drizzly rain continued for most of the way, making the narrow paths washed through the snowdrifts slippery, and low clouds further complicated their journey. Needless to say, the Irish cobs proved their worth; and the two women, clad in several layers of clothing under their breeches, warm coats with hats pulled down to shade their faces, were additionally covered by heavy waxed capes.

It was mid-afternoon when they made their cautious way down the final slope leading to Squilver village and already dark when they gained entrance to the farm. The gloom outside was to their advantage, for no one took notice when they left the horses in a derelict barn, and hung their wet garments in the shelter to dry.

Led up the backstairs of the farmhouse in silence by a servant, Meg met the lady for the first time since the previous autumn when she had learned of the pregnancy.

Donning an apron over her clothes, as was her practice, she assessed the state of labour and promptly gave a measured herbal potion. For a woman already tired, rest was essential if this, her sixth delivery, was to be successfully achieved.

When the husband looked into the bedroom at close of day, Meg knew he would not be seen before morning. Within minutes, she heard unconcerned snoring.

A maid-of-all-work stood by to run errands, but Meg told her to rest, an offer the girl gratefully accepted after she had bethought to bring them a crust of dry bread and cup of ale to wash it down. Thanking her, they ate the bread, suitably softened in ale, and left the rest to drink later. Then they waited for nature to take its course.

At four o'clock, a lusty boy was born, which was taken to a wet-nurse, while Meg and Nell attended the mother.

After two days of watching, they had done all they could do, and set off home before the physician who lived nearest to the hilly area arrived.

In fact, he passed them on the road back to the village. Meg guessed his identity by the arrogant way he drove his gig in the middle of the road, demanding that she should get out of his way. She shrugged, and took the big cob to the side while he drove past and Nell followed suit.

"Who's that?" Nell whispered.

"Dr Windermere, I suppose," said Meg. "He lives out Bredenbridge way. Our lady will be all right, as long as he doesn't start bleeding and purging her. The trouble is that's all that most of them do for their money. We're lucky with the physician at Middlebrook. He knows what he's doing."

They stopped at the village bakery to buy a freshly-baked loaf and a hunk of local cheese, offered by the baker's wife for hearing news of the baby's safe arrival.

At some places they were lucky with the food they received for the service rendered, but the housekeeper at the farm had been stingy in her portions. This morning, they were all but forgotten in the household's haste to prepare for the physician's arrival. That was why Meg wasted no time in acquiring victuals for they still had several miles to travel before they reached the vardo.

Meg knew, as she watched Nell nibble her portion in dainty bites, that the girl's mannerisms revealed her gentle origins. Irrespective of the male clothes she wore, she could never be seen as other than the woman she was. Her feminine ways were becoming increasingly difficult to hide from men. Therein was Meg's problem: to find Nell employment in a respectable household, and keep her safe.

Their hunger suitably assuaged, Meg wrapped the remaining half-loaf in a cloth, and put it in a pocket for later, before leading the way back up the hill with Nell following behind. The girl had done well, but she was tired, as was Meg if she cared to admit it. Never mind, when they reached the vardo they could take a rest.

More of the snow had melted since they had passed this way before, but some, sheltered by the trees, hung in the gully. Meg did not know what drew her attention to the shadow standing out against the whiteness. She stopped and looked again, hoping it was a stone, and saw her mistake.

She had sensed something was wrong riding up the path, but said nothing to Nell. Her nose warned her first what it might be as the slope levelled out for a stretch and she glanced down at the gully beneath the trees. Then she saw the outline of a boot protruding from the snow at an awkward angle, the sole uppermost, which could only mean someone still wore them.

She stopped the cob and slid to the ground. "Hold the horse for me, Nell," she said, not wanting to alarm.

"What is it, Meg?"

"I am not sure, but I'm going down to find out," she said, sweeping her hand in the general direction of the trees, hoping that Nell had not guessed her real purpose.

The ground cut away sharply from the path where they rode and the grass, slick before the rain, was like ice under her feet as she edged her way down with feet sideways one step at a time towards what could be a corpse. She might be wrong, but did not think anyone would abandon well-heeled footwear in the undergrowth.

If anyone else had seen them first, the figure that she guessed lay under the snow would have bare feet by now, based on the assumption that if the man was dead, he did not need boots. The question was, who was he and how did he come to die? Landing head-first in a snowdrift suggested there had been a horse from which he fell. In which case, there would be hoofprints, smaller than those of a cob.

"Are you all right, Meg?" Nell called anxiously down to her.

Meg reached the gully before she answered. "Yes. I won't be long."

Nor did she intend to be, but even though she was half-expecting it, the foul stench of decomposing flesh hit her nostrils the minute she touched the boot with her foot and the snow covering it fell away. She hoped the garish sight of his mottled skin was not visible to Nell from above.

She coughed as it caught in her throat, but forced herself to turn the body over, blotchy face uppermost. One look told her that the weather had done its worst, so she focused on the clothes, which were too tidy for a labourer, and the boots that had alerted her to the man's presence confirmed her assumption.

The style was not the plain black riding boot that she, out of habit, wore. Did that mean the man was an émigré? This was a lonely area where Bonaparte's agents might come to see people sympathetic to his cause. It was hard to say what the man had looked like before the snow covered the body, for he could have been lying here for anything up to a month.

Her nose twitched, anxious to be on her way, but she noticed his coat lay open, and quickly searched his pockets. A purse containing coins, so robbery was not the reason he lay here. A pocketbook, and although the pages were damp, she made out the word *Squilver* in ink with a date, but another word, which might have been a name, had smudged. Possibly that of someone in the area he had come to see. The date in the diary, two weeks before the heavy snowfall that preceded the rain, suggested that he had been alive.

The low crown beaver hat lying to the side had a London label. His drab-coloured driving coat with leather shoulder pads, and once fine linen shirt, told Meg that he was a traveller of some means, but his sad-looking cravat and shirt-points had lost the starch, which they no doubt had possessed when he ventured out. What was a well-dressed gentleman, doing in such a place in stormy weather? Not meeting a country wench, that was for sure.

"Meg…?" Nell called again, sounding more anxious than ever.

She turned away, and then glanced back at his dark, close-cropped hair, or what was left of it. Taking a handkerchief from his pocket, she touched

113

the side of the head, and it came back watery brownish-pink. Injured before the fall – or as a result? Meg's instinct said before. Dismissing speculation, she left him where he lay, knowing that if he remained here, carrion would find him and strip his bones clean before the spring.

However much she wanted to go home, Meg knew her responsibilities.

Reaching down, she replaced the purse and pocketbook out of sight, and pulled his coat together. A gold signet ring on his left hand gave her pause for thought, but she left it there, knowing that to have a second such ring in her possession could put a noose around her neck. Maybe the answer to the question of his identity lay on his finger – but that was for someone else to discover.

Tossing the handkerchief with the embroidered motif aside, Meg washed her hands thoroughly in the snow, to remove the tainted smell that clung to them, and replaced her leather gloves before climbing the slope, which seemed even steeper than on the way down.

"He's dead, isn't he?" said Nell, stating the obvious. "I saw his head wound. It was like the one that Artie Longden had. Did a horse kick him?"

"Possibly," said Meg, unwilling to speculate further. "We'll have to return to the village to find the nearest magistrate."

That was easier said than done, for they had to continue until the track was wide enough to turn the horses around and they made the journey back in silence. At the outskirts of the village, Meg stopped the cob and climbed down.

"Stay here with the horses and don't speak to anyone," she said to Nell. "Wait an hour, but if I get caught up in anything, make your way back to the vardo and head for the gardener's cottage at Hillend Rectory. I'll come there to find you."

She hesitated as she removed the strip of leather from around her neck. "If I'm not back within a sennight," she said, placing it in Nell's outstretched hand, "take that, and remember what I told you about the book."

"But what's happening, Meg?"

"I don't know, little one," she said, glad for the first time that she was not openly wearing men's clothes. "People can be funny with gypsies, especially where there's an unexplained death."

She could see that Nell did not like the idea, but having obtained the

114

girl's promise, Meg walked slowly towards the local tavern, set back from the road. Finding the door ajar, she called inside. "Where can I find the local justice? I've found a dead man in the gully on the hill."

The innkeeper, standing by the bar, hardly spared her a glance, but when she briskly repeated her question he grudgingly gave her his attention.

"Squire won't thank you for disturbing him about some blasted vagrant."

Meg noticed the assumption, thinking it too glibly made.

"Who's to say he was a vagrant," she said, knowing otherwise. "Surely that's for the justice to decide."

"Well, he must be, for none of the locals has gone missing."

"Please yourself," she said, shrugging her shoulders. "It's you that'll have to bury him, but it's a pity to leave a good pair of leather boots to spoil."

"Boots, what boots?" Instantly the man was alert.

"The ones he was wearing," said Meg, "they looked quite new to me."

"Did you touch them?"

"It'd be more than my life's worth to be seen with footwear like that, and it's not as if they'd fit me anyway…" Out of habit, Meg let her shoulders slouch, while watching, from his expression, the avaricious way the man's mind was working.

"You leave it with me," he said. "I'll make sure the squire knows about it. Did he have any papers on him, or money?"

"Papers mean nothing to me, when I can't read," she said, not answering the question, while knowing her understanding was probably better than that of the innkeeper.

"No, I s'pose not," the man muttered to himself. "What's your business here?"

"I've just delivered a live boy at the farm along the road," she said. "I have to go back in the morning to see all's well with the mother."

It was not strictly true, but he was not to know that and it gave her a reason to be here.

"You make sure that you do. George has been waiting a dozen years for this lad, with three girls and two boys lost before they was weaned."

The child had appeared healthy enough, but Meg knew the birthing chair would have made the process easier for the mother. With any luck, the woman would be all right, but she hoped the farmer would give his wife time to recover before he expected her to give him another son. She would know that for sure by the autumn.

For the moment, she was caught up in this business, waiting for the magistrate to hold an inquest. Then they would expect her to do the laying out. Other folks tended to be finicky about dead bodies found on hillsides, particularly with their head bashed in.

"Where does the parson live?" she said.

"Up at the rectory, but he's away in Bredenbridge visiting the Archdeacon on parish business. The curate will have to deal with the funeral."

"Won't the squire need to hold an inquest?" she said, knowing she was at a disadvantage speaking as a man, while dressed as a woman.

The man's eyes narrowed at her apparent understanding, then took the knowledge to himself. "Exactly," he said, "and I'll be the one to tell him – after I've taken a look for meself. Where did you say this body was to be found?"

"Half a mile up the hill in the gully under the trees," she said, watching his expression with apparent bovine simplicity.

He nodded, and said, "Over towards the Myndstone mines, you mean?"

"No, the one under Squilver Ridge."

"Just so I don't have a wasted journey going the wrong way," he said, with a smile to himself. "I wonder what he was doing up there?"

"Riding, I suppose, and maybe a rabbit startled his horse and he fell off."

"Was there a horse?"

"No," she said, "nor likely to be if it he was a stranger to the area on a hired nag." In fact, Meg had seen two deep sets of hoofprints on the path where riders had obviously met and talked, and the deep gash in the man's head, which ensured that he was probably dead before he left the saddle. Not that she was telling anyone what she saw.

"I'll attend to this," he said, and went off calling for his wife to attend the tap room; then he stopped, "What kind of boots did you say he had?"

"Fancy ones, like I've never seen," Meg said, omitting to say that they had a foreign look to them. "But if you're not interested, I'll be on my way and leave you to deal with the body. I daresay you'll find someone here that knows how to prepare him for burial."

"Wait a minute," he said. "What state's the body in?"

"Decomposing fast," she said, and had the satisfaction of seeing him gag, before he said, with difficulty, "Curate's up at the parsonage at this time of day. If you go there and tell him, I'll find some help to bring the body down from the gully. Squire can see him better down here," he said as another bout of nausea crossed his face.

"All right," said Meg, "I can go back to the farm afterwards."

If necessary, she would send Nell, where she was safe. Meg did not want the girl involved in things she did not understand.

★★★

The magistrate was duly informed of the find and the inquest arranged for the following morning in the tavern. Dr Windermere, the physician who saw the birthing mother, was recalled to give his opinion of the manner of death, and proclaimed that the man had slipped from his horse and broken his neck when falling down the gully.

Meg, sitting out of sight in a room filled with men, heard the learned scholar pontificate on the possible cause, and everyone hung on his words, but at no time was she required to speak. Women's evidence was inadmissible in court, and being a gypsy she had no right to have an opinion.

She suspected that the physician had done no more than lift the corner of the twill sheet covering the body and, having seen the degree of decomposition, stated the obvious. His nose could hardly fail to make him aware of the fact. The verdict, of accidental death, was unanimous and the magistrate signed a form to that effect.

Little time was wasted before Meg was ordered to attend the laying out procedure, for which she enlisted Nell's help, rather than call on people who might remark on the old, worn boots lying beside the pile of working clothes that were said to have been stripped from his body to aid the physician's inspection.

Even those were burned, before he was stitched in a sheet, and placed in a rough-hewn coffin ready for burial, within two days of him being found.

A few prayers were uttered and the wet soil replaced in the hastily-dug pauper's grave at the edge of the churchyard. When they left the church, none of the few people who attended the service gave it a second glance.

And certainly no one, quaffing ale in the village inn, admitted knowledge of the pocketbook Meg had seen on the body, which contained a hand-drawn map marking the place where the man met his nemesis; the distinctive Celtic signet ring on his finger or the handful of gold coins in the breast pocket. It was obvious that they, like the drab-coloured driving coat with leather shoulder pads and pair of fine black leather boots of foreign make that marked him a gentleman, would never be found. Whether he was a dandy or a spy, nobody knew nor cared for he was beyond anyone's help.

"Come, little one," Meg said, as she rode with Nell back up the hill, two days after their first attempt, "it's time we left this place to its intrigues, and returned to our own simple world."

Nevertheless, she knew things could not remain as they were. She could almost smell change coming. Ever since the tavern trouble over Neathwood way last autumn. In that area, Meg courted controversy, daring anyone to challenge her right to wear a nobleman's clothes. But one day someone would call her bluff and bring her before the local justice. Maybe that was what she wanted: to see him once more, and know that he recognised her.

She could not, however, continue her practice of open defiance with Nell unsettled. She was too pretty to pass unnoticed, and too intelligent to live with the lower orders as she had as a child.

A woman with Nell's looks always drew a gentleman's attention, but there had to be some way Meg could contrive to find her a safe haven. She recalled telling the old parson at Caitlin that the Middlebrook physician had shown a professional interest. She could but hope that the next time they met he would offer work.

Meg helped Maria's daughter as willingly as she and Mother Chapel had a young girl in her time of trouble, but she could not hold Nell back. She hoped one day to tell the true version of events, not the accepted part, which was little more than a lie.

Chapter 11

Early Summer 1811

After her experiences at Hillend Rectory, Nell knew that Miss Dinchope would have approved of her frequent attempts to keep her body clean. A regular strip wash in the shed or vardo sufficed for a time, but in the warmer weather, she made a point of slipping down to the stream and shedding her gypsy clothes to her shift before slipping into the water. Chilled though it was, she soaped a cloth and delighted in thoroughly scrubbing herself clean.

Usually, Meg stood amongst the trees to warn of any stranger's approach, and held a sheet ready for drying; but Nell never knew the time when Meg similarly availed herself of the opportunity – until she returned with wet hair. It seemed impertinent to offer to stand guard for someone older.

She did, however, come close on one occasion when she approached the river, but the sight of a tall, bare-chested figure with long black hair, standing waist-deep in the water, forced her to retreat in confusion and make her way back up the hill.

When Meg returned, with open-necked shirt and her jacket slung over her shoulder; her expression told Nell that she could read her mind – and Nell flushed at her suspicions that a Spartan lifestyle had stripped away all feminine traces.

"Mother Chapel couldn't decide what I was, when I was a nipper," Meg said. "She had a healthy boy, so she called me a girl, which is why she brought me here to learn a trade, rather than be made fun of as one of nature's misfits."

"Oh, Meg," said Nell, wrapping her arms around her friend. "I didn't realise."

"You weren't meant to, little one," Meg said, returning the hug. "Nobody was."

"I know that you wouldn't hurt me," said Nell, realising for the first time what she had not understood before about Meg's protective nature.

"Your Miss Dinchope might not have approved if she had known who it was that you used to visit."

Nell looked at her, surprised, wondering why Meg had mentioned the housekeeper from Hillend Rectory. "Does Mrs Hardwick know?" she said.

When Meg shrugged her shoulders, Nell understood why the carer did not let her daughter work with Meg – but in her case, there was no one to care if she had, unknowingly, lived for three years with a man. It also explained how Meg could smoke a pipe and slip easily between her big black boots and buckskins, and the guise of a midwife – after all, physicians were men who delivered babies with far less skill than Meg.

★★★

How could Meg admit that, in her teens, she had had warm feelings for Nell's mother, which were not those of one woman for another? Until then she had not known any different, but that was when she suspected the old lordship had two sons – but could never prove it – nor, as time went by did she want to.

As a child she had claimed her father's attention as her due, while her brother, as she thought him, looked on. She was the one to challenge the groom's dictate by riding ahead, climbing trees and getting them into mischief, yet Robbie took punishment in her place. When she protested, he had said, biting back his tears, "You're a girl, Maggie, and cannot be flogged."

But was she, or was it just Mother Chapel's claim at her birth? If she had been a boy, she, as her father's favourite, and the firstborn, would have been the heir and Robbie, the spare. He was closer to his mother, but could not have been a midwife – or could he? Meg had, in some situations, dressed as a man to deliver the wives of the gentry, because that was what some husbands

120

expected when female midwives were considered drunkards.

Meg had no feminine glands or ability to breed, but people saw what they wanted in one with a woman's name. As a midwife, she did a necessary job, and kept her little friend safe. Nell was the child she would never have, but one day she would have to let her go – and that time was fast coming.

★★★

Nell often thought that birth and death were two sides of the same coin. When she witnessed a birth, the scene filled her with awe, and she imagined that there could be no greater joy for any woman. Then she remembered the reality of her childhood where each new birth brought hardship to a family in straightened circumstances.

She also knew that infant death could strike without warning, taking babies that had scarcely time to breathe. Others slipped away in the early weeks, months or years, and if a mother developed the dreaded condition white-leg, she followed close behind and left the family to grieve and pick up the pieces as best they could.

Knowing that childbed fever had taken her mother, Nell buried her sorrow in the care of others. She knew that with death came sadness and loss, but for the old and infirm it brought freedom from suffering, so could that not be considered a blessing in disguise?

She had only seen one dead person before she lived with Meg. Looking at them in the coffins was not the same as touching the cold lifeless skin, knowing they could not feel the warmth of her hand or be aware that she was the person to wash their face the final time.

Whatever condition a person had been like in life, she now knew they had to be clean before burial; and once the cleansing process started it seemed disrespectful to speak until it was finished.

Nell knew that Meg did all her work with a soft hand and in silence, because she was convinced that it should be so not because anyone had told her. She doubted if Meg had been to a church service in her life, but she believed that her friend showed more respect for the dead than ever Parson Snitterfield at Hillend had done with ranting at the living; and he went to church twice every Sunday.

Sometimes, as they worked through the laying-out process, Nell wondered what colour the person's eyes had been and what their voice sounded like. Had it been loud or soft, when this woman called to her children or sang a lullaby? Whatever it was, the family would never hear it again and she felt sad.

She tried not to let it bother her, but it was not easy, any more than not having known what her own mother had looked like.

The thing she noticed was that when a person died they looked more at peace than in life. Away from their trials, tribulations and worries, the lines that marked a lifetime of cares relaxed.

Nell was thinking this about the old farm labourer's wife who had passed away after her final seizure. Several times in the last few weeks, she had visited the cottage with Meg, and thought it was sad to see the poor woman straining to make folk understand with her face and limbs stricken with palsy.

Every time she had tried to speak, the words slurred, and spittle dribbled from her mouth as she struggled in vain to form the sounds. Now no one would ever hear whatever it was she had wanted to say.

"Don't be sad, Nell. She's free of her suffering now," said Meg.

The tears that filled Nell's eyes were not for the deceased, but the mother she had never known, buried amongst the bluebells in the same area of woodland where Mother Chapel lay. At least, she assumed that was the place.

Not wanting anyone to see her weakness, she turned away to the darkest corner of the room and blew her nose on a cloth tucked in her sleeve. When she returned she realised they were not alone.

Normally, people left them in peace to complete their task, but on this occasion, the householder had brought a gentleman into the room whilst they were working. Nell looked at Meg, who gave no sign of having seen or heard anyone, and continued with her labours.

She could not understand why anyone would seek to interrupt at such a time. Surely they knew that it was disrespectful. Then she overheard the person speak in a loud whisper, and sensed that he must believe this.

"I will wait to speak with Mistress Chapel when she has finished."

It was only when she heard the widower's response that she understood the newcomer's significance: "Very good, Dr Althorpe."

Although she could not see his face, Nell recognised the name as one Meg had mentioned before, and it seemed strange that they were keeping him waiting. She did not know much about physicians, but imagined they would want attention as soon as they entered a room, but this one seemed to be content to wait.

Maybe he believed as Meg did that once the age-old custom began, it should continue in silence and due reverence. Nell did not know why she thought this, but the idea came clearly to her mind.

When the work was completed, she stepped aside to make the room tidy while the tall man in the black coat began to speak to Meg. It was hard not to hear their conversation, for his voice had a carrying quality, and she realised they were talking about her. What could it mean?

"The girl has no parents, sir; she is an orphan," said Meg.

"If you are her guardian, I must ask you to release her into my care. I have a project in mind, for which she would seem to be a suitable candidate," he said.

Nell froze, waiting for her friend's reply.

"No, sir," said Meg. "I'm not her keeper. Nell is well able to answer for herself, so you can put the offer to her."

She looked at them in amazement, desperately wanting Meg to say she could not spare her services. Instead, her friend called her to speak for herself.

"Nell, this gentleman is Dr Althorpe, from Middlebrook. He has something to say to you."

She waited nervously for the gentleman to speak.

"Mistress Chapel tells me that you have assisted in her work these last three years. If you are willing to work for me in my medical practice, I will pay you to do so," he said.

Overwhelmed by the physician's presence, Nell did not know how to decline his offer, so out of habit she bobbed a curtsy and murmured, "Yes, sir."

"Excellent. Now, I have to ask if you can read and write your letters."

Nell could not deny the fact knowing that, some months ago, he had heard her reading to an old lady at a farm in the valley. *A good reading voice* was how the farmer's wife had described her ability. But to her, the occupation was a delight, not a penance.

He nodded and Nell heard him give directions to Meg of where she was to report on the appointed date. "Bring her down to the surgery before the autumn fair."

Then he was gone, leaving her feeling forlorn. She wanted to stay with Meg, the only person to have taken an interest in her welfare and made her feel useful. Why did things have to change?

"Do I have to go with him? I'd rather stay with you, if I'm not a nuisance."

Nell could not stop the tears welling up when she thought she might have outstayed her welcome and made Meg want to get rid of her, even if she knew that was not the reason.

"No, little one; it's not that…"

She had never known her friend show emotion before, but it was obvious how affected the herbalist was, by the way Meg's hands gripped Nell's shoulders before the warmth started to flow through her.

It had never felt like that before, nor had Meg's humming sounded so much like a lament as it did that day, but it still had the effect of calming the sadness that filled them both.

Eventually, she heard Meg speak, and it sounded strangely muffled.

"You were never any trouble, little one. I've been glad to have you with me these last few years. I never thought that I would take to living with anyone else after Mother Chapel died. You have been more like family to me, but I was intended to live this life, and you should have a different sort of existence."

Nell stared at her, uncomprehending. "What do you mean?"

Meg took her time before answering. "The lines on your hand told me about the life you should be living, and it was never intended to be in a wood."

She thought about it for a few minutes, and then asked, "What kind of work does Dr Althorpe want me to do?"

"He didn't say what it involved, but will explain to you when you get there."

Nell bowed her head in acceptance, knowing that it would be ungrateful to refuse after all Meg had done to help when she was destitute.

"Think about everything you have learned with me," said Meg, in a firmer voice. "You have mastered all the tasks that we set out to do, so it will stand you in good stead when it comes to learning new things with Dr Althorpe. Never forget to use your senses and let those be your guide."

That helped Nell to feel better but she was still apprehensive. She hoped the work would not be too complicated or the physician would not expect more of her than she could perform. Although she felt sad about leaving, the prospect of making Meg proud helped make her feel better.

When Nell asked Meg where she was going to live, they walked from the wood along the side of Linmore Hill, and looked down across the valley towards the village of Middlebrook. It grew up halfway between the drovers' road and the water meadows that overlooked the confluence of Clee Brook and the River Linmore, and was the only place for miles, where vehicles could cross the river.

Meg pointed in the general direction. "Do you remember where we go to the autumn fair?"

"Yes, it's at Middlebrook," Nell said, recalling other times they had passed through the village.

Meg nodded, and then asked, "What can you remember about it?"

"I know there was a church and a coaching inn, because the stagecoach had stopped there. There was a street with some shops, and a village green with houses around it. Oh yes, there was a blacksmith and a miller as well; and on the outskirts of the village on the Norcott road, there was a tavern, called The Three Pigs. That's a strange name for an inn, but it seemed to suit it," Nell said, and chuckled at the recollection.

"Dr Althorpe lives in a big house, set back from the village green. There is a high stone wall around the garden." Meg pointed the way to look.

"I can see a house with high chimneys amongst the trees. Is that where I will be going?" she asked.

"Yes, I think that's the one, although there are a couple of other houses built in the same style. Can you see where the road crosses the bridge?"

Nell peered, and sure enough she could see it. "Yes, it comes in this direction and joins the drovers' track along the side of the valley."

"That's right, so you'll know how to find your way to the hill."

As they walked back towards the wood, Meg said, "I've known Dr Althorpe these fifteen years and more. He's one of the few physicians in these parts that still believe in the old ways of treating people with herbs."

"What do you mean?" said Nell.

"Most physicians think that herbs are poisons and want them banned from use. So they might be, to those that don't understand how plant extracts work, but in the right hands they have saved a good many lives."

"Then this doctor understands how you treat people?"

"Yes, we have worked together many times, and there are a few folk around that wouldn't be walking today if we hadn't done so."

Nell felt comforted by the knowledge that he understood Meg's work, but she was still puzzled about what her role would be. Having stood on the hillside and seen the rooftops of Middlebrook, she was able to believe it when Meg said it was not far away, and that they could meet up at the autumn fair.

She approached the day for leaving with trepidation, and on the afternoon before Meg was due to take her down the valley, she went out and picked some wild flowers for her friend. She had nothing else to give except her love and thankfulness for all the kindness she had been shown.

In return, Meg handed her a small twist of paper and advised her to take care of the contents. "Mother Chapel once took it in payment for her services, but I want you to have it because it was always intended to be for you. Keep it safe and if you ever feel the need, hold it and think of me and I will be thinking of you."

When Nell opened the paper, she gazed spellbound at a tiny cross and chain in a yellow-coloured metal. She had never seen anything so beautiful, much less possessed it, and could not believe that anyone would want to give her such a valuable gift. "How can it be for me, Meg? I'd be afraid to wear it in case anyone thought I had stolen it."

"It belongs to you, little one. Mother Chapel gave it to me to look after and it is time for you to have it. When you wear it, think of the good times we've had and be happy. If anyone asks, say that it was a present on your birthday."

"Is this the right day?" Nell said.

"Yes, it is seventeen years since Mother Chapel left you in the church at Hillend."

Meg's words had a touch of finality that she could not deny.

Nell felt a stranger when she shed her gypsy-style garments for the last time, and replaced them with clothes that Meg said would be more fitting for her new life. Her tidy clothes from Oak Apple Farm, which had given her confidence at the autumn fair, were faded but were all she had to wear. Preparing them for use, she had let out the side darts of the bodice and unpicked the hem to lengthen the skirt, but it was still short and crumpled.

What she needed was the use of an iron but had no means of acquiring one. Nell consoled herself with the thought that if they did not like her she could return to Meg – yet she knew that to do so would let Meg down.

Last night, Meg had advised her not to tell anyone that she had lived on the hillside with a gypsy herbalist, but however sad it made her, she promised just the same. Surely, no one in Middlebrook suspected the truth about Meg's origins?

It was a warm day in July, bathed in sunshine when they set off down the hill path in the vardo, but Nell's mood was sombre by the time they reached the outskirts of Middlebrook. Meg insisted that Nell remained out of sight until they had passed the church, and only when the road was clear did she allow her to alight. She looked around the vardo one last time and locked the scene in her memory.

Having climbed down, Meg pressed her hand to say farewell, and Nell began her slow walk along the drive to Dr Althorpe's house, a tall imposing building in local stone, on three levels – as precise in appearance as the gentleman who lived there.

Nell felt a brief moment of panic as she recalled the day, at the age of ten, when she started work at Hillend Rectory. Her first encounter with Miss Snitterfield had terrified her, and she hoped she would not have to face anyone like that again. She took a deep breath and exhaled slowly as Meg had taught her, and then taking courage in her hands, reached for the big polished brass doorknocker to summon attention. Her new life was about to begin.

Moving On

(1811 - 1816)

Chapter 12

Mid-Summer 1811

"Please, ma'am," Nell said as a servant opened the door a few inches. "I've been told to come here to see Dr Althorpe."

"He's too busy to see the likes of you," the woman said belligerently, and the door slammed shut before Nell could make out the other's features.

Used to Meg's kindness, the harsh words felt like a slap in the face. Rather than show the hurt, Nell raised her chin and turned away. Then, realising that her friend might be waiting by the village green, she sped down the driveway towards the road. But before she reached the gateway, a gig turned slowly into the drive, and a gentleman with a loud voice looked down at her and boomed, "Ah, you are the young person I was expecting. Follow me to the house."

Nell's heart sank, seeing her chance of freedom slip away.

"Please, sir," she said, "the woman at the house told me to go away."

All she wanted was to follow her instincts, and return to the wood, even if she had to walk all the way back.

He gave a dry laugh. "It sounds as if you have met Fish, the housemaid. She likes to guard us from all comers, but you will soon get used to that."

Nell was not sure she wanted to know, but had little choice in the matter. She followed the physician through a rear door from the stable yard, to the reception hall, and there found a tall woman with a spare frame and miserable face, looking towards the staircase as a small, darkly-clad lady with an air of fragility descended the flight on the arm of a manservant.

"My dear Elizabeth…" began Dr Althorpe.

The lady stopped, and raised her vinaigrette to her nose. "Who is this young person, James?" she said, her querulous tone rising.

Whatever Dr Althorpe intended to say was lost in his concern for the attack of vapours that followed. Ushering his wife towards the front of the house, the physician barked at Nell, "Go with Fish; she will tell you what to do."

Nell obeyed, knowing what to expect, and she was not wrong.

With venom oozing from every pore, Fish turned on Nell.

"I don't know what the master's thinking of, bringing you here to upset my lady. We don't need another maid, and so I shall tell him."

Nell would happily have walked out through the door without looking back, but the thought of letting Meg down stopped her. She waited quietly, while the maid fussed around in the kitchen, giving orders for a cordial to be made for her mistress. Only then did she speak to the scullery maid.

"Take this person up to the room at the far end of the attic corridor, Doris, and be quick about it. I can't be expected to run about after the likes of her."

"You can't put her in the store room, Florence."

"Why not?" said the housemaid. "We don't want her to be too comfortable. She won't be staying, if I have my way."

Nell was at a loss to know what she had done to deserve such a frosty reception, until the scullery maid, a gawky-looking female of indeterminate age, gave her opinion as they walked up the backstairs.

"You know your trouble, wench?"

She shook her head, and waited to hear her faults.

"You'm too comely by 'alf," said the woman. "Our Florence don't approve of pretty girls. Mind you, she doesn't like strangers, particularly if they have come from the other side of the hill and she cannot abide men either. Even Dr Althorpe has to think before he speaks to her, and he's known her these twenty years and more since he married."

Me, comely…? Nell looked at the woman in disbelief. Her hair might be a pretty colour, but that was all.

"Well, it stands to reason the mistress will object when he brings a strange young woman into the house without telling her first," the woman said, and continued as they reached the top of the first staircase, "and what the mistress don't like, Florence makes sure everybody else knows about."

She followed the woman in silence. At the upper landing, the scullion pointed to a door at the far end, saying, "Have a look in there. You might find a bed…if you're lucky."

Nell almost laughed at the notion of sleeping in a bed. Her first thought on opening the door was that Miss Dinchope would never have allowed a store room to be so dark and pokey. Or permit the accumulated pile of clutter in the centre to obliterate the furniture.

Leaving the door ajar, Nell made her way across the room intent on pulling back the curtains and easing open the dusty casement to clear the stuffiness. Once it was done she saw that far below was the back garden to the house, neatly set out with flowerbeds, trees and a kitchen garden. The view was a bonus she had not expected.

In the absence of her view from the hilltop, the sight of living produce would suffice, and if Fish effected her dismissal in the next few days it would not matter. Seeing a truckle bed in the corner, half-buried under a pile of boxes, and spare furniture coated in dust, Nell set down her bag with her few belongings and went downstairs to find out what her new role would be.

According to Fish, on a hasty tour of the house, it seemed that Nell was responsible for everything, as she had been in the early days at Hillend Rectory. Except, at Middlebrook, there was no Miss Dinchope to ensure fair play. No one told her the precise hours she should work, conditions of service or any payment she would receive, and Nell did not ask.

The first night, Nell did not disturb the clutter on the bed, but rolled herself in a coverlet and slept on the floor, looking at the stars through the open window. That way she could envisage Meg at the top of the hill. In assuming that all houses worked to the same routine, she rose at dawn, and reverted to the practices of her occupation that preceded her life with Meg.

She scrubbed the kitchen floor, cleared the ashes in the morning room, lit fires, heated water, made beds, washed dishes and prepared vegetables, and then, she took her duster, dustpan and brush, and went above stairs to begin again. In between, she snatched a few scraps of food to sustain her.

The greatest change was growing accustomed to victuals she had forgotten.

Fish dogged her footsteps, carping incessantly and checking every detail for faults. Nell determined at the outset that she would find none. Thank goodness for Miss Dinchope's training. It would take more than a harpy like Florence Fish to catch her out.

Used to living in the confined space of the vardo, Nell took the first opportunity she had to tidy the storeroom where she slept. Then she found a chair by the window, which provided sufficient light to do her stitching after she had wiped it clear of dust – something not done for years, despite Fish's claim to have personally cleaned every inch of the household.

Not in the last year, by Nell's estimation, or five more before that if the filthy rag provided by the scullion was a guide. Then she took a stiff brush to the mats and wiped a damp floor cloth over the wooden boards. Gradually, it started to resemble a room fit for habitation.

She had been three weeks in post before she encountered the physician again. During that time she had worn her own clothes with an apron to cover the frock she had brought with her, and a borrowed mobcap to hide her hair.

For a moment, he looked at her with scant recognition, before recalling her name. "Ah…it is Walcote, is it not?" he said, somewhat vaguely.

"Yes, sir," said Nell, bobbing her knees.

"Why are you dressed like that?" he said. "You should have a uniform."

"I have no other clothes, sir," she said.

"Why is that?"

When she remained silent, he said, brusquely, "I will speak with Mrs Althorpe. Go about your duties."

Nell bobbed her knees and complied, as he turned away.

Later in the morning, Fish appeared behind her grumbling, as Nell was setting the kindling alight in the morning room grate. "The mistress wants to see you, so you'd better hurry up and tidy yourself."

Stopping only to complete her task and wash her hands, Nell obeyed. Her first thought on entering the mistress's sitting room was of a sad little lady with lacklustre eyes and a downturned mouth, sitting at her writing desk.

All the furniture in the house was dark, solid and masculine, with furnishings that were plain coloured and functional. Even the lady's room was stark and cold, with few feminine touches. Nell sensed an atmosphere of sadness, and realised she had not seen any sign of children.

Was that the cause? She stopped her fanciful thoughts and concentrated on what lay ahead, only to find Mrs Althorpe staring at her with disapproval and Florence Fish open hostility. What had the woman found now to complain about?

"You should be wearing a uniform," said Mrs Althorpe, peevishly. "Fish will provide one from the store cupboard. I do not know why it has not been done."

While the maid favoured her with a look of dislike, Nell dutifully bobbed her knees and said, "Thank you, ma'am."

The following day the omission was remedied with great reluctance, as if the housemaid took it as a personal affront.

The plain grey uniform, intended to be worn in the morning for cleaning, was considerably too large for Nell's slender figure. A second, in blue stripe, for general duties in the afternoon was six inches too long, no doubt given that way in the hope it would defeat her.

Florence Fish, however, was not to know that Nell's skill with a needle had conquered worse things than the items reclaimed from the surgery ragbag. The uniform, hastily adapted, gave her a sense of belonging, which Fish did not intend her to have – much as she had felt at Hillend Rectory.

On anyone else the faded grey would have been dowdy, but on Nell, it simply looked subdued. Her fair skin led to the discovery of her tawny hair, and the subsequent humiliation by Fish, before the other servants in the kitchen, of having her bouncy curls cropped short. As a penance for having such a sinful colour, she was forced to sweep all traces from the floor and consign the offending items to the flames.

"There," said Fish with a grimace, at the smell, "that'll deal with the head lice that you're bound to have. Now it's the pump for you, my girl, out in the yard. Strip to your shift…"

Memories of Daisy Halford came to mind. It was as if she was in the room with her spiteful comments.

"Leave the girl alone, Aunty Flo…" protested the manservant.

135

"You mind your own business, Will Bucknole, and leave me to do the same. I'm in charge here."

"Dr Althorpe wouldn't approve…"

"And who's going to tell him?" the older maid challenged in a nasty tone. "Not you, if you want to stay here. I only have to tell the mistress that you're not doing your work, and you'll be out through the door before you can blink."

The young man, scarcely older than Nell, lapsed into a scared silence.

Nell, realising that she was not alone in being bullied, interceded. "Where is the pump, Miss Fish?"

The maid looked at her in surprise, evidently having expected her to argue. Instead, Nell looked the woman in the face and began to remove her fichu before the goggling eyes of the open-mouthed manservant – and continued, determined to hold the maidservant's gaze to see which one of them blinked first.

Fish responded immediately. "Stop that at once; it's indecent."

Nell stopped. "But the pump, Miss Fish," she said. "I thought you said I was to wash my hair." Cold water held no fears for Nell.

"I'll have none of your impudence, Walcote. Cover your chest and behave like a Christian woman while you're in this household."

"Yes, missus," said Nell, "but what about washing my hair?"

Exasperated, Florence Fish said, "Do it in the scullery sink, like we all do, with the door closed. Doris will tell you where to find the soap and a towel."

"Thank you," said Nell, as the older women turned to chastise the manservant.

"You can go and feed the pig, Will Bucknole. It'll give you something better to think about than gawking like a lecher at a half-naked woman."

"She weren't naked, Aunty Flo. Only showing…"

"Don't you answer me back," said Fish, delivering a slap to his ear that made his eyes water.

"Come on, Walcote," said the scullion, easing herself out of her chair by the kitchen fire. "Let's get your hair washed, and leave them to argue. One thing's certain, it won't take long to rub dry."

A few companionable words, intended as a kindness, which almost reduced Nell to tears.

★★★

A week later, Nell was summoned again to Mrs Althorpe's sitting room. Florence Fish stood beside her mistress, a self-righteous expression on her face.

Nell wondered what she was to be accused of now, but when Mrs Althorpe held out her hand, a shimmer of gold caught the light.

"Fish found this in your belongings, Walcote. From where did you get it?"

Recognising her precious gold cross and chain, Nell raised her chin and, with quiet dignity, met her mistress's eye. "It belongs to me, ma'am," she said, "and my mother before me." It was true for Meg had told her so.

At her words, Mrs Althorpe folded her hands, pursed her lips and said with asperity, "Give it back to her, Fish, and do not touch her property again."

The maid complied, but with such ill grace it was obvious the woman did not believe her version of events. Nell was thankful that she did not bring any of the coins which Meg had offered. That would truly have sealed her fate.

Having resolved one matter, the lady produced the rolled parchment containing Miss Dinchope's testimonial from Hillend Rectory.

"To what does this paper refer?" Mrs Althorpe's tone was cold.

"The time when I was in service at Hillend Rectory, ma'am," said Nell, knowing the inevitable question that would follow and the consequences.

Before it could be asked, the physician entered the room, and stopped in surprise. "What have you there, my dear?" he said, extending a hand.

As Mrs Althorpe relinquished the parchment, Florence Fish smirked.

He looked at it, eyebrows raised. "You must have worked at Hillend, before Reverend Snitterfield and his sister were taken…ill, Walcote," he said.

"Yes, sir," she said, guessing what would come next. But it was not what she imagined.

"It must have been an extremely difficult decision for Miss Dinchope to relinquish your services; but the circumstances in which she found herself made it inevitable."

Having only a vague idea of the details, Nell said nothing.

"Is it genuine?" said his wife, in surprise.

"Undoubtedly," he said. "I recognise the housekeeper's handwriting. A most efficient woman."

"In that case, what…"

Nell waited for the lady to ask what she had been doing in the intervening years. Fish looked on with avid interest. Dr Althorpe, however, ended the conversation. "We must not keep the servants from their duties, my dear, or Cook will not have luncheon prepared in time for me to go on my afternoon rounds, and that would never do."

No one argued with the master of the household. Nell silently thanked him for his intervention, but guessed that he, also, did not wish her previous occupation to be known. Meg, similarly, had been right to be cautious.

Fish scolded all the way back to the kitchen, but what mattered most was that Nell had her cross and chain; her only item of value. She was appalled that anyone would stoop so low as to take it from her belongings to cause trouble. Then she realised, too late, that the testimonial was still with Mrs Althorpe.

★★★

It was the same in the evenings after supper, when the servants gathered around the kitchen table to talk. Nell chose to sit in the furthest corner of the room from the fire and, as soon as she could, made the outdoor privy an excuse to escape into the garden. Once beyond the scullery door, she looked towards Linmore Hill and felt Meg's comforting presence. It was the only thing to make life bearable.

By now, she assumed the physician had forgotten the purpose for which he employed her, or regretted his impulse and relied on Fish to drive her away. It had to be something like that, for why else would Fish continue to harass her. Nell did her utmost to do her work, and the exchanges grew ever more acrimonious as she daily cheated the woman of her goal.

"You can't keep this up," Fish said, looking in the corners for dust and finding nothing. "I'll catch you out, and you'll be sent back where you belong, wherever that is – and don't think I believe that talk about you working at Hillend Rectory – even if you convinced the master that you did at some time."

Nell knew that it was Miss Dinchope's testimonial, and Dr Althorpe's knowledge about the parson and his sister being sent to the asylum, which did that. Not that he would discuss a patient's condition before the servants.

After a few more weeks of carping, the maid added the cleaning of the physician's surgery to Nell's workload. She learned the reason from Will Bucknole, who, amongst other duties, assisted Dr Althorpe in his surgery.

"Our Florence doesn't like cleaning the instruments that Dr Althorpe uses in his practice. She calls them heathenish. That is why you've got the job now, and I bet she hopes you won't like doing it either."

Nell realised what he meant when she entered the surgery and found a collection of bloodstained cups and sharp blades awaiting her. But working with Meg had inured her to such sights so she carefully separated the dirty items and set them to soak, whilst she cleaned the room.

It was not in her nature to give up so she worked all the harder, until one day she overheard Dr Althorpe saying the surgery was cleaner than ever and complimenting Florence on her tutelage. Nell smiled wryly, knowing that others had taken credit for her work at Hillend. Just as she accepted her early life, she did so again and tried not to let it bother her.

One evening whilst sitting in the kitchen, Nell noticed Florence's rheumy fingers struggling to cope with repairing linen. Each piece extracted from the workbox elicited mutters of complaint, but no one else seemed to notice. After watching the torturous process for a few minutes, Nell could stand it no longer.

"Is there anything I can do to help?" she said, half-expecting a refusal.

Fish glowered at her for daring to interrupt, and said in a voice full of doubt, "Can you darn stockings?" Evidently these were the bane of her life.

"Yes, ma'am," Nell said quietly, not wishing to boast.

"Make sure you do it properly," Florence muttered ungraciously, as she thrust at Nell a pile of knee-length stockings in need of repair. "Dr Althorpe will be the first to judge if you don't."

Having first consulted the maid on the size of needle and coloured yarn to use, Nell began to set neat stitches, just as Mrs Ferndale had taught her. Fish watched in suspicious silence, ready to ridicule Nell's efforts, until forced to concede. "Mmm, not bad," she said, before reaching for a beautifully soft garment. "There are a couple of loose buttons on this, but don't make a mess for it's the mistress's favourite silk blouse."

Nell knew she was being tested, but her skill surpassed anything Florence could do. Having received grudging approval, she continued sewing for the rest of the evening, whilst giving deference to Florence's judgement. Soon the workbox, long overflowing with items for repair, was empty.

The task reminded Nell of some of the farms she had visited on her travels with Meg, where she spent hours repairing torn sheets and nightshirts, stitching buttons on breeches, and darning socks, all for the cost of a loaf of bread. That was the value people placed on gypsies.

Whilst she did not expect thanks, Nell was surprised to hear that Florence had reported favourably to the mistress on the sewing work she had done. After that, Mrs Althorpe praised her for finding a quantity of dark-blue material purchased some years earlier and stored in the attic. No doubt she had Miss Dinchope's reference to thank for the change in her mistress's attitude.

During the search, she admitted to having received instruction from a dressmaker, and Mrs Althorpe gave her the task of making a Sunday-best outfit from the material. Being of slender build, Nell intended no vanity when she added discrete pleats and tucks to the bodice, but it changed the standard pattern from the ordinary to a very neat design.

From the remainder of the length of material she contrived to make a best dress with no frills for Florence and two working skirts for herself. After which, in gratitude to her employer, she neatly trimmed a handkerchief with fine lace, purchased in the haberdashery shop in the village, and bestowed it on the lady for her birthday.

Receiving it, Mrs Althorpe's pale face glowed with pleasure, and she, in turn, purchased a length of plain white cotton material for Nell to make two work blouses, and muslin for a fichu to complement the dark-blue frock she had made.

"It is essential that you have something tidy to wear to church," said Mrs Althorpe. "I presume that you were confirmed when you were younger?"

"Yes, ma'am," said Nell, unable to believe that the lady took such an interest in her. "It was while I was at Hillend Rectory."

Mrs Althorpe nodded approvingly. "Then you must attend early communion on Sunday with Fish. There will be plenty of time for you to do your work while my husband and I attend matins."

"Yes, ma'am; thank you, ma'am," she said, knowing that during the short walk along the road to the church, and back again, she would see Linmore Hill in the distance – and remember the time when she was free.

Once accepted into the household, Nell submitted with other servants to having her hair trimmed, with Florence Fish wielding the shears for men and women alike. There were even occasions when Fish decided that her curls needed a bit more time to grow – no doubt remembering the extra-close crop that she gave Nell on her arrival.

With their new understanding, she sensed that the older woman's fractious behaviour had probably stemmed less from the pain in her rheumy joints, than a fear that a younger servant would replace her.

Chapter 13

One day whilst cleaning the surgery, Nell found an open textbook on Dr Althorpe's desk and her curiosity overcame her. Normally she would not have touched it, but in recognising the picture of a foxglove was curious to learn more. She only intended to take a quick look, but became so engrossed in the description explaining how the plant was used to treat dropsy that she was still poring over the page when Dr Althorpe entered the room.

Mortified that she had taken liberties, Nell apologised and would have returned to her cleaning, but with a little encouragement she told him of the times when she had seen Meg using the plant extract, and before long he was answering questions on other things.

After that, he gave her permission to take a book from the shelf when she had finished work, and she was surprised to find various passages of text marked for her to read. Having completed her reading, Nell was amazed to see how often the answers to questions coincided with knowledge she had gained with Meg.

Initially, her learning was confined to the time she spent in the physician's surgery, and then one day when she had lived with them for almost a year, Dr Althorpe and his wife called her to their sitting room, and she waited quietly as her mistress began to speak.

"I am pleased with the way you have conducted yourself in your household duties, Walcote; but now, my husband wishes you to undertake some work for him as well. What do you say to that?"

"I would be honoured to do whatever Dr Althorpe wished me to do, ma'am," Nell responded.

"Well said, Walcote, but are you not curious to know what the work involves?" Dr Althorpe enquired.

The question surprised her. "It is not for me to be curious, sir. I am sure you will explain what you want me to do when the time comes."

He nodded approvingly and said, "I have been encouraged by your interest in learning, and would like to take you out occasionally on my rounds and show you the work I do in practice."

"Thank you, sir, and ma'am. I will do my best not to let you down," she said, bobbing her knees. She could not believe her good fortune, but then realised this must have been the physician's original plan when he employed her.

In preparation Mrs Althorpe purchased several lengths of serviceable material from the haberdashery shop in the village, for Nell to make a new uniform. On the occasions when she accompanied Dr Althorpe on his rounds, she wore a close-fitting hat large enough to cover her curls; a white blouse and grey skirt with a covering apron, and until she finished sewing her coat, wore the gentleman's cape that she had brought with her to the house, from which she would not be parted.

At first, she only assisted the physician on visits to the poor, but when she had completed a probationary period of three months, she was allowed to accompany him on daytime visits to the local gentry. As her knowledge and expertise increased, Nell went out on foot to the village to attend the basic needs of the common folk in sickness, and was careful to undertake her duties exactly as instructed, and on her return to the surgery reported her findings to Dr Althorpe.

After that, the groom taught her how to drive a dogcart to enable her to make visits further afield. Nell did not tell anyone that her gypsy friends had taught her to handle horses, and Meg to drive the vardo, so she became proficient in next to no time.

Soon she became a well-known figure driving around the area. It was obvious that she loved her work, for her patients reported to the physician that her cheerful smile and gentle touch made them feel better.

Irrespective of their status, Nell treated all her patients with respect, and was astonished when a lady of the local gentry, out riding with her groom, nodded acknowledgement on her travels. This was the highest accolade she could imagine.

Autumn 1812

Nell did not see Meg at the first Middlebrook Fair after she left the hillside. She was too scared to ask leave to attend, quite sure in her mind that if she left the house she would not want to return.

Things had changed by the following year, and she readily requested permission but made no mention of whom she was going to see. Florence Fish walked along by her side, but when the maid stopped for the third time to talk with acquaintances, Nell slipped away, walking apparently aimlessly towards the trees where she knew Meg would be waiting.

Their meeting was short; just long enough to reassure her friend that she was well and had no regrets. Nell made no mention of the difficulties she had experienced in the early months. Now she was accepted in the household and for that was grateful.

All too soon, people came to see Meg, so Nell said farewell and set off along the row of stalls wondering if she would see the country artist. It was three years since their last encounter, and she hoped that he had safely returned from Spain. Molly Hardwick had expected him to come home after his father's death.

To her delight, the gentleman, Adam Whitcott of Caitlin, was there with a selection of his work on display. Wanting to look at the pictures, but not draw his attention to her changed appearance, Nell scrutinised the local scenes, moving from one to the next until a small painting caught her eye.

The picture of a gypsy girl enthralled her, but she could not say why, for everything the subject wore looked faded. A gathered skirt and blouse, the old shawl around the girl's shoulders, and even the washed-out blue scarf that covered her head, and yet something held her attention.

At first she thought it was the girl's skinny frame, with fingers too thin to belong to a traveller, or the fair-skinned elfin features. As realisation dawned, Nell knew the truth about the cheeky red-gold little curls, peeping out of their hiding place, which gave the picture a glow of sunlight. They were the same ones that never stayed hidden, no matter how hard she tried to suppress their bounce, or contain them under a bonnet or starched cap.

This was no gypsy; it was of her, painted during the first full summer with Meg. Memories came flooding back from the time when she had sat while the artist sketched her likeness and received a few pence in payment for her trouble. A cloud shadowed the recollection when she recalled how she was treated like a pariah for wanting to purchase a tablet of lavender soap.

The last time she saw the picture, it was in pencil and looked like a collection of swirling lines, but now, seeing it painted and contained in a frame, it was a record of how she looked at the time.

Nell cast a quick look around to see if anyone else had spotted the resemblance, and caught sight of a tall man watching her. The artist looked older than the last time they met, with flecks of grey marking his black hair, but undoubtedly the same kindly person. She shook her head, looking in disbelief from the picture to the man, but before either could speak, a strangely familiar voice interrupted from somewhere close to where she stood.

"Is that picture for sale?"

Hearing the sound, Nell stood stock still and flushed to the roots of her hair. She wanted to turn and look at the newcomer, but the recollections associated with the last time she heard him speak would not let her. It surely had to be him, but she was scared to look in case he thought her presumptuous.

She did not know what to do. Caught between the two gentlemen and the picture stand, she pretended to be engrossed in studying other sketches. Even that was an effort, for his voice was tempting her to seek a glimpse of his profile. *What did he look like now?*

She closed her eyes trying to resist the temptation, but as the gentleman moved closer to speak with the artist, he almost brushed against her shoulder and his scent evoked a memory of the soft pressure of his lips. She touched her mouth and felt the kiss again. He was near yet so far away. What could she do, for she had never felt like this before?

Despite not wanting to listen, she heard them in the background discussing a commission to paint pictures, so she edged further away.

When Nell realised that they had finished talking she turned to watch the gentleman depart. She touched her lips and nodded, sure it was him.

The imperious line of his shoulders was the same and the shape of his brow, but the smile that won her heart was no longer there, and she felt sad.

Nell sighed, and recalled sensing something akin to sadness in him when he stood near her, and she wondered if the lines around his mouth might indicate his disappointment with life.

She recalled telling Meg of similar feelings. This time she chided herself for her presumption in having an opinion about the gentry, when it was not her place to do so. All the same, she remembered the gentle smile that lit the gentleman's face on that day five years ago when he rescued her – which, she supposed, calculating her age, made her about nineteen.

Suddenly, she realised the artist was speaking. "I can see that you recognised your sketch. It sold well, and the gentleman was pleased with his purchase."

Nell smiled absently at his comment, and wondered why the gentleman had chosen to buy her picture out of all the other ones on display – which was something that she would never know.

★★★

James Althorpe knew the herbalist had said that Walcote was an orphan, but from what he could see there was no sign of the peasant in her features, which suggested that she might originate from a gentlewoman who made a mistake. He knew it happened, even in the best-regulated circles.

Seeing her for the first time, he recalled another tawny-haired beauty, the wife of a fellow officer in Mysore, back in '82. In those days, he was a young and idealistic physician-surgeon in the East India Company Regiment, and like the rest of the officers and men, he loved her gentle nature and loving kindness. This girl was in her image.

Returning home on the death of his father, he escorted the same lady, tragically widowed, with her two children. Had he not been committed to undertake additional medical training to further his career, James might have waited for the period of her bereavement to pass. By the time his studies were complete, he had met Elizabeth and any thoughts of marrying another, however beautiful, had been forgotten.

This time, James responded to impulse. It was true, he had some vague notion of training a woman as a nurse to assist in his practice, but until that moment had no clear idea what she would be like. The moment he saw Walcote, on a visit to a patient at an outlying farm, he knew, and each successive sighting convinced him.

Not that she was aware that he had listened to the soft reading voice about which the farmer's wife had told him, or noted the calming influence she exercised over the patients. He, like them, was similarly charmed.

Whilst he guessed Walcote was not her real name, it was equally obvious that she did not have any idea of her true origins.

Initially there were problems in the household, due to a misunderstanding about his intentions towards the girl, but now she had integrated into the family. He was delighted that Elizabeth had made friends with Nell, because in so doing his wife had forgotten her tendency to imagine she was ill. A matter of concern for many years, but now she was taking an interest in the community.

It was gratifying to know that his instinct was sound. Nell was a natural nurse, and a credit to him. He also knew she had learned a great deal from the gypsy midwife, but it was better not to advertise the fact.

James remained true to his beliefs about traditional methods of healing, unlike some of his old colleagues who changed their ideas to fit whichever radical new theory prevailed at the time, and for which medicine was the poorer.

Such attitudes made him glad that he was working towards the end of his career rather than starting out. This was why he had wanted to try his idea whilst he still had time, and it was working well. Once the local gentry knew of Walcote's skills, several had paid for her services in the lying-in period and he knew that in those circles, one good recommendation could spread a long way.

As he grew older, James realised that he needed an assistant to support him, and if suitable, maybe the new partner might take over the practice when he retired. He had informed his acquaintances in the centres of medical excellence that he was looking for such a person and would await the outcome.

Chapter 14

By the spring of 1813, Nell had worked in the surgery for almost two years, and had overcome the initial difficulties. She was familiar with her working routine, and happy to have been accepted by the household and village folk alike.

She was polite to everyone, cautious in her dealings with men, and once Florence signified approval of her modest behaviour, was included in the family group attending Evensong. Nell had never sat near the front of a church before, but now, dressed in her Sunday-best clothes, she was allowed to join Florence in the family pew where Dr Althorpe and his wife sat, two rows behind the gentry. From there, she could see what was going on.

The church at Middlebrook was bigger and cleaner than Hillend had ever been, and there was no draught blowing under the door to catch the legs of the people who sat at the back. Nell knew and felt the difference, because that was where she had sat in the first few months that she worked at the surgery. Slipping into the back row near the font, and out again before the service ended, ready to hurry home while it was quiet.

That was how she knew the church from the back, looking towards the altar. Three rows of pews. A left one that ran the full length of the aisle, with the chancel beyond; another divided by a path from the door to the aisle, and a third, shorter one that stopped by the door, with the font in the back corner.

Now she had to walk halfway up the middle row of pews. Not up the main aisle, but along the second one and between the huge stone pillars that supported the roof. She could not see much from there, but was closer to the people at the front. That was when she realised that Middlebrook had aristocracy as well as different kinds of gentry.

They were the ones who came in when everyone else was seated, just before the service began. A lady and a tall gentleman, who walked with long leisurely strides towards the high-sided pew in front of the pulpit, and closed the door on the congregation for the duration of the service. Nell wondered who they were but had to wait for Florence to tell her.

When the sermon was over the gentleman emerged from the pew, looking profoundly bored, and waited for his lady to precede him down the aisle. Nell gazed at him open-mouthed, until she realised it was rude to stare and looked away. She felt quite dazed, not knowing what to think as the church started to empty from the front towards the back. When their turn came, Dr Althorpe and his wife left the pew by the main aisle, and Florence pushed Nell down the other flagstone path towards the door.

"What's the matter with you, Walcote?" she hissed. "Haven't you seen the nobility before?"

Nell shook her head, not daring to speak the thoughts that filled her mind.

"That's Lord and Lady Chetton," the maid said.

She would have liked to take a second look, but they had to wait while the parson spoke to the high-ups. When they moved on, everyone else made their way outside. Nell stood aside with Florence whilst the physician and his wife stopped to greet their acquaintances, but the conversations did not last long.

Dr Althorpe acknowledge everyone, irrespective of their station in life, while his wife approached an old lady with a maidservant in attendance, who had sat near the front of the church, but not in the first three rows.

"That's Mrs Fulmer from Elvington Place," intoned Florence in a loud whisper. "She's gentry, but not in the same way as Dr and Mrs Althorpe, if you know what I mean."

Nell did not know, but had learned that it was better to imply understanding, in case Florence lost patience with her. Life was infinitely better when she was kind. She walked back to the surgery, her mind awhirl, puzzling over things she did not understand. A face from the past, but where had she seen him before?

The tall, harsh-featured gentleman with black hair was clad entirely in black, right down to his immaculately polished leather boots, almost like...

A name came to mind, but that was ridiculous. Then she recalled seeing a similar-looking man, riding a brown horse through Hillend village when she was a child, and assumed it was he or someone similar that she had seen.

I had a brother once, but he's too grand to know me...

Did he live at Neathwood, the village where Meg stopped on her travels?

Perturbed by the recollection of Meg's words, Nell concentrated on the lady clad in black silks, with whom Mrs Althorpe had spoken. Perhaps Florence had meant that she was almost-gentry, an expression used by Mrs Jemkins, the gardener's wife at Hillend Rectory, for the tenant farmers.

She immediately dismissed the idea, knowing there was nothing *almost* about a person who brought her maid to church and rode in a fine carriage. Or wore a proliferation of coloured jewellery on her fingers and pinned to her corsage. The effect was quite overwhelming and gave Nell the impression of someone with so many rings that she could not decide the ones she liked best.

Nell knew that Mrs Althorpe often went to visit the old lady, but was surprised to hear that Mrs Fulmer had invited her as well. So Dr Althorpe took her on a formal visit to his patient.

Situated on a rise above the village, Elvington Place was the finest house Nell had ever seen. Built in a classical style of red brick with white sash windows, and porticoed entrance, it had an undoubted air of grandeur.

Similarly, the uniformed servant that opened the door and took Dr Althorpe's hat and coat ignored Nell. But she did not expect anything else.

Following them through the reception hall and up the staircase, she had a fleeting impression of pictures lining the walls and delicate porcelain bowls on tables. There were glass cabinets filled with intricately designed ornaments, and the pale-coloured carpets were so thick, she was almost afraid to walk on them.

Keeping it clean must be a nightmare, and she was glad the dusting was not her responsibility in case anything was broken. It would take forever to replace.

At the door of Mrs Fulmer's apartment, the butler left them in the care of the lady's companion, an unsmiling woman of indeterminate age, clad in black bombazine. Nell followed closely on Dr Althorpe's heels, expecting to hear grave news, but soon realised on seeing Mrs Fulmer's welcoming smile that the visit was of a social nature, one that Dr Althorpe repeated several days a week.

It lasted no more than half an hour, but on the journey home, he hinted that apart from a touch of dropsy, there was little the matter with the lady, other than she liked company.

Mrs Fulmer must have been pretty in her youth, but now she was plump and white-haired, and huffed with effort when she heaved herself out of her seat. Although costly, her clothes were of an older, more flamboyant style to those worn by Mrs Althorpe, who was always neatly dressed, and on whom Nell modelled her own plain attire.

After the initial visit, it was arranged that Nell went on her own to undertake small procedures, which pleased the lady. She drove the dogcart on morning rounds to see her other patients, but preferred to walk the half mile to Mrs Fulmer's house in the afternoon. Discovering this, the lady provided her with transport for the return journey.

Sitting in the gig beside a uniformed groom reminded her of the times when she drove the vardo with Meg, and the thought brought a lump to her throat. She did so miss her.

Nell learned that Elvington Place was named after the house in which Mrs Fulmer was born near Bredenbridge, and from where she was married at the age of thirty. An unhappy state that lasted twenty years and from which an apoplectic attack, a dozen years before, eventually freed her from a drunken husband.

Since then she had been free to please herself, but her health had suffered, and her only regret was that she did not have a daughter. Taking a fancy to Nell, the lady offered her presents, which she resolutely declined.

"Let me give you this, my dear," Mrs Fulmer said, tugging a pretty bracelet with blue stones from her chubby wrist and pushing it over Nell's slender hand where it hung loosely. "It matches your lovely eyes."

"Thank you, ma'am, but I cannot accept it," she said, as she handed the bauble back. "It is a pleasure to serve you, and that is enough."

Despite her disappointment, Mrs Fulmer said, "I suppose you are right, my dear. I doubt in your present position that you'd have the chance to wear it, but one day, life might give you something better."

Nell was glad that her refusal did not offend the lady. Such valuable items were not for the likes of her, for she would not have known what to do with it.

The situation made her aware that Mrs Fulmer had everything that money could buy, except friends. Even the house, elegant as it was, had a sad feel to it. Despite the cheery face that the lady showed the world, Nell sensed she was lonely, for when they were alone she was happy to talk and have her hands held. Recalling the comfort she derived from Meg's hands, Nell willingly complied.

Accepted as confidante, she learned that the lady's father made his fortune in trade, but was at a loss to know why, when Mrs Fulmer lived in a big house and employed many servants, she did not have the same social status as the local gentry. She gave up trying to understand, and accepted Dr Althorpe's word, when he said that he liked the woman's broad speech and blunt manner, and although she might not be a lady in the accepted sense, to his mind she was worth two of the rest. His opinion was good enough for Nell.

On the day of the visit, Nell wore her Sunday-best clothes and accompanied Dr Althorpe and his wife to Elvington Place. Shortly after their arrival, Mrs Fulmer rang a bell to summon the butler. Within seconds, a stiffly attentive individual entered the room, followed by two obsequious footmen and a sullen-faced female, pushing an overloaded tea trolley.

Nell had never before seen such delicate tableware, but she recognised the astonished face of the uniformed housemaid who poured the tea. Their eyes met for a brief second and then each looked away; Nell to study the floral patterns on her teacup and the maid to attend her teapot.

It was someone Nell never thought to see again. The last time she saw Daisy Halford was just before the girl left Hillend Rectory, claiming to have acquired a post as personal servant to a lady of fashion. Mrs Jemkins, however, said the housekeeper dismissed the girl when she stole Nell's wages.

One thing was certain: Halford was a minion in Mrs Fulmer's household. Nell sensed her chagrin, but for once felt no pity.

The amount of food on the table made her feel uncomfortable, and she could not eat more than a morsel without remembering the poor people she visited with scarce enough to eat. She noticed that Mrs Althorpe was similarly occupied in studying the confectionaries, and wondered if this was what she meant by "vulgar displays of ostentation".

Several times, Nell saw Mrs Fulmer looking at the clock, and eventually, she called her butler to tell her late husband's nephew to join them.

When he entered the room, Nell realised she had seen the young man with Mrs Fulmer at church the previous weekend. Now, he seemed anxious to make her acquaintance, going out of his way to include her in the conversation.

His attention embarrassed her more than the overloaded table of food. She felt his eyes running over her body like a spider, and it made her skin crawl. Even his aunt seemed to notice her discomfiture, for she said in her blunt way, "Leave the girl alone, Spencer. I know she is a pretty little soul, but you can't eat her. Have one of these cakes instead."

Nell flushed at the implication, but was glad of the woman's perception. Then she glanced at Dr Althorpe and saw concern in his gaze, and wished she had not come.

It was a relief when the two men began to talk, and from parts of the conversation that she could hear, Nell gathered that the young man had completed his medical studies in London and was seeking a post.

She knew that her employer was considering taking an assistant, but hoped he would look further afield than the room where they were sitting. To her regret, Dr Althorpe agreed to meet the man in his surgery to discuss the matter.

Nell made sure she kept out of sight when the younger man arrived at the surgery, but later from her vantage point at the top of the staircase, she saw his face, flushed with triumph as he left the house.

Afterwards, she heard Dr Althorpe saying to his wife, "I am sorry, my dear, I know you dislike the man, but the testimonial from Mr Windsor-Hardgrave states quite clearly that Frogg was one of his best students. There was nothing on which I could fail him. Naturally, I have stated that it will only be for a year in the first instance, and I will of course write to my old friend and apprise him of the situation."

Nell's heart sank as she realised that for the next year, she would be working with Dr Frogg and for some reason it scared her.

The differences between the two men were evident from the beginning.

Dr Althorpe's refined origins were apparent in the way he behaved and dressed, and from what Nell could see of the newcomer, the opposite applied.

Despite the correct attire that Dr Althorpe insisted be worn for morning visits and professional calls, Dr Frogg shunned the breeches of a country gentleman, and wore straight-legged trousers to denote his modern outlook, but his scrawny physique let him down.

Irrespective of what Dr Althorpe wore, it was obvious to Nell that he was a gentleman. She had learned from Florence that he was the younger son of a baronet, who trained as a physician and surgeon and joined the army in India, until he married. He had spent several years in London, before taking a country practice and had lived in Middlebrook ever since.

Dr Frogg's swaggering manner betrayed his origins, which Nell suspected might belong lower down the social scale than those of his wealthy connections. His voice had a nasal sound, almost a whine that set her teeth on edge.

For the first few weeks, Dr Althorpe and his assistant went out on introductory visits together, dined on their return, and held long discussions in the surgery late into the night. Nell hardly saw them and continued with her regular rounds. With Dr Frogg in the house she was more than happy to eat in the kitchen with Florence and the other servants, because it meant she did not have to speak with the newcomer.

Several times, she found a posy of flowers with her name attached, lying on a side table in the front hall, and then a verse of poetry singing the praises of her eyes. Some of the other servants teased her about having a secret admirer. Nell knew whom they meant, but did not want anything to do with him.

With each proclaimed endearment, she grew more nervous about his intentions, and when they met he tried to kiss her hand, but as soon as his scent filled her nostrils, she felt frightened and wanted to run away.

She did not know how to refuse his gifts without giving offence, but could not help feeling uneasy. Why should she feel threatened by such a puny little man, so slight and unprepossessing? Then she realised, his eyes were devoid of warmth. How different he was to...

Nell blushed, remembering how she had once fallen under the spell of a pair of smiling grey eyes, full of kindness, because her rescuer cared enough about her state of undress to give his cape to cover her modesty.

She would never forget him, and it was no wonder she did not want other men to kiss her, because none could match her secret ideal.

★★★

Each day after she finished work, Nell slipped up the backstairs to change her uniform dress. One evening as she came downstairs, she met Dr Frogg waiting on the landing. As she viewed him with dismay, his pallid cheeks flushed red and bulging eyes lit up.

"My goddess," he said. "I have been looking for you everywhere." His speech slurred, as he leaned towards her, and she smelled spirits on his breath.

Nell recoiled, but could not avoid the slobbering lips pressed against her mouth. She tried to push him away, but her struggles inflamed him. He laughed without humour and his hands seemed everywhere at once; snatching the fichu from her dress, pawing her breasts, pulling at her skirts.

"No, Dr Frogg; please…don't…" She tried to scream.

"Don't worry, my lovely, you'll get used to it. There'll be plenty more of this when we are married," he boasted, thrusting his slimy tongue inside her mouth.

Nell gagged as the sudden blockage deprived her of air. She felt her senses slipping away, and then retched. Suddenly, she was free of him, and knew the rancid taste in her throat had stopped the beast before he did worse than paw her legs.

From somewhere nearby, she heard Florence's voice calling, "Dr Frogg, are you upstairs, I think Dr Althorpe is looking for you."

Frogg cursed and mopped his splattered clothes. Before leaving, he said savagely, "If you repeat one word of this, I will kill you."

Nell felt sick with relief as he disappeared down the staircase, and then realised that Florence was beside her. "And I will see that you don't, my lad," she muttered, "because we'll sort you out first."

Thank goodness for Florence's hatred of men. Nell had never before seen the woman so angry. It was obvious she witnessed everything, and would not remain silent.

Autumn 1813

James Althorpe felt outraged, because he had based the appointment of his assistant on a testimonial purportedly written by an eminent physician of his acquaintance. Now, he had received the professor's response denying the existence of such a reference, and hinting at grave news that he could not commit to a letter. In the circumstances, he urged his friend to visit London at the earliest opportunity.

The news could not have come at a worse time. To do this, James knew that he would have to trust an untried assistant with his practice, at a time when the creature was mooning around Nell Walcote like a lovesick swain.

As he prepared for his journey, his assistant invaded the privacy of his study, claiming the need to communicate on a personal matter.

"Yes, Dr Frogg, and what might that be?" James's tone was brusque.

"I am sure that you cannot be unaware of my admiration for Mrs Althorpe's niece, and wish to seek your permission to pay my addresses to the young lady."

James frowned as he pondered the request and then asked directly, "When you say that you wish to marry my wife's relation, are you perhaps referring to Nell Walcote?"

"Indeed, sir," said Frogg. "I am sure that she would be a great asset to me in my career now that I am in the practice."

James's fury knew no bounds for the man's impertinence in thinking he could secure tenure on his post by using such devious methods.

"You are precipitate in your assumptions, Frogg. You would do better to convince me of your worthiness to be my assistant, than presume to the hand of the young woman in my care. Miss Walcote is my nurse, not a member of my family."

He saw the man's look of revulsion, and knew his guess was right. Afterwards, he felt obliged to call Walcote to speak for herself. He knew that her honesty was beyond question. The answer was clear, even before he asked.

"Have you inadvertently implied that you are related to Mrs Althorpe?"

Nell looked puzzled, and then shook her head. "No sir, it would not be honest to do that," she said. "I was a foundling."

Seeing the bleak look in her eyes, James felt sad that he had to pursue the matter. "Dr Frogg implied that you encouraged him to form an attachment."

A look of revulsion crossed her face. "I would not marry him if he were the last man in the world. I have no expectation of ever being married."

Seeing her distress, James felt tempted to offer comfort, but resisted the impulse knowing that if he did so he would be as bad as Frogg.

Chapter 15

"Trust your instincts." Nell remembered Meg's words, and knew that they told her to be careful where the new medical assistant was concerned.

When Dr Frogg found out Nell was not Mrs Althorpe's niece, he turned his spite against her. She guessed that Florence had told her mistress about the foiled attack on the landing, but was terrified that he might try to harm her again.

The news of Dr Althorpe's impending visit to London left her feeling bereft of support. It was a sudden decision, caused by the arrival of an urgent letter that forced Dr Althorpe to plan his journey by the night mail coach, the fastest means by which he could reach London. His wife, nervous of staying in the house without him, opted to visit her married sister in Norcott, the nearest town from which the physician could set out, which left Nell in the house with the servants and a creature that preyed on helpless women.

However little she relished the prospect, she had no choice but accept her employer's dictate. She knew from his list of instructions, what work to do in the surgery and which patients to visit. If it had not been for Dr Frogg, there would be no cause for alarm.

Dr Frogg's inability to ride a horse necessitated him using Will Bucknole as his groom to drive the gig. In fact, Florence insisted, so they always knew where he was, which left Nell free to attend her patients. That effectively dealt with the daytime. When Dr Althorpe set out he told them to expect him back within a sennight, but no one expected him to return in less than nine days.

At night, Nell hardly dared close her eyes for fear of waking to find her tormentor in her room. Not that it was her own bedroom at the top of the house, but a truckle bed set up in the corner of the room where Florence slept.

She struggled to keep awake during the daytime, but even after three nights, being tired was no guarantee that slumber would claim her tonight. The lack of sleep made her feel colder than ever, just like the times as a child when she shared a blanket with three siblings, which left scarcely the edge to cover her skinny limbs. Even the dog had more comfort, and eventually she had shared his shelter.

As with other nights, Nell heard every chime of the grandfather clock in the front hallway, and with every creak on the stairs, she buried her head further under the bedclothes, not least to escape the gentle purr of Florence's snores.

She must have slept awhile, for as she emerged to take a breath of air, Nell heard the unmistakable scrape of the squeaky handle of the room next door where she normally slept. She listened, hardly daring to breathe, and almost fell out of bed with fright when Florence bellowed, "Who's that next door? Is that you, Will Bucknole? Get back to your own bed, or I will tan your hide for you, disturbing me at this time of night."

Until then, Nell had not realised Florence was awake.

Still scolding, the maid rummaged amongst the contents of the bedside table to find a tinderbox. Even before the tallow candle was alight, Nell heard the sound of a second door opening along the corridor and footsteps running down the attic staircase. Only then did she exhale.

"It's all right," Florence said in her blunt voice. "I was expecting something of the kind. William can go down and see that creature leaves us alone tonight, so we can sleep now."

In the morning, when they investigated the disturbance, they found the coverlet on the bed next door cast aside and the bolster that Florence had placed down the bed discarded on the floor.

"That must have been a disappointment for him," said Florence with sour satisfaction. "Teach him not to come sneaking up here disturbing our sleep."

During the daytime, Nell went warily about her work, peeping around corners to ensure that no one was waiting to pounce on her, and in the evening, Florence saved her the need to speak with the doctor. Six days slipped by in this manner. One evening, the bell rang from the front of the house while they were sitting in the kitchen. Will Bucknole went to answer, but he quickly returned.

"He wants to see you," he said, nodding towards Nell, "says he needs to tell you about one of the patients."

"Ha," Florence snorted her disbelief, but Nell had no choice but to obey.

Gathering her courage, she knocked firmly on the surgery door; and found when she entered the room, the assistant sitting behind Dr Althorpe's oak desk. At his right hand, she saw a brandy bottle and glass, and on the other side, a dark-coloured bottle that he held up for her inspection.

Viewing her through bloodshot eyes, he sneered, "I don't suppose you can read can you, *Nurse Walcote?*"

"Yes, sir," she said. "I can read. It contains Laudanum."

"Note the name well, Walcote, for you will need the oblivion these contents give when I have finished with you. Only an imbecile would waste time teaching the likes of you to read. Althorpe should know that women were put on the earth to serve their menfolk, not to have their brains addled by learning." Frogg's voice was icy cold, but underneath, she sensed his passions were seething.

Then he started to taunt her. "You common slut, I told you what would happen if you betrayed me. Now that I know where you sleep, you had better lock your bedroom door at night, if you can – for I have the master key. It doesn't matter where you try to hide, you will never be safe."

His words chilled her to the core, and his cruel eyes reminded her of the bad times when Ted Walcote came looking for her when he had been at the tavern. It scared her as a child and she ran away to hide. Now she was terrified of the consequences because here there was nowhere for her to go.

Instinctively, she looked towards the door, but he said, "No, Walcote, you will stand there until I have finished, or you won't live to regret it."

She tried to speak, but her mouth felt dry from over-breathing. Her feet did not seem to be part of her any more – they felt strangely heavy, like blocks of wood fixed to the floor. The effort of standing in one place whilst he vented his spleen sapped her energy, but his accusation that Dr Althorpe was a disgrace to his profession for introducing her to gentry as a nurse, brought an unaccustomed surge of anger.

"Nurse...?" he said. "More like his doxy by the way he looks at you." The venom spewed from his foul mouth. "Ah, yes," he wiped spittle from his chin and nodded, "I expect he charges extra for your special services in the bedchambers around here. The so-called country gentlemen would be happy to pay for what passes for a virgin. Of course, you, with your innocent looks would insist on that."

Despite her fear, Nell sensed his impotent resentment of the world of the gentry to which he could never aspire, and it gave her strength.

"It isn't true," she burst out. "How dare you suggest such a thing about Dr Althorpe? He is a good man."

"People will believe whatever I tell them," Frogg snarled. "With his reputation ruined, I'll be the Middlebrook physician."

It was obvious that Frogg liked the sound of his own voice for he used it a lot, but nothing good came out of his mouth.

"Althorpe has convinced his patients that he's a gentleman, but they'll change their mind when I tell them about what he does with his nurse in the surgery when you are supposed to be working. Studying, he calls it, and his hen-witted wife believes him. Fornication, more like. What d'you think she would say if I told her what really goes on in this room?"

Nell closed her eyes and tried to shut out the obscenities. As he ranted, the contents of the bottle diminished, and she remembered hearing the cook complaining about the amount of wine he consumed each night. Now, he was drinking the bottle of brandy that Dr Althorpe kept for medicinal purposes.

What had she done to deserve this kind of persecution? It was not as if she sought Dr Frogg's attention, because until he came to the house she had been happy in her work. Now, he had spoiled everything. Worse than that, he wanted to destroy the people who made her welcome, and had given him employment.

"Are you listening to me?" Frogg bellowed. "I said that if it pleases you to lift your skirts for Althorpe in this room, then you can do it for me now and see what pleasures a younger man can give you."

Nell started in surprise – realising she had closed her mind to the raving some time ago. Then her mind registered what he was suggesting.

"Lift my skirt – for you?" she said in distaste. She knew what he was implying, for it was something she had often seen in Oak Apple Cottage when Ted Walcote came home. Either Peggy was used to it, or else she had not the strength to oppose it.

Then there were the times when she had seen him using other women behind the woodshed or in the coppice at the bottom of the garden. Any female would do to sate his needs, even the girls who were little older than she was.

That is what had scared her most, and made her hide, but now, this beast wanted it of her. Nell looked for somewhere to run, but not even the corners of the room provided shelter. She felt cold, and glanced towards the fireplace.

For some reason, her mind registered the fire was burning low, and noted the box of logs alongside the fire tools. The poker on one side, and tongs the other, both of them just out of reach. If only the poker was nearer, then at least she would have something with which to defend herself.

"I will never do that with you, I'd rather die than let you touch me again," Nell spat at him, and turned to go.

Scarcely had she moved when he shouted, "Stand still, I haven't finished yet. It's up to you whether Althorpe is ruined or not."

Nell raised her weary head and felt her gorge rising at the sight of his thick lips rolling back over his yellow teeth.

"All you have to do to save him the humiliation of being cast out of his profession in disgrace, is to raise your skirts here in this room tonight. You know there is no one to save you this time, so why fight it?" he bragged.

Nell stood, shaking her head, but he insisted, "Pick your skirts up, now."

Wearily, she grasped the material to her sides, and then raised the hem to show her ankles.

"That's better; now, higher, I want to see your knees next." His leer broadened in anticipation.

As he talked, Nell was judging the distance to the fireplace, and knew that there was only one way she could reach it. She guessed that the sight of her bare flesh would inflame his passions, so she raised her eyes slowly, and lifted her skirts. She needed him to think she was too frightened to refuse his demands, so she took a chance and felt the cool air reaching her thighs as she moved between him and the fireplace.

This close, she could smell his foul stench, and felt tainted for her apparent complicity. She could not allow herself to run away, knowing that until he had passed the point of no return, he might still catch her before she reached the door.

"Please...don't hurt me," Nell forced herself to whimper, and watched transfixed as his fumbling hands moved down to his belt, thankful he did not wear breeches, for the front opening flap would have defeated her plan. She moistened her dry lips, as he started to open the buttons, and instinctively swayed her hips to move her tired legs, while he let his trousers fall around his ankles. The sight of his puny limbs filled her with revulsion.

She waited until Frogg bent down to step out of the garment, then dropped her skirts and grabbed the poker. The clatter of the falling firedogs startled him, and in his haste, he stumbled towards her, just as the poker in her hand caught him a glancing blow on the head. He crashed to the floor, struck the fender and lay perfectly still.

Nell took one look at his limp figure on the hearthrug, dropped the poker and dashed towards the kitchen corridor, just as Florence emerged through the door, shouting, "What's going on here?"

"I have killed Dr Frogg," Nell sobbed. She was terrified of what the consequences of her action might be, but knew there was no alternative.

Florence seemed unperturbed.

"If you have then it's no more than he deserved, after what he tried to do to you."

Nell did not want to return to the surgery, but the maid insisted she went with her. When they entered the room, Frogg was sitting on the floor with his bleeding head in his hands. At the sight of Nell, he struggled to get to his feet.

"That bitch hit me with a poker. I'll have her arrested for trying to kill me."

From the safety of the door, Nell watched in disbelief as Florence methodically picked up the poker with the other firedogs and set them straight on the hearth. Then, giving the man a dismissive glance, she said, in a pious tone, "I expect the shock of banging your head has made you forget, Dr Frogg. I don't know what you were doing with your trousers around your ankles, but whatever it was, this is no place for God-fearing women to be with you in that state of undress."

Frogg blinked uncomprehendingly as the maid continued, "Now, be a sensible man and let Will Bucknole help you up to bed. He's assisted the physician enough times in the surgery to know how to bind up your head for tonight and Dr Althorpe will be home by morning." Turning aside, she shouted, "*William!* Oh, drat the boy, he's never here when he's needed."

No sooner had she uttered the words than her nephew appeared in the doorway and asked, "What d'you want me to do now?"

Nell thought she ought to attend to the wound, but Bucknole shook his head and whispered, "I'd be glad if you'd sort out the things I need, but it would be better if you keep out of his sight."

Having done as he asked, Nell returned to the kitchen. Heedless of the tears streaming down her face, she sat by the kitchen fire, hoping Dr Frogg did not die in the night, and wishing Meg were there to help. She was still sitting there when Florence returned.

"William can stay with him tonight, to make sure he's all right. He's done this sort of thing before, and knows what Dr Althorpe would order."

"What are we going to do now?" Nell asked.

"I don't know about you, but I think that dirty fender needs cleaning before we go to bed, or we will have the devil's own job to move the blood in the morning. Oh yes, and we had better give the poker a wipe as well."

"No, I meant, how will we explain this to Dr Althorpe?" said Nell.

"What you heard me tell Dr Frogg, of course. He must have had his own reasons for undressing in there, but I don't want to know what they were, and I'm not going to lose any sleep over it, and neither will you."

Their task completed, Florence carried the medicinal bottle of brandy back to the kitchen, poured a measure into a cup, and handed it to Nell.

"Go on," she said. "Take a sip of this. It'll help you sleep."

"I'd rather have some warm milk and honey," said Nell.

"And so you shall," said Florence, "when you've drunk this. Go on, it is hardly a mouthful. A mouse could drink it."

Believing her, Nell took a sip and then grimaced as the scorching liquid trickled down her throat. She shook her head, not wanting more, but Florence was adamant so she obediently drained the dregs.

"Thank you," she said, and within minutes felt a warm glow seeping through her, and a weariness she could not resist.

She awoke the next morning, wondering how she came to be lying in her bed. The sun streamed through a gap in the curtains. As she lay back on the pillow, the memory of a poker in her hand and the crumpled body lying on the surgery floor came flooding back. *Was Dr Frogg still alive…?*

Scrambling out of bed, she splashed her face with water from the jug and quickly dressed. She ran downstairs to the kitchen, and found Florence and Will Bucknole sitting around the table with the cook and scullery maid.

Florence looked up as Nell entered and gave her a warning glance.

"I was just telling them about Dr Frogg's accident."

"How is he?" she said, turning to look at the manservant.

"Fast asleep," Florence said, and sniffed. "Not surprising with all the brandy he drank. I filled that bottle up only the other day."

The cook shook her head and tutted. "The demons are in the drink," she intoned. "You'd think he'd know better, with him being a physician."

"Ah, but he's not a gentleman, is he?" said Florence, her voice echoing the other woman's pious tone.

Nell flopped down on a wooden chair, feeling hollow inside but not wanting food. Florence supplied the answer by saying in a firm voice, as she added a heaped spoonful of Mrs Althorpe's chocolate to warm milk, "Drink it up, for it's what Dr Althorpe would prescribe."

To maintain appearances, Nell dutifully went out on her rounds, but it was the hardest morning she could remember. She hurried back to the surgery, hoping to hear of Dr Althorpe's return, but they had to wait until four o'clock in the afternoon before a hired post-chaise drove up the drive. A lot had happened in the time since the physician and his wife had set out for Norcott.

Nell was never more relieved to see anyone, but explanations had to wait until the physician had examined his assistant, and made decisions about treatment.

Earlier, when Frogg was asleep, she had peeped into the sickroom, and guessed from his high colour that he was probably running a fever. Knowing the usual medical treatment was to have a pint of blood drained, she went into the surgery to ensure the apparatus was clean and ready for use. She knew that Meg would have used willow bark, a herbal remedy, but Dr Frogg would not appreciate it.

She waited whilst Dr Althorpe talked to Florence and the manservant, but eventually it was her turn. At first, she felt nervous, going back into the surgery, but when she saw the physician's weary face she wished he could have had a better homecoming. She did not really want to explain how his assistant was injured, but knew if he asked a direct question, she would tell the truth.

For once, Nell was glad that Mrs Althorpe had a headache, and retired early to bed, because of the distress it would cause her to hear accusations made about her husband. Even though they were untrue, it would still be offensive and might cause a rift between the physician and his wife, and with Nell. She did not want that to happen.

"Is this where the accident happened?" Dr Althorpe asked.

Nell sat as far away from his desk as she could without causing comment. She nodded without looking at him, trying to keep her eyes tightly closed, to shut out pictures in her mind of the time when she thought she had killed a man.

She choked on her tears, sniffed and tried to speak, then glanced in his direction and saw he was leaning on his desk, with head in his hands, and could see that he too was distressed.

Nell wished that she could offer comfort, but dared not go near him for fear of someone seeing them. Instead, she looked away and waited until he was ready to talk.

"Florence seemed to be rather vague about what happened to Dr Frogg, so I thought you might know. Do you?" he asked.

"Yes, sir," she said, choosing her words carefully. "I think after the last time, he decided to punish me whilst you were out of the house."

"I take it from his present state of ill health, that he did not succeed in his endeavour? You are obviously a very resourceful young woman," he said dryly.

Nell did not know what to say, but his next words provided her with an opening. "I gather that my name was used as a threat against you."

"He made foul accusations about you, saying he could ruin your practice if these things became known. I couldn't let him do that, because you have been kind to me," she said.

"I know what he said, because he was rambling in his sleep, and maligned you more than me. I can withstand such things, but it could have spoiled your life. I am glad you hit him. I only wish I had been here to thrash him myself."

★★★

For the first time in his life, Dr Althorpe was at a loss to know what to do. During his stay in London, he had learned from his old colleague, Windsor-Hardgrave, the sordid truth about Frogg's elopement with the professor's niece, and when she was pregnant, he left her destitute to die in childbirth.

James was appalled by what he had learned, but knew he had to tread carefully, for to accuse a medical man of being involved in the death of another unrelated person was not something he would do lightly.

It was not that he lacked the courage, but he could not without just cause throw the blackguard out of his home, simply on the say-so of even one of the most eminent professors of medicine in the country. Yet all the time, there was an innocent young woman living in his house, within reach of a lecher.

James's head had ached all the way back from London, and since his return. Before he left, he had been glad that he had dealt with the matter of the proposal, which Frogg attributed to his being bewitched by a young woman seeking to entrap him.

Now it seemed that his intervention had made the bounder persecute Nell more, even trying to rape her in his surgery. He had also heard of an earlier attempt on Nell's virtue, but on that occasion, Florence intervened to stop it.

The trouble was that scandals spread quickly in a village, so how could he be sure that the man would behave in a professional manner with his patients. That was the problem, because Frogg was not a gentleman and never had been.

In the light of what had happened, he could not cast an injured man out of the household. By the time he recovered, James needed to have a plan to cover the remaining months of Frogg's practice in Middlebrook.

James would have to ensure that Nell Walcote only worked in the surgery when he was there, and she accompanied him on all but the most insignificant visits, when she could do her own round as she had been accustomed to doing.

It was obvious he would have to make plans for the girl's future. He knew that his wife loved her as a daughter, and would happily adopt her, but he had reservations about whether that was best for Nell, because it would not protect her from abuse when she was alone.

In his opinion marriage was the best option for any woman, but he did not want to entrust the future of that gentle girl to any common man, or a lecher like Frogg. Then James recalled some years earlier, meeting a clergyman from Caitlin Vale, and decided to write to him to solicit clerical guidance on the matter. If he was right, he seemed to think the cleric had an unmarried son. Maybe that would provide the answer he sought.

Chapter 16

Remarkably, Mrs Fulmer showed little emotion at the sudden, violent indisposition of her late husband's nephew. She even offered to transfer Dr Frogg to Bredenbridge and pay for his treatment.

"Better for everyone to have him there out of our way, than causing trouble for you, Dr Althorpe, as I can see he will if he stays here. I presume it was Nell Walcote that he was chasing when he fell and hit his head," she said in her shrewd way.

"Indeed it was, ma'am," James said, knowing that prevarication would not serve, "and not for the first time. I would, however, understand if you felt the need to report the matter to the magistrate."

"Nonsense," she said in a brisk tone. "It is a pity he didn't break his neck, and we would have been rid of him once and for all. As he did not, we must keep him out of harm's way and away from our little girl."

In the event, they settled for a few months recuperation in the Westbridge Infirmary, conveniently attached to the Asylum. That way, Dr Althorpe could oversee his care. It was a situation that suited everyone.

Once agreed, it did not take long to put the plan into action. James ensured that Nell visited Mrs Fulmer during the afternoon when a commodious travelling coach with a team of four sturdy horses drove up to Middlebrook surgery, and two burly attendants climbed out and went into the house.

Within minutes, they emerged carrying the patient, suitably sedated to withstand the journey. When they set off again, Dr Althorpe followed behind in his gig, with Will Bucknole at his side. They returned three hours later.

★★★

Nell heard the news from Florence Fish when she ate her supper in the kitchen. Her normally taciturn face wore a distinct smile of satisfaction.

"There you are, Nell, you've seen the last of Dr Frogg. He won't come back here to bother you again."

Nell wished that she might believe it, but the incident bothered her. She had caused the head injury, and yet no one seemed concerned by his infirmity. Mrs Fulmer certainly was not bothered, for she had said as much during the afternoon. Maybe she was silly in taking Daisy Halford's words to heart.

It was two o'clock when Nell arrived at Elvington Place. The housemaid admitted her to the house and escorted her towards Mrs Fulmer's sitting room. At the foot of the staircase Daisy Halford stopped, and said in a nasty voice, "You're Nell Walcote, the foundling from Hillend Rectory, aren't you? Dr Althorpe wouldn't let you go anywhere near his rich patients if he knew who you were. I won't say a word if you make it worth my while. Half a crown would do…this time."

Nell looked at her in disbelief, for she never carried money on her person. Before she could reply, a sharp voice came from the upper landing.

"Halford, who are you talking to?"

Agnes Woodville, Mrs Fulmer's dresser, was standing on the landing.

"Don't you dare say a word of this to anyone," Halford hissed at Nell, then simpered. "The nurse has come to see the mistress, Miss Woodville."

"Come upstairs, Nurse Walcote; Mrs Fulmer is expecting you. Go and make the tea, Halford," the dresser ended on a dismissive note.

It was more than six years since she left Hillend, but Nell still felt the same sense of not belonging as when she went with Meg to Middlebrook Fair, dressed as a gypsy. She felt like weeping, but could not indulge herself when a patient needed her care.

She looked away when Halford brought in the tea trolley, expecting

170

the maid to expose her as a fraud, but under Woodville's gimlet stare, the woman did not utter a word. As soon as she had left the room, Mrs Fulmer said, in a soothing voice, "Don't worry about that spiteful cat, my lovely girl. I know everything I want to about you, and you are worth a dozen of her."

At her words Nell's tears overflowed. She was accustomed to harshness, but kindness was something she could not withstand.

A few days later

"The reason I asked you to call, Dr Althorpe, is not for me, but to talk about your little nurse. I want to find out about her origins."

When Dr Althorpe received a summons, he rushed back from his morning visits, convinced that Mrs Fulmer was in desperate need of his medical skills. He went immediately to Elvington Place, and found her lying on a daybed in her boudoir, surrounded by expensive finery. She looked thoughtful, but the sight of him brought a broad smile to her face.

Contrary to his expectation of ill health, it seemed that all she wanted was to talk, but from what she said, he was not sure it was in his interest to tell her.

"Nell Walcote? Why do you want to know about her?" His tone was sharper than usual, but he moderated the pitch knowing he could not afford to offend his wealthy patient.

"You only have to look at her bones to know she is gentry born. Has she any family, because if she hasn't, I would like to adopt her?" she said, indicating he should take a seat.

This was becoming more bizarre by the second. James chose the chair nearest to where she sat, for he suspected her hearing might be impaired.

"I know little of her history," he said, deciding to say nothing about the gypsy connection, "other than to say that she is an orphan, or as she freely admits, a foundling."

"Fathered by the gentry, if I'm any judge of things," she said bluntly. "Poor little soul, it's not her fault if she is. That poisonous spider, Halford, hinted as much, but it will do her no good. I detest tittle-tattling, and there are many respectable households that deliver seven-month babies. I daresay they've had a few of those at Linmore Hall, but that is no concern of mine. Nell Walcote is."

That was plain speaking indeed.

Ignoring the diversion, James resumed his discourse. "Nell has lived with us for about two and a half years, half of which she has worked in the surgery, and proves her worth every day." He took a breath before adding, "Adoption is a huge step for someone that you do not know."

He did not admit to having considered the same option. Nor that he had his own ideas about the girl's origins, based on an enigmatic likeness that Nell had to a gentlewoman he once knew. The lady he would have gone to the ends of the earth to serve, and taken half the regimental officers in India with him.

"I know it is," she said. "Maybe, we should see how well we get on first. I like her, and she is a kind little soul, but she doesn't know me. She's very polite, and says her loyalty belongs to you."

When he looked surprised, she added, "I asked her if she would like to be my companion. My only concern is that being with me she would be without anyone to protect her, whereas with you she would be safe. You might be in a position to find her a husband of your class, for she will need someone strong with what I have a mind to leave her."

"Are you saying…?" he was incredulous.

"Yes, Dr Althorpe, I was thinking of giving your little nurse some money and a few trinkets as well," she said, waving a wrist adorned with bracelets.

She stopped abruptly, then raised a finger to her lips to halt any reply and tilted her head to listen. With barely a second between, a hand knocked, and the door opened to reveal a housemaid wheeling a tea trolley, and under Mrs Fulmer's guidance, filling and distributing teacups.

"Thank you, Halford," said Mrs Fulmer in a crisp tone. "You can leave the rest to me."

It was obvious the girl was burning with curiosity, but her mistress was not going to oblige her with as much as a hint of gossip. Dr Althorpe waited for the servant to leave the room, but he suspected that her ear was pressed firmly against the door. The lady evidently thought the same. "Halford," she shouted.

The door immediately opened, and the maid, flushing to the roots of her hair, all but fell into the room. Mrs Fulmer viewed her with distaste. "This tea is cold. Go and make a fresh pot, and this time make sure the kettle is boiling."

As the door closed for the second time, Mrs Fulmer said, "I have a feeling that wench is still spying for that so-called nephew of my late husband. There was bad blood in the Fulmer family, but my dear papa did not learn of it in time to stop the wedding, only to ensure that he left me in full charge of my money. It caused no end of arguments, but Fulmer couldn't touch a penny without my consent. I want, similarly, to leave it in trustworthy hands."

"If your servants are spying on you, ma'am, why do you not dismiss them?" he said. That was the obvious way of dealing with the matter.

"If I did, I have no doubt that Halford and others like her would take out more than they brought in, and I want to prevent that."

She raised her hand to her ear, just as a tap on the door indicated the maid was about to return, so it was decided that they had a better chance of discussing the matter in private outside the lady's house.

Dr Althorpe waited until the door opened, before saying in a loud voice, intended to be heard by someone hard of hearing, "I think the best thing, ma'am, would be for you to come to the surgery so that I can examine you, and we will discuss your concerns in the proper place. Would tomorrow at eleven o'clock be convenient?"

"It would indeed, Dr Althorpe. I will bring my dresser with me for assistance."

★★★

Mrs Fulmer came to Dr Althorpe's surgery at the appointed time, accompanied by her personal maid, who was left to sit outside his consulting room.

"Woodville's as good a servant as I could have," she said. "I have known her since I was a girl, and she will be well provided for, but it is better that she plays no part in this, then no one can blame her."

Opening her capacious reticule, she said, "I have a letter here for Ernest Bassingbourne, my man of business in Bredenbridge. I would be obliged if you could send it from here, as I don't want anyone at my place to know. With your permission, I will see him here and give him instructions. Once the deed is done, no one can interfere."

"If you are absolutely sure this is what you want, ma'am, I will undertake to do it for you," said Dr Althorpe. "Now, as you are here, I think that we should listen to your heart. As I recall, it was causing you some concern."

"A few flutters, my friend," she said, "but when you are over sixty, you expect something of the kind. It will tell me when it is time to go. That is why I want my business in order, with everything set out clearly in black and white. I intend to leave Fulmer's nephew ten thousand pounds. I always intended that it should have been five, but after this trouble we won't quibble."

Having escorted the lady and her servant to the carriage, Dr Althorpe returned to his office and called for Will Bucknole. As he signed the corner of the envelope, to ensure payment, he said, "I want you to take this to the postal collecting office, William, and make sure that it reaches Bredenbridge by tonight. There must be no delay."

James knew that he had a problem. Mrs Fulmer was an exceedingly wealthy woman, and to be involved in the settling of her affairs did not come within his remit as a physician. Conversely, her fluttering heartbeat did, and he was in full agreement that she should meet with no obstructions, before, as she said, her heart told her it was time to leave.

That could come at any time. He was not surprised that she liked Nell Walcote, for many people did, but to leave her money was another thing. Still, he would not be involved in the wording of that document, except as a joint executor with the man of business.

Having sent Nell out on her morning rounds, James knew he would have to ensure that he made the same arrangement when the solicitor was due to come. Mrs Fulmer had stressed that she did not want anyone to suspect her intentions.

He had no doubt that the man of business would advise her to reconsider, but from what James could see, Mrs Fulmer intended to add the final codicil. At a stroke, Nell Walcote would change overnight from a foundling to an heiress and when it became known, her troubles with fortune hunters would start.

No, it was James who would have the unenviable task of finding an honest man to be her husband. A difficult task at the best of times, but in this situation he would say it was almost impossible. *Someone of your class,* the lady had said, and she was right, for nothing less than a gentleman would do for Nell. But what would she think?

Only when the manservant returned could James start to relax.

"It's on its way, sir. It will be there before close of business tonight."

Now he had to wait for the response, and a reply from Reverend Whitcott at Caitlin, about a matter that could solve his problem and keep Nell safe.

It was just as well that she was booked to attend a tenant farmer's wife during the lying-in period. That would keep her occupied for the rest of the month, with the likelihood of another booking to follow.

The solicitor's reply was not long in coming, and James found himself obliged to act with subterfuge, something he abhorred, but there was no alternative given the delicacy of the situation. He knew that, with care, Mrs Fulmer could live for many years, but urgency added to the strain on her heart. He must act with caution in case anyone thought he had a vested interest.

A week later, Mrs Fulmer visited his house to advise her man of business of the amendment she required him to make. Not wishing to be involved, James left them to talk, but on his return, he heard the solicitor caution the lady on what he thought imprudence, an action that brought a sharp rebuff.

"It is not your money, Bassingbourne," she retorted. "It is mine, and you're here to act on my wishes, so don't you forget it."

"Of course, ma'am." The man immediately modified his features to a more conciliatory expression.

Hearing the high-handed manner in which the woman dealt with opposition reminded James forcibly of his paternal grandmother, a veritable dragon when anyone opposed her will. Mrs Fulmer's father had obviously been in trade, but her mother's origins might have been genteel.

Afterwards, they took afternoon tea with Mrs Althorpe and arranged another meeting for the following week. When everything was completed, Mrs Fulmer was tired but triumphant and spent several days of the following week resting, time in which she had a daily attendance from her physician, and the promise of several visits from Nell Walcote on her return to the surgery.

Fortunately, everything went to plan.

Chapter 17

Mid-April 1814 – Linmore Dale

"I thought physicians were supposed to look cheery for their patients," said Mrs Fulmer in a teasing voice, "particularly when you bring good news about the war ending."

"A cessation in hostilities does not come without its problems, ma'am." James Althorpe thought he had hidden his concern, but evidently not from this acutely sharp-eyed lady. "They will appear once the celebrations are over."

"With the homecoming soldiers, you mean?"

"Yes," he said, glad to have someone with whom to share his thoughts. "Those who return will not be the men they once were, nor will their wives and families be as they remember. Some wives, thinking they were widowed, might well have remarried."

"Who can blame them?" said Mrs Fulmer. "The lot of a lone woman with children is hard, and just because I didn't have any of my own, doesn't mean I am unaware of the difficulties. I saw plenty of hardships when I lived in Bredenbridge, a dozen years ago. I did what I could to help by employing women as servants, but it was precious little. That's why I don't readily turn people out of doors even when they deserve it."

James nodded, knowing her kindly nature would not allow her to create poverty in the lower orders.

"What kind of problems do you envisage in Linmore Dale?" she said.

176

"You might as well tell me, having aroused my curiosity."

"I do not think that you were resident in Middlebrook at the time of the Peace of Amiens, ma'am," he said.

"No," she said, "I came two years later, by which time the war had resumed."

"It was a productive time, when many men who returned found work. Both the Neathwood Park and Linmore Hall estates took advantage of the influx of labour. When the war resumed, former soldiers re-enlisted, and their sons took their jobs."

"So you think that will happen again?"

"Yes," he said, "I think people will come seeking work, but we will probably have more casualties with which to contend."

"I see," she said, "so we'll have to make plans on the off-chance that you are right."

"We...?" he said, surprised at her ready acceptance of his opinion.

"You didn't think I would be left out, did you? What kind of facilities will you need, and how much will it cost."

"I was not asking for money, ma'am," he said, trying to regain control of a situation of which she was rapidly taking charge.

"Nevertheless, you will need it," she said bluntly. "You have medical expertise and I have money, so we will make a formidable team."

"We cannot do this alone," he said firmly, "but there are some people that I might speak with on my visits, who would be ready to help."

"Members of the gentry who would think it strange for me, a relative stranger in the district, to be involved, you mean? Don't worry about upsetting my feelings. I can be a secret benefactor to your fund, if you like."

Embarrassed at her perspicacity, James said, "It is probably best if I speak with Squire Norbery of Linmore Hall. He is the local Member of Parliament, so his voice will be heeded by others."

"Was it his son that married Miss Annabel Bradstone from Bredenbridge?"

"Yes," he said, "Joshua and his wife live at Linmore Manor."

"I was acquainted with the Bradstone family before I came here, so it is better if my name is not mentioned. I will also make my donations to the fund in cash."

Knowing the lady's reclusive tendencies, he was not surprised at her reluctance to be known. "I would not divulge your name without permission, ma'am."

"What problems do you anticipate?" she said, resuming their previous topic of conversation.

"From a purely medical viewpoint, I daresay that many wounded soldiers will require care in the next few months. Looking towards the winter, we will need a good supply of food, warm clothing, and shelter."

"And a few shillings in their purse; otherwise they will not want to leave."

"What a shrewd businesswoman you would have made, ma'am," he said.

"My father used to say that, when I kept his accounts in the early days," she said softly, bowing her head to contain her emotions. "My mother died when I was young, so he educated me as he would have done a son."

"I did not know that, ma'am," he said, touched that she trusted him enough to share a secret.

"Very few people know anything about me – and that's the way I prefer it."

"In which case, you will indeed be my secret benefactor, Mrs Fulmer."

"Shall we call it the *Poor Fund*, for which I will give you a hundred pounds?"

James found, when he spoke on the subject with his wife, that she was in full agreement. Similarly, when he saw Lady Chetton of Neathwood after church and she expressed a wish to consult with him at his surgery but not, he discovered about her health. Apparently she had returned from London.

"Celebrations are all very well; Dr Althorpe, but people in London have no idea of the hardships that country folk endure," said her ladyship, almost before he had made her welcome. "Thinking back to the last time this happened; we must plan for the reality."

James started to murmur his agreement, which she cut short.

"With many discharged soldiers coming home, plus an unknown number of casualties, we will need money. Therefore, we must set up a committee of which I will be a fund-raiser. There have to be some benefits to having a title, and extracting money from the tight-fisted is something I will relish. I intend to let it be known discretely that I am arranging an evening of dancing to celebrate the victory, for a select few, by invitation only."

"Which everyone who considers themselves gentry in Linmore Dale will wish to attend," he said with a dry laugh.

"Of course," she said. "And a few others besides, I daresay."

"Will your husband not mind?"

She looked at him in surprise. "Robert will hate it," she said, "but as long as we have card tables as well, he will not complain. Once they are at Neathwood, I will announce my latest fund for the poor, for which I hear that you already have a donation. May I be permitted to ask the name of the benefactor?"

News travelled fast. He wondered from whom she had heard a whisper.

"One of my patients, a lady, whose name I am not at liberty to divulge."

"How much was her gift?" Lady Chetton asked bluntly.

"One hundred pounds," he said, "and she is willing to give more."

"That is extremely generous," she said with a nod of approval. "I will equal it – in guineas. What else do you need?"

How fortunate he was to have found another practical lady like Mrs Fulmer. He wondered if they were acquainted, but thought it unlikely.

★★★

The hastily organised Ball, held in June at Neathwood Park, was deemed to have been a great fund-raising success. Similarly, a pig roast and firework event held for the village folk in the Middlebrook and Linmore-in-the-Dale area was enjoyed by all.

To James, the victory at Toulouse, which led to Bonaparte's abdication, had a hollow feel, as did the soon to be forgotten celebrations. He knew, only too well, that twenty years of war did not end in an instant. The suffering and hardships caused went on, which were not evident at the time of the short-lived Peace at Amiens. Men with broken bodies had yet to come home, and sons who shouldered responsibilities would be expected to step aside as head of the household.

He said as much to Lady Chetton, who shared his concerns when she came with lists in hand to apprise him on the fund-raising total.

"We now have eight hundred and fifty pounds in our account to approach the winter season, Dr Althorpe, with promissory notes for two hundred more. Part of that came from the Faro Bank, which is one of Robert's favourite card games – hence his co-operation."

Planning their campaign had evidently given the lady a purpose.

"If discharged soldiers come here in any numbers, they will be hungry and need to be fed," she said. "Beasts on the hoof can be kept at Neathwood and probably Linmore as well. I will discuss the matter with Joshua Norbery."

"From where would you acquire them, my lady?" said James, feeling he was being swept along, much as he had with Mrs Fulmer.

"Obviously, we must not deplete the local markets of supplies for fear of causing shortages," she said. "I do not know if you are aware that every year in the spring and autumn, drovers bring herds down from the Welsh hills.

"When they reach Linmore Dale, I will purchase fifty head of cattle, and a corresponding number of sheep," she continued. "In fact, it would draw less attention if I sent my bailiff to negotiate the sale in advance."

"Is that not possibly an excessive number?"

"Not really," she said. "We can fatten them here, and sell them on later if they are not required. Personally, I think it possible that more might be needed by the late autumn. Beef stew is a warming meal, for which vegetables will also be needed. I will set the gardeners to increase the vegetable patches."

"What about pigs?" he said, knowing salt bacon would supplement the stores.

"Undoubtedly they will be required. I will make enquiries."

★★★

Having established the basic requirements, Lady Chetton turned her attention to which of the ladies of Linmore Dale might be approached to support the venture. While she ran through a list of names for his consideration, James gave a nod or shook his head.

"I believe that Mrs Joshua Norbery is a lady with an extremely wealthy father," she said with a smile. "Do you think her parents might oblige me by attending the next function? Robert calls him an infernal mushroom, but as I tell him, the man is a wealthy mushroom. I trust that you will not betray my indiscretion, Dr Althorpe?"

"I hear many things in the course of my work, ma'am," he said. "But would be hard pressed to recall exactly where it was."

Lady Chetton smiled her understanding. "I would be pleased if you were to attend the soiree with your wife. And I rely on you to tell me the names of the people at Middlebrook Grange. It is remiss of me, but I have quite forgotten and it is only a month since the woman approached me at church."

"I think you mean Mr and Mrs Doverdale and the lady's sister, Miss Edgton."

"Ah, yes, they must be included. Otherwise she might be offended and give me the cut direct. That would never do."

"I think it unlikely, ma'am."

"What about Squire Norbery's wife from Linmore Hall?"

"No," he said in a decided tone. "Miss Kate suffers from melancholia and has not gone into society since the death of her eldest son about fifteen years ago. She lives retired in her own apartments at Linmore Hall."

"Miss Kate?" Lady Chetton's brows rose in surprise.

"As opposed to Miss Jane Littlemore, her sister. That is how she is known in her own private world – and by the servants at Linmore."

"So who is the lady that I have seen with Squire Norbery? I assumed, from their demeanour, that she was his wife."

"No," he said again, choosing his words carefully. "Miss Jane runs the household at Linmore Hall in her sister's absence. It is said that she declined several offers of marriage to attend Miss Kate." In this case, James chose to repeat gossip that he had heard. "I think you could safely include Tom Norbery's daughter, at Shettleston Hall, and his two nieces, who married tenant farmers on the estate. I will have to ask my wife to clarify whether it is Lucy who is Mrs David Buttercross, and Julia, who married Sebastian Dinham. Being identical twins, I cannot recall."

"In that case, I will invite the three ladies and their aunt to join our fund-raising committee, Dr Althorpe. I trust that you will not mind if I mention your name?"

He inclined his head in agreement, as the peeress prepared to depart.

"I will leave the task of compiling a list of medical equipment, beds and suchlike, to you. If you tell me what additional help is required, I will make enquiries when I convene the ladies meeting."

"One might almost suspect that you relish the task, ma'am."

"Yes," she said, "it is good to feel that I am doing something practical again. It is not the done thing for Lady Chetton to clean out the stables these days, but in Ireland before my marriage, my guardian insisted it was one of my daily duties."

Late Summer 1814

After almost a year, Dr Althorpe had given up hope of receiving a response from his old acquaintance, the rector of Caitlin. Of course, it could be that he had passed away, and in the light of Dr Frogg's absence, and recent events with Mrs Fulmer, he decided that the gentleman's personal involvement was not imperative. James had set aside any notion of adopting Nell Walcote in favour of making contingency plans for homecoming soldiers.

Some of the walking wounded who had passed through the valley en route to their homes in Wales brought news of the less able who were heading that way, and in return received a hot meal and a bed for the night before moving on.

Everything possible was prepared for a situation in which they had no way of judging numbers in advance. A cruck barn on the Neathwood estate, across the post road from the River Linmore bridge, had been cleaned together with a lean-to store which now contained a supply of army tents and pallets with straw mattresses that had arrived with piles of surplus blankets, courtesy of Mrs Fulmer. The old barn, offered by Lady Chetton, was deemed far enough away from Middlebrook village to avoid trouble with the locals.

Similarly, a field stove had been set up in readiness. Not for the cooking of food, which arrived in cauldrons from Linmore, Shettleston and Neathwood, but to keep it warm after being in transit. Everyone had a daily portion of beef pie, rabbit stew, and a thick crust of bread and cheese, with ale or cider to drink in moderation.

James continued on his rounds, keeping the locals informed of the news, and giving reassurance of the good behaviour of people of whom he had no knowledge.

As the number of casualties increased, two army surgeons came from Bredenbridge to help – James presumed at the behest of Squire Norbery – men of sound common sense, whose task was hindered by foolish local girls who were intrigued by their uniforms. It was a tense time, with husbands and lovers standing jealously by to repulse the slightest advance on what they considered their property.

He would have welcomed the arrival of some chronically sick. He did his daily rounds of patients, and in his attempt to keep Nell Walcote safe was forced to use Bucknole as a groom, when the man would have been better used as a ward orderly.

They had all their preparations made, and for a while it seemed they might not be needed. Summer came and a few passing soldiers, with good intentions, offered to help with the harvest. There was an uneasy peace.

★★★

On the day of the Middlebrook Fair, James received a visit from a stranger, who apologised for the intrusion and requested the privilege of a few moments of his time. Receiving the visiting card from the manservant, James noted the name, *Whitcott*, and the place of residence, *Caitlin*. When he agreed to delay his departure, he found that his visitor was not the elderly cleric he expected to see, but the rector's son.

Captain Adam Whitcott was a tall, dark-haired man, of medium build and a military bearing. His features were unremarkable, but his voice was distinctive, almost compelling in its sincerity, and James liked him on sight.

Shaking hands, he said, "I must apologise for my tardy response to your letter to my late father, Dr Althorpe. His demise was three years ago. My mother followed him this last Whitsun, hence the delay."

Offering condolences, James wondered at the purpose of the visit.

"I appreciate that you requested clerical guidance from my father, but maybe I can be of assistance. I trained for the ministry after my discharge from the army, but found it was not my calling," Adam Whitcott said with wry good humour. "I spend much of my time painting portraits and am not often at home."

With Mrs Fulmer's remit in mind, James looked at him with different eyes. He was undoubtedly an officer and gentlemen, who might, if agreeable, be a suitable match for Nell Walcote. He proceeded to explain his requirements.

"When I wrote to your father, I wished to seek his opinion on the advisability of adopting a young woman in my employ."

His visitor's brows rose slightly, but he uttered not a word.

"Since then, another person whose identity I cannot divulge has expressed the same interest and wishes to make the young person her heir. The lady has also charged me, as one of her executors, to find the girl a husband in what she calls my class. She makes no excuse for the fact that her father made his money in trade."

"I see," said Captain Whitcott. "Not an easy task, without seeing the young woman and knowing more of her background. You may be assured that I will respect the confidentiality of anything you tell me."

James explained in brief terms about Nell's origins, and his personal belief that she was of good stock, a sentiment, her wealthy benefactor had seconded.

"I would have thought that as your adopted daughter, the young woman would become acceptable to people of our class, particularly if she had a dowry."

James agreed.

"I suppose that I am eligible for the position," the younger man said with a smile, "but am not seeking a bride, with or without money. However, I will make discrete enquiries on my travels and let you know if I hear of anyone suitable."

Having reached an agreement, they shook hands and Captain Whitcott departed, leaving James to wish that Nell had been available to meet him, instead of at the fair seeing her old friend, the herbalist, as she did every year.

Once seen, he might have reconsidered his decision not to wed. She was a delightful girl who would make some man a good wife, if only she could overcome her sense of unworthiness and the belief that marriage was not for her.

Chapter 18

Early July 1815 – Middlebrook Surgery

"A plague on all battles…" The words burst from James Althorpe's lips.

He sat in his study, staring with unseeing eyes at the crumpled news-sheet in his hands. The information it contained was, he supposed, good for England, but a disaster for the families like his own that had borne the brunt and lost their future generations of manhood.

The battle at Waterloo, the place where Wellington and Bonaparte had finally met face-to-face, was over. And by all accounts, there had been horrendous losses on both sides.

James wondered if the outcome would have been different if Wellington had retained the best of his Peninsular army, instead of half of them being in America. Too many had been killed, injured or sold out last year, when Bonaparte was exiled to Elba. Why the blazes could not the man have remained there?

Twenty years of war had wreaked havoc on his family. A younger brother lost in America, who would have been better to have stayed at home. A nephew blinded and two more maimed that would not make old bones. At times like this he was glad that he had no surviving children to weep for.

Every day in his work he encountered the hardships endured by some, and others for whom death would have been preferable to the awful sense of uselessness that shattered limbs or lost sight instilled in them. With no way to resume normal lives, all they had left was time to dwell on the horrors of battles fought and lost comrades. For some, drink led to oblivion, while others begged him to help them out of their misery. Sometimes James was tempted, but had not yet succumbed.

Only this morning he had heard that his sister's youngest daughter, Drusilla, had lost her betrothed, an enthusiastic young man who, like countless others, had rushed off to fight for his country. This brought home the futility of war; the fact that this lovely girl who had eagerly anticipated her bridals in the autumn, was bereaved before she was a bride. James brushed away a tear, remembering that she was the same age as his daughter Harriet would have been, had she lived.

He shook his head in sorrow at the wasted lives and then roused from his contemplations. There was no time for maudlin thoughts. If the same thing happened as it had a year ago after the Battle of Toulouse, the army would disband regiments and discharge soldiers in their thousands. But this time there would be more injured and, inevitably, more to bury.

★★★

Once again, plans were being made that needed practical solutions. James remembered the day last year when the previous delivery of stores arrived in three large covered wagons. In the first were a dozen wooden pallets. Another contained a score and a half straw mattresses, forty canvas sheets and army blankets, while the third vehicle carried fifteen tents each large enough to provide shelter for four men.

Army suppliers were only too pleased to release stores that might otherwise not be sold. James knew to whom he was indebted when he visited Mrs Fulmer.

"Have the stores arrived yet?" the lady asked with the enthusiasm of a child.

"Indeed, ma'am," he said, "but your generosity…it is too much…"

"That's nothing to the point, for you will need more. Take these before anyone else realises there is a demand and buys them up."

Within another week, as many items again followed the first order.

James could not deny that Mrs Fulmer had been more animated at the time than he had previously seen her, and she was almost sorry when it was over. He began to wonder from where she had acquired her unexpected thirst for knowledge.

While the towns of Norcott and Westbridge were overwhelmed by their numbers, the villages of Linmore and Middlebrook pooled their resources, and coped with the practical organising skills of Sergeant Percival.

Meeting him, James had suffered a slight shock, but schooled his expression to impassivity. Whilst the man's smoky-black hair and distinctive hawkish features were undoubtedly reminiscent of the old Lord Chetton of Neathwood, Percival had the war-hardened look of a soldier. He wondered how Lady Chetton would respond when Miss Jane introduced the man, but the peeress, in her well-mannered way, showed no surprise.

★★★

James made no complaint when he learned that Mrs Fulmer had supplemented her order for stores of the previous year with three dozen rolls of canvas sheeting. He also welcomed Lady Chetton and Miss Littlemore's offer to again provide victuals for the men. Similarly, the extra hands offered by the various estates for sundry duties when the time came to dig graves.

Most of the casualties from the previous year had been buried in a newly designated war cemetery near the cruck barn. The bishop was first outraged at the suggestion and then he pontificated, as the clergy were wont to do, but Squire Tom Norbery's brusque words held sway.

"My Lord Bishop," he said. "Surely you do not expect us to fill the local churchyards at Linmore and Middlebrook, and then demand that you provide us with cemeteries for local people who die in the coming winter season? Give us the consecrated ground that we now need to treat our dead soldiers with respect. I know what I, as a member of His Majesty's Parliament, would prefer to happen."

Suitably shamed by the quiet voice of authority, the Bishop had complied.

James stirred from his reverie. Soon, the canvas tents and army blankets, gathering dust on neatly stacked wooden pallets in the cruck barn would be brought out again. A visit to Mrs Fulmer this morning had reminded him of their existence, and he had little doubt her mind was already working out the number required to replace stores disposed of last year.

For a lady living in seclusion, she had a remarkable number of business contacts, and not for the first time he wondered about the kind of trade in which her father had made his fortune. Such was the magnitude of her wealth he had a feeling that it was connected to the war. Hence, her wish to make recompense.

Closer to home, he wondered if Micky Bouldon, the handyman-cum-groom at the surgery, would return to the job that James had given him in payment for his caring services – employment that he, together with twenty-five other former soldiers taken on by local estates, had abandoned when the call to arms came.

James knew that he was not alone in hoping the man had survived the recent battle. His sweetheart in the village, Charlotte, the granddaughter of the old Dr Tilbury, was also awaiting the man's return. Miss Tilbury, the village school teacher who taught Micky his letters through the long winter evenings, had secretly wept at his departure. Would she also be bereaved before a bride, like James's niece?

He had little doubt that the ladies of Linmore Dale were even now organising another fund-raising event for the poor and the needy. Mrs Shettleston had offered to host a Summer Ball, and Squire Norbery volunteered Linmore as the venue for the next year, though goodness only knew what state the country would be in by then.

It was inevitable that in peacetime, a much reduced army of occupation was needed in Europe, which meant that the army would discharge more soldiers in coming months. James had little doubt that, when the army cancelled orders, the Bredenbridge foundry master and munitions manufacturers would turn off workers at a time when there were more mouths to feed.

Similarly the weather, growing increasingly inclement in recent months, was likely to destroy the harvest. The people of Linmore Dale had not failed to meet the challenge before, but this time, following the victory over the French aggressor, would test their resolve.

The autumn weather continued cold and wet. The village fair had been washed out, and those folk who had brought livestock to sell looked in vain for a buyer until Sergeant Percival arrived to buy a sow with a dozen or so piglets in a pen; a cow in milk with her two calves, together with six breeding goats and their kids. He paid a good price for the whole and even the most cantankerous of villagers went home satisfied. No doubt the poor families of the parish would be the beneficiaries.

★★★

By mid-September the influx of casualties was making its presence felt. The cruck barn could not take any more, so James required an alternative building to use as an infirmary. Mrs Fulmer had, when he explained his plan, ordered sheets from a linen warehouse. He suspected that his wife had discretely mentioned his intention to use the house for wounded officers.

Within days, an empty house near to the surgery was made available for his use. By the time James looked inside, it was in the process of being cleaned, and a few days later, six metal beds were installed with sufficient mattresses and linen to accommodate half as many more in relative comfort. Elizabeth told him that she had arranged for local washerwomen to attend the laundry.

A separate room was set aside for him to undertake surgery, and the village apothecary provided such medication as might be required. James still had his favourite remedies, but when the offer was extended he made no mention of these.

When the first of the wounded officers arrived, he was glad that Nell felt able to undertake an occasional shift to supervise the village carers, after she had finished her daily routine in the practice. He also discovered, quite by chance, that she made a detour around by the cruck barn, but was glad to hear that she was sent home, under the escort of a Linmore servant.

This meant that he did not have to pretend when Mrs Fulmer asked about her presence. "I hope you're not expecting my little friend to work with the common soldiers, Dr James."

"No, indeed, ma'am," Althorpe said. "She works but a few hours in the infirmary."

"With the officers?" she said sharply. "Let us hope they are gentlemen as well."

"They are sick men, ma'am; and as soon as they are fit to be moved, they will be dispatched home to their families. I personally will arrange it."

"Good night, Mrs Althorpe. I hope you sleep well." Nell had little doubt of that, knowing that the physician's wife took a small dose of valerian.

"Good night, my dear. I hope that you will take the opportunity to have an early night as well."

Nell watched the lady and her maid ascend the front stairs, and saw Florence Fish look back from the landing. "I'll prepare your warm milk when I come downstairs, Nurse Walcote."

She heard the words but did not stop to answer. Knowing that Florence would be occupied for quite half an hour, Nell sped up the backstairs to her bedroom, cast off her tidy clothes that she wore in the evening and dived under the bed for a bag where she kept her breeches that she had brought from her life with Meg.

Whatever the physician's wife might wish, there would be no early night, or sleep in a bed if the previous ones were any guide. Confined by daylight within the limits of her role as the physician's assistant, Nell spent a few hours each night in the infirmary, as the once-empty cottage where Dr Althorpe accommodated the injured officers was called. A necessity on which Lady Chetton insisted was fitting for their rank.

Tonight, however, her destination was the cruck barn beyond the post road, which ran between Norcott and Westbridge. Once there, she could help the other carers by checking the wounds of sick and injured soldiers, or offer comfort to dying men, simply by being there. Often it was all she could do, other than to hold a hand as their breath ebbed away. Death was, as she had learned whilst working with Meg, a desolate place to approach alone.

The house was quiet as Nell crept along the corridor towards the surgery door. She noticed there was no light beneath, which meant that Dr Althorpe was probably at the infirmary taking a last look at his officer patients before returning home. Nell checked in her pocket for her spare key, and nodded. All would be well as long as no one slid the bolt in place at the end of the day.

Having closed the outer door, she made her way along the path to the stables, hoping she would not meet Will Bucknole, who constantly grouched about being expected to do his daily work and assist the surgeon in the infirmary. Nell knew that he took it as a matter of pride to be trusted, but being Florence Fish's nephew it was in his nature to grumble.

Entering the stable, she guessed from the snoring in the hayloft that the stable lad had fallen asleep awaiting the physician's return. But she did not need his help. She found the halter hanging on the hook, and with a few whispered words of reassurance, led the physician's spare horse out through the door to the mounting block.

This was her most vulnerable moment. No one knew that she could ride, and to be caught mounted astride like a man would shock the neighbourhood. Intending to avoid being seen near the surgery, she guided the horse through the trees by the back gate and along the lane leading to the bridge. She had to trust the horse's sense of direction as she passed a few houses with darkened windows, but a soft word here and there ensured its compliance.

Once across to the other side, she nudged the animal with her knees as it lengthened its stride to an easy pace. Nell longed to canter, but knew that in the half-light of the waxing moon she must take care. It was like being out of doors with Meg, but without the warm companionship that she missed so much.

Being late September she imagined that by now Meg would have finished the hedgerow harvest and be preparing for her trip to Caitlin. Their last, hastily contrived meeting had been at the autumn fair, which meant it would probably be another year before they met again.

She sighed, regretting the necessity on which Dr Althorpe insisted that her former life as a gypsy be kept secret. Nell was not ashamed of the connection, nor, she suspected, was he. It was what local society as she had heard it called, expected of her present position. Knowing that Meg had been in full agreement, Nell complied.

Ten minutes later she approached the post road, ready to cross. She knew the place by the sound of water cascading over rocks under the River Linmore bridge, and stopped for a moment to listen. But seeing it in the half-light, it felt a place of desolation. She shivered, as an unaccountably cold feeling ran down her spine, and then urged the horse onwards.

All was silent as she reached the improvised circle of tents pitched to give shelter to homeward-bound soldiers, or those recovering from the wounds sustained in the war. A lone fire burned to give light and warmth.

She slipped to the floor and led the horse to the makeshift stable at the back of the cruck barn.

A disembodied hand reached out to take the reins from her grasp, and a half-familiar voice said, "Evening, Nurse Walcote. Just you leave him with me. I'll see that he's ready when you want to leave."

"Thank you, William Rufus," she said, knowing it was one of the Linmore Hall servants that she had met when visiting the barn with Dr Althorpe.

The man spoke to an unseen helper and followed her inside the barn. A glow of light from a lantern lit the space, indicating the area at the one end where the most serious casualties lay, divided by a screen from the rest. She listened to the pitch of moans and sensed that by morning there would be fewer to attend. "Where am I needed most?" she said, ready to take his advice.

"If you don't mind taking over from Jessie, while she takes a drink," William Rufus said, pointing in the direction of a stiffly-built woman that she knew to be his sister, kneeling at the side of a wounded soldier.

Nell moved forward to touch the woman's shoulder, and indicated the silent figure of the man waiting in the doorway.

"Thank you, Nurse Walcote," said the woman. "I could do with a breath of air."

"How is he?" Nell whispered, indicating the man on the floor.

Jessie shook her head. "Moithering about summat, but I can't make out what he's saying. Maybe you can make sense of it."

"I will do my best," she said as they exchanged places.

Nell looked around and counted six figures on wooden pallets with straw mattresses, all covered by a canvas sheet and thin army blanket, which gave little warmth to the body lying between the covers at a time when it was most needed. Basic comfort was the only word to describe it.

Beyond the screen she heard the murmur of William Rufus's rustic drawl, followed by the clipped tones of another man in response, and then a softly spoken third one in the background intoning a prayer. She had heard the physician say that a new surgeon and army chaplain had arrived, but had little expectation of being noticed by them in the few hours she would spend here. It was better if her presence did not come to Dr Althorpe's attention.

"Mary…" a failing voice called in the shadows.

"I'm here," said Nell, moving forward to grasp the dying man's hand, as she had done for so many in their final moments.

"Please…tell Mary and the children…" The man's voice ended on a cough.

She leaned closer to hear the words and smelt death on his breath, and knew that it was only minutes away.

"Take the paper from my breast pocket, but don't let anyone see…"

With a surprisingly purposeful hand he guided her fingers to the inner pocket of his tunic, and held it there. She felt the edge of a leather pouch and a crumpled sheet of paper.

"What must I do with it?" Nell whispered.

"Give it to Mary," he said, "it will prove her right to have…" The soldier's voice faded into oblivion with the effort, leaving Nell's hand in his pocket. She withdrew the contents and looked at them, wondering who Mary might be, and where the woman could be found. Then she recalled his words, *don't let anyone see…*

Slipping the whole into her pocket, she felt for his pulse and closed his eyes for the last time. She stood up intending to call William Rufus, but found herself under the scrutiny of a hard-faced stranger wearing an officer's uniform.

His piercing eyes took in every movement, and she realised he must have watched the last scene but, too far away to hear the conversation, misinterpreted it.

"Sir," she said. "He's…"

"Dead…and you could not wait long enough to close his eyes with a modicum of respect before you picked his pocket."

"No, sir," she breathed, in disbelief.

"Come here, woman, and show me the contents of your pocket."

As she moved towards him, the scene in the darkened barn shifted back to the occasion at Middlebrook Fair when a stallholder accused her of stealing. She closed her eyes to shut out the painful memory.

"What…is…your…name?" he ground out the words. "Tell me, or I will wring it out of your thieving mouth."

"I am Nurse Walcote," she said, knowing that wearing breeches did not help her situation. "I did not steal this. The man asked me to give it to Mary." Nell held out the soft leather pouch that she now realised contained coins, and the still warm, folded sheet of paper, much crumpled from the long hours it had been in the soldier's inner pocket.

"Nurse Walcote...?" he said, injecting every syllable with contempt. "What right would a doxy like you have to use the title?"

"She uses it on my authority, Gideon," said a quiet voice, none the less welcome for its chill tone. "And I will thank you not to insult my employee."

She had not heard Dr Althorpe's approach, but was glad of his presence.

"If you will excuse me, sir," the surgeon's manner was rigidly formal. "A patient has just died, and I must confirm his passing." With that he turned away.

"Nell, it is not fitting for you to be here amongst these men," said Dr Althorpe.

"I don't know who the man was, sir, but he wanted his family to have this," she said, still clutching the contents of her pocket.

Dr Althorpe led her to a table in the lighted area near the stove, where the surgeon had been writing his report. "Sit down," he said, "while I sort this matter out."

Nell felt sick, and not only from the tiredness of a long day. She wanted to cry, much as she had been tempted at school, but the thought of those bad times gave her strength. *Oh, Meg, where are you?*

From nowhere, a hand touched her shoulder, and as she felt its comforting warmth, knew the origin of the voice that came to her in the darkness. "It's time that you were home in your bed, little one."

At the sound, Nell's tears of relief began to flow.

"Mistress Chapel, you come at an opportune moment," said Dr Althorpe.

"I came to offer my help, sir," said Meg, "but the girl should not be here."

Nell heard the thinly veiled anger in Meg's tone, and felt protected.

"Indeed, you are right, Mistress Chapel. However, there is a matter for Sergeant Percival to resolve, and then I will take Nell home."

"Nurse Walcote," said a deep voice, from the shadows. "Captain Hawser tells me that you have something that belonged to Private Easthope."

Nell looked up in surprise, but the face she saw was a mirror image of the woman holding her shoulder. Somewhat older, with shorter hair streaked with grey at the temples, but undoubtedly a close likeness. Similarly, the man looked astonished.

"Good God, a female in the old gentleman's likeness," he said, with a humourless laugh. "Now I've seen everything."

"It happens to us all sooner or later," Meg Chapel said with equal dryness.

Nell offered him the leather pouch and folded paper. "The man that died, Private Easthope, asked me to give these to Mary. He said to tell her and the children…" Her voice broke, knowing the endearment the man had intended. She turned and buried her face against Meg's chest.

"Leave her alone," Meg growled.

"What about the manner in which she acquired it?" the surgeon's accusing voice came from the darkness.

"There is nothing to discuss, Gideon," said the physician wearily. "Sergeant Percival will deal with the matter. It probably relates to Easthope's army pension, and his farewell to his family. The man was lucky to have retained it so long on the road." He turned aside, "I leave it in your hands, Mr Percival."

"Yes, sir; I have the man's details, and will ensure that they receive it."

"Come, Nell," he said. "We can safely leave Mistress Chapel to attend the patients in your stead. I am sure that Captain Hawser will wish to give her a report on their condition. He and I will communicate at the surgery tomorrow."

"The horse is in the stable," she said, remembering how she had come.

"Yes, I know," he said. "I recognised it when I arrived. William Rufus can tie the reins to the gig."

★★★

James could not deny that he was pleased with the outcome, but not the means by which it was achieved. He knew that if ever Mrs Fulmer heard a whisper, she would not be happy, nor would his wife. Nell was to be

195

protected, and in that moment, he had failed to do so. Not least because she had gone out riding a horse wearing breeches, not only alone but in a manner that no lady should ever be seen doing.

He was relieved that Nell accepted his dictate that Elizabeth should not be told of her absence from the house. And even though he suspected that Florence Fish guessed the dirty footprints in the hallway were too small to belong to him, she did not allude to the fact.

Whilst he could imagine how chafed Nell must feel by the restrictions placed on her movements, Mrs Fulmer's intention for her to be a lady sealed his lips. At least he could be sure after their unexpected meeting that Gideon Hawser, a charmer with the ladies, would be circumspect in his behaviour towards Nell.

Flirtatious he might be, but Gideon was also a gentleman and would not attempt to seduce James's nurse, under the physician's roof. Not least because the young man was committed to undertaking a year or two of medical study in London before he could afford to take a wife of his own class. Similarly, Peter, his twin, would return to Oxford to complete his studies in Divinity. With those facts in mind, James was content to rest easy.

***

Instead, he was reminded of the event the following morning. Hardly had James entered his surgery at nine o'clock, than Will Bucknole showed a visitor through the door. "Captain Hawser wants to see you, sir."

From the officer's less than pristine appearance, he had obviously come from the cruck barn, without stopping to shave or change his clothes.

"Good morning, Gideon," said James. "Do you have a crisis to report?"

"May I ask for a moment of Nurse Walcote's time?" his tone was jerky.

"Why?" said James. "If it is to torment her further, then I ask you to stop for you have already caused great offence."

Shock at his blunt reception was replaced by embarrassment. "Sir, I come to offer my profound apologies for the embarrassment I caused you last night; and, if you would permit me to speak with Nurse Walcote, the distress to her. My only excuse being that I had no expectation of seeing *a lady* dressed like that. Such women are usually…" He stopped, at a loss to

196

know how to continue.

James ignored the inference and said, "What you saw, in fact, was a kind soul helping a dying man to find peace."

"I wish to make my apologies."

"It is better for you to do so through me, Gideon, and leave it at that."

"I ask your pardon and that of Miss Walcote – if that is how she is known."

"It is," said James, intending to close the conversation.

"May I ask what you know of her connection with the gypsy woman?"

"What is your reason for asking?"

"There was *a closeness* between them." His words came out as accusatory.

"Mistress Chapel is an experienced midwife and herbalist, Gideon. Nurse Walcote is one of her students, whose skills are well regarded in my practice. She is also an orphan, and I would take it as a kindness if you would refrain from probing further into her history."

"In that case, sir," said the officer stiffly. "Maybe it would be better in the circumstances, if I do not visit the house."

"Nonsense," said James. "That course of action would cause distress to my wife, and I do not think that is your intention. I will convey your message to Nurse Walcote, and we will consider the matter closed."

James sensed, from the younger man's expression, that he had inadvertently fuelled, rather than quelled his curiosity. A thought reinforced when Gideon visited with his brother, later in the day, to take tea, and Elizabeth said, "James, where is Nell? I would like to introduce her to…"

"Bucknole is taking her to see Mrs Fulmer, who is quite counting on her company." He turned aside to explain. "Nurse Walcote is a favourite with one of my private patients, a person who takes a great interest in the care given to wounded soldiers."

"The lady was so taken with Nell that she asked her to be a companion," said Mrs Althorpe. "Fortunately, she declined. She is such a dear girl – almost like a daughter to me."

"We must not bore our visitors with local matters, my dear," said James, watching with interest the look of astonishment on one twin brother's face, and chagrin, changing to speculation, on the other.

He had little doubt that Gideon Hawser would view Nell Walcote differently the next time they met. Whether she stopped to allow him to speak was another matter.

Chapter 19

Autumn 1815

"Elizabeth, I have excellent news," said Dr Althorpe over luncheon. "Bouldon has returned from the war. I met him at the cruck barn last night when I did my last round of the day. He is sadly malnourished at present, but I thought to help him find some useful occupation when his injuries heal."

"Bouldon?" said Mrs Althorpe. "Do you mean the former groom that showed promise and then let us down, when we needed his services?"

"His departure may have been inconvenient at the time, my dear, but his return, relatively unscathed, is a matter for celebration."

"Does Miss Tilbury know of this?"

"No, and the man is fearful that she would not acknowledge him again."

"Who can blame the poor woman for that, believing herself abandoned?"

"Nonsense, my dear," said the physician. "The man re-enlisted with his former comrades and fought for his country, but he survived as many did not."

"Charlotte believed that they were coming to an understanding, James. He left without telling her of his intention," said his wife.

"Would that have made their parting any easier? The call to arms came and he answered it. She should be proud of him, not scold him."

Listening to the physician's conversation with his wife, Nell thought of a different version on the same topic she had heard in the kitchen when

Will Bucknole and Florence Fish learned that the soldier, home from the war, was already lodging in the Middlebrook surgery stable. Something the physician omitted to tell his wife.

"I suppose that Bouldon chap thinks, by sidling up and talking to Dr Althorpe last night, he'll get his old job back," said Fish.

"Maybe," said Bucknole, "and maybe not. It's not as if he was anything more than a groom when he was here, for all his fancy ideas about learning his letters."

"It was Miss Tilbury who encouraged him to be book-learned, although what a lady with her background in the gentry had in mind I really can't imagine."

Nell smiled ruefully at the interchange and remained silent. In her case, having the ability to read and write was what had drawn her to Dr Althorpe's attention, so why should a man not wish to better himself?

She was pleased that Bouldon had survived the battle, but having seen him talking with Dr Althorpe it was obvious that he had not escaped the conflict unscathed in body or mind. Never of large build, he seemed to have shrunken in stature and acquired a nervous twitch on one side of his newly scarred face, presumably as a result.

Miss Tilbury, however, was the granddaughter of the old physician from whom Dr Althorpe had taken over the surgery. When her grandfather's death left her with a home and independent means this lady had, much to everyone's astonishment, become a teacher in the village school.

Now a mature woman of about forty, she gave half-hourly lessons after school to people in whom she saw the potential to better themselves. Although this predominantly applied to women entering service, for Micky Bouldon it was a means by which the man might redeem his self-respect.

"What did we know of him?" said Florence. "Other than he was passing through Linmore Dale with the rest of the raff and scaff from the war. Now he's back again, he'll expect to take up where he left off with his courting of the school teacher. As if a respectable woman like that would look twice at him. I'm sure I wouldn't if I was in her position."

Nell almost laughed at the thought knowing Florence's dislike of men, but stopped herself in case the housemaid demanded to know the cause of the hilarity.

The room went suddenly quiet as she realised that Micky Bouldon, was standing in the doorway listening to the conversation. His expression was bleak and Nell felt his sense of hopelessness. Florence, similarly, changed her tone.

"Well, look what the cat's brought in," she said bluntly. "I hope you've taken your boots off by the back door, Mick Bouldon, and you can wash your hands in the scullery if you want some supper. You know where to find the soap and towel – and make sure you rinse the scum from the bowl when you've finished," she called after him.

Minutes later he returned to have his hands inspected before being allowed to "put his feet under the table", as Florence called sitting down to eat his food.

"So you came back," said Florence.

"It takes more than the Frenchies to finish me off, Miss Fish, and they tried hard enough."

Nell sensed that facing Florence would be as much of an ordeal as the battle, for which he had left his job.

"I s'pose you went off breaking all them French women's hearts," said Bucknole, with all the tact of a countryman.

"No," said the groom, flushing to the roots of his hair, "only Boney's dream to rule the world. That's what we all went for."

Florence had not finished her interrogation. "Are you just passing through the area, or stopping this time?"

The man looked at her and said quietly, "I was hoping to find my half-sister that used to work for a parson in this area, just as I was last year."

"Oh, so you have family hereabouts, do you? What's her name?"

"It was Dora Peckledy, when I last saw her," he said. "Me own ma died, and me pa remarried. Dora was born when I were about three year old."

"It's not a name that I know," said Florence, shaking her head dismissively.

Nell knew, but she remained silent until after the supper was over and the dishes washed. Bouldon was making his way out through the scullery, when she made an excuse to go to the surgery and met the man as he opened the back door to go back to the stables.

"Mr Bouldon," she said. "I knew Dora Peckledy several years ago when I worked at Hillend Rectory. She left when the mistress died, but went as nursemaid with the parson's children to their grandmother, Lady Ullingswick. I can't remember whether she lived in Norcott or Bredenbridge, but I will give you the name of the gardener's wife who can tell you."

He looked at her with a weariness that made her want to weep.

"I'd take it as a kindness if you'd write that down for me, Nurse Walcote."

Nell entered the surgery office that she used, and drew out her notepad from the desk. She wrote the words in a clear hand, *Mrs Jemkins, Hillend Rectory* – and then added as an afterthought, *this man is looking for his sister, Dora Peckledy.*

"It's some years since I worked there, but I think she would remember me. Tell her that Nell Walcote sent you."

"I'm obliged to you, miss," he said. "Dora's all the kin that I have left, and having family gives me some roots. I'd like to see her once again."

"Yes, I know what you mean. I hope you find her," said Nell, who had no one to call her own. Meg was the closest to family she had, because she had known Nell's mother.

Two weeks later

Nell said little when she heard gossiping tongues linking the village school teacher with a soldier, newly back from the war. A man assumed by many to be seeking to ingratiate himself with the purpose of taking gross advantage of the lady's innocence.

She, however, was better placed than most to be aware of both sides of the situation. It was obvious that, with shelter and a nourishing diet, Bouldon was returning to health. Florence might grumble about his ugly face, but she was not proof against the sight of a clean bowl that, only minutes before, had been filled with steaming beef stew.

A favourite, he said, much as his stepmother used to make. Now aware of his early life, Nell knew such moments were precious. Similarly, Dr Althorpe had taken her into his confidence, as much as he was capable of so doing, by way of thinking aloud in her presence when in the surgery and then asking for her opinion.

Whilst Nell knew that any decisions would be made by him, she listened with interest when he asked, "What do you think of Bouldon's reading and ability to count, Nurse Walcote?"

"In what sense do you mean, sir?" she said, not having any reason to discuss the matter with the man.

"Do you think he might be capable of applying his knowledge if he had, perchance, the opportunity to obtain the post of a clerk?"

"I'm sure that he would do his utmost to be of service, sir," she said, wondering if he meant in the surgery. Then she realised it would mean coming into conflict with Bucknole, who jealously guarded his domain.

"Mr Skimblescott, the apothecary, was telling me that one of his apprentices was completing his tenure, and wondered if I knew of anyone who might fill the space until he could find a replacement. He did admit that the payment he was able to offer is insufficient for anyone with a family, and the situation unlikely to encourage a young man to stay.

"I asked if he had considered retaining one apprentice, and training a clerk to attend the paperwork. When he agreed, I wondered if I might also consider a similar remedy to the matter of finding a medical assistant," he mused.

Nell waited to hear what he had decided.

"I suggested to the apothecary that Bouldon might be an option, but stressed that it might be wise to arrange for the man to have additional tuition. Do you suppose he would be prepared to accept a nominal wage during his training? He will, of course, be expected to work regular hours and study in his own time."

She looked at him in surprise, realising that he was truly asking her opinion.

"I know that he would like to find honest occupation, sir," she said, not liking to mention the stepsister of which Bouldon had told her.

"I have no doubt he is concerned about how people in the village receive him."

"Yes, sir," she said, knowing to whom he referred.

"Then we must do our utmost to assist the man to restore his self-respect."

Somehow, Nell guessed his plan would involve her as well.

"Goodnight, Nurse Walcote. Thank you for coming; I have so enjoyed your company. Are you sure you will be safe crossing the road to the surgery garden?"

"Of course, Miss Tilbury," she said, "I have my *night-eyes*."

When the lady laughed, she was unaware that bright lights in a house were more unfriendly to Nell than the night sky. This was a time of day when she thought of Meg, and felt safe. Needless to say Nell held the lantern aloft to light her way across the road before slipping through the solid wooden gate and locking it, then leaving the key in the alcove of the high garden wall where another lantern hung.

It was a cold clear night, but she stood looking up at the stars, thinking back to other times and places where she had done likewise. Nights when she had slept on the ground, rolled in a blanket with Meg for company. She shivered as loneliness touched her soul, and drew her grey cape closer, the one without which she would not travel. The colour was faded and worn, and the cloth had long since lost the scent of its original owner, but she kept it as a talisman – a memory that she would treasure to her last breath, even if she never saw him again.

She sighed and stepped forward along the path, then stopped, her senses tense with awareness. Her nose twitched with distaste, smelling tobacco smoke, and knew she would have to run the gauntlet of seeing one of the two Hawser brothers.

Nell had hoped that by saying she was going to Miss Tilbury's reading class on the evening before their departure, she might avoid seeing them again; assuming she would be out on her rounds before they finished breakfast. Now it seemed that one of them was in the garden, and she guessed who it would be.

Lieutenant Peter Hawser, the army chaplain, was rigidly polite, which suited her well. He had not spoken of seeing her in the cruck barn, but his twin brother's dark eyes followed her every movement, full of condemnation. She could sense him in the shadows, awaiting his opportunity to scold. Why could he not have left her alone for one more night?

Tomorrow, he could think as many bad thoughts as he chose – without her knowing – or possibly caring what he thought of her. Maybe if she stood here a while longer he would grow tired of waiting, but she knew if she delayed, Florence would eventually send Will Bucknole out to find her, and he would scold her for the inconvenience of being sent out in the cold night air, when he was comfortably ensconced by the kitchen fire.

As she made a move to step forward, Nell heard the sound of her name being called softly, gently, almost caressingly from the shadows. She shivered, feeling a frisson of awareness, but not of fear, running down her spine.

"Nurse Walcote," he repeated her name. "You should not be out here… alone."

She turned towards the sound and found Captain Hawser, tall and imposing in her path. His presence surrounded her with a masculine scent that was particularly his own mixed with a faint hint of cigars – but not in a threatening way that she had felt in Dr Frogg's company. Strangely, it was quite the reverse.

"I have been attending Miss Tilbury's reading class, sir," she burst out, knowing it was only half the truth, for tonight little reading had been done.

"Tilbury?" he said questioningly.

"The lady's grandfather was physician before Dr Althorpe, sir," she said, wondering what else he had to say before she could escape to the warmth of the kitchen and Florence's inquisitive questions. He had not moved but she felt that he compelled her to stay.

"My brother and I leave Middlebrook tomorrow to return home before resuming our various studies. It is unlikely that I will have another chance to speak with you in private for some time."

"*Sir?*" she said, wondering why he wanted to single her out if only to scold.

"I wanted to express…my apologies for my behaviour at the barn. It was unforgivably rude, and I crave your pardon. The kinds of females who wear breeches and ride astride are not considered gentlewomen."

"Why are you saying this to me, sir? I am Dr Althorpe's employee, not family. In my position I do not expect…" She almost said "courtesy".

"Then you should expect to be admired; but seeing you wearing such clothes, it was for all the wrong reasons," he said, taking her hand and raising it to his lips, and then turning it over to press a gentle kiss to her palm.

"Go indoors, sweet Nell, before I forget that I am supposed to be a gentleman and take advantage of your innocence. The memory of you in breeches haunts my sleep. I cannot think of any other woman – even for pleasure."

Nell turned away confused by the passion in his voice.

"Please…don't give your heart away before I return. Save it for me."

She ran away before he could ask more of her than she could promise.

Rather than face Florence's probing questions, Nell pleaded a headache when she reached the kitchen, but accepted a drink of warm milk and honey before slipping up the backstairs to bed. But it was long before she slept.

Her thoughts were on the scene in the garden and the confidences that Miss Tilbury had shared with her, having begged for an hour of her company. Nell had visited the lady during her morning rounds thinking she went to offer a remedy for women's problems, and discovered that it was a confidante the lady needed to tell of a secret love, which she supposed unshared.

Nell had explained, in the same vein of secrecy, that Micky Bouldon, although his name was not mentioned, had come to Linmore Dale originally to find a long-lost sister, and stayed for different reasons.

Having survived the war, he was drawn back to Middlebrook for the same reason he had stayed, and Dr Althorpe, knowing that the man wished to better himself, had suggested that the village apothecary trained him as a clerk. The news drew tears from the lady and a hug for Nell.

Then Miss Tilbury drew back. "Are you sure it was his sister that he was seeking? Do not spare me if it was not. I would rather know."

"He told me that Dora Peckledy, his half-sister, was born from his father's second marriage. I knew her when I worked at Hillend Rectory, but she moved to work with Lady Ullingswick's grandchildren before I left…" Nell stopped, afraid of being asked why she had given up an apparently respectable job.

Miss Tilbury, however, was smiling. "Lady Ullingswick and my mother were friends in their youth. I wonder if Mama realised how closely we were situated to the lady's daughter when she lived at Hillend. It cannot be more than six miles away," she said. "I still have her address somewhere, so will write to enquire about the nursemaid's whereabouts. Mr Bouldon might find it useful…"

Nell had been thinking of the strange coincidence when she had locked the garden gate. Now, cocooned under the bedclothes, she spared a thought for Captain Hawser's plea, knowing that the gentleman was too late, for Nell's heart had always been in the care of another. Someone who did not know she still existed – although he had for some inexplicable reason purchased her picture at the Middlebrook Fair.

Chapter 20

Spring 1816

Linmore Dale seemed strangely quiet in the spring when the last of the old soldiers, as James still called them, had gone on their way. Before leaving they had packed up the stores of beds and pallets, and cleaned out the cruck barn. Stained mattresses were burned, and everyone hoped they would never be needed again. The cruck barn looked lonely in the rain, with the adjoining cemetery filled with simple wooden crosses that no one would give a second glance.

When he heard of violent scenes of unrest out beyond Norcott and Bredenbridge, James hoped that Linmore Dale would remain unscathed. Amongst it all, babies were born, old people and the not so old died, and the gentry called him to attend their needs, real and imaginary.

The long cold winter had been relentless in filling the Linmore and Middlebrook churchyards. More often than not, when James prescribed lungwort for patients with chest complaints and willow bark tea for fevers, Skimblescott, the apothecary, concurred that the old remedies were best.

He could not recall how many times Meg Chapel had slipped away under cover of darkness, presumably to deliver babies for the poor. He wondered if she ever stopped to eat or sleep, for he had never seen her close her eyes or a morsel pass her lips. He only knew they could not have coped without her poultices for the war wounds.

When Easter came and went the cold damp weather continued to seep into everyone's bones, filling the churchyard as surely as any war. As did hunger, but that was insidious. Usually, Linmore Dale was ablaze with ripening corn and barley fields in the summer, but a year on from the Waterloo battle, it presented a different picture.

The deep winter snow left waterlogged fields in the spring and now stunted growth rotted in the soil. Farmers did their best, and the old soldiers had offered to help but a wet spring was not the time for digging drainage ditches – while farm workers, already disgruntled, saw them as a threat to their jobs.

Last year's mediocre harvest was bad but this year would be considerably worse if the sun did not show its face.

Micky Bouldon, however slight and unprepossessing in appearance, thrived in his new occupation, a better clerk than ever he had been a groom. One day, James could imagine that he might, with a little prompting, propose marriage to his lady love – or if he did not, Miss Tilbury would arrange the matter so smoothly as to make him think it was his idea.

When Skimblescott, the apothecary, first dropped a hint in James's ear, he suspected that Nell was already privy to the plan.

The wedding day was dull and overcast, with a prospect of rain in the evening, but the mood was cheery. The couple, quiet and plainly dressed, celebrated their nuptials in the physician's house with tea and cakes donated by Mrs Fulmer after Nell mentioned her inability to attend the lady on that particular day.

Children from the village school attended the service, as did the apothecary's apprentice who acted as best man for the groom, with Nell as bridesmaid.

Dr Althorpe gave the bride away in memory of her grandfather, a recollection that left not a dry eye in the church. And a lullaby through which the schoolchildren warbled their happy little way similarly brought a lump to James's throat.

Watching the bride and groom make their vows, he observed Nell in attendance, and wondered how long it would be before he, in loco parentis, led her up the aisle. First, he had the difficult task of finding her a husband of his class who was acceptable to her. That was the problem, for she needed someone who would not crush her gentle spirit. Better by far to leave her unwed than risk that.

When Miss Tilbury told Nell the news, she begged her to be her bridesmaid. "Oh, please, Nurse Walcote, stand as my friend, for I have no others."

In accepting, Nell wondered what it involved, and found that she must attend the reading of the banns in the bride-to-be's company, visit the haberdashery shop in the village to help choose material for a new gown of serviceable quality, and accept new ribbons to trim her Sunday-best dress and hat in thanks.

Clearly this was not going to be an extravagant event. A jacket and trousers was cut down to size for the bridegroom from one stored in mothballs, which had belonged to the lady's brother before his untimely death. The sentiment brought tears to Bouldon's eyes, never having worn anything of such good quality.

When Dora Peckledy came to her brother's wedding, Nell saw her for the first time in ten years. She arrived, thanks to Lady Ullingswick's kindness to Miss Tilbury, in the lady's second best coach to support her newly reacquainted brother – and told Nell that he was an apothecary's clerk.

"Oh, but you'd know that, for he said it was you who put him in touch with me. Fancy you knowing Miss Tilbury as well. I suppose she's now my sister Charlotte, but I don't feel that I know her well enough to call her that."

Nell nodded agreement.

"How old were you when you came to the rectory?" said Dora, who had a carrying voice.

"About ten, I think," said Nell, knowing it was twelve years ago.

"And I left two years later, when the mistress died," said Dora. "But I'll never forget how scared you were on that first day when you looked in through the scullery door at the rectory – poor little thing that you were, coming to see the housekeeper with your grubby clothes and tangled hair…"

"Ah, Nurse Walcote," a familiar voice interrupted Dora's recollections. "This must be Bouldon's sister. Introduce her, if you please."

"Miss Peckledy," said Nell. "This is Dr Althorpe, my employer."

At the introduction to gentry, Dora's tone became obsequious and all thoughts of Nell as a foundling were forgotten.

"Indeed," he said. "You were not at Hillend Rectory, I think, when I last attended Reverend Snitterfield?"

"No, sir," said Dora. "I've been with Lady Ullingswick ever since she took her daughter's children into care. Miss Petunia Snitterfield not having the patience."

"Quite so, Miss Peckledy, I recall the lady's temperament, but this is a day of celebration for your brother, not a recollection of past misfortunes," he said, and moved on to speak with other guests.

"Very gentlemanly," said Dora, congratulating Nell on her good fortune in having secured the physician as an employer.

Nell hoped the woman would not ask what happened in the intervening years to prepare her for such a position. Fortunately, Miss Tilbury, now Mrs Bouldon, called her. "Nurse Walcote, will you be coming for your reading practice this evening?"

"But I thought…" she said. "You have Mr Bouldon…and Miss Peckledy as a visitor." It sounded a lame excuse.

"Bouldon says that he must make up for lost time in the office this evening, and his sister is quite exhausted by the journey, and needs to rest before returning to Bredenbridge tomorrow."

"If you are sure, ma'am," she said, guessing the lady might need some advice about the changes in her life with having a husband. Dr Althorpe was better placed to give that, but Nell, despite never having been a bride, would…do her best.

When she arrived after supper to find the lady alone, Nell learned in a heavily whispered confidence that Bouldon, having been affected by the war, could not be a husband in the accepted sense. That relieved her of the necessity of explaining the physical side of a relationship in which she had no experience – only the delicious tingle she felt when a gentleman's lips touched her own as a girl. And more recently, the warmth in Captain Hawser's voice when he told her of his yearning for her company – but she was not entirely convinced he meant that in a respectable way.

"You say that Miss Peckledy is returning to Bredenbridge tomorrow?"

"Yes, she feels that she cannot leave Lady Ullingswick for longer, and it will take her another day or two to recover her spirits."

211

"Will she visit again?"

"I think it unlikely," said the lady. "Bouldon is content to have seen her again, and his sister agreed that it should be just for the one occasion, the distance and expense being too great to make it a regular occurrence."

Nell sensed that this situation was to everyone's benefit. She, also, was relieved that Dora would not be in a position to tell anyone of her background. She was, however, puzzled by something Dora had said when asking about the former housekeeper at Hillend Rectory.

"What happened to Miss Dinchope?"

"I think she went as housekeeper for a member of the local gentry, but I don't know where it was." Nell could, however, have told her about the testimonial, which Mrs Althorpe still had in her possession, but left it unsaid.

"Best thing too, for her," said Dora. "I always thought she was more of a lady than Miss Petunia claimed herself to be. That's probably why she dressed herself up to look older than she was – on account of the parson's inclinations and Miss Petunia being jealous of younger women. She had the prettiest coloured hair when she first arrived – it was a bit darker than yours was after we washed it."

Nell tried to visualise the housekeeper with a younger face, without her black bombazine and white-frilled cap – and failed. Then she dismissed the notion knowing that the time to which Dora alluded was before her arrival at the rectory.

"Do you know what happened to Reverend Snitterfield's older children?" she said, wishing to change the subject.

Dora frowned for a moment. "The mistress, that's Lady Ullingswick, told me that they went to live with his first wife's family, but I don't know what happened after the parson and his sister went to live at Worthing, on the south coast. It seems that they decided all of a sudden to live by the sea, for their health, and both died there."

Nell, having heard a different version of events, remained mute.

★★★

212

It was soon common knowledge that Mrs Bouldon and her husband lived separate lives apart from attending church together twice on a Sunday. People understood that, because she was a lady and he was still in training as the apothecary's clerk.

Within two months of the marriage, Nell heard the latest gossip from Florence that Mrs Bouldon, in her generosity, had adopted the three children of a woman who had died in childbirth, and whose husband had since gone off to join the militia. The rumour was that she had paid the man to relinquish his claims.

"It's a bit much to bring three of them in the house, and one no more than a few weeks old," said Florence, "particularly with her knowing nothing about children other than what she teaches in school. They say she has a wet-nurse and a nursemaid to look after them. I half-expected her to have asked you to go and live with them, although I daresay Mrs Fulmer would have something to say about that."

"I'm quite happy where I am, Florence," said Nell.

"Maybe you are for now, but the mistress would love to see you married with children that she could call grandchildren. To a gentleman who'd treat you with respect, not like that Captain Hawser who looked like he wanted to eat you, when he thought nobody was looking – but I saw him. All that smouldering dark-eyed passion leaves them in need of a physic. His brother was much more polite."

Nell flushed, but knowing there was some truth in the pronouncement, she said, "I'm not likely to get married, Florence, now or in the future."

"So you're going to be like me, then? Quite satisfied with your lot?" Florence said, tossing down the challenge that made Nell laugh.

"I'm happy as I am," she repeated, knowing it was not quite the truth but she could not have everything.

Having satisfied Florence's curiosity, Nell faced Mrs Bouldon on their next reading night, which occurred several times a week without opening a single volume. She looked around for the absent husband, and learned that he had stayed in the office to study the apothecary's accounts. Nell sensed, without being told, that he wanted to make his wife proud of him. That was probably why he had all but cut the connection with his stepsister, not wanting to be reminded of his humble origins.

"Marriage is not quite what I imagined, Nurse Walcote," said the lady, "but it is better than loneliness, And being a mother, even though the children are not my own, is beyond my wildest dreams."

Nell smiled, guessing what was coming next.

"Maybe it will happen to you one day."

She knew the lady entertained hopes after Nell had caught the bridal bouquet of roses on the day of the wedding.

"Loneliness has its own sound, but I grew accustomed to that," said Mrs Bouldon. "That was why I took pupils in to help them better themselves and their presence gave something back to me."

Nell sensed that the lady's marriage fitted the same category. Living in the open air with Meg, she had never felt lonely, but with people around her it crowded in on her. She smiled, talked and gave comfort to her patients. That was a world she understood, but dressing up to go to church in full view of the gentry frightened her. And if she married, it would get worse.

Chapter 21

Late June 1816

As the treasurer of the poor fund, James had responsibility for keeping accounts. Every time he looked at the dwindling reserves in the record book and thought of the means to restore the levels, he knew that the Linmore Ball was the logical way for it to be achieved. Similarly, he knew that even the most mediocre painting on Mrs Fulmer's walls would restore the fund to a healthy balance, with money to spare.

She had so many and gave no thought to their value, but she did think about people. Only this morning she had asked about the house, which had been used as an infirmary for wounded officers. James, knowing it belonged to her and assumed that she wished to have it returned, had said, "It is empty now, ma'am. I will have it cleaned and restored to you."

"That is not what I meant," she said. "It's already been cleaned, and I wondered what other use you might have for it."

He looked at her and, recognising the warm glow of enthusiasm in her eyes, which he had seen at the beginning of her fund-raising, said, "Have you any suggestions, ma'am?"

"What's the state of the Westbridge poorhouse?" she said without hesitation.

"Overflowing," he said, "and it could be filled several times more."

"That is what I heard and the same applies to the ones in Norcott and Bredenbridge."

James did not know from where the lady acquired her information, but he knew it to be faultless. He waited to see what suggestions she might make.

"How many children from families broken up in this area are being crammed into those dreary dormitories? And how many more will be there before the autumn?"

"I would think a dozen at least, and probably more."

She nodded. "So why do we have an empty house if there are families, or children at least, who need a roof over their heads?"

"Are you suggesting…?"

"That we use the one that was lately an infirmary and the one next door and fit them out with the metal beds that the officers used. Each house has a garden where children can play. They would, of course, need supervision, so we should have to employ male and female attendants, or maybe some of the older children might be trained to assist. We must also ensure they have an hour or two each day for schooling to learn their letters and numbers."

"How many houses have you in mind to use, ma'am?" he said, feeling she was beginning to sweep him along again, just as she had with the equipment for the cruck barn and infirmary.

"One or two initially," she said. "Introduce the idea slowly, to avoid upsetting the neighbours. I know from Bredenbridge that folks can be a bit funny about helping the poor, but this is no time to worry about them. If they must blame anyone, let it be me. There is no need for your name to be mentioned, except when you protest and I overrule you in my high-handed way."

"Must I protest when I think it is a sound idea? Might I also ask if we could consult with Mrs Bouldon to see if she is acquainted with anyone who might come in to teach the children?"

"Ask whoever you like," she said, "but don't take too long about it. Call it an orphanage if you want to and say it is run by a charity. As well as their letters and numbers, we must ensure that the girls are taught housework and laundry, with woodworking for the boys. Maybe the local coffin-maker could use a trainee apprentice or two.

"Let me know when you have assessed the rooms to see how many can be accommodated. I will send the numbers to Bassingbourne's office in Bredenbridge, for him to order the household fittings. Don't worry; we know what we are doing. We've done it before."

"So I perceive, ma'am," James said, wondering what the ladies of the poor fund committee would have to say when he told them. He could imagine that Lady Chetton would sweep all before her if anyone raised any protests. "Whilst the orphanage is an excellent idea; I must admit that I did find it useful to have local facilities…"

Mrs Fulmer looked at him sharply. "Keep the one house for the village, and use the one next door for the orphanage. When it is full, we will consider where we go from there. Maybe Linmore Dale should have one of its own."

James smiled at her enthusiasm, but knew there were others to consider. "I will, with your permission, ma'am, mention it to the ladies of the fund-raising committee for the poor. And there we must leave the matter for today, for I think all this excitement will overtax your heart."

"Oh, yes," she said, "I had forgotten about that. It would be inconvenient if it told me it was time to leave before we have found our little friend a husband of your class. I don't suppose you have any ideas yet?"

"I am afraid that I have had a few other things to think about recently, ma'am," he said, knowing the lady would not rest until she had her way on this particular point. Nell seemed equally determined to oppose such a suggestion.

James was aware that Mrs Bouldon had, in her newly married state, enumerated the benefits of surrogate motherhood. He also knew that Nell had listened politely but remained unconvinced. Surely there must be someone who could persuade her to change her mind. The question was: who?

★★★

"An orphanage, Dr Althorpe – in Middlebrook?"

James had known that he would face incredulity, but he could not allow that to deter him. Lady Chetton had, of necessity, to be the first person told. The fund-raising meetings were each held at a different member's home – except for James who travelled wherever he was required.

Today he was at Neathwood Park ahead of the other members who had further to travel than Middlebrook, intending to broach the subject muted

217

by Mrs Fulmer. Once he had the peeress's agreement the others would invariably follow.

James would leave when the main business for which he was responsible had been completed and let the ladies take afternoon tea and enjoy a cosy chat.

"Yes, my lady. The infirmary property is no longer required, but I have the option of the lease to use it for homeless children rather than letting them go to the poorhouse."

"Your anonymous donor, I presume?" Lady Chetton said shrewdly.

"I believe it is some kind of business associate, my lady," he said, knowing he could imply that Mrs Fulmer's man of business was the person concerned. Having met Bassingbourne on a previous occasion, James knew he would be involved.

"I think you should apprise me of the facts before the Linmore ladies arrive," she said, straight to the point.

"My contact was instrumental in the house used for the infirmary being made available for the wounded officers last year. Having discharged the last gentleman to his home I did not feel that we could justify retaining the property."

Lady Chetton nodded her understanding. "What did *she* say to that?"

"They asked how many children from families in this area were crammed into the poorhouses at Westbridge and Norcott. And how many more would be there before the autumn."

"Could you tell her?" she said, ignoring his change of pronoun.

"I do not have precise figures, my lady, but it is too many," he said. "That was when they made the suggestion about Linmore Dale accommodating its own. When I said that I must discuss it with you, she told me to call it an orphanage, and said that it could be run by a charity – or something to that effect."

Mrs Fulmer's blunt advice brought a smile of appreciation.

"What put that idea in her head?"

"A lady in the village recently adopted three children from a home that had lost its mother; one was a newborn, the mother having died in childbirth." James knew that this, if nothing else, would convince her.

"Is that the schoolmistress? I had heard some mention of the fact. Also that she is recently married. Is she not likely to have children of her own?"

"No," he said. "Mrs Bouldon, the granddaughter of the physician from whom I took over the medical practice, is more than forty years of age, and her husband was, for many years, a soldier."

"The apothecary's clerk, I believe."

It appeared there was little that Lady Chetton did not know.

"My contact thought that if one person could accommodate three children, why could not Linmore Dale rescue a dozen?"

"A charity would need to have a committee and chairperson, Dr Althorpe."

"Indeed, ma'am," he said, thankful for her understanding.

"Someone with experience of fund-raising, I suppose?"

James nodded.

"I will put the idea to the ladies this afternoon after we have discussed the financial state of the fund and our plans for the Linmore Ball. That is why Miss Jane will be here, for she can apprise Joshua Norbery in his father's absence. You would be most welcome to stay for tea, but if you have other business…"

"Thank you, my lady. As you so rightly surmise, I have visits to make."

"There is no need for our neighbours to be told about the orphanage before the Linmore Ball," she said. "It might impede their generosity, and we want them to come for an evening of entertainment with full purses and an open mind."

"How true, ma'am," he said. "May I tell my *contact* that you are giving the matter some thought?"

"Can you not reveal the person's name?" she said, not answering his question.

"Let me say that I think you would deal extremely well together, ma'am; but she does not wish her involvement to be known. I am not privy to know the reason."

James suspected that it related to the man who, without the proper training, called himself Dr Frogg, but could not betray a confidence of this nature.

"Then we must respect her wish."

When the ladies from Linmore arrived, James thanked them for their unstinting use of their time during the previous winter, and made special mention of the diligence of the Linmore and Neathwood servants in providing care to the sick.

"I doubt if we could have kept Jessie or her brothers away, Dr Althorpe, and likewise Sergeant Percival," said Miss Littlemore, to which her three nieces nodded agreement.

James sensed a slight tightening of Lady Chetton's smile at the mention of the sergeant's name and guessed that she had recognised the Neathwood connection, but she gave no hint as she continued, "We must not forget Mrs Althorpe's family connections, Captain and Lieutenant Hawser, who worked between the cruck barn and the infirmary. I hope you will convey our thanks to them."

Having completed the pleasantries, James explained that the fund contained less than two hundred pounds, the drain being caused by the provision of clothing and fuel for the poorest of the district during the exceptionally long cold winter. He saved the monies expended on the homecoming soldiers, together with funerals, until last.

"Things are becoming more difficult by the day, ladies," he said. "Conditions beyond Linmore Dale are considerably worse, and are unlikely to improve."

Miss Littlemore brought his unspoken thought to the surface. "Which begs the question about the wisdom, at such a time, of whether or not we should hold the Linmore Ball in order to raise funds? I think that is what Dr Althorpe was too tactful to say. Am I right, sir?"

"You are, ma'am," he said.

Her three nieces objected with gasps, hands aflutter: "But Aunt Jane… we must…it is the only way…"

"I cannot deny it is the best option we have to raise a large amount of money," she said, "but it is how we, the privileged people, are perceived, which concerns me."

When the lady's nieces protested once again, James interceded, "I think Miss Jane means that she recalls the situation in France, over twenty years ago, before the war that brought Bonaparte to power – as I do."

There was a thoughtful silence before Mrs Shettleston asked, "So what do we do? I am told by my sister-in-law that the arrangements for the Ball are well in hand. The invitations have been sent out and acceptances received, including your own, Dr Althorpe. To cancel now, without a valid reason, would damage our chances of receiving funds for the coming winter."

James had heard rumours that Squire Norbery had asked his daughter-in-law to act as hostess in his wife's absence – a matter of contention with Mrs Shettleston, his daughter. He had also gathered, on his visits to reassure Mrs Joshua that her frail nerves would survive the ordeal, that Miss Dinchope had full authority to oversee and implement the planning.

Left to her own devices, Joshua Norbery's wife would hand over the arrangements to her bombastic father, but the involvement of their highly efficient housekeeper would ensure she did not succeed. He would not, however, like to be in her husband's shoes if, for any reason, the function was cancelled.

Joshua had broad shoulders but his wife was a spiteful woman who had spared not a single thought for the poor. Usually, when fund-raising was mentioned, she disappeared to Bredenbridge to stay with her family. And for all his wealth, her father had a similar blind spot.

Aware that plans for the Ball would continue, whatever the outcome, James left the meeting unsure that the right decision had been made.

Similarly, knowing that Lady Chetton had deferred making a decision about the orphanage until after the Ball, he was caught between two strong-minded ladies unaccustomed to having their word questioned. For the moment, one of them would have to accept the other lady's dictate – but for how long would Mrs Fulmer do so?

"Never mind, Dr James," she had said. "Bassingbourne can set up the trust in readiness for when her ladyship agrees, as she will." Mrs Fulmer seemed equally sure of herself.

Driving home in his gig, James recalled the way in which Mrs Fulmer had introduced the subject of the orphanage.

"Lizzy Onnybrook and I were at school together, as were our mothers, and they shared an interest in the Bredenbridge orphanage. We did the same when we were older but both married hard men with no interest in helping the poor.

"We could do something similar here on a smaller scale. Lizzy doesn't do much now. That husband of hers doesn't approve of charity – but the less said about him the better."

In not knowing the man's name, James felt that he had missed a significant part of the conversation. Three pieces of information with a connection, which escaped him, and yet he was sure it was there. And then she said, "When Fulmer died, he cut the ties with me – or so he thought."

James did not think that Mrs Fulmer would cut a connection that she wished to retain and guessed that secret communications still passed between Middlebrook and Bredenbridge. The orphanage link explained her interest in Nell Walcote, a child from a poor background.

Three weeks later

"Such a shame about that poor gentleman…Squire Norbery, I mean."

James, on his daily visit to Mrs Fulmer, wondered what else the lady would say. He was used to her strange little outbursts but this, coming a week after the event, was a surprise.

"I mean with the news, arriving in the middle of the Linmore Ball, about a rabble attacking his coach just out of Bredenbridge…"

Yes, thought James, knowing that speculation was rife, *but who told you the precise details?*

"I don't suppose it's the kind of event that you would attend, Dr Althorpe," said the lady, gently probing.

James looked at her with interest but remained mute.

"If you're wondering how I came to hear about it, then I'll tell you," she said, with the look of a child conferring a secret. "My friend Lizzy told me, because she was at the Ball. The family had expected to stay at Linmore for a few more days, but when Bradstone started raging at Annabel in front of the guests, it was better if they weren't there."

James gaped at her as the final piece of the puzzle, a name, slid into place.

"Oh," she said, with a chuckle, "did I not tell you that Lizzy's eldest daughter was Mrs Joshua Norbery?"

"No, ma'am," he said, ruefully, "I think you omitted to mention the fact."

"Never mind, you know now, so you will understand what I mean when I say about that *ghastly* man rushing back to Bredenbridge ahead of Mr Joshua Norbery. Lizzy was mortified that they delayed the gentleman's coach, just out of Norcott, by hogging the middle of the road. When they reached home, Bradstone demanded that Squire Norbery be taken up to Fallowfield Court to be attended by one of his fancy physicians, who are all talk and no action.

"It seems, however, that Mr Joshua took the militia surgeon's advice and refused to move his father after the operation on account that it might have killed the gentleman. That put an end to Bradstone dictating to everybody," she said gleefully.

"Indeed, ma'am, it would have been most unwise," said James, wondering how he could acquire more recent news of Squire Norbery's progress.

James and his wife had, in fact, attended the Linmore Ball and the family dinner that preceded it. He had seen Mrs Joshua's parents and sister, but not made the connection. His attention was on his patient Mrs Kate Norbery who attended the family function at the insistence of her brother-in-law, Lord Cardington of Rushmore. Something that James would have advised against, had he been consulted.

He knew that, in taking his father's place as host, Joshua Norbery's patience had been sorely tried whilst being harassed by his mother and spouse. It was left to Miss Jane to support him. No sooner had Joshua declared his intention to travel to Bredenbridge, than his aunt decided to go with him.

There were no megrims from Miss Littlemore, as there had been with the other two ladies. Kate Norbery had a hysterical fit and her daughter-in-law a tantrum of monumental proportions, which was silenced by her father who effectively ended the Ball. Remarkably, it was Mrs Shettleston who, with the housekeeper's help, dealt with the situation, giving laudanum to her mother, and a sharp public scold with a strong dose of hartshorn to Mrs Joshua who was taken home to bed in tears.

James had never experienced an evening like it. He had stayed long enough to ensure that Miss Kate's sedation was effective, and had assured Joshua that his services were available to attend Squire Norbery, if required.

"Thank you, sir. I don't know in what state I will find my father. It appears that he sustained a shotgun wound by some person unknown. I will apprise you of his condition when I am in a position to do so..." Joshua's voice broke, and he turned away to begin his journey.

★★★

James had visited both ladies the following morning. Miss Kate seemed quite her usual self, and oblivious of her husband's situation. A fact that he reported to Lord Cardington who subjected him to cross-examination and said that, in Squire Norbery's absence, all matters relating to the lady's treatment should be referred to him. Whilst James acknowledged the peer's presence with a stiff bow, he considered the demand impertinent.

For the lachrymose Mrs Joshua at Linmore Manor, he prescribed complete rest in bed, when it was obvious she had already decided on that course of action. Abandoned by her family and friends, it was left to the housekeeper, who had witnessed Mr Bradstone's humiliation of his daughter, to attend the lady.

James could see that Miss Dinchope was concerned, but it was not, he suspected, for the lady under her care. Whilst her manner was polite when speaking to her mistress, there was a hint of disdain unlike the woman's reserved manner when the master of the household was present.

Miss Dinchope was efficiency personified, and the Linmore servants afforded her the respect that she deserved. Even Miss Sparrow, the haughty dresser to Mrs Joshua, treated the housekeeper with caution. Hayton, the butler, deferred to her judgement in all things. That could have been because she took complete charge of the household, which relieved him of his worries.

The housekeeper was not a motherly soul, and yet something about the woman puzzled James. He knew that he had met her at Hillend Rectory, but did not think it was the only or most significant place. More than that, she reminded him of someone to whom he could not give a name, and it annoyed him. Mysteries of this kind were meant to be solved.

On subsequent visits, James was indebted to Hayton for telling him that Mr Joshua had written to Lord Cardington and to his wife, to say that he and Miss Jane would remain at the militia hospital until his father was safe to be moved. From that James deduced that the gentleman's condition was critical, which meant that whether he recovered was in the lap of the gods.

He maintained his visits to Linmore as much to hear news as to see the patients that were in no real need of his attention, beyond that which Mrs Kate Norbery regularly had. His presence gave Mrs Joshua's claim to be ill-used undeserved credence.

A strange silence settled over the estate, as if everyone was bracing themselves for unwelcome news. Letters came with requests from Mr Joshua in Bredenbridge, which were promptly dealt with and returned; but no information to indicate his father's condition.

Even Mrs Fulmer was at a loss, when he visited her for much the same reason. She did, however, say, "Bradstone is in a sulk, so poor Lizzy has taken to her bed, which is always the wisest thing until it's over. These things can go on for weeks and are most unpleasant."

What a strange world the wealthy folk must live in.

Similarly, at church, Lady Chetton asked for news of the invalid, of which James was not in possession. Then she raised the subject about which he had forgotten.

"What are we going to do about the orphanage, Dr Althorpe?"

What indeed? James had not thought about it for several weeks, but he imagined that Mrs Fulmer would have been thinking of little else – apart from how she could obtain news from Bredenbridge.

Whilst James knew that Tom Norbery had been a fit man for his age; the outcome of gunshot wounds, even with the best care, was unpredictable. In the wrong hands, they were invariably fatal; hence his concern.

Needless to say the peeress wanted an answer to her question.

"I was not aware that the committee had made a decision, ma'am."

"The ladies were all in agreement, and want to know how soon the arrangements for the orphanage could be implemented."

No one had thought to apprise him of the fact. "Miss Jane is not here," he said.

"That will not deter us," she said crisply.

"In that case, ma'am, I will ask…"

"Your anonymous lady donor for information about the lease of the property, as my man of business wishes to peruse the conditions."

"Yes, my lady," he said, "I will do so this afternoon."

"Poor Dr Althorpe," she said, "you are in the unenviable position of being caught between two determined ladies. Might I suggest that your contact's man of business sends the details to mine at Neathwood Park?"

"Thank you, my lady. I think that would be infinitely the best idea."

They parted company and James made his way to Elvington Place to apprise Mrs Fulmer of the request, knowing the matter was out of his hands. Now he must contrive somehow to acquire news of Tom Norbery's condition.

Chapter 22

August 1816

James heard nothing more until the third week, when a letter came to the surgery from Joshua Norbery. He paused before breaking the seal, hoping it did not bring the worst possible news. Several times, he had considered writing to the military surgeon at Bredenbridge, a distant cousin of his wife's family.

He knew the man by repute, but was reluctant to ask a fellow medical man to break a confidence. What excuse could he offer?

In theory, Tom Norbery was his patient, but that was all – so he waited, and it grew harder every day. He tried to recall what Joshua had said about his father's accident. Incident was a better word if he had received a shotgun wound from an unknown person. Most likely looters were responsible. Civil unrest was rife in other parts of the country – even rioting in the eastern counties.

He shook his head, tore open the letter and perused the message. He read it again to establish the facts. It stated quite clearly that Tom Norbery was coming home; not to Linmore Hall where he resided, but Miss Littlemore's cottage on the far side of the estate near the drovers' road.

Joshua begged for the physician's assistance, and said he would inform James of the day when they would travel. Then he read the postscript. *Colonel Hawser will send a report of my father's care.* That was all the preparation he had, and must ensure that everything else was organised. He looked back at the heavily underscored postscript.

I would appreciate if you would treat this in the strictest confidence.

That meant that James could not solicit help from other physicians, and just when he needed her most, Nell Walcote was not available for the next few weeks. The lying-in period for the wife of a tenant farmer had overrun, and he could not count on her being available sooner. Will Bucknole would have to undertake some of her normal duties, to ease the pressure in the practice. It would probably work, as long as no one else went into labour. James did not know how he would contrive, but he must, and in secret.

He knew that Linmore had servants capable of nursing, and would have to rely on them. Miss Littlemore's servant, Jessie, had helped to care for the wounded soldiers, as did her brother William Rufus. James was making plans, without knowing for what he planned, and would not until he saw Colonel Hawser's report.

Gunshot wounds were invariably messy things, contaminated by dirt, grease and clothing through which the shot passed. Then there was mauling about and trauma during the extraction process, with debilitating blood loss. He had seen many such cases in the Mysore Wars.

A memory flickered through his mind of the widowed lady who reminded him of Nell Walcote. If only he could remember her name, but it was so long ago. Was she Helen…or Nell…? What was her family name? If he recalled, there were two children, a boy and girl, with auburn hair like their parents. James escorted them on the sea journey to England, but had to leave them soon after arrival. He wished he could have seen them safely to their family.

Why did that memory have to come now? He was being fanciful, trying to fit a long gone situation to his thoughts, because a sniper had shot and killed the lady's husband, an officer in his regiment.

★★★

A week later, James received a visit from a Linmore groom. Bucknole admitted him through the side door to the surgery, and one look at the newcomer's face, told James the time had come.

"Dr Althorpe? I'm Ed Salter, come with a letter from Mr Joshua Norbery."

James gave no sign of having recognised the groom as a former patient, but gave his attention to the letter. It was short and to the point. *Please come immediately to Linmore. My groom will escort you.*

James's work was finished for the day, barring any emergencies. He had hoped for a quiet evening spent with his wife, but that was by the by.

Bucknole waited outside the door for instructions, the only member of the household to know where James was going. Someone he could trust to be discrete, and not disclose his true destination.

"I must go out, my dear," he said, to his wife. "Do not hold back dinner. There is a problem at Linmore Hall…Mrs Kate Norbery, I believe."

Mrs Althorpe sighed, but accepted his explanation. It was a valid excuse, used many times, and not one anyone could disprove.

"Oh dear," she said. "I suppose that means you will be there half the night?"

"I will not know until I arrive," he said, "but quite possibly."

★★★

The groom set off through Middlebrook, and continued past the river bridge, and the coaching inn opposite, as if heading towards the back drive to the estate. James followed a short distance behind in his gig, with his medical bag stocked for every eventuality.

Once clear of the village, they increased the pace, and reached the lodge gates barely a quarter of an hour later. On the way, James saw a lone labourer walking home, but there was no one in sight when Salter looked back and indicated, with a sweep of his hand, his intention to ride through the gates. A minute later, James followed him along the drive.

The August evening seemed unnaturally quiet, but maybe that was just the impression James had. It was humid after the rain of the afternoon, and barring another downpour, would be light for several hours yet.

"I'm to take you to Miss Jane's cottage, sir. They thought it best," Salter said, leading the way along a track that disappeared into the coppice of trees that edged the red brick walls, which formed the boundary to the park. They drove for half a mile before emerging into a clearing, to stop before a single-storey house. Built in local limestone, it was simple in design, and looked compact, but James knew from previous visits that it was surprisingly spacious.

The front door opened immediately, and Jessie, Miss Littlemore's servant, emerged, smiling a greeting. "You're a welcome sight, Dr Althorpe."

Inside, Joshua Norbery moved forward to extend a hand of welcome. "Thank you for coming so promptly, Dr Althorpe."

Returning the greeting, James said, "Tell me what happened, Mr Norbery." He knew the urgency, but needed facts before seeing his patient.

"We found my father desperately ill, having just come out of surgery. He has had many bouts of fever, and several times required bleeding. He received excellent care from Dr Hawser. I have no complaints about that, but…he wanted to come home…" he ended on a sad note.

James knew that if Tom Norbery was likely to die, he had wanted to be somewhere familiar, not in a cold hospital bed. He nodded understanding.

"I will let you read Colonel Hawser's letter, sir. That will explain the treatment better than I can."

James read of the events of which Joshua spoke. "Do you know how your father acquired the gunshot wound – in the shoulder, I think?"

"Yes," said Joshua. "The left one and it looks as if Drakestone, our groom on the box, discharged the blunderbuss when my father was dragged from the coach. A band of brigands stopped them a mile before the approaches to Bredenbridge. According to Kilcot, the coachman, the leader of the group struck my father a blow to the head. Horace fired on the man, but caught my father in the blast. It was a well meant action, with devastating consequences."

James knew the groom in question. A country lad, reduced to simplicity by a head injury, sustained in a driving accident at Rushmore Hall, many years ago. A tragedy indeed, for only Squire Norbery's kindness had provided him with occupation, when Lord Cardington dismissed him.

"If you would be so kind, Mr Norbery," said James. "I would be obliged if you would take me to see your father."

★★★

"Here is Dr Althorpe, sir," Joshua said, leading the way.

There were three people standing in the room when they entered. Miss Jane, her maidservant, and a strangely familiar profile in the shadows, half turned to the corner. Someone that James felt he should know, but whose identity escaped him.

He guessed the sickroom was usually Miss Littlemore's bedchamber, a feminine room, with its white walls and curtains in soft shades of blue, and few adornments on the plain furniture. A cool room, designed for rest. The bed in the centre took his eye. It was larger than he imagined a maiden lady might use, but eminently comfortable for a sick man...or any man. The thought crossed his mind, before he dismissed it and turned his attention to his patient lying in the same bed that was used by another inexplicably injured man some years previously.

In health, Tom Norbery was a fine-looking man, with broad shoulders and long limbs, without an ounce of spare flesh. Frailty made him look considerably older than the sixty years since his birth. Pallor accentuated his aquiline features, and his eyes looked sunken. In this state he looked close to death.

James contained his horror in a blunt tone. "I am glad you arrived safely, Mr Norbery," he said. "I think it was foolish to embark on such a journey in your condition, but now you are here, I need to know whether you are any the worse for it."

A ghost of a smile crossed his patient's face, making him look younger.

"Thank you for coming, Dr Althorpe," he whispered. "You had better get on with the job then, but you will not find me complaining."

"I would recommend that you wait until I have finished, sir," James said gruffly, and embarked on an examination of the shoulder wound that would have made a fit man weep. Even looking at it was exquisite agony.

James schooled his expression to impassivity, and let his expert fingertips confirm what his practised eye told him when he saw the puckered skin around the stitches. He had seen many angry-looking wounds, but none so full of tension or with such a vivid flush tracking across the chest.

A detached part of his mind recited the classic signs of inflammation – *rubor, calor, tumor, dolor* – redness, heat, swelling, and even though Tom Norbery scarcely flinched, pain.

James knew that a wound full of poison would not heal. Ideally, it needed poultices to draw it to the surface. At the optimum time when it peaked, but before it burst, he must cut the stitches to release the foul contents.

Knowing time was crucial, James spoke his mind.

"Colonel Hawser told me in his letter that you had some fever, Mr Norbery, and I expect after traipsing all over the countryside, you will have more before too long. If it happens, I may have to bleed you, which I would rather not do. In the old days, we used herbs to deal with such things. The current medical establishment calls such practices pagan, and extols the virtues of modern methods of practice, whatever they might be. I know of a herbalist, if you are prepared to put your trust in her, and if we could find her at this time of year. The choice is yours."

Instead of looking shocked, Miss Littlemore smiled.

"Dr Althorpe," she said. "Would your herbalist be Mistress Chapel, because if so, she is already here waiting?"

Now he knew to whom the profile in the shadows belonged.

"If that is the case, ma'am, I am pleased, but will not ask how you came to hear of her. It is sufficient to know that Mr Norbery will benefit from her expertise. Normally, I have in my service a nurse who has worked with Mistress Chapel. At present, she is staying with a newly delivered lady for the lying-in period, but will come here after she has finished. Now, if I may, I would like to speak with Mistress Chapel alone."

As they prepared to leave the room, James overheard Miss Littlemore speaking with her nephew. "Joshua, would you mind staying with us please? I do not want anyone at the Hall to know we are here, and if you return home it would be apparent. There are several reasons why I ask, not least because of our herbalist. Can you imagine Lord Cardington's face if he knew we had engaged the services of a gypsy?"

James could not have wished for a better helper. Had Tom Norbery remained at Bredenbridge, he would undoubtedly have died. He still might, but with Meg Chapel's mysterious herbal potions and poultices, he stood a fighting chance of survival.

"I think you probably know which potions to use better than I do, Mistress Chapel. And I would be much obliged if you could instruct Jessie in their use."

A woman of few words, Meg Chapel nodded.

Although in theory, the herbalist needed his approval to proceed, James guessed that everything was prepared, even as he walked through the door. He did not know the contents of the potion Tom Norbery drank, but could tell from his grimace that it tasted disgusting. The most effective ones always did, and he guessed that it contained willow bark to combat fever.

He watched in silence as Jessie helped Meg to apply a warm comfrey poultice to the chest wound, and a second one on the shoulder blade, then bandaged them securely in place. Now, all they had to do was to lower the light and wait for the shivering attacks that they knew would come.

Tom Norbery was already exhausted from the journey, and each one drained him more. After each episode, tepid sponging refreshed the skin, and fresh bed linen replaced the damp. The supply of clean linen seemed inexhaustible, but it appeared that Miss Jane had anticipated the need by visiting a warehouse in Bredenbridge to purchase extra bed linen. This, according to Jessie, was to be removed each morning and clean laundry brought back every second day.

Despite the crisis, the sickroom had a companionable atmosphere. While Meg and the servant withdrew to an outer room, James stayed with his patient, in company with Joshua Norbery and his aunt, sitting on either side of the bed. It was a strange situation, for these gentry behaved differently to any he had seen.

During the long waiting hours, Jessie supplied James with coffee, but there was little to do after three o'clock when Tom finally lapsed into a deep sleep. Equally tired, James gratefully accepted Jessie's offer of a reclining daybed in the adjoining room. "We'll call you if we need you, Dr Althorpe," she said.

He was asleep in minutes, but awoke two hours later feeling refreshed. All was quiet when he returned to the sick room. The door was open, but a tapestry curtain provided a screen through which he passed unhindered. Only now did he understand the reason for Jessie's discretion.

Tom Norbery slumbered on the bed with Miss Jane lying beside him, their fingers interlinked, as if by so doing she anchored him in the living world. In the far corner, Joshua sprawled in an armchair, oblivious, while Meg Chapel stood watching from the shadows.

"Is all well?" James mouthed and received a nod in reply.

He backed silently out through the curtained door, aware of seeing an aspect of the gentry that had nothing to do with Miss Kate or Linmore Hall.

Sensing that someone was watching him, he turned and met Jessie's eyes. She smiled, and nodded her understanding. "I'm making some more coffee, Dr Althorpe," she said. "Would you like some?"

"An excellent idea, Jessie; but I need to see Mr Norbery first."

Having assured himself of his patient's condition, James left the cottage at six o'clock, promising to return later in the day. He washed, shaved, and changed his clothes, before taking breakfast. Afterwards, he set off on his morning rounds, with the intention of resting in the afternoon. He made no mention of his nocturnal visit to his wife and she, out of habit, asked no questions. Elizabeth was the perfect life's companion, the soul of discretion, and James had no wish to deceive her.

In the evening he visited the cottage in the wood, to observe Tom Norbery's progress. He noted the inflamed condition of the larger wound, but guessed it would be several days until it needed lancing. He was right. It peaked on the fourth evening, and he carefully removed the end stitches to drain the foul smelling fluid; an unpleasant, if satisfying event.

When it was complete, Meg inserted thin strips of linen into the cavity to absorb the residue. Having repeated the process for two more days, James closed the wound with boiled linen thread, knowing that it should heal.

They had overcome the first hurdle. Almost a week had passed and Tom Norbery was still alive. He looked a different man to when he travelled from Bredenbridge, and James cautiously predicted a more optimistic outcome to the one he had anticipated at the outset.

"Mistress Chapel," said James, taking the herbalist aside. "I have a lady living out at Hollytree Farm beyond Middlebrook, who is due for her fourth delivery within the next sennight. I do not anticipate any problems and wonder if…"

"You want me to attend her, sir?" she said.

"With the situation here I cannot be sure that I will be readily available," he said, glad of her quick understanding. "Nurse Walcote is due to attend for the lying-in period, but I would be happier if she had your support."

"I'll be leaving here in the morning to see a couple of other people this side of Middlebrook. I'll make my way on from there. Jessie knows what to do with the dressings, and I'll leave her a plentiful supply of herbs."

"I am obliged to you, Mistress Chapel," he said, not knowing how long his care would be needed at Linmore, in addition to his regular visits to Mrs Fulmer.

James guessed that it would please Nell Walcote to work with her friend again. He had little doubt that the pregnant woman would be safe in their hands, but would need to justify Walcote's absence to Mrs Fulmer.

At least, Nell would not encounter Dr Frogg whilst attending a lady for the lying-in period. Nor did James want to place her in the confined space of a woodland cottage with a gentleman estranged from his wife.

Every day James saw an improvement in his patient's condition, but he became increasingly aware of the limitations placed on Joshua's movement. Constraints imposed by the need to maintain his father's presence a secret had forced him to conduct all matters of estate management by writing to his agent. But he could not go home to see his children, while he was supposed to be in Bredenbridge with his father and Aunt Jane.

It was the strangest situation James could recall. After the first night, he did not question the need for Tom Norbery to be where he was, for it was evident that Miss Jane was a vital component in his state of health. The gentleman had made great strides in a relatively short time, but it was early days yet so the deception must continue. No one at Linmore Hall must suspect that he was at the cottage.

Rather than put female distractions in his way, James decided that it was better to give Joshua something positive to anticipate in his father's recovery.

"Progress will undoubtedly be slow, but if we can be sure the wound healing continues at the present rate, we might start sitting your father in a chair next week. I am not an advocate of letting a patient lie abed for weeks on end without good reason. A change of perspective would benefit him. If he suffers no ill effects, he could sit out of doors for a short time each day before taking a wheeled-chair ride through the woodland. How do you view that itinerary?"

It was a prospect to which they all looked forward with great anticipation.

Chapter 23

"James, where have you been? A message came from Linmore Hall, calling you to see Mrs Norbery. I told the groom I thought that you were already there."

Dr Althorpe groaned inwardly. It had been his dread for the last three weeks since Tom Norbery returned from Bredenbridge, that someone at Linmore would summon his attention. Now, it had happened. He was tired, weary and fearful about what would happen next.

"No, my dear," he said, choosing his words carefully. "Not Mrs Norbery this time." He almost clarified the statement with *"that"*, to imply Joshua Norbery's wife, but could not lie. Elizabeth did not deserve to be told an untruth. He sensed that trouble lay ahead, but did not know the direction from where it would come. "What time was this?"

"Three hours ago, soon after you left," she said. "But if you were not at Linmore Hall, James, where have you been...?"

Three hours ago, which left plenty of time to ensure that he was not at the manor also. He sighed, seeing her look of distress and could imagine what she was thinking. Once, many years ago, she had accused him of having a mistress, and she had been right; but since that time no other woman had come between them. It was a dark time in the months after their daughter died, when, unable to console his wife he took comfort for himself, and had regretted it to this day.

"I beg that you will excuse me, my dear," he said. "I will tell you everything later. Now, I must go to see Miss Kate at Linmore."

It was the worst possible way to leave her, but he could not break faith with his patient, and explanations of this nature would take a considerable time.

At Linmore, he was met by Lord Cardington; still there, more than seven weeks after the Summer Ball. "My apologies, your lordship," James said in a brisk tone, hoping to allay suspicion. "I regret that I was called elsewhere to another patient."

"Who is of more significance?" The words barked out.

James frowned at the man's impertinence. "I hardly think the details of a lady's confinement are a matter for discussion with unrelated persons, Lord Cardington." He strived to maintain a civil tone.

The man snorted. "Are you telling me…?"

"My monthly nurse is in attendance with the lady, and requested my opinion on a problem." It was not exactly an untruth. He was due to visit Mrs Birchwood later today. "Now, if I may be permitted to see Mrs Norbery, sir…"

"You are too late, Althorpe."

"Too late…?" The words fell ominously flat.

"Your services are no longer required. In your absence, I summoned Dr Frogg from Westbridge to attend my sister-in-law. He is the newly appointed consultant of such matters."

"I presume that you mean from the asylum?" James was dumfounded. How the deuce had Frogg wormed his way into such a position? He was not fully qualified as a physician, let alone a specialist of mental health.

James left Linmore knowing that later today he must allay his wife's fears. First he would validate his claim to have visited Mrs Birchwood. If he took Nell Walcote home, then Elizabeth would have to believe him.

★★★

"Ah, Dr Althorpe, I expect that you've come for your little nurse. I don't mind telling you that she's a joy to have in the house."

Nell heard Farmer Birchwood's booming voice at the top of the staircase, and Dr Althorpe's response. "Indeed, sir. If your wife is fully recovered, another lady needs her attention. I am expecting a call to come at any time."

She smiled, guessing the lady in question was Mrs Fulmer, not one about to give birth. It was always the same when she was away from the surgery for more than a few days, and this time it had exceeded a month. She would be glad to be home, for she had missed the family as she now thought of them.

No doubt, Florence Fish would reach for the shears as soon as she saw that Nell's tawny hair had grown considerably longer.

She stopped her musings as Dr Althorpe entered the room. He looked strained around the eyes. A sure sign of tiredness, but there was something else as well, probably anxiety. His previous visits were brisk and she sensed he was involved elsewhere, but they had little time to speak in private.

Her heart went out to him, imagining him working every hour that God gave in her absence, while she sat amusing Mrs Birchwood, who did not need to have her attention for a full month. It had been her fifth confinement in as many years without a single problem, but she liked company, and Nell had attended her for three of those.

"Well, my dear," said Mr Birchwood to his wife. "I suppose we can't be selfish when other people need our little Nurse Walcote. Never mind, I have no doubt that we will be seeing her again, ere long."

He was one of the tenant farmers on the Neathwood estate, a jovial man, full of apparent good nature. "Thank you for your kindness to my wife, Nurse Walcote," he said, covertly stroking Nell's hand as he pressed a coin into her palm.

Somehow she suppressed a shudder, as she dutifully bobbed her knees and murmured words of thanks, guessing without looking that the coin was a guinea. Farmer Birchwood's fulsome compliments and offers of more coins had embarrassed her for several days. It was a relief to be going home, for she could do without the disturbed nights listening for his shuffling footsteps in the corridor and furtive rattling of locked bedroom doors.

"He gave me this," she said, holding out the gold coin to the physician, as she sat beside him in the gig.

"I have received payment for your services," he said. "That is for you to use as you wish."

"But sir," she said. "I have no need of his money. I love my work."

"And I have plenty awaiting you. Welcome home, Nell. Mrs Althorpe will be delighted to see you, as we all are."

★★★

Nell was happy to be home. Florence Fish made her welcome but Dr Althorpe left almost immediately to see another patient. When she went into the surgery, she found a note bearing her name.

Nurse Walcote, Dr Althorpe wrote. *Please ensure that Mrs Fulmer receives a daily visit in my absence.* She frowned. Who was he visiting? She turned her head, hearing the outer door open and Will Bucknole's voice.

"Oh, you're back, are you? About time too," he said. His surly tone made her feel guilty. "We could have done with your help last week."

"Where is Dr Althorpe?" she asked.

"It's in the letter," he said, not answering her question, "but if anybody asks, you are to say that it's the old lady at Linmore who takes his time."

Nell turned back to the letter, searching for the missing details. "How long has the lady been ill?" she said, unsure to whom he referred.

Bucknole shuffled his feet and avoided her eye. "Three weeks or more…"

And she had been away from the surgery for almost five, so everything fell on Dr Althorpe in her absence. It must have been a difficult time.

"I've been doing some of the visits," the man said. "That Mrs Fulmer from Elvington calls almost every day, but 'er only wants you or Dr Althorpe."

Nell nodded her understanding. "I'll go to see her now," she said. "There are a few hours of daylight left, and it is better if I don't leave it until tomorrow."

She felt the need to walk after being confined in the farmhouse. The last week had not been necessary, because Mrs Birchwood employed a woman from the village to breastfeed the baby.

Nell did not understand why a mother with sufficient milk did not feed her baby. If she ever had a child, she would feed it. That was unlikely, which was just as well for she had no opinion of men – except one. She smiled, recalling that she still had the cape given by the gentleman who rescued her. Maybe she should have returned it, but knew not where to find him. No, she thought, better forget him and do her work.

Mrs Fulmer greeted her with a glowing smile, and called for the tea tray.

"I'm so glad you have come, my little friend," she said. "Now I can be well again."

Nell sat and talked while holding her hands.

"Where is Dr Althorpe these days?" said Mrs Fulmer.

Nell hesitated before answering, long enough for the lady to say, "It is all right, my dear. I know you are not supposed to talk about your other patients. Quite right too, for if he is seeing the old lady at the Hall, then it is not my business. I doubt if Mrs Norbery would want to know about me either."

"I don't know," Nell said. "He left the surgery as soon as I came home."

"Never mind, as long as you come to see me again tomorrow."

"Yes, if I possibly can," Nell said, knowing the lady had missed her. Most likely Mrs Birchwood would feel her loss as well.

★★★

Keep our little girl safe… James heard an echo of Mrs Fulmer's voice. He had also seen the farmer's lustful expression and Nell's recoil when he touched her hand. How the deuce was he going to fulfil his obligation to keep her away from married men?

Nell's return to the surgery pacified his wife, as did James's explanation, when he finally had time to give it. He deeply regretted the upset caused by Linmore. Elizabeth was horrified to hear of his dismissal as attendant to Mrs Norbery. The trouble was, he could not carry tales of this to his patient at Miss Littlemore's cottage, at least not until Tom Norbery was in a stronger frame.

The meeting at Linmore had left James with a deep sense of unease, but he had other things to concern him. The necessity of seeking another medical assistant was becoming increasingly important. The present situation proved that he could only achieve so much, even with Nell Walcote and Bucknole to help.

The manner of losing Miss Kate as a patient had disrupted his routine.

Only a husband had the right to dismiss his wife's medical practitioner, as Lord Cardington well knew, but James let it stand. He had to, knowing that he trod a slippery slope, and one step either way out of line could betray his knowledge of Tom Norbery's whereabouts.

He was thankful that Jessie could cope with the dressings. Nell would probably have done it better but he wanted to keep her away from gentlemen who might find her attractive. That presented him with another problem in choosing an assistant, as Frogg had proved.

James knew that he had to find her a husband. Adam Whitcott would have been the ideal person, if he could be persuaded to make an offer.

If he implied that Nell was an heiress, and a vague but distant connection of his family, she might almost aspire to marry anyone. Even someone in Joshua Norbery's position would not be too far above her, if he were not already married. But he was, and a man of the world who James imagined had known many women, while Nell was an innocent maid.

He could not take a chance of having them meet unless Tom Norbery suffered a relapse and that was his worst nightmare. The strain was beginning to tell and he began to think that discovery would almost come as a relief. But when it came, he was anything but thankful.

★★★

What was going on? Nell knew she was booked as monthly nurse at a farm, two miles beyond Middlebrook, following a delivery that Dr Althorpe was due to attend. It was a lady, having her fourth baby that probably did not really need her to stay longer than a fortnight, more a case of the almost-gentry, as Mrs Jemkins of Hillend used to call them, wanting to be in the fashion of having a nurse.

She must not be cynical when there were people who needed attention. Nor could she choose her patients, even if she knew that Mrs Fulmer would want to see her tomorrow. She hoped that Dr Althorpe would explain her absence, but it would not please the lady.

The knowledge that she was leaving again put Will Bucknole in a bad mood. She wondered how Meg would have dealt with the situation.

"Dr Althorpe left another note for you," said Bucknole. "He said when you're ready; I'm to take you out to Hollytree Farm."

"Thank you, William," she said, opening the sealed letter, marked with her name and labelled, *With reference to Mrs Greenfield.*

> *Nurse Walcote, I am committed to attend another patient, so Mistress Chapel has agreed to undertake the above delivery in my absence. I want you to be there in advance of her arrival to examine the lady. Send word to the surgery if you have need of me. I will contrive to come.*

What did he mean that Meg was delivering the lady? When did he arrange it? Nell read the letter twice, wondering if she had missed something.

"Which patient is Dr Althorpe attending, William?" said Nell as she absorbed the information.

"Stop asking questions, woman, and do as he tells you," he said bluntly.

"In that case, I will speak with Mrs Althorpe," said Nell, knowing she would not get any sense out of him.

"Don't you go upsetting the missus, Nell Walcote; 'er's had enough to put up with when you wasn't here."

"I must see Florence about my clean uniforms," she said, turning her back on his grouches. Something was going on and the house was not comfortable.

"Florence..." she called into the kitchen.

"Come and have your tea. It's all ready for you, and I've got your uniforms packed as well. The mistress told me what you need, and to say that Dr Althorpe will visit the lady as soon as he can."

"Is Mrs Althorpe here?"

"No, she's out visiting Mrs Fulmer, as she has done every day these last three weeks. Don't waste any time, William's waiting to take you out to the farm."

Having finished her meal, Nell ran upstairs to change her uniform, and then back down to the surgery as she had an idea.

If Meg was going to be there, all would be well, Nell thought as she dusted off the birthing chair in the store room. If Bucknole was determined to complain, he could do it whilst carrying the contraption that had helped

242

more ladies than it hindered. She had learned of such things when living with Meg, and if they would be working together on a delivery, this was her contribution.

★★★

Nell entered Hollytree Farm through the back door and was taken straight up to the mistress's bedchamber. Mrs Greenfield reclined on her daybed, attired in a flowing nightgown, looking bored. She was an attractive woman with pale russet-coloured hair, but her indolent disposition and three previous births by the age of five and twenty had left her comfortably proportioned rather than the sylphlike pose she liked to strike.

Nell had met the lady several times before, and was received as an old friend. "Hello, Nurse Walcote. I'm glad you're here early. We can play cards while we're waiting for things to happen."

That was not what Nell had rushed to hear. "Is anything happening yet?" she said, changing the subject.

"A few niggles. Sometimes a bit stronger," said the lady.

"Is it all right if I examine you?" Nell said, knowing that she could assess the contractions with a touch if any progress was being made, but she needed to warn the lady in advance that Meg was a substitute for Dr Althorpe. The best there was, in her opinion. She placed her hands over the lady's expanded belly and immediately the questions started to interrupt.

"What time is Dr Althorpe coming to see me?"

Nell concentrated on her palpation before answering. "I'm sorry," she said, excusing her lack of response. "I needed to know what was happening."

"Is everything all right?"

"Yes," she said, having felt the baby moving, some tightening and relaxation of muscles, and seen a few changes of expression on the lady's chubby face.

"I'm afraid that Dr Althorpe may be delayed, Mrs Greenfield, but he has arranged for an experienced midwife to help me with the delivery."

"Do you know what to do, Nurse Walcote? I thought you were only his monthly nurse, who stayed after the delivery."

"I often assist him," Nell said. "I have brought the birthing chair that we used last time."

"Anything that helps to shorten the time is welcome."

"I will need to change the bed linen and prepare the crib for the baby," Nell said.

"Just ring the bell over there, and Matilda will bring whatever you need."

Nell gave the servant a list of her requirements, and spent the next hour preparing the room for the delivery. She always wore a wraparound apron and mobcap for deliveries and set aside a longer gown for Meg, of the type worn by Dr Althorpe. It was not an affectation, more to keep his clothes clean knowing that he moved on to visit other patients.

By the time Meg arrived, three hours later, the evening shadows were closing in. The room was warm and the equipment prepared. Water boiled in the kitchen, and Nell was happy with the progress in labour that Mrs Greenfield had made, but it was time for another examination. As she registered eight chimes on a clock downstairs, she heard firm footsteps approaching along the landing and wondered whether Meg or Dr Althorpe would arrive first.

Nell turned in anticipation and smiled as a familiar figure in a long black cape swept into the room escorted by the housemaid. Wearing her black hair tied back under a tricorn hat, polished boots and breeches, Meg could have passed, in the candlelight, for the physician. When Nell assisted her to don the wraparound apron to protect her clothes, no one, certainly not her patient, knew the difference. Even her demeanour was confident and masculine, which explained why Meg had arrived under cover of darkness, no doubt on horseback.

Mrs Greenfield was still reclining on her daybed. Nell was glad that she had taken some food and drink, and that her husband, a bluff, red-faced countryman, had looked through the door some time ago, but came no closer.

"Ah, you're getting on with it, m'dear," he said. "I'll leave you to your women, but I expect James Althorpe will be along before too long to take charge of things."

At the time, Nell had bobbed her knees and made suitable noises to suggest agreement and he went away to spend his evening drinking brandy.

"Dr Althorpe told me to expect you," said Nell, when she had sent the maid downstairs for her supper, with instructions to bring victuals and drinks for her.

Meg nodded, and proceeded to examine the lady, before approving Nell's inclusion of the birthing chair. "Useful contraption to have," she said. "Where's the husband?"

"Downstairs," said Nell, lowering her voice. "He came in earlier to see his wife, and went down for his supper."

"Good," said Meg, "It's unlikely that we'll see him again tonight."

The minutes ticked slowly by and the chiming clock marked each hour. In between contractions, Meg and Nell helped the lady to walk around the room before settling her on the birthing chair with the adjustable back, and grips on the arms and footrests to brace her feet against.

Meg sat before the lady on a lower seat; the maid stood at her mistress's side sponging her face with a damp cloth, and Nell waited with a bowl to hand for the afterbirth and warm towels set aside to receive the baby. By eleven o'clock a baby girl had been born and cried, the cord clamped and the afterbirth delivered complete, which left the new mother extolling the virtues of the birthing chair and the excellent care of the man-midwife.

"That was the easiest of all my deliveries," she said, with a drowsy sigh as she slid into the comfort of her warmed bed. "The chair made such a difference. I could do it all again tomorrow."

"Will you be breastfeeding the babe?" said Meg.

"Oh, no," said Mrs Greenfield, caressing her ample breasts. "My husband always wants these for himself. The wet-nurse from the village is coming to feed the baby as she did the other three."

"In that case, Nurse Walcote will give you a potion in the morning to dry the milk," said Meg, and turned away from the bed to allow the lady to sleep. "I daresay she'll be pregnant again within a month when her husband hears that she's given him another daughter."

Nell nodded agreement, wishing that ladies of the gentry realised that breastfeeding could give them a break from a perpetual state of pregnancy.

"Never mind, Nell, they do what they choose to do; and you need to rest. I'll keep an eye on her."

The house was quiet all around. The maid had gone to her bed more than an hour ago when they cleared the sheets from the floor. Nell did not realise how tired she was until she sat in an armchair behind the screens by the fireplace and closed her eyes. When she opened them again, Meg was sitting in a chair nursing the baby, but at Nell's movement, she replaced the infant in its crib.

"I'm sorry, Meg, I didn't mean to sleep," she said.

"There's no harm done, little one," Meg murmured. "All's well with the lady. She's still asleep, but I must be on my way soon."

The reassuring sound brought tears to Nell's eyes. It took her back to the other deliveries that they had conducted together.

"I've told her that you will bind her breasts in the morning and give the herbal tea for three days to stop the milk coming in. You know how much to give of the other herbs if the lochia looks heavy or smelly. And make sure you keep a close eye on her legs for any sign of clots. She doesn't look very active, so be extra careful."

"I will, Meg, and thank you for everything. I expect Dr Althorpe will visit us later."

"I daresay he will."

"I'll tell him that you had to leave."

Meg slipped away before dawn broke, or any of the servants were stirring. The housemaid, who had insisted on being called Tilly, entered the bedchamber, rubbing her eyes just after six to find her mistress still sleeping. She looked behind the screen at the newborn cocooned in the crib, and then back at Nell. "Where's he gone?" she said in a disappointed tone.

"Who do you mean?" said Nell, while guessing to whom she referred.

"The tall chap what was here last night," she said, "the man-midwife with the lovely voice."

"Oh…" said Nell with a little smile. "*He* had another delivery to attend, but never mind about him; we have to prepare the lady for Dr Althorpe's visit. I expect Mr Greenfield will come to see his wife as well."

"Not before he's been out riding and had his breakfast, he won't," Tilly scoffed. "It's not as if it's the first baby or even a boy; although I daresay he might have made an effort for that."

246

Nell wondered if he had ventured into the room and seen Meg. How else did he know it was a girl – unless one of the servants told him?

When Mrs Greenfield awoke, she was similarly disappointed by the absence of the "man-midwife". Nell made his apologies and offered the same excuse of another delivery that she had given Tilly.

"He was so handsome, Nurse Walcote," said the lady with a girlish giggle. "His voice sent a little quiver down my spine. It made me feel quite unnecessary. I almost felt as if I should know his features, and yet I can't be sure. I don't want to offend Dr Althorpe, but I shall certainly ask for the other man to attend me the next time I'm brought to bed. What did you say his name was?"

Nell almost laughed, knowing that no name had been given, and similarly that the lady would not accept any excuses. "Meggins," she said on the spur of the moment. "John Meggins."

"You're teasing me, Nurse Walcote," the lady scolded, "he didn't look like a John. He looked deliciously autocratic, so I think I'll call him Vincent."

"As you wish, ma'am," Nell said. "Maybe Dr Althorpe can tell you when he comes. Before that, I must bind your breasts and give you the first dose of herbal tea that *Vincent* prescribed to dry the milk flow."

As she expected, there was no resistance. When she asked Tilly for assistance, the girl obliged, but shook her head and tutted at her mistress's suggestion for a name. "What's wrong with John?" she said. "I've a cousin of that name, and he's footman to Mr Joshua Norbery at the old manor at Linmore."

"Nothing, Tilly," said Nell softly, wondering if the gentleman was the son of Squire Norbery, about whom Mrs Grimble had told her when she was a child.

★★★

When Mr Greenfield entered the room with Dr Althorpe at ten o'clock, he looked at his wife's breasts in eager anticipation of their lushness and his face fell.

"What's going on with all that binding?" he said bluntly. "Take it off and leave them natural so I can enjoy seeing them."

"Nothing untoward, sir," said the physician. "We are merely suppressing the milk before the breasts become painful. It is much better to do that when the lady does not intend to breastfeed."

"If you say so, Althorpe, but I don't like it," Mr Greenfield said, disgruntled.

"But Anthony," said his wife, "Vincent told me it was necessary, and you know you don't like squalling babies in the bed with us."

"Who the devil is Vincent?" her husband said.

"The man-midwife Dr Althorpe sent to deliver me. Nurse Walcote stood by to help him, but he did everything that was necessary."

Nell met Dr Althorpe's look of enquiry. "It was Meggins, sir," she said.

"Ah, yes," he said, nodding his understanding, "one of the best midwives of my acquaintance."

"If he was so blinking clever, it's a pity he couldn't have delivered the son I wanted."

"Excellent though he was, sir," said the physician blandly, "that particular requirement is beyond the ability of our man-midwife."

"It's just as well, Althorpe, considering the fuss that Mrs Greenfield is making about the fellow. I don't think we'll have him attend her for the next confinement. It's not good for her nerves."

"No, indeed, sir," said Dr Althorpe. "I think I can assure you of that."

During the exchange, Nell kept her eyes fixed on the floor, and hoped that within three weeks the lady would be fit again.

In fact, her husband did not wait that long. Two weeks to the day after the delivery, Mr Greenfield appeared in his wife's bedchamber, clad in his nightshirt.

"Oh, Anthony," said his wife, "It's too soon for any of that."

Nell came forward, "I'm sorry sir," she said, "your wife is right…"

"In that case, my wench, you'd better take her place in my bed. It's all the same to me."

Before Nell could reply, his wife railed at him. "Indeed you won't have another woman in my home, Anthony Greenfield, and certainly not one that we are paying to attend me."

Nell looked from one to the other, and bowed to the inevitable clash.

"On your head be it, sir," she said. "If your wife bleeds as a result, you must take responsibility. And I trust that you will inform Dr Althorpe of your decision."

"Oh, must I, Miss Clever?" he snarled. "We'll see about that tomorrow when you pack your bags and go back to the surgery. That's what I'll tell Althorpe, and I won't pay for any time you and that man-midwife, or whatever he was, spent here."

Nell waited as the farmer stomped from the room and slammed the door with a resounding thump, and then turned back to face her patient's outrage.

"Oh, Nurse Walcote," said the lady, visibly shocked. "It was most improper for someone in *your* position to speak to my husband in that manner."

Know your place and do as you are told...

"In that case, ma'am," Nell said quietly, "I suggest that you get some sleep whilst you can. It doesn't sound as if you will tomorrow."

Meg had been right to anticipate the husband's carnal intentions and his wife's acquiescence. Thankfully, the lady had no complications so there was nothing of concern to keep Nell there, but she wondered what would happen the next time the farmer's wife needed a monthly nurse.

Chapter 24

For many nights, James had little sleep between his visits to Miss Littlemore's cottage. At dusk there were few people to see him, or in the hours after dawn before farm labourers were abroad. Joshua Norbery had adopted the same tactics when riding on the hill. His father almost ordered him to go, but softened the directive with, "You can be my eyes today when you ride across Blackthorn Ridge." That was on the far side of the hill.

James was the first to approve the measure, for it kept Joshua active and gave his father something to which he could look forward. The only problem being the distinctive Norbery profile, and the bay gelding Joshua usually rode at home. Hence the need for a horse that would pass unnoticed. Fortunately, the grooms contrived to bring a roan within a few days of his arrival.

It was half past five when James approached the back drive to the Linmore estate. The morning was dry, but the sun was undecided about whether it would shine. He stopped to look around not wanting to be seen entering the park, but all was quiet as he moved forward again. Then he heard the muffled sound of hoofbeats on grass coming down the ride from Linmore Hill, and guessed the identity of the rider.

The drovers' road was clear of traffic when he turned the gig along the path towards the trees, but before he reached the coppice, Joshua Norbery was riding alongside and he signalled his intention to go forward. James followed, knowing that within minutes the horse would be hidden in the stable behind the cottage.

But it was not. A groom had taken charge of the roan, but Joshua stood rigid, staring at the unmistakable figure of Lord Cardington waiting by the door of the house for admittance. James brought the gig to a halt, and handed the reins to the outdoor servant, William Rufus, before reaching for his medical case.

"It appears that your father has a visitor, Mr Norbery," he said dryly, and turned to address the irate peer who looked ready to suffer an apoplectic attack. Maybe, James's presence was fortuitous.

"Good day to you, Lord Cardington," he said.

Joshua similarly addressed his uncle.

"You may well look surprised to see me, nephew," Cardington snapped, completely ignoring James. "It is no thanks to you that I am here."

There was no time for further speech, because Jessie interrupted without preamble from the open doorway.

"If you care to follow me, Lord Cardington," she said firmly, "Miss Jane's in the parlour. Doctor Althorpe, I'm to tell you to go straight in to see Mr Norbery: and Mr Joshua, you had better go with him."

Everyone complied. James knew they had solved the problem temporarily, but it would not take long to return.

"Good morning, James," Tom Norbery said before addressing his son, as they entered his bedroom. "How was the view from the ridge this morning?"

"Much sunnier than the visitor I found waiting outside the cottage," said Joshua, "and I do not refer to Dr Althorpe."

"Oh dear," Tom said, ruefully. "I thought I heard Cardington's voice."

"I am sorry, sir, but he was here when we arrived. I don't know how he discovered our whereabouts."

"It cannot be helped now. Please tell Aunt Jane that I will see our illustrious visitor when the good doctor has finished with me."

Joshua accepted his dismissal and left the room. Jessie stood inside the door ready to assist, while James completed his examination in silence. When he had finished, he said, "You do not have to see him if you do not wish, Mr Norbery."

"If not today, then Jane or Joshua will bear his tirade. I will speak for myself." He nodded to Jessie. "If you would be so good as to tell his lordship that I will see him now."

Lord Cardington swept through the open door and stopped, thunderstruck. Everyone else stood behind him, waiting for his outburst.

It did not come, for James spoke first. "I am loath to permit you so many visitors, Mr Norbery, but as you insist, I trust that no one will upset you."

He watched Lord Cardington's face crumble with shock.

"Tom, my dear fellow; I had no idea..." He had recourse to wipe a kerchief over his eyes before he continued. "It was foolhardy of you to leave the care of your surgeon." He then turned savagely on Joshua. "Now do you understand why I was concerned?"

James noticed, as the tableau played out before him, that Miss Jane's response was instinctively maternal.

"Humphrey," she said. "It is grossly unfair to blame Joshua. It was my decision to bring his father here, and Tom supported me. We have been proved right because he is still here. Even you would have wept if you had been in the camp hospital with us, watching him getting weaker every time the doctor bled him. I could not bear to see him slipping away from me."

"Jane, my love, you must not be distressed because our brother-in-law is showing his concern, albeit in his usual grumpy fashion."

As James prepared to tell the aristocratic interloper to go to the devil, he sensed that Tom Norbery, sick as he was, intended to assert his authority.

"Tom, please," Lord Cardington protested. "Not in front of the servants."

"What do you mean, Humphrey? These people know everything there is to know about us. You cannot tell me, when I have been close to death, that I should not acknowledge the lady I have always loved. I will do it where and when I choose."

Joshua moved to his father's side. "I wholeheartedly agree."

Cardington cast him a look of disdain, but his tone was conciliatory.

"Tom, I beg your pardon for speaking to Joshua like that, but he knows well enough that we arranged when he left Linmore that he would keep me fully apprised of your condition. The least he could have done was to warn me that you had embarked on a foolhardy journey, which could have cost you your life."

"At least I would have died in my own bed," Tom Norbery said.

"No, for it would have been in Jane's bed and that is the trouble. What would the neighbourhood have said if such a thing had happened?" Lord Cardington literally spluttered the words.

"It is nobody's business where I choose to die. I don't give a damn what people think of me any more. When I get back on my feet, there will be a few changes made at Linmore that are long overdue. Now, I would like to rest," he said, with dismissal in every syllable.

"Well said, sir," James remarked when the door closed behind the visitor.

"Well said indeed, but I have little doubt that he will take it out on Joshua."

"Your son is well able to cope, I think. He has a broad back."

Nevertheless the tirade they could hear outside, to which Lord Cardington gave vent, caused distress. James waited until the peer departed before he left the house. His patient declined a small dose of laudanum, but accepted one of Jessie's calming drinks of camomile tea.

The unwelcome visitor returned on three successive days, and pointedly ignored James and Joshua Norbery on each occasion. After which, Tom Norbery declared the situation intolerable and announced his intention to return to Linmore Hall.

When James heard of the proposed change, he shrugged his shoulders and said, "I suppose it was inevitable. I should have expected something of the kind to happen. It would have had the same outcome if Lord Cardington had set out to visit you at the militia hospital in Bredenbridge, and found you had already left."

"I suppose so, but now my brother-in-law has made us feel like naughty children. It annoys me to feel as weak as a kitten and unable to assert myself to tell him to leave. I trust that you will continue my care at the Hall?"

"Indeed I will. The only difference is that we must work towards your recovery from a different venue. There should not be any damage done as long as we remain true to our herbal plan of action. Mistress Chapel was most insistent on that and the one stitch on the shoulder wound is looking inflamed again."

"I expect that you are right, but I was looking forward to taking a wheeled-chair ride in the woods."

"Do not worry, Tom," said Miss Jane. "I promise you that Joshua and I will take you in the gardens instead."

Tom Norbery reached out to take her hand. "As long as you are with me, Jane," he said, "I will survive."

Once the decision was made, the grooms brought the large travelling coach out of storage behind the lodge. James was there to oversee the journey, as Joshua and his father elected to approach Linmore by way of the post road.

"If Norbery of Linmore is going home, we will travel up the front drive in the proper manner, not scuttle across the park as if we have done something wrong."

Watching the sadness in Tom Norbery's face, James knew what it cost him to pretend that all was well as he looked around the cottage. *No doubt wondering when he would return.* James shivered at the thought.

"I'll tidy up here first and come along this evening to attend your dressings, sir," said Jessie.

The Linmore coach set off in a silent procession towards the front drive with James driving his gig and Joshua riding alongside until they reached a fork in the road, when Joshua moved forward to the window of his father's coach.

"I will leave you here sir, but will look forward to seeing you both tonight."

With that, Joshua turned the horse towards his home at the manor, and James followed the coach to Linmore Hall. He supervised the transfer of Mr Norbery to his bedchamber, and promised to return in the evening.

When James arrived, he was directed, not upstairs to the master's bedchamber which he requested. Instead, Lord Cardington received him with great pomp and unpleasantness in Squire Norbery's library, by keeping the desk between them, and looking at him with extreme disapproval. James felt at a distinct disadvantage.

Something did not feel right. There was no sign of Joshua, which bothered him. Not for himself, but for his patient. It was an icy exchange.

"You are a disgrace to your calling, Althorpe," said Lord Cardington. "I can accept that ladies, such as Miss Littlemore, are prone to fanciful ideas, but I will not accept your complicity in the disgraceful events that took place across the park. As a professional man, you had a duty to inform me what was happening."

Watching the peer, James could imagine him delivering a speech in the House of Lords, full of bombastic arrogance, and exhibiting the same belief in his own omnipotence as James's older brother, who was a knight of the realm, and a complete bore – someone from whom he would not tolerate any impertinence.

"Lord Cardington," said James, looking him in the eye. "If I were your physician I could acknowledge the justice of your words, but I am not. Mr Thomas Norbery has complete faith in my ability, and he requested that I continue to be his medical attendant, only this morning. If you will excuse me, I wish to see my patient. He is my concern."

"Not so fast, Althorpe; I dismissed you in this room once before, and take great pleasure in doing so again, at my sister-in-law's instigation."

James could not allow that to be the case. It beggared belief to take her word in a matter of this severity. "Mrs Kate Norbery is not sufficiently aware of her husband's condition to make a decision, Lord Cardington," he said. "Only he or his son can do that." And Miss Littlemore, he said under his breath.

"I am her representative, Althorpe; and on her behalf, I am telling you to leave Linmore Hall, never to return. Dr Frogg will replace you."

Looking at the implacable face before him, James realised that this stupid man was more concerned with salving his pride than about Tom Norbery's health. Realising the futility of further argument, he gave a curt bow and turned to the door. "I only hope that you know what you are doing in allowing this outrage, Cardington," he said, very softly. "The consequences of this decision could be extremely grave and far reaching. On your head be it."

James's face was set as he took the reins of the gig, knowing that he could not allow this to happen. Joshua Norbery had the power to overturn this appalling decision, and Miss Jane, but where was she?

After what he had witnessed in the cottage, he could not imagine her permitting anyone to threaten Tom Norbery's life. Similarly, he understood why she had been so insistent on going to her home. She must have known this would happen. Now she needed Joshua's support.

Turning the gig around, he headed for Linmore Manor, but was destined for disappointment. Hayton, the butler, was as garrulous as could be.

"I'm sorry, Dr Althorpe, but Mr Joshua's resting," he confided. "No sooner did he lie on his bed, than he was asleep. He didn't even stay awake to take a bath after the water was heated."

James could not blame him for that, for he had slept on a truckle bed, in the corner of Miss Littlemore's parlour, for the last three weeks.

What else could he do? Taking a visiting card from his pocket, he said to Hayton, "When Mr Joshua awakes, I would be obliged if you could give him this card, and ask if he can contact me at the Middlebrook surgery. It is imperative that I speak with him on a matter of grave importance."

"Oh, yes, Dr Althorpe," said Hayton, slipping the card into his pocket, "I'll take it upstairs to his room directly and leave it at his bedside."

That was all James could do, and to wait. Surely, Joshua would visit his father this evening, for he had heard him say so...

The following day, James returned to Linmore Manor, hoping for a better outcome, but once again he was unsuccessful in tracking down Joshua Norbery.

"He's with the estate manager, Dr Althorpe, and will be out all day," Vernold, the first footman, said.

"Do you know if he received the card I left yesterday?" James said.

"If you gave it to Mr Hayton," said the man, "then I expect he did, sir."

Other than offering another card with the same message, he had to be content. He could accept that Joshua Norbery had much to do after a protracted absence. It was only as he drove down the back drive towards the drovers' road that James realised his error. He should have spoken to the housekeeper, Miss Dinchope, instead, for she would have ensured the message was delivered. Now he would have to wait.

★★★

A week passed without news from Linmore, before James finally accepted that his services were no longer needed, but he could not dispel the sense of foreboding that came to him in the dark of the night. It was an instinct that he had had about patients on other occasions, which had been proved right. He hoped it would not be the case with Tom Norbery.

Two days later, Ed Salter, the groom who had delivered the letter from Bredenbridge, rushed into the surgery. The message he brought was short and to the point. *Dr Althorpe, please come at once. My father is in urgent need of your attention. Joshua Norbery.*

"Tell Mr Joshua that I will be there directly."

"No, sir; begging your pardon," said the groom. "He said that I'm to drive you in the chaise. It'll be quicker. I'll be outside when you're ready."

James nodded, knowing that time was of the essence.

"I must apprise my wife of events," he said, reaching for the medical bag he had packed ready for such an eventuality. Hearing a woman's voice outside the office, he called, "Elizabeth, I must go to Linmore. Mr Norbery has suffered a relapse. Depending on what I find, I will probably return for Walcote. Tell her to be prepared to stay at the Hall."

How fortunate that her lying-in duties at Hollytree Farm had been curtailed.

He followed the groom with a heavy heart, knowing that Frogg had had a free hand in Tom Norbery's care for over a week, and shuddered to think of the damage that might have been done. Pray God he was not too late.

The journey took less than fifteen minutes but it seemed interminable. James was admitted to the Hall by a subdued-looking butler. Of Lord Cardington there was no sign, but Joshua Norbery awaited him on the landing, worry etched in his face.

"Thank you for coming so quickly, Dr Althorpe," he said. "I hardly know how to explain what has been happening in your absence."

"Let us not delay, Mr Norbery," said James. "I will see my patient and make my own assessment."

His sense of smell, honed by years of medical practice, came into play as he walked up the staircase. Stale blood had its own sickly odour, as did other bodily functions. James thought himself half-prepared, but as the bedroom door opened, the sight of the figure in the bed made the gorge rise in his throat.

Tom Norbery lay silhouetted against the pillows, his eyes closed. The man's pallor looked frighteningly similar to the colour of the sheets. His arms hung limply at his sides, wrapped in white cloth from elbow to wrist.

Knowing what he would find, James carefully turned back the edges of the dressing, and looked at the crude venesection scars from which blood had trickled and congealed in puddles on the bed. Someone had evidently tried to clean the worst of it, but the evidence was clear.

He felt anger and abject disgust in equal measures, that anyone who purported to be a physician should treat a patient with such disrespect. Not that he needed to be told the perpetrator for he recognised Frogg's handiwork.

"When…was this…act of barbarism…inflicted?" James said, hardly trusting himself to speak.

"I was told that Dr Frogg came during the morning," Joshua said. "He brought two attendants from the asylum several days ago, who kept visitors at bay including Aunt Jane and Jessie. When I visited my father last night, I was told he was asleep and could not be disturbed, which I now realise was due to having been dosed with laudanum. Roundthorn the butler met me at the door with news of this situation, an hour ago, but did not think to send for me sooner."

"Where are the said attendants?" James said, glancing around the room.

"I found them in a drunken stupor, and had them forcibly ejected from the house. I presume they are outside somewhere, and if Frogg shows his face, he too will be…removed."

That explained the mixture of foul odours that pervaded the room.

When James had completed his examination of his patient, he said aside to Jessie, "What is the state of the herb supply? I hope we have some left."

The woman looked almost in tears. "No, sir," she said. "We haven't had any since just after you left. The other doctor threw them in the fire. If I'd known he would do that, I wouldn't have left the packets close at hand."

James's hands curled like claws at his sides, and then he took a deep breath. "You cannot be blamed for his actions, Jessie," he said to reassure her. "I would not have expected anyone to have done that either."

His mind was seething. Frogg deserved to be horsewhipped for his vandalism, but James supposed that he was no more to blame than Lord Cardington, whose interference had sabotaged all the good work that had been done in the cottage. It made him angry to think that such arrogant people had the power to make laws and dictate to other folk.

"Surely we can obtain more herbs?" Joshua Norbery interrupted his train of thought. "Where does the herbalist live?"

"Up in the big wood on the hillside," said James, "but it is not that simple. She visits Caitlin Vale at this time of year and may already have departed. In the meantime, I will bring my nurse, for she is familiar with the herbalist's methods."

"No, we must contact Meg," insisted Miss Jane, from the bedside where she was quietly talking with Tom Norbery. "William Rufus found her before, so we will send him again."

Once again James wondered from where Miss Jane's original knowledge of Meg Chapel stemmed, but he forbore to ask. Faith was a strange thing and in a situation like this it was all one had to cling to.

Joshua immediately left the room to make arrangements.

As the door closed behind him, James said in a quiet voice, "May I enquire the whereabouts of Lord Cardington, ma'am?"

A look of distaste crossed the lady's face. "Well may you ask, Dr Althorpe. Having destroyed our peace, my sister and her husband left Linmore within a day of our return, to visit friends in the area."

It was obvious from her tone that Miss Jane's anger was directed towards Lord Cardington, for the manner in which she instilled the word *husband* with contempt exactly summed up her feelings.

She stopped, and then resumed in a calmer voice. "Dr Althorpe, this room is untenable; I cannot leave Tom here. Have I your permission to move him to the adjoining bedchamber?"

He nodded agreement. "If you have it prepared, Miss Jane, we will move him when I return with my nurse."

"Thank you, Dr Althorpe."

James guessed that she needed to be active in order to release her sense of outrage. Even without seeing it, he could imagine the appalling state of the room before his arrival. They had obviously changed the bed linen, and cleaned the rest of the gore, but the damning evidence of gross malpractice remained.

When the Linmore groom offered to drive him home, James accepted, realising the man wanted to feel useful, but idle hands left him with time to think. Profanities rose to his tongue but he did not utter them. What was the point?

Giving vent to his anger would not replace the blood that Tom Norbery had lost, or the nourishment of which he had been deprived whilst under the influence of laudanum. Somehow, that must be reversed.

The manner in which Meg Chapel's plan of care had been wantonly disregarded made him want to weep. A week ago, Tom Norbery stood a good chance of recovery. Now James did not want to put his doubts into words. He hoped that Nell Walcote was awaiting him at the surgery, for in Meg Chapel's absence her knowledge of herbalism was their only hope.

For once, Mrs Fulmer must take second place. The thought of the lady and her beneficent wishes for Nell brought his mind a complete circle to the man who claimed to be her nephew. He shuddered to think where it would all end when a great deal of money was involved?

Chapter 25

You must be ready for when Dr Althorpe returns.

That was what Mrs Althorpe said when Nell came home from her visits. Without knowing for what she prepared, she packed her work bag with bundles of cotton squares to use as dressings, rolls of wool padding and bandages, before replenishing the supply of salves that Meg Chapel taught her to use.

Be ready to stay… she was told. Whilst Nell did not know for how long, she packed three clean aprons and Florence added a nightcap and gown.

"Take a shawl as well," said the maid. "These autumn nights are chilly."

It was only mid-September, but Nell knew all about feeling cold, having had her sleep disturbed by the nocturnal wanderings of a lustful spouse in a recent household. She hoped she would not encounter anyone like Farmer Birchwood again, even if he did give her a guinea in appreciation of the care she gave his wife. Mr Greenfield, by contrast, had been decidedly argumentative when his will was challenged.

When Dr Althorpe arrived there was no time to ask questions before they were on their way again. To her surprise a groom driving the horse rode postilion, leaving her to sit beside the physician.

Almost from the time they climbed into the chaise, Dr Althorpe started talking. "I must tell you about the patient we are going to see at Linmore Hall. Several weeks ago, Squire Norbery suffered a violent attack whilst he was travelling near Bredenbridge. Fortunately, he was taken to the militia hospital where a surgeon operated on him and undoubtedly saved his life."

Whilst Nell recalled hearing of the town on her travels with Meg, the gentleman's name was familiar for a different reason.

"I expect Bucknole told you that I was attending a patient on the Linmore Estate. This is the same gentleman. The care he received whilst there was excellent, but for reasons best known to them, the gentry took him back to Linmore Hall and he has not done well since. I will not say why that is because I cannot think of it without becoming angry."

Although she nodded agreement, no one had told her the details.

"Essentially, Nell, he is a very sick man, and I want you to do your utmost to make him comfortable. That, I believe is all we can do for him now, because he was shamefully treated by one of whom we both know. However, I will not say more than that."

Engrossed in listening, she did not notice the direction they took out of Middlebrook village, and after that she was lost. It was lucky the unknown groom knew where he was going because even in the darkness, he negotiated a sharp turn off the drovers' road through park gates, and across a metalled drive.

It was only when Dr Althorpe finished speaking that she noticed the vehicle had drawn up outside a large house with many lighted windows. From the moment the front door opened, Nell felt she was entering a different world. Normally when she arrived at a patient's house, she used the servants' entrance, but on this occasion, she followed Dr Althorpe through the front door.

Apart from an impression of a reception hall with a marble tiled floor, she had no time to look around before a uniformed footman escorted them up two flights of a mellow oak staircase. As they approached the second landing Nell became aware of a strange earthy smell that reminded her of Oak Apple Cottage when Ted Walcote was at home. Not at all the kind of thing she expected in a mansion.

Then a door opened and a rosy-faced woman emerged, bringing with her the heady scent of lavender to replace the odour. How much more pleasant it was for the patient.

"Hello, Dr Althorpe," the woman said, "I'm glad you have come. Mr Norbery was asking for you."

Although Nell waited for the physician to introduce her, she recognised

262

the woman as a carer from the cruck barn who had attended wounded soldiers.

"This is my nurse, Nell Walcote."

"Hello, Nell, I'm Jessie. I am glad you've come to help. Dr Althorpe said you're a friend of Meg Chapel, who was with us in Miss Littlemore's cottage a few weeks ago. We could do with her now, because we were working wonders then."

That explained the excellent care about which Dr Althorpe had spoken. She did not know why the gentleman was in a cottage, but she knew that Meg would not have come here.

Nell was astounded when she followed Jessie into the patient's bedchamber. Even in the candlelight, she could see the room was at least twice the size of those in the Birchwood or Greenfield farmhouses, and wondered how many other such rooms lay beyond the doors set in the broad walls.

Dr Althorpe moved to the bedside, and beckoned her to follow.

"Mr Norbery, I would like to make Nurse Walcote known to you. I wanted to bring her to the cottage when Mistress Chapel was there. Now she is here I am sure you will feel the benefit of her care."

Nell bobbed her knees in acknowledgement, and waited. She had not expected the gentleman to greet her, so it came as a surprise when he said, "Welcome to my home, young lady. I hope that I will not cause you too many problems." The gentleman's voice sounded weary.

"Thank you, sir," Nell whispered, "I will do my best."

Shortly afterwards, Dr Althorpe returned to the surgery, and left Jessie to explain the care they were giving. Observing her patient across the room, Nell could see that he must have been a fine-looking man before the accident, but now his condition was weak. Even so, his grey eyes were sharp and his silver hair thick and glossy, which belied the frailty of his constitution.

As she watched, she had the strangest feeling that like the gentleman's name, his face seemed familiar, but chided herself for imagining any such thing.

Before they settled the patient for the night, Jessie showed Nell how she checked the wounds for any seepage.

"I know you are familiar with this, but I always make a point of inspecting the dressings before Mr Norbery goes to sleep, then I will know if there has been any oozing in the night. We haven't had any for a while now, but I like to be sure he's comfortable."

Nell sensed that she was hearing two versions of the situation. One from Jessie, in the patient's hearing, and what she had already been told by Dr Althorpe. The truth was somewhere between the two.

She watched as Jessie carefully eased back the binding that held the dressing pads, and then nodded approval before replacing them again.

"That's quite clean, Mr Norbery, so I think it will be all right for tonight," she said whilst securing the bandages around his shoulder.

"Goodnight, sir," Jessie said, "I expect Miss Jane will be along to see you shortly. I'm going to show Nell the dressing room and then we'll come back and see if you need anything."

When they entered the dressing room, Nell saw a truckle bed made up along a wall, and did not have long to wait until Jessie provided an answer to her unspoken query. "Now that we are sharing the watch, it means we can both have a few hours' rest."

"I didn't think we would be allowed to sleep," said Nell in surprise.

Jessie smiled and continued her explanation: "Most of the time we can sit and watch him from the chairs next door, but you still need to have a break from it as well, particularly in the early hours when you are most tired."

Nell hoped they would not leave her alone tonight, and was relieved when Jessie said, "Don't worry; nobody expects you to know what to do straight away. Most of the care will be in the daytime, but one or other of us must be here at night in case he needs us. We'll take it in turns and if you take the first rest, I'll come in here later."

She waited for Jessie to continue.

"I could see you were shocked when you saw Mr Norbery's injuries. I felt as you do when I saw them first, and I expect you are wondering how he came to be injured."

She nodded, trying to remember what Dr Althorpe had told her.

"It's a bit of a mystery really," Jessie said, "but from what we can gather, he was attacked by a crowd of ruffians just outside Bredenbridge. We are not sure who it was that shot him, but he needed an operation to remove the gunshot. It was a wonder he survived at all, considering the amount of blood he lost. He was in the militia camp hospital for almost a month before Miss Jane brought him back to Linmore. That was when Meg became involved in his care, and she showed me how to treat him with herbal potions and poultices."

Jessie's voice sounded matter-of-fact, but her expression was anxious.

"He was slowly getting better and if we could have continued with your friend's treatment he might have recovered by now. The trouble is, someone who ought to have known better interfered and it all went wrong. Now Dr Althorpe says his internal organs are failing," Jessie ended with a sniff.

During the night, Nell tried to piece together the snippets of information she gleaned from Jessie. There were many questions she wanted to ask, but thought it better to watch and wait until she saw Dr Althorpe.

The physician returned early the following morning. Soon afterwards, a younger man entered the room, and Nell had to stop herself staring, for his likeness to the man in the bed was unmistakable. Fortunately, Dr Althorpe spoke to him first and she passed unnoticed, but when the physician mentioned her name, she averted her gaze, bobbed a curtsy, and they continued their conversation without further reference to her.

Nell knew, as soon as she heard his voice, that he was the gentleman who had bought her picture at Middlebrook Fair; and the one who rescued her as a girl. Her mind was awhirl with the realisation of his identity. She imagined that gentlemen kissed lots of girls, so it would have meant nothing to him, but for her it was the gentlest touch, and she would treasure the memory forever.

"That's Mr Joshua," Jessie whispered. "He's Squire Norbery's son."

Nell hugged the name to herself. Yes, she thought, it suits him.

Once started, other memories came floating back and she realised that his father must be the same Squire Norbery about whom Mrs Grimble had spoken when Nell was a child; the one who took an interest in her welfare. How strange that she should come here to care for him at such a time.

Despite her determination not to watch Mr Joshua, she found her eyes straying in his direction. She noticed that he spent a lot of time looking out of the window, checking his timepiece, as if waiting for something.

Later in the day, she saw his expression brighten and he left the room, but he looked sad when he returned. Immediately, Jessie went to speak with him, and then came back to explain to Nell.

"Mr Joshua was waiting to see if my brother had found Meg, but by the looks of things she wasn't in the wood."

"What did he want from Meg?" said Nell.

Jessie replied in a whisper. "More of the herbs she used to clear up the inflammation in Squire Norbery's wounds when we were in the cottage. When we moved to the Hall, the other physician threw them away before the treatment was complete, and it is because of what he did that the squire is so poorly now."

Nell shivered. "That sounds like Dr Frogg."

"I can see that you know him, and it doesn't look as if you think much of him either."

"No, I don't."

Nell hoped she would not be asked to explain her dislike, but realised it was not necessary, when Jessie said, "That was only one of the bad things he did to the squire, but whatever his name was, he's not worth calling a doctor."

However much she agreed, Nell could not openly say so.

"Dr Althorpe says that you know many of Meg's secrets, so we'd better do what we can with what we have. Please, Nell, do your best for Mr Norbery. He's a wonderful man, but his body can't take any more." Jessie turned aside to hide her tears. It was the first sign she gave of knowing the likely outcome.

Nell closed her eyes, and saw in her mind the brown stone storage jars for herbs on the shelves in the woodsman's hut. *Oh, Meg, if only they had told me sooner, I could have told them where to find what they needed.*

In the absence of which, she set out to compensate her patient for the ill-usage he had suffered. She took extra care to cleanse the wounds, apply salves and new dressings, and encourage him to drink a few spoonfuls of broth or calf's foot jelly. For a few days, he showed signs of improvement.

Having been used to attending the needs of common folk, Nell imagined the reason she was excluded from the room when Squire Norbery was washed and shaved was because such grand folks might think she did not know how to do the job properly.

"Jessie, please tell me if I have done something wrong, because I have not intended to offend the gentleman."

"No, it's nothing like that," said Jessie with a chuckle. "It's because Squire Norbery said it wasn't right for a young woman to bathe him when Raven, his manservant, was here to help. The old chap felt that he'd let his master down when the others pushed him out."

Sensing that it was more about the valet maintaining his dignity than thinking her unworthy, Nell waited in the dressing room next door until the task was completed. Then she brought in her collection of salves to prevent her patient's skin becoming sore.

"Thank you for making me comfortable, Nurse Walcote," the squire said, "you are a kind soul, and your little face cheers me greatly."

Nell did not know what to say, so she bobbed her knees and scurried back to the safety of the chair in the corner, just as his son entered the room. She heard them speaking together and noticed Mr Joshua glance in her direction, but she continued her observations from afar. Later, she went to the squire's bedside when he was restless.

"Please, Nurse Walcote," he whispered, "let me feel the comforting warmth in your hands."

Nell reached out and cupped both her hands around his fingers, then waited until the heat spread through her just as she had received from Meg, and within minutes, he was asleep.

As she stood at the bedside, she glanced towards the other side of the room where his son sat in a chair, watching her. His smile brought tears to her eyes, for she knew there was little else she could do to help his father.

Nell noticed that the only other person that brought Squire Norbery pleasure was a gently spoken lady called Miss Littlemore. At first, she assumed it was his wife, but then noticed a special closeness that defied description, and was glad that Mr Joshua was part of it. She felt privileged to be there, sharing the time they had together.

Jessie told her the names of other visitors who came to the room.

"That's Squire Norbery's sister, Mrs Pontesbury, who's come from London; and Mrs Shettleston, his daughter." Another time she looked cross when a portly, self-important gentleman visited, and would have stayed. "I don't know what Lord Cardington is doing here for we can do without his interference. It's because of him calling in Dr Frogg that the master is in the state he is. He'd do better to stay away."

Gradually, Squire Norbery's condition deteriorated, and as the periods between somnolence and waking grew longer, it became increasingly difficult to ensure that he took a few sips of boiled water before sleep claimed him again.

Nell did not want to intrude into the time his loved ones were with him, but it was unavoidable, so she waited quietly in the corner of the room with Jessie, and thought back to other such times spent with Meg.

Maybe it was the recollection of those occasions, but as she sensed the pain of their separation drawing closer, Nell directed her prayers towards them.

At the end Mr Joshua and Miss Littlemore sat with hands linked across the bed, each holding one of Squire Norbery's hands. Seeing them in the half-light of the candles, the likeness between the two bowed heads was remarkable.

Nell had never seen such a loving or peaceful farewell, and it surprised her to find that the gentry wept in their grief just as Jessie did beside her.

Once Dr Althorpe had confirmed the gentleman had passed away, Nell helped Jessie to render the last offices, and it was good to know that others showed the same degree of respect that she had learned with Meg.

When all was complete, she climbed into Dr Althorpe's gig and on the way home to Middlebrook, wept silent tears of sadness for the people left behind. Nell included herself in their number, for she realised that Squire Norbery of Linmore had always been part of her life, and in her prayers. Now he was gone. It was little wonder that she felt bereft.

A few days earlier

The shadowy figure that approached the woodland cottage in the hours of twilight did so with decided steps, intending to fulfil a purpose. Meg Chapel had set out for Caitlin but, halfway across the top of Linmore Hill, stopped the caravan in response to a deep sense of foreboding.

Knowing that something was not right and she had the means to restore the balance, she parked the vardo amongst some trees and unhitched the

268

horse intending to ride back the way she had come. At the bottom of the slope near the back drive to Linmore Hall, she left the cob to await her return. From there it was easier on foot.

Reaching the drovers' road, she listened for the night sounds, which were strangely absent in the cold air. The moon coming to the full was a good thing for some, but others, like poachers who wished to remain hidden, welcomed a few fleeting clouds to obscure movement for which a waiting gamekeeper would look.

Meg Chapel, similarly, was of their number. Not for any nefarious means, but to deliver herbs for which she sensed there was an urgent need.

Finely attuned to Nell Walcote's moods, she could almost feel her anxiety. But where was she now and what had caused it?

The last time they met, a couple of weeks ago, was on a farm out beyond Middlebrook. When Meg had, in Dr Althorpe's absence, played the part of a male-midwife, slipping in under cover of the dark of the moon, and out before dawn. A trouble-free delivery, which Nell could have managed alone and had done in the past when two babes arrived on the same night and both midwives were needed in different places to give a helping hand.

By rights, according to the ways of the gentry, Nell should still be at Hollytree Farm, but Meg sensed that she was not. So strong was the feeling it had brought her here to the back drive of Linmore Hall, near the cottage where Meg had attended the injuries that Squire Norbery had sustained in an attack on his coach. She stood, sensing a voice calling, *Where are you, Meg?*

"I'm here, little one?" she whispered, "but where are you?"

Where also were the three members of a family, bound together by love? The same folk, which Meg had watched from the shadows when Mother Chapel had delivered a baby boy in the late spring over three decades ago? The absence of lights or smoke from the cottage chimney told her that they were not here now, nor the loyal servants who had hidden their presence in recent weeks. Meg sensed betrayal in the woodland clearing. A perception of malice chilled her as she moved through the trees, and looked out across the park towards Linmore Hall.

Yes, that is where they were – and where Nell was too. She felt in the pouch at her waist for the waxed packet of herbs, wishing that she could hold it out and have someone take it. But Meg knew that it would achieve nothing if she ventured across the park, for gamekeepers would shoot a gypsy on sight.

At the sound of approaching hoofbeats along the drive, she turned back towards the cottage, hoping they would come, but the horse galloped on beyond the woodland path and faded into the distance.

I'll leave them here, Nell, she thought, and then realised that Nell had not been to the cottage. Surely, if she left the pouch in full view, one of the servants would return and find them. In the end all Meg could do was hang a double portion of the herbs Jessie had used over the front door handle – and to hope.

Deep in thought, she made her way back through the silent woodland past the lodge, across the drovers' road, and up the lower slopes of the ride. Finding the cob, she mounted the horse and made her weary way to the top and out along the hill path, trusting his instincts to take her back to the vardo.

Tomorrow, she would continue on her journey to Caitlin, but never had she felt less inclined to go.

Chapter 26

It was, Meg remembered when she reached the Caitlin side of the hill, two years since her previous visit. Her involvement in the cruck barn at Middlebrook after the end of the war, and then the Waterloo battle, had come at the time when she should have picked hedgerow fruits, ready to go to Caitlin. By the time she had finished winter was fast approaching and it was too late for travelling.

That was why she set out despite the mizzling rain and low clouds that covered the hill and left a chill feeling in her bones. Starved she was to the core and unusually hungry. The thought that it was long since a morsel passed her lips made her draw the vardo aside from the path to break her fast with a dry crust of bread.

She dozed awhile, surrounded by a world of dampness, and then suddenly awake heard the sound of galloping hoofbeats passing within feet of the vardo. Soon they receded into the distance, travelling the way she had come from Linmore.

What kind of foolhardy rider gave so little thought to his mount as to risk a strained fetlock in a rabbit hole – or worse for himself? If the horse stumbled and threw him, he might lie injured for days without being seen. Or until spring, covered by snow, like the man she had found below Squilver Ridge.

Cupping a hand to her ear, Meg listened to the silence of the mist before resuming her journey. Several times on the slow descent to the valley her thoughts returned to the invalid at Linmore, hoping that someone had found the herbs.

Similarly, she debated the wisdom of changing into her women's clothes, knowing that folks she wished to avoid might see her. In the end she did so, knowing that Molly Hardwick would view a man clad in black with suspicion.

★★★

"Good heavens, Mistress Chapel. You're a welcome sight. We thought you must be dead with nobody having seen you these last couple of years," Molly Hardwick said in surprise.

"I was tied up with things on the other side of the hill," Meg said.

"We could have done with your help with the old soldiers coming home to die. And the parson saying they didn't belong, when they were born here. It's five years since he came to Caitlin, and never once shown an ounce of Christian charity. Not like our sainted Reverend Whitcott…" Molly stopped to wipe away a tear.

Meg waited for the woman to compose herself. Words of sympathy did not come easily to one who had never known kindness.

When Molly had recovered, she let the conversation drift as the carer chose, knowing it was the best way to hear the news without asking.

"You'll have to be careful on your travels, Meg. The militia are in the area on account of this by-election that followed the attack on Squire Norbery of Linmore, the parliament member."

"He's not dead, is he?" said Meg, instantly alert.

"No, but close to it the way I heard. Even if he isn't he can't do the job now, but they're a bit quick in finding a replacement. Not that it affects the likes of us, as it does the folks at Caitlin Hall.

"No sooner did Squire Whitcott's wife hear the news than she claimed a family connection through her great-aunt, to Mrs Norbery's relations at Norcott Abbey."

"You mean the wild ones that burned down Myndstone Manor?" said Meg.

"Yes, and a rum lot they were too; but it don't do to say that in the gentry's hearing," said Molly. "I suppose that might explain Mr Cedric's

272

wild ways. Although to be right, he's Lieutenant Whitcott now, being as he's in the militia."

Meg noted the news with a grimace, but passed it off with a wry comment.

"Too much lead in the water poisons the mind. Red clover or garlic might help those that understand the need."

"Yes," said Molly, "but he's not one that's likely to be amongst their numbers. He's more than likely afflicted with the great pox."

Having agreed on the failings of the Squire's younger son, Molly continued. "It's a bad time for folks going into winter with food in short supply, except in households where there was always plenty. Elsie gets her meals at the rectory and brings a few victuals home for me, but if the parson's wife knew she'd be out of a job.

"It's no wonder there's rioting in the towns with so many folks turned off from the factories. It was bad enough with the war going on for so long, but this is worse. I doubt if you have many herbs this year, with the wet spring and summer."

"Not many," Meg said, "but you can have what I can spare."

"With this kind of autumn, I reckon I'll need them."

"It's the same everywhere," said Meg.

She started to see the attack on Squire Norbery differently. It was tragic, and he was a good man, but starving folk saw him as part of a government that made bad laws and kept them hungry. The aristocracy were the same, with no idea how poor people lived or any interest in finding out. Maybe it was for the best if the gentleman from Linmore Hall gave up politics and stayed at home.

As long as he recovers… said a little voice that made Meg shiver.

"Elsie says that Mr Cedric and his friends in the militia use the attack on the politician as an excuse for blood sports. They chase the common folk like foxes on the hunting field. Many locals are afraid to leave their houses, and yet if the ones with jobs don't, they lose everything."

"Was he the one that increased the use of our herbal tea a few years ago?" said Meg, recalling a bully riding a thoroughbred that she had taught a salutary lesson in horsemanship.

"Yes," said Mollie with a grimace, "that's the one."

"But if he's in the militia, surely he's based out by Bredenbridge?"

"Yes, but he volunteers for militia duties out here, so he can hide away at home. He and his friends have stirred up so much trouble that Squire Whitcott is ordering his nephew, who was a Captain in the regular army, to join the militia, but Mr Adam says that he has other things to do besides play at soldiers like Mr Cedric."

Meg wondered if they, or others like them, caused the attack on the politician.

"I sometimes wonder if he's still involved in army work, but without a uniform."

"A spy?" said Meg.

"I suppose it does sound fanciful. He's not the type to do anything underhand. He's as good-natured as his father was."

You never could tell who a gentleman in fine leather boots might meet on the hills, Meg thought, recollecting the body she found in the snow a few years before. *Maybe that was why he had been there.*

"The Squire's wife called him a coward," said Molly. "She's never forgiven her husband for making no secret of the fact that his twin brother won the lady that he would have wed – or that Mr Adam is the kind of son he always wanted."

"It happens a lot in their world," said Meg dryly.

"Yes, but it made her spiteful. That's why the rector's widow was turned out of the parsonage before her husband was cold in his grave. Squire Whitcott was ashamed, but it's his wife's money they live on, even if she has no class."

"What's the gentleman going to do about it?"

"I don't know. Mr Adam rides about the countryside looking at things and talking to the old soldiers. I think he'd like to help them, but I can't see how."

"How do you know all this?" said Meg.

"Elsie hears the news from the housekeeper who has a sister working at the Hall. She says that the rectory isn't the same as when Parson Whitcott was alive, and now his widow's died as well, these last twelve months."

"What about their son?" she said, knowing Molly wanted to tell her.

"Mr Adam lived with his mother after he left the army, but since her death he moved to a house that he was supposed to inherit from his grandmother. It only came to light when his mother's will was read. That upset the lady at the Hall because she wanted to sell it to one of her friends.

"And," said Molly, warming to the theme, "it seems that a clause in his grandfather's will says if both of Squire Whitcott's sons die without a legal heir, Mr Adam will inherit the estate. That was why they hoped he'd die in the war."

"I doubt if Mrs Squire Whitcott relishes that prospect," said Meg.

"What happened to Nell?" said Molly, suddenly changing the subject.

"The physician at Middlebrook offered her a job."

"I daresay you miss her company," said Molly.

Meg nodded, but said nothing of the aching loneliness she felt.

"Elsie said she'd like to work with you if you ever had another apprentice."

"It wouldn't be easy for an ordinary girl to live with me," said Meg.

"Nell wasn't a local girl, was she?"

"I knew her from the day of her birth," said Meg, not answering the question. "In which direction are the militia patrols likely to be?"

"They'll probably stay out on the Bredenbridge to Norcott side of the hills."

Meg grimaced, knowing that was the most direct route home.

"What about the villages under the Devil's mountain?" she said.

"I haven't heard of any recent trouble out that way. Elsie said that a new brigade major has taken charge of the area this side of Bredenbridge. A proper soldier, like Mr Adam was in the war."

As long as the hunting-mad officers of the militia don't stir up trouble. The thought came to Meg's mind of its own volition.

"It sounds as if he's the kind that's needed," she said.

Meg set off again, undecided on the route she would take. It was a long haul back over Linmore Hill and there might be nothing to avoid. Preparing for a longer journey home she parked the vardo out of sight of prying eyes. From a box under the bed she extracted, cleaned and loaded a small pistol that fitted neatly into the pocket of her cape. As she worked methodically she hissed gently between her teeth.

Afterwards she slipped a long thin blade inside her boot, and kept the swordstick close amongst an innocuous basket of wooden pegs in case of need. Possession of quality items belonging to the gentry could put a noose around her neck. But Meg knew it would only take one of them, in a dark moment, to save her life. Before any of them saw the light of day, she had other means to use in her defence.

Everywhere she went people talked about the forthcoming by-election as if changing one politician for another would provide a miracle cure. Meg listened to many stories as she weaved her way along country lanes between farms and hamlets, hearing of different incidents each one more vicious than the last. None that people had seen first-hand, but always something that someone else had told them.

In the end she heeded Molly's advice to avoid the road between Bredenbridge and Norcott. It was out there that Squire Norbery had been attacked, and she had an uneasy feeling that the militia would target the driver of a gypsy caravan. Especially one who had caused a huntsman that was now an officer to take a toss into a duck pond. He cursed her at the time, but if she met him again, he would do far worse.

★★★

Within an hour Meg knew that it was not a good decision. Rain came down in torrents, washing mud out of fields, and streams overflowed the roads. Progress, such as it was, was slow, and she had doubts of finding shelter for the night. Even the thought of turning back was impossible, for there was nowhere to turn the vardo. It was one of the most difficult journeys she had encountered travelling alone. When the horse tried to refuse to ford the stream, she urged him on and afterwards knew she should have trusted his instincts.

The steep road that ran up to the wood was awash with rain and mud, but Meg wanted to reach the shelter of the trees. Dry kindling to make a fire was looking unlikely, but she had a few crusts of bread that Mollie Hardwick had given her. Those, soaked in rainwater would be her supper. After that, she would have to forage as she went along.

Farmer's wives were unlikely to open their doors, and no one else had anything to spare. Meg thought longingly of the bowls of broth offered at farms a few years ago, but things were different now.

She noticed when she reached the wood that some of the bigger trees had been felled, leaving parts of the hillside open, while others previously overgrown had been stripped for kindling. It was stark to contemplate the difference, and when she thought of her woodland clearing she wished herself back there.

The threat of darkness forced her to call a halt, but she was on the road at first light intending to pass the villages in the shortest time. However, the heavy mist and low cloud that enshrouded the hill dictated her pace. When she set off, Meg debated whether to shed her skirt for the breeches she wore beneath, but did not.

In one of the mining villages, she saw a funeral procession with a handful of mourners, and noticed that the school doors were closed. No one had time to tell her who had passed away, nor did she wish to intrude. Further along the road, people standing around in groups watched her approach with suspicion.

Men with dust ingrained in their skin, pregnant women, white-faced and weary before their time, and hollow-eyed children with skinny limbs: hunger stared her in the face, and she had nothing but a few pence to offer them. Even with rain running off the brim of her hat and waterproof cape, she was better protected than they were.

The rain eased along the way but resumed before she started to descend the long winding slope to the corner overlooking the Myndstone mine. High above her, to the right, the side of the hill was cut away by the mining. The ore, having been ripped out during the wars, was needed less now.

It was always an area of hard work, but now, an air of discontent hung over the valley. "Whoa, boy..." she said, pulling on the reins, feeling suddenly alone.

As she jumped down from the bench to apply the skid-lock to slow the wheels, Meg remembered the legends of the devil's stacks of quartzite and could feel *his* presence sitting up there in the heavy cloud, as if determined to torment her.

Rounding the corner by the mine, she saw a group of miners with desolation in their eyes and no hope of work. Men with a stark choice of watching their families starve, or steal a rabbit and face the militia. No choice really.

She felt in her pocket for a few loose coins and tossed it at their feet. Better that they had them to feed their children, than be forced to steal and suffer the consequences. Her future concerned no one.

Receiving a nod by way of thanks she drove on towards the corner that would lead down the slope to the wooded hillside and the village at the bottom of the hill. Before that she had to pass the site of the old Myndstone Manor, or what was left of it these days. She saw the rusted gates ahead that had once been black paint.

A shrill cry, more like the screech of a bird of prey, broke the silence, followed by one of human terror warned her there was trouble ahead, but the wheels of the vardo rolled relentlessly on around the corner and stopped.

In the distance amongst the trees, Meg saw the slight figure of a boy prostrated on the ground and two militia officers on horseback with a girl of about fourteen, which they were taunting with naked blades, stripping the clothes from her back as she tried frantically to escape their devilry. And nearby two subordinate militia soldiers looked impotently on.

Meg recognised, in one of the officers on horseback, the voice of her nemesis and knew, as a witness to Cedric Whitcott's villainy, that she was caught with her back to the steep hill. What would he care for one more body discarded on the hillside for carrion to peck clean her bones? Calling it civil unrest was an excuse for terrorizing women and children – a militia cleansing.

Some might seek to escape but Meg remained and the girl, seeing her, drew their attention with a plea for help. Recognition between her and Cedric Whitcott was instant and explosive.

"*You,*" he roared, wheeling the horse around. "Hold the whore in check, Monty, while I deal with this old witch. She will not escape me this time."

A look of bewilderment crossed the other officer's face. "Let the gypsy go, Cedric. She is nothing to us."

A slight movement, amongst the trees, caught Meg's eye but was gone too suddenly for her to know if what she imagined was true. She could only hope that someone had gone to seek help. If not, the officers would leave no one alive.

"She is to me, Monty. This old crone bewitched my best hunter and tipped me into a stinking duck pond, when I gave her no cause for offence."

Except to Nell, by threatening me, thought Meg.

"I vowed then that, if I ever saw her again, I would kill her." He sheathed his sword, and drew out a pistol, and then hesitated. "What do you say to a twenty-guinea bet that I hit her straight between the eyes; and then torch her miserable caravan and any others of her kind with it?"

"You can't kill someone for a paltry bet."

"You are right; she is not worth that amount. Let's make it fifteen guineas."

"That's not what I meant," the second one argued. "It would be murder."

"Are you disputing the bet or the reason for it? I'm the one with justification."

"I won't be a party to it," said the second officer.

"That's a pathetic excuse for refusing my bet," Whitcott taunted. "Why not admit that you are scared I will win and you'll have to pay?"

The threat to the second officer's honour proved impossible to resist.

"I'll take your bet, Whitcott, but you will lose your money and answer for the consequences. You are no gentleman. You're not even fit to wear the uniform," he said in disgust.

"That's more like it, Monty. I was afraid I would have to shoot you as well."

Meg stared, knowing that he meant it. The other man looked uncertain.

Their momentary distraction gave the girl a chance of freedom, but instead, she gawked in disbelief at the mention of so much money.

Similarly, Meg considered her options for escape. On the horse she might achieve it, but would lose the vardo to his spite. She thought of the book hidden inside and its inscription, *To Margaret on your seventh birthday, from Papa Chetton* – the name by which she had known him – though whether he really was, she could not be sure. Nevertheless, she would not abandon his gift.

It was true that she carried his ring as a token of security, but in her

279

present situation she would be deemed to have stolen it. They would use it as evidence, and sell it for a pittance.

Something for you or the girl to send to Neathwood in time of trouble, the old gentleman had said when he pressed it into Mother Chapel's hand, a few weeks before he was laid to rest. And a pouch of guinea coins that paid for the new vardo after her mother's demise. *Maybe today she would meet them again.*

Meg knew the kind of trouble that she faced, but it was too late to act.

"I will enjoy this," said Cedric Whitcott. "This day has been a long time coming, but my revenge will be all the sweeter."

With nothing to lose but her life, Meg held the officer's gaze as he balanced the pistol against his forearm and squinted along the barrel. As the gun exploded into life, her hiss caused the officer's horse to rear, unseating him, and she flinched as the shot whistled over her head, splintering the wooden frame of the vardo. Free of its rider, the terrified animal bolted, leaving the other mounted soldier with his sword unsheathed.

Cedric Whitcott lay on the floor, too stunned to do more than scream to his colleague, "Shoot her, damn you, Monty. Tell the others to torch the caravan."

When the other man failed to move, Cedric Whitcott struggled groggily to his feet and grabbed his gun. "You see, she's done it again, but this time, old witch, will be your last breath." He raised the weapon to fire again.

Meg's hand crept to the leather thong around her neck, that held the ring, as she watched the man approach with right arm extended, determination in every debauched line of his face.

She faced him alone but only for a moment. Another rider, a stranger, galloped down the slope and halted beside the vardo, with a drawn pistol levelled at the officer.

"Then you will have to shoot me as a witness, Cedric, if you can aim straight and have enough ammunition," he said in a quiet voice, full of menace.

"Most willingly, I have always wanted to kill you. But what the blazes are *you* doing here giving orders?" bellowed the militia officer.

"Stopping a murder, by the looks of things," said the newcomer.

Seeing the two together, Meg recognised the family likeness between them.

"You have no authority without a uniform, cousin. If you wanted to give orders, you should have re-enlisted." Cedric Whitcott's words came out as from a petulant child. "I can have you arrested for threatening me."

The other man viewed him with disdain. "If you know so much about war, Cedric, why did you not join earlier and learn proper discipline? This is not a hunting field, and these people are not vermin to be torn to shreds by a pack of hounds."

"Because my father favoured you in purchasing a commission," snarled the younger man. "If he had considered my needs, I would have worn the uniform you did."

Meg felt somewhat detached from the argument – about her at the outset, but which now bore the hallmarks of a family feud.

"And been a better man for it – am I not right, Major Cobarne?"

Hearing the name, Meg looked down the road to where a group of marching soldiers was approaching, led by a lean-faced officer on horseback. Was this the brigade major about whom Molly Hardwick had spoken?

"You are, sir," said a voice with a distinct hint of Irish accent. "You have obviously known active service?"

"Ten years in the lowlands and three more the Iberian Peninsula. I left after Badajoz."

"That was a bloody battle. I was injured there but went back on Lord Hill's staff until the end. I thought, on hearing your cousin's name, that he was the officer who dragged me from the battlefield. Now, I realise it was probably you that I must thank for saving my life."

Meg watched, with mild interest, the interchange between the two gentlemen.

"Yes, I remember, and wish you well in this present venture, Major Cobarne. It is not war as we knew it."

"Some aspects are but, as you can see, there is no honour at this time," said the officer. "A moment if you please, sir; I must ascertain the facts from my Lieutenant." He turned to the junior officer, ignoring Cedric Whitcott.

"Our patrol came upon this person and a group of agitators, who took to the woods on our arrival." The second officer sought to justify his presence. "We followed, intending to apprehend them."

"How many were in the group and where are they?" the brigade major said, looking towards the woodland.

"About five, sir, but they got away."

"All of them?"

"Apart from the wench," babbled the junior officer, "and the boy…"

"Who, it seems, can no longer give his version of the encounter."

"This old woman was the agitator, sir. Lieutenant Whitcott had seen her before. He said that she was known to be a witch."

"You will be telling me next that she lives up amongst the Devil's quartzite stacks," Major Cobarne said with heavy irony, before turning aside to ask, "Well, woman; tell me your name and what business you have on this side of the hill?"

Meg knew if she admitted to being a gypsy herbalist, they would equate that with a witch's brew. "I'm a travelling midwife," she said.

His dark eyes bored into hers. "What is the name of your patient?"

"I don't have one no more, sir," she said, lapsing into the local dialect as she pointed towards the village, "she's up there in the churchyard with her dead baby."

"Did she die in labour?"

"Hunger more like," she said. "A body can only take so much, and when the mother dies so does the baby."

"She's lying…she came here to agitate the men at the mines," said the young officer. "This gypsy was one of the ringleaders, sir. We were about to arrest her."

"Having already dealt savagely with the other woman and a young boy foolish enough to try to protect his sister?"

"What do peasants like them matter?" Cedric Whitcott interceded.

The senior officer cast him a look of disdain and said aside to the former army officer, "Captain Whitcott, can I leave the gypsy woman with you while I deal with this matter of discipline?"

"No, you can't do that," shouted the rebellious lieutenant. "That witch will stir up trouble amongst the enemy. She should be clapped in irons."

There was a murmur of dissention amongst the ranks.

"Don't you know it was people like this crone who attacked Thomas Norbery, our local politician?"

"I am well aware of the facts, Lieutenant," said the brigade major.

"If you'd lived in this area all your life, as I have, it would mean something. But you are only a blasted Irishman."

The silence that followed the insubordination could be felt.

"Yes, Lieutenant Whitcott," said the brigade major in a dangerously quiet voice, "but I am the blasted Irishman who grew up at Linmore Hall with Squire Tom Norbery as my guardian. Unlike you, I have seen him since the attack, and will do so again when I have finished this spell of duty. Furthermore, Lieutenant, I will remind you in front of witnesses that I am the senior officer of this brigade."

Meg, listening, wondered if he knew of the recent events on the Linmore Estate. She could have told him, but knew that he was more interested in establishing who was in charge than listening to her. The girl from the mining village looked to be in a sorry state, with blood oozing from the slashes to her breasts that she tried feebly to cover with the tattered remains of her clothes.

Ignoring the menfolk, Meg reached into the vardo and tossed her a shawl.

"Cover yourself with that, girl," she said, "and I'll put some salves on the cuts." Then she climbed down and improvised a dressing, and bound it in place before bringing the girl forward, while the soldiers ignored her and continued their dispute.

"Sergeant," Major Cobarne barked out an order. "This officer is to be relieved of his command with immediate effect. I want you to take him into protective custody for his own safety. And similarly, Lieutenant Clevedon will relinquish his weapon."

"Yes, *sir*," came the response, with alacrity.

Despite the ensuing noise, Meg heard a quiet voice at her side.

"Mistress Chapel, I must speak with Major Cobarne on a matter of some importance, but it would be better if we do not remain here afterwards. If you are ready to depart, I suggest that you stay close to me."

"Yes, sir," said Meg, grateful for the first time in many years to a member of the gentry. "You, I think are the son of Reverend Whitcott of Caitlin, and the young officer must be your cousin."

He looked weary. "Yes, on both accounts, and it will be my unpleasant duty to inform my uncle of his son's predicament. He will not be happy."

"I met your father several times on my travels. He was a good man."

He nodded and compressed his lips, before saying, "Stay close to me. The soldiers will not harm you whilst under my protection."

Chapter 27

Stay close, Captain Whitcott had said, but how could Meg do that when he was riding beside the brigade major, and the soldiers holding the humiliated junior officers under restraint took their place in the procession back to the brigade camp?

In any event, her mind was on other things. "Where do you live?" she asked the girl, whilst dressing her wounds.

"Up there, in the village." The girl's voice was shaky; as well she might be after the murderous things she had witnessed that day.

"I'll see that you get home safely."

"But he said...the gentleman said..." the girl began, only to be interrupted.

"Captain Whitcott said you was to stay close to him," a man's voice asserted.

Meg turned to the soldier, a private by his militia uniform, but a seasoned soldier in his manner and tone.

"And so I will," she said, "just as soon as I have finished dressing the girl's wounds and taken her home. I can hardly run away up the hill. You can come as well, if you like."

"No," he said quickly. "I'll stay with your horse. He looks to be going lame. You might need to find a farrier."

Meg could not argue about "William Brown", as Nell used to call the cob: his feet needed attention. Nor would she dispute the danger in which the soldier might stand if he followed her and the girl to the village, particularly when the villagers discovered that one of their numbers had been killed, albeit by a so-called officer of the militia.

Rank did not count to anyone ready to apportion blame. Murder was murder and one uniformed soldier was the same as another. The militia, however, would see things differently. It all depended on the viewpoint it suited them to use.

The private probably suspected that she was an agitator, off to seek reinforcements, or ready to lead him to a certain death. It was a chance he was not prepared to take. In leaving him with the vardo, Meg took the risk of having her treasures found and her reason for being in possession misinterpreted. That was her dilemma. But as the girl needed support, she readily gave it.

"Don't worry," the soldier said. "I won't hurt him."

"Nor he you, although he has been known to bite," she said, recalling the original owner's description before she made her choice to buy the cob.

By the time she had walked around the corner to the village near the mine, explained to the girl's family about the dead boy in the wood, and retraced her steps down the road again, the soldier had completed his examination of the cob's foot.

"He's got a splinter caught under the shoe that'll fester if it's not dealt with," he said. "There's a smithy half a mile along the main road."

Meg nodded her thanks and led the horse and vardo down the road to within sight of where the brigade camp was pitched. Most likely, the cob had picked up the splinter in the woodland where she parked the vardo overnight and in the rain this morning she failed to notice the problem.

"You took your time, soldier," said the sergeant waiting at the gate.

"The gypsy woman took the girl home and told the family about the lad in the wood," he said, looking shamefaced. "I stayed with the horse to see she didn't run off into the hills."

"A bad business, that was," said the sergeant, shaking his head. "Leave the gypsy woman here with me. The major might want to question her."

As the private saluted and marched away, the sergeant said, "How's the girl?"

"She'll live," said Meg, "which is more than she would have done if I

286

hadn't happened along to take your officer's attention. Killing me would have been more fun for him than a defenceless youth trying to protect his sister."

"He's not my officer – Major Cobarne is," the sergeant let slip the information, and then recollected to whom he spoke. "I meant to say the Lieutenant wasn't in the real army."

Hearing the scorn in his voice, Meg could see the scant respect in which the militia officer from Caitlin was held.

"Captain Whitcott asked me to look out for you," he said, without meeting her eye, as if talking to himself. "I knew the officer in the war. He was one of the decent ones, like the Major, that can be trusted."

"Not many of those left by what I can see."

His lips twitched to show his appreciation of her comment. "I daresay if you waited over by those trees, the Major might want to question you."

Meg nodded and moved the vardo in the direction he pointed to where two gentlemen stood aside in conversation, the one handing documents to the other.

The officer's voice was quiet, but Meg's hearing was sharp, and she recalled the name he mentioned in an instant. "Ledwyche" was the one she had read in a dead man's pocketbook found in the gully above Squilver village…she stopped to calculate…going on five years ago.

"He disappeared without trace," said Major Cobarne, "which was unlike him. I am convinced that something serious prevented him from reporting back, but the authorities chose to believe that he defected to the French."

"Was he a friend?" Whitcott asked.

"We trained together from the beginning, and were the last of our group to survive. I would stake my life on him not being a traitor."

"I am glad," said Adam Whitcott, "for his father was my late mother's brother. Uncle George believed in his son's innocence when Peter was accused of treason. When he died, soon after, Peter's twin brother inherited the Barony, but never married. The stigma of having a spy in the family made him a recluse. It is sad to think that their name will die with him."

"He wore a signet ring that he said was a family heirloom, and vowed to take it to the grave," said the officer.

"Yes, the one with the Celtic knot fashioned from Welsh gold. If we

287

knew where it was now, I daresay it could provide us with some answers."

Meg could have told them, but now was not the time for such disclosures, or to admit she had listened to their conversation. She was still in a precarious position, but maybe if she spoke with the gentleman from Caitlin again, she might drop a hint about where his cousin lay buried.

Their conversation faded into the distance, but only minutes later the private that had seen to the cob's feet returned.

"Major Cobarne says as how you're to travel with Captain Whitcott. I told the gentleman about the cob going lame, and he said that if you wanted to start slowly, he'd catch up with you," said the soldier, and went on his way.

Meg nodded and, assuming that was the last she would see of the soldiers, gathered the reins together and turned the vardo around. If she could reach the right-hand fork in the road, which led to the old standing stones, she could deal with the splinter. Minutes later, she heard hoofbeats following her. She slowed to a halt expecting the gentleman to ride past but he drew level.

"Your horse will not travel far with that foot," he said.

"I will attend to it," she said, in a brusque tone. "I've done it before."

"I daresay, but which are you, a midwife or a farrier?" he said.

"I have many trades," she said, "but none of what they accused me."

He asked no more questions, and Meg wondered how far he would insist on staying with her. The road they travelled was quiet, but the signs of poverty showed everywhere they went. Hungry eyes followed them from the shadows of houses.

"It's true that I'm a midwife, and I travel around the hill country," she said. "This time I found an area sorely in trouble. Men who worked in the mines are out of work, their families starving; the churchyard full of old people: dead children and mothers that lost their babies and succumbed themselves. The few that survive are so thin they have no flesh on their bones, or hope of ever having any. That's what I found, sir, if you care to listen." Her anger, too long suppressed like her origins, hovered beneath the surface seeking an outlet.

"Who are you…really?" he said. "You do not speak as one of the common folk."

"I'm Meg Chapel, sir. That is how I'm known hereabouts."

"But I suspect that you were not always so named?" he said.

"That was a long time ago, sir," she said.

"Do you have proof of this other identity?"

"I have a book," she said, reaching into the vardo for her treasured memento. "A gift from someone, whose name I thought could be trusted."

"Would you permit me to look at it?" he said.

After a brief hesitation she placed the book of sermons in his hand and looked away. Hearing an intake of breath, she turned back almost defiantly to face him and saw incredulity in his expression.

"Thank you for showing it to me," he said, reverently stroking the ornate leather cover. "It is a treasure beyond compare, and you are right to keep it safe."

Meg nodded, and gave her attention to the cob, which was limping badly.

"Your horse needs to have its hoof dealt with," he said. "The smithy is not far."

"There's no need for you to be involved with the likes of me," Meg said, knowing that she would not take the horse to a farrier while dressed as a gypsy woman. "I'll attend to the animal."

"I think not," he said firmly. "I gave Major Cobarne my word that I would see you safely to the main road, and will not leave you with the horse incapacitated."

Meg acknowledged the justice of his words.

"It might be easier if we park the vardo amongst the trees and take the horses to the smithy. I don't mind waiting if you prefer to attire yourself differently," he said, turning aside, "I will speak with the farrier and order a tankard of ale from the inn next door."

Two things struck Meg simultaneously. She had not realised how thirsty she was until he mentioned ale, and it dawned on her that Captain Whitcott must recall seeing her at Middlebrook Fair clad in her breeches and boots.

Having parked the vardo along an old bridleway through the trees, Meg shed her women's drapes and tied back her hair with black ribbon. And then, hoping that her weathered skin would hide the absence of stubble, she pulled the black hat down over her eyes and, with an air of nonchalance, slipped the book of sermons into an inner coat pocket beside a few shiny coins that a man would use to pay the blacksmith. Female she might be, dependent she was not.

"Come on, William Brown, let's get that splinter out of your hoof," she said, as she unhitched the cob from the vardo, and led him slowly down the road towards the smithy.

Understanding her wish for privacy, the gentleman had found a lone table in the shadows of the inn garden, away from prying eyes. It pleased Meg to meet him on equal terms when they sat down to quaff ale and share a crust of bread and cheese. Never had she enjoyed company more or liked a man so well. This might have been her life had she not been born a girl.

"What happened to the young person that travelled with you some years ago?" His question broke through her reverie.

"She took a respectable position in Linmore Dale, and is well thought of."

"I am pleased," he said, "The sketch that I did of her sold well. Such delicate features and fine colouring are rare."

"Unusual in these parts," said Meg, meeting his gaze, "unlike my own."

Her comment drew a smile of understanding.

"I knew her mother," she said softly.

"And she was…?"

"A lady from a good family, fallen on hard times."

"In that case, it is best if her daughter does not come to Caitlin – or you for the present time for we do not yet know the outcome of this infamous day."

They both knew that he referred to his cousin's evil influence.

"Why do you risk being seen with me?" she said.

"Because my uncle would wish me to make recompense for his son's disgraceful behaviour. We cannot change what happened now; Cedric will have to face the consequences of his actions."

"You can't be held responsible for him," she said.

"His mother will apportion blame, but if he had been allowed to join the army when he was younger; he would be a different man now."

"Or dead," she said bluntly.

"Yes," he said, "there is that aspect to consider."

"Does the farrier know he is shoeing a horse for me?" she said.

"He will recognise the Irish Cob breed but being a former soldier is unlikely to refuse the work. Farriers do not pick and choose which horses they shoe."

"You'll let me pay for the service?" she said.

"I think not," he said, firmly. "It is better for me to be seen to do it."

Meg knew that although the gentleman understood why she dressed in men's clothes, it did not mean that he approved.

As he prepared to collect the cob she knew that she had to speak.

"I couldn't help hearing a name that you and the major mentioned, sir."

"You listened to our conversation?" he said. His voice had a wary edge.

"Not listened, but my hearing is keen. It has to be, living as I do. You spoke of your cousin being missing, and I might have information about his whereabouts."

"Tell me what you know and I will decide what it is worth, if that is your purpose," he sounded disappointed.

She ignored the inference of bribery.

"Five years ago, last spring, I found a body in the gully below Squilver Ridge, half a mile above the village. It had been there a while, hidden by the snow."

"What were you doing there?"

"I was attending a birthing mother in the area. I don't normally travel that way, but flooded roads forced me to cross the hill on horseback. I found the body when I rode back towards the ridge."

"What did you do about it?" he said.

"I thought it best to report the matter to the local magistrate. Your cousin's name was in his pocketbook, and he wore the ring the officer mentioned."

"Did you notice anything else?"

Meg could visualise the book in her hand. "It said, *Squilver*, on the date a few weeks before I was there; and another name, but with the book being damp, the writing had smudged."

She looked the man in the eye. "He didn't die by natural means," she said. "Someone cudgelled him from behind, and he must have fallen from his horse down the steep slope into the gully, out of sight."

"So he had arranged to meet someone, and died at the spot."

"Yes, it looks that way."

"What happened to the body? I would like to be able to tell his brother."

"There were gold coins in his purse, but he had a pauper's funeral and was buried in an unmarked grave at the edge of the churchyard near the yew tree."

"What happened to the money?"

"Probably what happens in any of these situations? It went into someone's pocket with the ring and pocketbook, but being distinctive they would mark a local man as a thief. The innkeeper agreed to bring the body down to the village, but only after I told him about the fine pair of boots lying in the snow."

"And greed did the rest," he said.

"I stayed to lay out the body for burial, and there was no sign of the clothes he had worn – only a pile of working men's rags and shabby hobnailed boots – hence the pauper's grave. Sad, but at least the carrion didn't pick his bones clean."

He flinched visibly, and then said, "Surely, there must have been an inquest."

"Yes," said Meg. "Squire Myndham took the chair, and Dr Windermere, from out Bredenbridge way made what passed for an examination. He was in the village attending the lady I delivered. They recorded a verdict of accidental death."

"Do you dispute that, Mistress Chapel?"

"I'd be surprised if anyone could see a head wound, when they only lifted the sheet covering the body by a few inches."

"That was what he did?" he said in disgust.

She nodded. "In fairness to the physician, the man on the table had been dead sufficiently long to make the task unpleasant."

"And decomposing, I suppose?"

"Yes," she said, "but I doubt he'd soil his hands touching any of the lower orders. If he'd known a gentleman was involved, things might have been different."

It took a moment to sufficiently control his emotions to speak in an even tone.

"Thank you for telling me, Mistress Chapel. I can, at least, tell my cousin that his brother died in service to the nation. But we do not know what happened to the ring and pocketbook."

"It's a while ago, but I daresay the innkeeper's tongue might be loosened by the hint of a reward asking for news," said Meg. "The boots were probably sold, but he might still have the ring and book hidden away. The one was too distinctive to pass unnoticed, and the other considered insignificant. That's why I left things as they were. If I'd removed anything, they'd have called me a thief, and hung me."

"What a wonderful spymaster you would have made, Mistress Chapel."

"You learn a lot about people travelling the roads, sir," Meg said with a grimace. "Your other cousin, for one…"

"Ah, yes, the unlovable Cedric," he said. "I had forgotten him. If he had killed you today, as he intended, I would never have heard your news of Peter. Now, I must return to Caitlin to report Cedric's situation to his father, for which his mother will insist I am responsible," he said with a shrug of the shoulders.

They continued in silence until they reached a side road that Meg knew led up over the long hill of the quartzite stones towards Caitlin.

"I must leave you here, Mistress Chapel," he said. "When I have resolved the matter of Cedric, I will investigate the Squilver incident and report my findings to people in authority. It would be good to clear my mother's nephew of the infamous charge of treason."

Meg was surprised that he offered his hand for her to shake. When she took it, the thought came that here was a man who would keep Nell safe. *A prediction,* she believed, *set in motion by the strange energy of the stones.*

She watched him ride away, knowing that she had trusted him with her secret, and given him news of a family connection brought low by dishonour. She wished him luck, but suspected that his investigations might yet unearth more unpalatable facts about another member of his family.

As she drove on, she recalled Molly Hardwick's words about Cedric

Whitcott having friends out by Squilver Ridge, at the time when the missing groom from Caitlin Hall was found in a gravel pit. Another unexplained death that left a grieving family looking for reasons. She wondered if they were connected.

What would have happened if two distant family connections had met unexpectedly, to conduct nefarious business on a lonely hillside? With one of them purporting to be a spy – the other a villain in truth.

Thank goodness Nell had not been with her today.

"I trust that your friend is safe?" Captain Whitcott had asked before leaving. No doubt he recalled the disrespectful way that Nell had been treated at the Middlebrook Fair.

"Yes, sir," Meg said, "she works with the Middlebrook physician."

"A good man of medicine, by all accounts. I met him once and my late father spoke well of him." His look of relief on hearing the name of Nell's employer, changed to one of dawning realisation, although to what she could not say.

"Better than most I've seen hereabouts," Meg said.

"With Dr James Althorpe as an example, I can see why Dr Windermere's standards fell short in your estimation."

Much as the former assistant at Middlebrook surgery had done in his treatment of Squire Norbery of Linmore. Such men were not fit to touch a patient, but society deemed them worthy, whereas physicians of Dr Althorpe's calibre were rare.

★★★

Meg continued along the lower track, until the ridge of Linmore Hill came into view. She felt old as she passed the drive that led to the manor house of the raven, which brought back memories of a girl that once worked there and the troubles she endured. Helping Maria and making a friend seemed so long ago.

When her thoughts turned to Nell, she wondered if the manservant from the cottage at Linmore had found the pouch of herbs, which Meg had sensed might be needed yet hoped she was wrong.

Tiredness almost forced Meg to stop when she reached the crossroads near Hillend, but she pushed on along the drovers' road towards Linmore. She saw the lodge on the back drive under a darkening sky, and started up the slope of the first ride leading towards the wood.

Meg stopped at the top to listen to the sound of the stable clock at Linmore Hall chiming the hour in the distance. A lone barn owl hooted in the dusk as it winged its way across the estate. *Too late...*it seemed to say... *too late.*

Too late for what? Meg wondered. She had survived today, but could not turn back the clock to a time when the old gentleman from Neathwood had visited the hillside in the months after his wife had died.

An old groom they had known had ventured into the clearing and announced that his master wished to have speech with Mother Chapel.

Meg was in the woodsman's hut when the servant came and she heard them speaking before the deeper voice, remembered from childhood, broke in. Impetuosity told her to make herself know to him, but caution forced her to heed her mother's words. A cowardly inaction she had regretted ever since.

She could hear their voices now as clearly as if it were yesterday.

"You have the son you wanted to bear your name and title, sir," her mother had said. "And now would take the girl from me. What can you give her? At least with me she has a useful occupation."

Meg had heard him own her as his daughter, but it meant little for he had many such baseborn children in Linmore Dale. She was just one of them, even if for a time she was the favourite he used to sit on his knee and read to. A memory that she kept locked inside.

"It is not simply for me that I want her to come home," he had insisted. "Her brother pines for her. I want you both to come home with me. We should all be together."

Meg had sensed Mother Chapel's hesitation, but she did not weaken.

"That was our agreement. The boy for you and I would keep the girl."

"Can I see her once more...please?"

She heard anguish in a voice more used to command than pleading.

"No, it would serve no purpose." Mother Chapel had been adamant.

"I see," he said sadly. "Then I would be obliged if you would give this to the girl when the time comes. I would ask her to think kindly of me."

Wanting to approach but afraid, Meg had watched them through the trees and heard the jingle of coins in the pouch that he handed to her mother.

"The book and the token you wear are for her. If she ever needs help, send the ring to me...if I am still here. If not, then the next Lordship will answer its call."

Little more than a month later, the same loyal servant brought news telling them that his master had died after a hunting accident. And before two more weeks had passed Mother Chapel was struck down with a malady for which Meg did not have a remedy.

She looked at the green stone, remembering the moment she had taken the still-warm ring from her dead mother's hand and strung it on the leather thong around her neck. Then she laid her in the fresh-dug earth beneath the trees, and spoke a few words from the same book of sermons her father had brought.

Several times in the succeeding years, Meg had risked discovery by visiting his tomb at Neathwood, wearing the black clothes and boots he bequeathed to her. Now she had shown the book he had given her to a stranger, knowing that if anyone saw the tome in her possession they would claim she had stolen it and her life would be forfeit. After the events of today, she felt a need to go there again.

Meg knew that she was not ready to die. Her purpose was to help Nell bring her children into the world; the ones she had seen in the lifeline on the girl's hand. After that whatever happened would do so, for Neathwood was far beyond her reach.

Chapter 28

Late September 1816

Squire Norbery's funeral was a dark day for the people of Linmore Dale, and the heavy skies matched the sombre mood of the occasion. When James Althorpe arrived, the church was almost filled to capacity, with hardly a space to be seen in the churchyard. Grown men, standing shoulder to shoulder, bowed their heads and wept, with no distinction between the gentry and working folk of Linmore Dale who came to say farewell to one of its most respected sons.

Undeterred by the rain, Joshua Norbery walked behind the cortege down the drive to the village church. His face was gaunt, and his eyes bleak. He looked lost, and yet, James noticed, there was a squaring of the shoulders to bear the responsibility of stepping into his father's shoes as Squire Norbery.

Joshua's brother-in-law, from Shettleston Hall, and the husbands of Tom Norbery's two nieces, followed close behind with a variety of cousins, all clad in the traditional unrelieved funereal black, with one notable exception who wore his dark military dress uniform as a sign of respect.

Of the older gentlemen, only Mr Marcus Pontesbury walked the distance with his sons, whereas Lord Cardington and Arthur Bradstone, the father of Mrs Joshua Norbery, travelled in closed carriages, separate from the other.

Earth to earth, ashes to ashes…and the ceremony was over.

When the mourners gathered at the Hall, James was pleased to see that Kate Norbery was conspicuous by her absence and Mrs Pontesbury took charge of the occasion, as she had in the hours preceding Tom Norbery's death.

Observing from the sidelines, he noticed that in the frosty atmosphere dividing the family into opposing groups, Mrs Pontesbury gathered her husband and sons around Joshua and Miss Jane. Similarly, Lord and Lady Cardington tried to take precedence, but their sons, Major Frederick and his brother Viscount Atcherly, excused themselves and joined Miss Jane in the Pontesbury circle. This left Annabel Norbery to sit with her parents and sister, a situation that clearly did not please her.

When James went to make his excuses to leave, Mrs Pontesbury took the opportunity to publicly acknowledge him to the assembled wake.

"Dr Althorpe, I speak for myself and my dear sister, Jane, when I say that those of us who wished my brother well thank you for your excellent care. Regrettably, not everyone who is present felt the same attachment."

He noticed the latter comment was directed at Lord Cardington, and that Joshua acknowledged his aunt's words with a bow.

Noting her inclusion of Miss Jane, he realised that Tom Norbery's sister was privy to the true state of affairs. Similarly, she regretted the short-sightedness of those who should have known better, and pointedly ignored Lord Cardington's snort of protest. Truly she was a formidable lady.

★★★

James had little time after that to think of the folk at Linmore. The necessity of finding an assistant that he could trust was foremost in his mind. Even without Nell Walcote and Bucknole to help, his hands were tied and losing Miss Kate as a patient disrupted his routine.

Mrs Fulmer was delighted to have more of Nell Walcote's time. Similarly, Mr Greenfield of Hollytree Farm demanded Nell's attendance on several occasions, for trivial matters on behalf of his wife. When James considered the degree of insult she was offered and subsequent non-payment of his account, he felt obliged to deny them and suggested the gentleman looked elsewhere for medical services. It was, he realised, a high-handed attitude, but as a member of the almost-gentry, Mr and Mrs Greenfield left much to be desired.

Other things took their place and it was several weeks later and well into autumn before James made his way up the front drive to Linmore Hall. Having first enquired his whereabouts at the Manor, he found the new Squire Norbery in the library, surrounded by books and boxes filled with papers. He saw that Joshua had aged. Grief showed in the bitter twist of his mouth, turning down at the edges.

"Mr Norbery," he said, extending a hand in greeting.

James had never seen the room in such a state of disarray. The oak desk had all but disappeared under the sheets of paper, which Joshua was in the weary process of sorting into piles.

"You find me alone, Dr Althorpe, apart from the servants, and these ancient documents for which I must now take responsibility," Joshua said with a rueful smile. "There is no pleasure to be had in a house of bereavement, so the children are staying with their grandparents at Bredenbridge, as is their mother. I was hoping to spend time with them." His tone was devoid of expression but his eyes were sad.

It was no wonder the couple were estranged, if Annabel Norbery was using the children that he loved as an excuse to punish her husband for the prolonged absence, which he could not avoid.

"Lord Cardington...?" James said to break the silence that followed.

"My esteemed relative has finally returned to his home, and taken my mother with him. A pleasant change for her, but unfortunately he coerced Aunt Jane into going too, which she did under sufferance. She had planned to help me sort out this," he waved a hand to indicate the paperwork that littered the desk. "Now I must contrive to make what I can of it."

"I must not stay," James said, starting to rise from the seat in which he had recently sat, "for I have interrupted your work."

"No, I am grateful, for I needed someone with whom to talk. It will take time to adjust. I never suspected there was so much I did not know about my father."

James wondered what he had learned about his origins. He waited to see what Joshua would say next, but it was not what he expected.

"In the absence of Aunt Jane and Martha, I thought Jessie might be able to help." His mind seemed to drift from the subject. "I rode out to Aunt Jane's cottage this morning to see her maid, and discovered that Meg Chapel did not abandon us. She left a supply of herbs at the cottage, which Jessie found hanging from the door latch on her return. Had we known in time, I would not now be doing this."

The precious herbs that might have saved Tom Norbery's life, if not for the interference of Lord Cardington.

"He would have been here to explain everything in person. If only I had thought to send William Rufus to the cottage instead of chasing over the hill." Joshua shook his head, overcome by the recollections. "I am sorry, Dr Althorpe."

James dismissed the apology with a wave of the hand. "Have you eaten today, for if not I recommend that you take a luncheon?"

It was well after two o'clock, and from the empty jug and tankard at Joshua's elbow, it seemed likely that any nourishment was of the liquid kind.

"Will you join me? If you don't mind me sitting down to eat, dressed as I am."

Having been riding in the morning, Joshua had discarded his coat over the back of a chair, and sat in his shirtsleeves and waistcoat, buckskins and top boots.

"With pleasure," said James, "if only to see that you eat a reasonable meal. There is a matter that I wished to discuss with you, which has been troubling me."

They retired to the morning room, where a table was prepared with cold meats, cheeses and bread.

"When I am alone, I live between here and the library," said Joshua. "There is little point in making extra work for the servants."

What a strange notion for a man of means with many servants.

"Does your wife plan to make a long stay at Fallowfield Court?" James said. "Or Mrs Kate Norbery at Rushmore Hall?"

Joshua shrugged his shoulders. "Like any other man, I am not privy to know their plans. They have been away for over a month already, and will return when they decide, but I could wish the children were here," he stopped. "What was the matter that you wished to discuss?"

James readily accepted the abrupt change of subject.

"While we were at the cottage, Lord Cardington sent for me to see Mrs

Kate Norbery. When I failed to arrive at his command, he consulted Dr Frogg who works from the Asylum at Westbridge, and I was summarily dismissed as her physician. I should have told you at the time, but did not wish your father to be distressed. Although Frogg was formerly my assistant, there had been some difficulties."

He was reluctant to divulge the nature of these.

"I can imagine that was extremely unpleasant, and outside Lord Cardington's remit. He had no right to interfere, but that has never stopped him from doing so," said Joshua.

"He dismissed me again when we brought your father back to Linmore Hall, which prevented me from attending Mr Norbery. I went immediately to the Manor, but Hayton your butler said that you were resting. I left my visiting card and asked that you contacted me. I did the same the following day."

Joshua raked his fingers through his hair. "Damn, I saw your card but received no message. Having been absent from the estate, I spent several days sorting out problems. I visited my father in the evenings, and assumed that you had attended him earlier in the day. I subsequently learned what was happening from Jessie, who slipped in under cover of darkness when I arrived. It was not only you who was prevented from seeing my father, but Aunt Jane also. A gross impertinence to set a man's servants to deny him access to the people he most wanted to see."

I will be all right, as long as you are with me, Jane.

The words that Tom Norbery had spoken before they left the cottage came to mind. How prophetic they were. Deprived of Jane's loving support, he failed.

It would be a long time before Joshua trusted Lord Cardington again.

"Having made these arbitrary decisions, his lordship left Linmore to visit friends at Winterton Hall. It was from there I called him when my father's health deteriorated. The rest you know."

"The matter of Dr Frogg as your medical attendant…?"

"Aunt Jane would refuse to allow him near her, and I feel the same way. My mother and I, as you well know, have never seen eye to eye. If I decided that you should be her physician, she would refuse; but I would be obliged if you would consent to visit if the need arises."

James nodded in agreement. "I understand your position exactly, Mr Norbery, and am more than willing. Regarding the time when I tried to contact you. I realise now that I should have spoken with your housekeeper, Miss Dinchope."

The first hint of a smile lit Joshua's eyes. "Yes, that would undoubtedly have been the best course of action, Dr Althorpe, for she is a truly estimable person."

How different things might have been if they had known that Meg Chapel had come back to the cottage before leaving for Caitlin. Looking back over events, and what he had known of her in the past, James should have realised the herbalist would ensure they had an adequate supply of herbs. He was not a fanciful person, but for all he knew she might have special powers to anticipate problems, and set in motion ways of dealing with them.

Having seen Joshua Norbery, he could imagine that the paperwork with which he was occupied would absorb some of his grief, but he would miss his daughters even if his wife's absence did not concern him quite so readily.

Looking back to the day of the funeral, James wondered if the content of Mrs Pontesbury's conversation with her nephew's wife had provoked the lady to fly to Bredenbridge when the event was over. He suspected that it might be the case, particularly when he recollected hearing Joshua's aunt enumerating the social restrictions that his wife must endure during the bereavement year, and advising her to spend the time being a dutiful wife by bearing him a son and heir.

Any woman of sense would know it was not an unreasonable request now that Joshua was Squire Norbery of Linmore, but evidently the suggestion did not find favour with his wife. James wondered what the lady's father would have to say if the estrangement between them became permanent. It was a situation to be observed with interest.

Acknowledgements

To the growing number of readers who follow the Linmore Series. I thank you all, including my long suffering husband and two sons who have lived with me in Linmore Dale from the beginning; my editor, Doug Watts, who gave me a belief in my creative ability when my confidence was fragile. I am also indebted to Jenny, my community midwife whilst in training, who shared her knowledge of natural therapies; and Jane Noble Knight, whose Shropshire workshop empowered me to take the first step along the publishing pathway.

www.ingramcontent.com/pod-product-compliance
Lightning Source LLC
Chambersburg PA
CBHW071004280626
47160CB00016B/2421

* 9 781910 100851 *